ABOUT THE A

Des Mason was brought up in th_   _don
in North Somerset, leaving home at   work in
a variety of occupations including lect_   _ teaching in
London and West Africa, North America a_ _ Cumbria. He has
also worked as a steward on the cross-channel ferries, as an
amusement park attendant, a building site labourer and a school
inspector. For the last ten years Des has been working happily
for the South Wales Fire & Rescue Service, where he has been
touched by the support of so many of his colleagues who have
purchased copies of this book.

He started work on *The Scrimshaw of Sable Island* during a year
spent teaching at a college in Nova Scotia. His imagination was
originally fired by the stories of Captain Kidd's treasure, reputed
to be buried on Oak Island, combined with his meeting with
the Nova Scotia novelist Thomas Raddall, who described to
him in vivid detail the strange and sinister landscape of Sable
Island – graveyard of the Atlantic. He finished the first draft of
the book ten years later and has since rewritten it several times
in the course of trying to find a publisher.

Des Mason has been friends with the artist John Gooch since
they met as boys at school. It is also as a result of John's faith in
the book, evinced by his illustrations, that Des decided to self-
publish and donate all the profits from sales to the children's
hospice, Ty Hafan.

For further information go to www.troubador.co.uk

A tale of land and sea

The
Scrimshaw
of
Sable Island

Desmond *Mason*

Illustrated by John Gooch

Matador
9 Priory Business Park,
Wistow Road, Kibworth Beauchamp,
Leicestershire. LE8 0RX
Tel: (+44) 116 279 2299
Fax: (+44) 116 279 2277
Email: books@troubador.co.uk
Web: www.troubador.co.uk/matador

ISBN 978 1780884 134

British Library Cataloguing in Publication Data.
A catalogue record for this book is available from the British Library.

Typeset in 12pt Bembo by Troubador Publishing Ltd, Leicester, UK
Printed and bound in the UK by TJ International, Padstow, Cornwall

Matador is an imprint of Troubador Publishing Ltd

To Caroline, Rowena & Conrad
Richest of all treasures
and in memory of my friend
Danny Caines

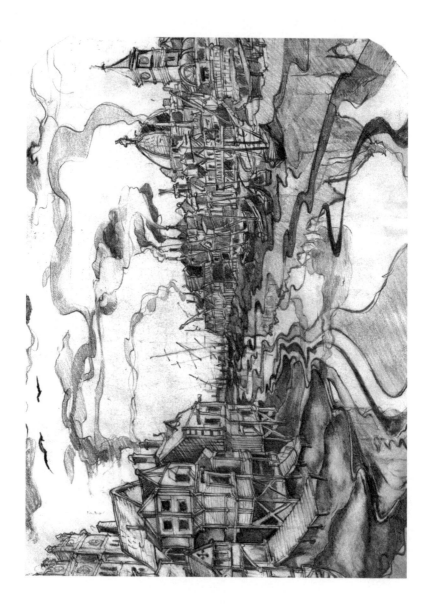

CHAPTER ONE

The Climbing Boy

Limpets and weeds clamped onto the wooden pilings of the docks. The river shifted, whispering in the darkness at low tide. Rats scurried across the flat slopes of mud. Sitting on the dock of Hangman's Reach, Owen Davies was deeply unhappy as he stared out over the river across the forest of masts and ships crowding the busy port of Bristol. Eleven years old, he was thinking about death: all the more frightening because it was his own death he had in mind. He was thinking about killing himself. The mud and the musk of the river, mingled with rotten food and rubbish, smelled like the breath of an old witch. He was overcome with a sense of helplessness and a fear of the uncertain future that stretched out in front of him like a prison sentence. He only knew that he could never go back to the way things were before death had come to visit his home.

Owen and his family were from South Wales. His father had moved them all to Bristol in the hope of finding work when Owen was only seven years old. With their tiny farm taken by moneylenders and no land left to live on, his father had decided to move to England rather than starve in Wales. Life was hard for the Welsh in Bristol. Their lilting accent was mocked and mimicked and Owen had lost count of the number of fights he had braved, rather than put up with the mockery of the jeering Bristol boys. Owen's father became a dockside labourer.

In the great days of sailing ships, with Britain's Industrial Revolution powering the world, Bristol was busy sending out the riches from Britain's factories to every corner of the growing British Empire. In return, the wealth of the world poured back into the great port of Bristol. An army of labourers was kept busy humping baskets, bags and buckets of cargo up from the holds of the ships to the dockside.

It was hard, grinding work, but it had kept the roof over the family's two rooms in the sprawling slums of Bristol's Welsh Back, where seven children and their parents lived and ate and slept. Now, Owen's father was dead. He had fallen from a ladder when a sack of melons carried by the man above him had burst apart, raining the heavy globes of fruit down onto his head. His neck had broken in the fall.

As the weeks passed by following his death, food had become scarce and Owen's mother had grown brooding, tearful and fretful. Then, that very morning, a stranger had called round, knocking with great ham-like fists on the door of their home.

He was big, rough and dirty, with enormous hands and a beard of black bristles. His cheeks flamed with a maze of broken veins and his eyes were red and bloodshot under a single heavy black eyebrow. Every bit of him that could be seen was dirty. With his bottom lip sticking out and his forehead creased in a frown, he looked like a man having trouble thinking. He brought into the room with him a strong smell of soot. He spoke briefly to the boy's mother then he bent down to speak into Owen's face. His breath stank of rum and bad teeth.

"You'll have plenty of grub and a roof over yer head, see," he said to the boy. His voice was deep and hoarse with the broad accent of the West Country. "And if yer a good lad, like yer Mammy says, you can have duff on Sundays. There now. I can't say better than that, can I? Duff on Sundays! What do you say to that then?"

Never having eaten Plum Duff pudding, Owen had not the faintest idea what the man was talking about. He stayed silent until his mother chipped in.

"This is Mr Jem Noggins, Owen," she said. "He's going to take you to live with him and learn to be a chimney sweep like what he is. It's not what I want Owen, but since yer Pa died we got no money." Her voice cracked on the edge of tears. "I just can't feed all of us no more. So Mister Noggins will look after you, and you be a good boy now and do what he tells you."

The sweep pulled back his lips. It looked like he was exercising his face rather than smiling. His teeth were yellow and green. "Duff on Sundays!" he said, rubbing his great hands together. "Why, every week will be like Christmas to you, Boy!"

So tonight… tonight he would be spending his last night at home. Owen sat hunched by the river, looking at the ships riding at anchor, and thinking dark thoughts about an uncertain future. But the more he thought about it, the less he fancied snuffing out his own candle. It might be a hard life in front of him, hard and uncertain, but it was better than no life at all. Finally he made his way back to the dark alley and the two rooms crowded with sleeping children, to spend his last night at home with his brothers and sisters.

He awoke with the foot of his brother pushed against his head and the foot of his sister right beside his nose. With four of them to a bed, they always slept top to tail as the easiest way of ensuring something like a night's sleep. The fusty smell of the blankets and old coats on top of him was as comfortable to him as the smell of its den to a fox. His first thought: he was leaving home forever on that very day. With his father dead, his mother penniless, and his brothers and sisters in need, Owen knew he had no choice but to go. His last day at home flew by. As the afternoon wore down to a shadowy ghost of the day, Jem Noggins rapped at the door and took him away, leaving his mother three guineas richer and with one mouth less to feed.

Jem Noggins lived in the basement of an old house perched on the side of the River Avon above the busy docks of Hotwells. The Sweep's home was one enormous room with a heap of bedding and a table and chairs at one end. From what Owen could make out in the dim light of the candle lit by the Sweep, there was nothing much but a bundle of brushes and a litter of empty bottles at the other. Tucked away in a corner, an old sack filled with straw ticking was shown to Owen as his bed. The walls of the room were covered in dirt and mildew and a pot-bellied iron stove at the end of the room gave out equal portions of heat and smoke. His own home had been anything but grand, but his mother had always done her best to keep it clean. Owen's heart sank as he looked around at the murky den and the shambling giant with whom he was to share it.

A pot of greasy stew was soon burning on the stove and the Sweep filled two bowls, pushing one across the table to Owen.

"Eat hearty boy," he said, "and don't turn yer nose up at it because it's all yer getting."

Spooning up the burned offering, Owen watched the Sweep tearing at a loaf of bread with his big green teeth, slurping and slobbering over his food like the old pig they had kept back in Caerwent.

The Sweep looked up sharply to find the boy staring at him.

"What you looking at Boy?" he growled. "You finish yer stew then get to sleep. We got an early start in the morning."

The smiling act he had put on in front of Owen's mother had vanished, along with any mention of duff on Sundays. Owen felt as if he was locked up with a dangerous animal. As the evening wore on, the boy's fears grew. The Sweep lit a new tallow candle that spluttered and flickered, giving off a light that only seemed to bring out the great gulfs of shadow darkening the room. Lying on his itching mattress wrapped in a stinking blanket, Owen pretended to be asleep as he watched Jem Noggins drink his way through a whole bottle of strong Navy rum.

Every now and then the Sweep would stagger to his feet, his shadow reeling across the wall as he tottered about like a dancing bear, singing a few lines of song and letting rip with his guts as though his breeches would explode. Then he would sit down and mumble to himself, banging his fist on the table and snarling. At last he grew quiet and sat staring stupidly at the guttering candle in front of him. His chin slumped on his chest and his lower lip trembled as his shoulders heaved. Tears ran down his dirty face. Then, with a curse, he was on his feet again, weaving his way to the other side of the room as he growled at some invisible enemy. His giant shadow reared crazily across the walls, from one wall to another.

The Sweep took no more notice of Owen than if he had been a stone, and the boy finally fell sleep.

Dreaming he was being shaken by a great black dog, he awoke to find himself being dragged from his bed by Jem Noggins. The Chimney Sweep was telling him to wake up. The first traces of morning light came from the grimy window high on the wall as the Sweep pushed a hunk of bread into Owen's hand and tottered off through the murk, groaning like a wounded bear as he gathered together his brushes and mats. Owen scarcely had time to cram the bread in his mouth and wash it down with a drink of water before he was thrust into his jacket and found himself stumbling through the streets as the cold dawn light was breaking.

The big Chimney Sweep carried a great bundle of

brushes on his shoulder. Owen trailed behind him under a roll of mats that were almost as big as he was. The April wind whipped through his thin clothes and his teeth were chattering like dice in a tumbler.

Around them, the city was coming to life. Window shutters were opened and curtains pulled back; the clopping of hooves mingled with the clamour of milk churns and the rumble of iron wheels over the cobbles as the carts and drays began their long day's work. At the bottom of Christmas Steps, they stopped at a steamy little eating house full of noise and people and the smells of food and sweat. The Sweep bought Owen a slice of bread and dripping and a cup of beef tea then slurped and guzzled his way through seven bowls of thin barley broth. With his red eyes and purple cheeks, Owen thought he looked as if a fire was raging inside him, a fire he was trying to put out by drowning it in soup.

Then they were back out onto the street again in the full light of the morning, with the city buzzing and bustling and the gleaming spire of St Mary Redcliffe Church rising above the morning mist. Leaving the river behind them, Owen followed the Sweep as he turned into a crescent of fine houses. They stretched round in a graceful curve, all spotless paint and shining windows. Jem Noggins knocked softly on the door of one of them. A grand looking old man appeared and told them to go to the tradesman's entrance.

"Yes, My Lord." The Sweep bent his great loaf-like head and pulled at a greasy forelock of hair.

"I am not My Lord," sniffed the old man. "Sir Michael does not answer the door to anyone, never mind common tradesmen. Go down to the basement door – and take your urchin with you."

A serving maid showed them in and took them through

the house. Walking along passages lined with elegant wallpaper and fine paintings, Owen marvelled at the soft rugs and carpets with their colours glowing against the shine of the polished wooden floors. The house gave off a feeling of comfort and money that was a world away from that of the boy struggling along behind the Sweep under a heavy pile of mats. They were led into a light, airy room with tall windows draped by curtains of blue velvet.

Dominating the room was a great marble fireplace. It was a massive thing, supported by two carved columns. The servant pulled the carpets back and Jem Noggins took out the iron fire basket before he started to lay down his mats in front of the hearth.

"There you are," he said to Owen. "A nice easy big one for your first chimbley. Just you get in there, and up you go like a monkey up a tree. Duff on Sundays! What a lucky little shaver you is, and no mistake!"

Feeling anything but lucky, Owen shrank back and began to snivel and sob.

"What's this? Parping!" cried the Sweep. "I'm not having no boy of mine parping! You just stop that now afore I gives you something to parp about!"

Grabbing the boy by the arm, he put a brush into his hand and shoved him bodily into the fireplace.

"Look up boy," he growled. "D'you see any light?"

Raising his eyes the boy could at first see only a funnel choked with soot and dark as pitch. Then, impossibly far away, high, high above, there was a tiny circle of blue light.

"Well boy? D'you see the sky?"

Owen admitted he could see a bit of sky.

"Good," grunted the Sweep. "Now – Git up with you!"

With that, he took hold of Owen by both ankles and stuffed him headfirst up the chimney.

"Get climbing boy," he yelled beneath him. "Climb! Or

by the powers, I'll light a fire under you to roast your liver!
Climb, you little devil, or I'll pull your head off and use it as
a door stop!"

Owen's eyes were full of soot. Soot was in his mouth and
up his nose and down his collar and in his ears. But he was
more scared of losing his head than he was of the soot, and
away up the chimney he went. Bracing his back against one
side of the chimney, he used his hands and legs to push
himself upwards, with the brush held above his head. The
higher he climbed, the more the idea of running away from
the Sweep seemed like a sensible kind of a plan. He could
almost see his severed head acting as a doorstop in the
Sweep's gloomy room, and he wondered what had
happened to his last apprentice. There were stories a-plenty
of apprentices who had been killed by their cruel masters.
And the more Owen learned about chimneys, the less he
liked them.

The climbing itself wasn't too hard, but with every foot
he gained, he seemed to scrape more skin from his knees

and his knuckles, scrabbling against the rough bricks under their coating of soot. And added to his fear of the Sweep was the thought of the tremendous drop opening up beneath him. What if he should suddenly lose his footing!? Down, down he would fall, to land in a broken heap on the marble slabs far below. He didn't want to spend the rest of his life going up chimneys. He decided there and then. Anything would be better. He could run away to sea. He could simply run away. Moving through a suffocating storm of soot, Owen climbed through the blackness that blinded him and drowned him until it seemed he had been lost for years in a world made up of equal parts of soot, fear and pain. Up and up he climbed, pushing the brush before him. Each jerk of his body brought a fresh cascade of soot pouring down on his head, choking and blinding him. He felt the yawning pull of the sucking drop so many feet below him. Then suddenly the brush was free.

With a final push, Owen heaved himself up until his arms reached over the rim of the chimney pot. Coughing and spitting soot from his mouth, he hung there high on the rooftop, blinking weakly in the morning sunlight.

CHAPTER TWO

Buffers and Codgers

Hanging limply from the top of his chimney, Owen hawked and coughed the soot from his throat and waited for his head to clear. Once he had stopped gasping for breath and his streaming eyes blinked back into focus, he looked around him. He was dangling in the middle of a world of rooftops.

In all directions, the roofs of Bristol stretched away into the distance: gables and gutters; shingles and church spires; tiles, turrets and trees. It was a bird's eye view of the world, and Owen let his eyes wander over it. The river shone gunmetal grey, busy with its traffic of sails and masts winding towards the great rocks of the Avon Gorge. The woods and the green hills west of the city rolled away to the far horizon. Then a yell came up from below him.

Jem Noggins was standing down in the road shouting. He was waving his arms. The wind carried some of his words away, but Owen was able to make out some of what he was saying.

"Good lad… Down the same way you went up… Look lively now Taffy. . Duff on Sundays…"

Remembering his miserable supper of the night before, Owen held out little hope for the chance of Duff appearing in a month of Sundays. He grew more certain in his decision. He didn't want to spend his days stuck up chimneys nor his nights wrapped in a smelly blanket watching Jem Noggins go mad with drink. He didn't want to breathe soot, taste soot and smell soot for the rest of his life. He never wanted to climb another chimney – and he didn't want to go back down this one.

He pulled himself up over the rim of the stack and dropped down from the chimney to stand unsteadily on the ridge of the roof.

In the street down below him, Jem Noggins started to dance up and down. He was shaking his fists in the air and shouting at the sky like a man angry with God.

"You gerroff that roof now! …Rip yer lights out, so 'elp me I will. Get back in your chimbley! Break your spine, I will! I swears it on my Muvver's life! No Duff for you this Sunday!"

Leaving his threats and his Duff to blow about in the wind, Owen dropped onto his hands and knees and scrambled along the spine of rooftops, crawling fearfully among the windy heights. Dodging around each chimney stack, he worked his way along the crescent. All the way, the Sweep followed him on the road below, yelling and cursing blue lights. Then a grand looking man came out of one of the houses and told him to stop his awful racket. It was while Jem Noggins was dealing with the man that Owen saw his line of escape. The house at the end of the crescent backed on to another line of houses that seemed to lead into a perfect warren of roofs: a labyrinth where he could hide from the anger of the maddened Sweep. Sliding down one roof and clambering over another, he caught one last glimpse of Jem Noggins before he vanished from his sight.

He made his way along the maze of roof tops, deeper and deeper into the tangle of houses until the excitement of his escape began to fade. A chill wind was biting through his clothes and his teeth were clattering in his head. Just

below the ridge of roof tiles he was scrambling along, a gable window jutted up out of the roof. Spreading himself across the slates like a spider, Owen crawled down to it until he could peer over the top and look inside.

He was looking into a room filled with a strange assortment of bedclothes and ornaments, bookshelves and boxes, furniture and animals. In one corner of the room, a bright coloured parrot in a gilded cage sat pecking at itself. Sprawled on a mat in front of a fire of beaming coals, a tabby cat lay sleeping. Sitting writing with his head down at a desk just beneath the window, a man with a bald patch at the back of his head suddenly sat bolt upright and looked straight into Owen's eyes.

The man's eyes widened and his mouth dropped open and the two upside down faces looked at each other for a full fifteen seconds without moving. Then, pushing his papers to one side, the man in the room climbed up onto his desk, opened the window and popped his head through to look at Owen right side up. A kind, bearded face topped off with thinning brown hair looked at Owen and frowned with concern.

"Are you training to be a sparrow, or have you just lost your chimney?" the man said. His voice lifted and sang with the familiar accent of the Welsh valleys.

"Please, Mister," said Owen desperately, "I'm running away, I am. I don't want to be a chimbley boy."

"Really?" The man raised his eyebrows. "Well, I can't say as I blame you come to think of it. I don't think I should fancy climbing chimneys much myself. I can't leave a fellow Welshman out there shivering on the roof. Would you care to come into my parlour? Or do you prefer sitting up there where there's an even chance of breaking your neck or catching pneumonia?"

Holding out his arms, Owen was glad enough to grab the first chance he had of getting down off the freezing heights of the rooftops. The man took a careful hold of him and then swung him through the window to put him down on solid ground. It was only a bit of carpet on a creaky wooden floor, but Owen sighed with relief to be off the slippery roof tiles and out of the chill of the wind. The room smelled of tobacco, burning coal – and kippers. The cat was stretching itself in front of the fire.

"My name is Tudor Glendower Jones," said the man. "And may I ask who it is I have the honour of addressing?"

Tudor Jones was a man of about thirty with a face like a good-natured monkey. One eyebrow arched higher than the other above bright brown eyes. He was a tall, well set man, wearing clothes that were a mix of bright colour and shabby age, with colour having the best of the match. His battered slippers were of fine red leather while his trousers were mostly blue: the rest being made up of an assortment of patches. A white shirt was tucked into a scarlet sash around his waist and an old velveteen waistcoat, looking like a coat of green mould, draped over his shoulders. Owen noted that the front of his shirt and waistcoat were spotted and stained with scraps of egg yolk, smears of ink, and tobacco burns.

"Pirate gold!" squawked the bird in the corner. "Food for the sharks!"

Owen looked from the man to the parrot and back again in some confusion. He had never heard a bird talk before.

Tudor Jones smiled at him. "That there is old Methuselah. He's a talking bird, he is. He doesn't understand anything mind. He just copies noises he's heard from sailors. Swear words mostly. What did you say your name was again?"

"Owen Davies, please Mister."

"Owen Davies is it? A good, strong Welsh name." Tudor Jones looked at him thoughtfully. "Well, Owen Davies, you certainly are a very grubby little boy and no mistake. I don't know whether you're a boy who's half made up of soot, or a lump of soot that's half boy."

"I can't help it," Owen told him. "I been stuck up a chimbley half the morning. How would you like it?"

"You are so dirty," said Tudor Jones, "that lumps of you are falling off and making a mess all over my nice carpet."

Looking down, Owen saw that the 'nice carpet' was a knotted Welsh rag rug with a ring of soot on it that had shaken loose as he was put down on the floor.

"What are we going to do with you then, eh?" Tudor Jones squatted down so that his face was on a level with that of Owen.

Owen had been taken away from his family the day before – a family that just couldn't afford him. He had spent a frightening night in a strange and filthy basement watching the behaviour of the drunken Chimney Sweep. What with the cold and the climb up the chimney; the mad scramble across the roof tops and his fear of the chimney sweep catching him and ripping off his head: Owen was a boy on the outer borders of desperation.

He managed to blurt out, "Please can I stay with you, Mister Jones?" before bursting out into a great flood of tears.

Between sobs and gulps and pats on the back and a cup of hot blackberry cordial, Owen told the listening man the whole story of how he came to be running away from the Sweep. From what Tudor Jones said in reply, it was a story

not too far removed from that of his own. Bristol was full of runaways from all over the country – and the distant shores beyond: young vagabonds who survived as best they could. The burial grounds of the poor were filled with the unmarked graves of those who failed. By the time that Owen had finished with his story, the pair of them were kneeling on either side of the sleeping cat, staring into the glowing embers of the fire. Tudor Jones was filled with pity and fear for the future of the boy. Owen was still enmeshed in his memories and his fear of the Sweep.

The parrot broke the silence. "Six steps from the parvis!" it squawked. "Food for the sharks!"

Tudor Jones rose to his feet. "Us Welsh have got to stick together," he said firmly. "I think the first thing to do is to get you washed. One thing at a time is best. Follow me. This is a job for Mother Ryan."

Then Owen found himself clattering down an echoing wooden staircase behind Tudor Jones, past walls of bare plaster patterned with cracks and great blotches of mildew and damp. Down and down they went until they reached a floor of hard flagstones, at which point a door opened and a billowing cloud of warm steam swirled about him as he stepped into the washing room.

"Allow me to introduce a young man to you," said Tudor Jones, stepping forward and bowing to the person who emerged from the steam. "This is Master Owen Davies. Master Owen Davies, this is Mother Ryan."

Mother Ryan, Laundry Lady, was up to her elbows in soap suds, her face dripping with moisture. The steam came from a row of tubs and sinks and half a dozen kettles hissing over a dancing fire. Her face was lined, lean and hard and her mouth puckered as she looked at him. Then she smiled.

"Jaysus! Did you pull him out of a chimney Mister Jones? Well if you did, it's the blessings of Saint Anthony and

Saint Michael be upon you!" She spoke in a soft Irish accent and began to poke around in a steaming vat with a long wooden pole.

"Now this Master Davies is in need of a bit of laundry," said Tudor Jones. "In fact he's in need of a lot of laundry. Soap him and scrub him, rinse him and rub him, then put him through the mangle to dry him off!" With those alarming words, Tudor Jones was gone.

Mother Ryan stood with her hands on her hips, staring at Owen through bleached blue eyes. Her thin lips suddenly cracked into a smile.

"Don't you look so worried Macushla," she said with a laugh. "For isn't a hot bath a great thing on a cold morning like this. And haven't I seven children of me own that I've

bathed and babied and seen fully grown. Take off your dirty clothes now and let's be getting you washed."

So it was that Owen, pulled free of his filthy clothes, found himself plunged into a vat of warm water that quickly came to resemble a pot of ink. From there he was pulled into a fresh tub and rubbed with a pumice stone and scrubbed with a scrubbing brush until his skin was smarting. Then his hair was soaped and his head was pummelled until the soot in his eyes was replaced by soap and his head felt like a clapper inside a bell. Finally he was plunged into yet another tub of water and emerged half drowned but clean and tingling, to be rubbed down briskly with a coarse towel and placed in front of the fire to dry.

Mother Ryan, with a dew drop dangling from the end of her nose, looked at Owen as if he were a painting she had just finished and she was well satisfied with the result.

"Well aren't you the broth of a boy!" she said, in her lilting Irish accent. "Now we need some clothes. Let's see what I have in me oddments."

With that she vanished inside a large cupboard, leaving Owen steaming in front of the fire, along with the row of hissing kettles. When she came out again, she was carrying a wicker basket filled with an assortment of clothes that she proceeded to fling at him one at a time.

"Drawers," she said, hurling across a pair of ragged linen pants that he quickly put on to cover himself up. "Britches and stockings," she said, throwing across a pair of grey breeches and two woollen stockings, one red and one blue. "Vest." Owen pulled over his head a grey rag of flannel. "Shirt." A blouse of faded blue fitted Owen perfectly, apart from one sleeve which was chopped off at the elbow. "Jacket." An ancient brocade jacket, hopelessly stained with red wine, was so big that Owen had to roll the sleeves back before his hands appeared, while the tail of the coat hung nearly to the floor. "Scarf," said Mother Ryan, and proceeded to half throttle him with a threadbare cravat the colour of seaweed. "Hat," said the laundry woman, rummaging around in her basket until she pulled out a knitted sailor's cap that she pulled down over his ears and fixed in place with a rap of her knuckles on the top of his head. "There!" she exclaimed. "Aren't you the very picture of a fine young blade." Then, poking her bony head outside the door she called out loudly, "Are you there now Mister Jones?"

Tudor Jones strolled back into the room and looked at Owen with a critical eye, circling around him as if the boy was a horse he was thinking of buying.

"Very good Mother Ryan," he said finally. "He makes a very impressive scarecrow."

"Take no notice of his blathering," the old woman told Owen briskly. "Them clothes will do you as good as your own until I get them in the wash. Now be off with the pair of you, for I've work enough to do – even if some of us haven't." This last said with a loud sniff in the direction of Tudor Jones.

"Don't you worry your head about that, Mother Ryan," said Tudor Jones. "We all have our work to be getting along with. Especially this boy here has a job to do. How much does he owe you?"

Old Mother Ryan tilted her head towards the ceiling, pushed out her bottom lip and closed one eye. "Sixpence," she said. "And another sixpence for washing his dirty clothes. That's a round shilling you owe me Mister Jones. And no offers. My price is my price."

Tudor Jones, who had been about to offer less, agreed. "Right you are Mother Ryan. A shilling it is. He'll have it for you tonight."

He tapped his finger on the side of his nose and winked a bright brown eye at Owen. "Buffers and Codgers," he said mysteriously. "Come on boy, we've got work to do."

So it was that Owen found himself back on the streets of Bristol, washed and changed and filled with relief at his escape from Jem Noggins and the choking tunnel of soot that was the life he offered. As the two of them passed among the shops, the taverns and the market barrows thronging the city, Tudor Jones explained about Buffers and Codgers.

"You have to be careful Owen," he said seriously. "There are some nasty, wicked people around mind. You never let anyone touch you or grab hold of you, and always be ready to run. You never go off with anyone and you stick to busy streets with lots of people. Then, if you pick your mark carefully, you're safe and you'll have money. It's Buffers and Codgers you're looking for, and leave everyone else alone. Trust me. It's how I made a living when I first run away to Bristol."

Tudor Jones suddenly tightened his grip on Owen's shoulder and they stopped. They were standing outside the busy Corn Exchange building looking up towards the church by the river.

"Look over there boy," he said, pointing across the street to an old gentleman who was peering through his spectacles into the window of a jeweller's shop. "You see that Buffer in the blue frock coat: that old Codger looking at the rings and watches. Go over there and ask him for threepence. Tell him you haven't eaten for three days. Tell him your stomach thinks your throat's cut."

Owen picked his way across the road, avoiding the piles of horse dung, until he was standing beside the man. Then, uncertain how to begin, Owen shifted from one leg to the other until the gentleman turned to look at him.

"Please Mister," he blurted out. "Can I have threepence for some dinner? I haven't eaten for three days. My stomach thinks my throat's been cut."

"Well goodness me!" exclaimed the old gentleman, leaning back and hooking his thumbs into his waistcoat pocket. "We can't have that now, can we." And with a smile, he pressed a silver threepence piece into Owen's outstretched hand: "Off you go then, and fill yourself up with as much steak and kidney pie as you can eat."

Dazed and amazed at his good fortune, Owen wandered back across the street and followed Tudor Jones until they turned a corner and were safely out of sight of the old gentleman.

"Well done Owen," he said. "That's the way of it. Now, when you've got enough for both of us to have something to eat, we'll go and have a bite and I can tell you a bit more about spotting Buffers and Codgers."

Over lunch of a hot pasty with pickled onions and ginger beer, Tudor Jones explained his theory about Buffers and Codgers. They were elderly men whose good nature had not gone sour with age: men who had done well in life, but to whom kindness was still a habit.

"They always got fat little bellies," said Tudor Jones, "which shows that they got plenty of grub and they don't mind eating it. They always got a sparkle in their eyes and lines on their faces what shows they smile a lot and they got something to smile about. And they're always a tad on the old side, the kind what are grandfathers to some little nipper about the same age as you."

"What about women?" asked Owen. "Don't you get women Buffers and Codgers?"

"Waste of time boy," said Tudor Jones. "Women are suspicious of men in general, and to them, a boy is just a man not yet grown. They always think we're up to some mischief and that they can see through it. There's no getting to the bottom of women," he said gloomily. "You'll find out what I mean when you get older."

During the long afternoon spent wandering around the

streets of Bristol, Tudor Jones directed Owen towards no less than seven Buffers and Codgers, each of whom gave Owen some money towards telling his stomach that his throat hadn't been cut. But whenever he tried to pick out one himself, Tudor Jones would point out some reason why he was unsuitable.

"No. He won't do. Mouth like a rat trap."

"No. His shoes are too worn out."

The reasons that he gave for turning down Owen's choices were strange in their variety, ranging from wrinkles in the wrong places to dyed hair; from being too scruffy to being too smart. Tudor Jones took pride in his ability to spot the genuine article among the hordes thronging the city streets, and he was always right in his choice.

At the bottom of Christmas Steps, they turned and

headed towards what Owen was now thinking of as his new home.

"You see Owen," said Tudor Jones, "your real Buffer isn't too vain of his appearance. He doesn't think that much of himself. And he's not bothered about dressing to show people how much money he's got…"

Owen suddenly grabbed his friend's hand and whispered to him in a voice hoarse with fear.

"Help me Mister Jones! Here comes the Sweep! Don't let him get me! Please!"

Slouching towards them along the opposite side of the street was the bear-like figure of Jem Noggins. A scowl of baffled fury sat on his sooty face and his great black head turned from side to side, endlessly searching – searching for something the Sweep had lost.

CHAPTER THREE

The Scrimshaw

Fairly dancing with fear at the sight of the Sweep coming towards them, Owen pulled frantically at the hand of Tudor Jones.

"Run!" he begged. "We have to run!"

Then the restless eyes of Jem Noggins fixed upon the pair of them. He saw them. With a roar of rage, he came surging across the road towards them. A passing coach checked him for a moment, blocking them from his sight.

In that moment, Owen suddenly found himself lifted into the air and flung over the shoulders of Tudor Jones as if he were a sack of flour. Then he was bumping along as fast as that man's long legs could carry him, away from the bellowing threats of the Chimney Sweep. The distance between them widened as they ran through the crowded streets towards the church of St Mary's on the Quay. Owen watched the sweep falling further and further behind. Tudor Jones moved like a racehorse while the Sweep blundered along, lurching and staggering like a blinded bear. But he showed no sign of giving up the chase. Stubborn as a disease, he followed on behind them. Across the bridge over the river, down streets filled with barrows selling fruit and pans and clothing, Tudor Jones ran. With Owen bouncing on his shoulder, he ran and ran.

Turning down a side alley, past a row of hovels and a reeking opium den, he ran. They came out into another busy road, alive with shops and people and moving carriages. But before they reached the next turn off, the Sweep came lumbering into view, chasing along behind them like a bad dream.

Tudor Jones was losing his breath. As they turned another corner, with the Sweep again out of sight for a few moments, he gasped.

"Can't keep going like this. Got to drop you off. Wait until I get back. Got to lose Sweep. Stay and wait. Keep out of sight."

And then there was the Sweep again: his massive body lurching around in the middle of the road; his face purple and running with sweat.

Putting on a desperate burst of speed, Tudor Jones again spurted ahead to increase the distance between them. He turned into a street filled with barrows and yelling hawkers by Old Saint Paul's Market.

"Penny a pound for taters. Get yer taters here, my lovers…"

"Pots and pans from Merthyr Tydfil…"

"Hot black pudding. Three slices for a penny…"

The faces and the voices blurred by.

Then a door was pushed open and Owen found himself thrown inside. The door slammed shut behind him before he knew what was happening. Looking around for somewhere to hide, he burrowed in among some coats hanging on a railing. Then the black head of the Sweep went past the shop window without a pause or a glance in his direction.

For a second he was in front of Owen, etched against the glass in shadow. Then he was gone.

Owen went limp with relief. Then he froze once more

as a hand gripped his shoulder from behind and pulled him out from his nest of coats.

The man he turned to face was a tall, burly man dressed in a rust coloured frock coat with a spotless white cravat tied under his neat chin beard. The great dome of his head was topped with a sparse growth of grey hair. Behind a pair of gold rimmed spectacles, soft hazel eyes looked down at Owen with a mixture of pity tinged with suspicion.

"Well now, look at you," said the man softly. "Do I detect a boy in trouble? What might you have done to get into trouble, eh?"

His voice was calm and gentle. Owen hoped he had found a genuine Buffer and Codger. The words came tumbling out of Owen's mouth without him thinking.

"Please Mister, can I stop here for a minute? There's a man chasing me. Trying to stick me up a chimbley, he is. My friend…My friend, he's coming back for me once he's lost him. Please Mister! He'll rip my lights out he will. Said he'd break my spine. Don't give me away to him…" Owen was sobbing with fear.

The man patted him on the shoulder. "Calm yourself boy. Calm yourself. Don't fret. Be still. Be calm. Don't tremble so. Nothing bad will happen to you here." He spoke in the lilting accent of the Welsh Valleys. His hand on Owen's shoulder guided him towards a chair.

Owen sat down, still panting with terror.

"Take deep breaths," said the man. "Go on. Breathe deeply. That's the way now. Take deep breaths and have no fear."

The calm and soothing tone of the big man's voice and the deep breaths that he took calmed Owen. He forced himself to stop shaking and he started to breathe more easily.

"A runaway climbing boy out of Wales eh?" the man mused. "Well now, what have we got here that might be of interest to a Welsh climbing boy? Oh, but, pardon me Sir! Allow me to introduce myself. My name is Adrian Obsidian Bell. I am a fellow Welshman, at your service, young man." His eyebrows arched up and his whiskers twitched. "And this," he continued, spreading his arms wide, "this is my emporium: The Odds and Ends Shop."

Suddenly he reached behind his ear and pulled something out of nowhere between his fingers.

"Now, there's a thing!" he exclaimed, holding out the object for Owen to look at. "Where did that come from?"

It was a large white disc with a picture of a church scratched upon its surface in black ink. The big man squatted down beside Owen and held it between his finger and thumb, turning it so that Owen saw some writing on the back. But Owen couldn't read.

"You see that, boy? That's a mystery, that is. That's a slice across the middle of a sperm whale's tooth. Do you know what a sperm whale is child? Have you ever heard of the great Leviathan: the mighty giant that roams across all of the seas of this Earth?"

The man squatting beside him talked on quietly. Just listening to his voice, Owen began to feel warm and comfortable, even though he didn't have the faintest idea what the man was talking about.

Adrian Bell continued in his soft, hypnotic voice, turning the disc around between his long fingers.

"Well now," he continued, "I am going to tell you about one of the most extraordinary creatures in the world. Listen carefully, for I am going to tell you about the Sperm Whale. The sperm whale is one of the biggest animals that have ever lived upon God's good Earth. It swims the sea like a fish, but it is bigger than any fish in the world. It breathes the air like a human being, but it can dive a mile underwater. Then it stays there for half an hour or more, eating the monstrous serpents that live in the ocean deeps. The whale is as long as a row of houses. This thing that I am holding is just a slice of its tooth. Can you picture how big the thing itself must be?"

Owen looked at the tooth, imagining a creature many times the size of Jem Noggins. The thought was somehow a comforting one.

"Just think my young friend. This whale, this giant of the oceans – whose tooth we have here – roamed all the seas of the Earth, from side to side and from top to bottom. This whale saw the far north of our whirling planet, where there is nothing but endless snow. The dark seas would be studded with drifting icebergs moving silently past the great cliffs of ice that glimmered blue in the moonlight."

The voice was low and soothing. Owen felt safe and comfortable as the voice of Adrian Bell continued.

"Then the whale would move on. Who knows but a month or two later, this whale was swimming past islands a-sprout with palms, near the shores of sunny Africa, where

the black men fish from canoes dug out of solid tree trunks. The whole world of the seas was this whale's home. Just as a man on dry land can't see far under the surface of the water, so a creature swimming in the sea can only know the shores of the land: the bays and headlands, cliffs and crags where the land meets the sea. But what did this whale need of the land? His world was deep under water, fighting great monsters at the bottom of the sea, on the mud of the ocean floor. This tooth," he continued, turning the flat disc round and round; "this tooth bit into the mighty swordfish and the savage sharks and tore them into pieces. Here. Feel it."

He passed the thing into Owen's hand. It was cool to the touch and smooth, except where it had been scratched to make the picture and the writing.

Adrian Bell continued talking dreamily. "The whale must have lived for a very long time to grow a tooth of that size. For years he must have wandered the oceans as the spirit took him. In the tropics seas, they tell me, the sea is warm and turquoise blue, scattered with islands of coral and filled with fishes all the colours of the rainbow. And in all of this world, from the ice-clamped waters of the dark, polar seas, to the sunlit oceans of the Equator at the middle of the Earth, there was nothing that the whale feared. Sometimes he would come up from the calm, green depths to find the surface of the sea whipped by a furious hurricane. It held no terror for him. He would sport and play in the raging waves, then sink down once more to the calm beneath and the storm would pass over his head. In all the deep green ocean, there was no fish nor storm that could harm him, so vast was he; so strong and so brave. And he was clever too. He must have been clever: his brain was so big and so heavy. Who knows what thoughts moved through his mind as he pushed his great body through the waters of the Earth? Did he have names for the strange creatures that live in the dark abyss: for the birds and the flying fishes: the cliffs and the bays of the land? Who knows what he made of the moon shining down on the sea and the million stars of the night? He might have imagined himself to be the Lord of all the Oceans: The Eyes of God in the waters of the Earth."

Owen, lost in the magic of the man's words, was far away at sea as the dreaming voice of Adrian Bell continued thinking aloud.

"But the whale didn't know the ways of the human beings who lived on the land. He knew nothing of little boys forced into lives of misery: little boys who would grow into rough, hard men and take to the sea in wooden ships. The whale did not know of the oil that men burned to lighten their darkness, or the money his body was worth to the merchants and the sailors: men who were clever at making knives and spears and cunning in ways of using them.

"So one day this whale came up for air, came rising through the green depths as he had done countless times before, and there, floating near to him in the sunlight was a ship.

"What was a ship to a whale? It was a floating curiosity: a thing: something like a tree washed out to sea. Was he, the Storm Leaper, the Shark Slayer, likely to be afraid of a tree floating on the water? So he spouted, emptying and filling his great lungs with sweet air and watching the ship as he breathed.

"A small boat pulled away from the ship and began rowing towards him. It meant nothing: a little creature with many fins that scurried towards him over the surface of the water. As it came nearer, he saw the sunlight glint on something that looked like a long, sharp tooth. It was held by a man.

"The waves rocked him gently and the albatross floated high overhead in a sky of azure blue. The great whale rolled easily in the ocean swell, puffing and blowing as the water washed over him and the odd creature drew ever more close to where he lay in the water. Then the long, sharp tooth came darting at him and bit deep into his lungs, wiping out the sunlight in a black explosion of pain. Although the whale dived and swam, he could not get free of the long tooth inside him, or get rid of the men in the following boat. He surfaced again, sending a red froth of blood spouting through his blowhole. Men were still beside him. More harpoons were slammed into him. Nothing but pain and terror remained until the great whale died."

There was a silence. Looking up at last, Owen saw that Adrian Bell was misty eyed.

"So it was that the mightiest of God's creatures fell

victim to the harpoons of the whaling men. Then they cut up his carcass and opened his head for the oil it contained. One of the whalers took a tooth from the great jaw, and perhaps that man made this."

He took the object from Owen's hand and held it out in his palm. "See, by there. The tooth was sliced cross ways. Then it was polished. Then a picture was scratched onto it with the point of a needle, and soot was rubbed in to make the picture stand out. It's called a Scrimshaw."

"And here's a mystery for you now," the man continued. "On the one side here, as you can see, is a picture of a church. What church is it? Where is this church to be found?" He turned the Scrimshaw over. "And what is the connection between that church what is written on the other side? For five years I've been waiting for an answer to that question."

"What does the writing say?" asked Owen.

Then the door of the shop clattered open and Tudor Jones, red-faced and sweating, closed it behind him.

"I lost him Owen," he said, panting. "He's half way to Stokes Croft by now. You all right boy?"

Pleased as he was to see his friend return, Owen was still bound up in the story he had been listening to. "Mister Bell has been telling me about whales and scrimshaws and things about the sea."

"Ahem. Yes indeed. Adrian Obsidian Bell at your service," said that gentleman, rising up onto his toes and inclining his great head in something like a bow.

"Tudor Glendower Jones, Sir," the other replied, with a similar nod of his head.. "It's always nice to meet a fellow Welshman. Thank you for taking care of the boy. We were in a bit of a tight spot. Diolch yn fawr."

"Croeso. My pleasure I assure you."

"What does the writing say Mister Bell?" piped Owen. "You was telling me what was written on that Scrimshaw."

"Ah yes. Of course. It says, 'Listen to Methuselah.'"

In the silence that followed could be heard the measured ticking of a clock and the rumble of wheels rolling over the cobbles outside.

"Can I have a look at that?" Tudor Jones spoke with sudden interest then moved towards the window to look at the object in the light. "Where did this come from then?"

"Curious story altogether." The big man pulled at his whiskers and wrinkled his nose. "An old seaman brought it in. Man by the name of Salt. Daniel Salt... Er, excuse me."

The door of the shop had opened to admit two identical women wearing the same dresses of startling peacock blue. With a smile and a tip of his domed head, Adrian Bell moved over to greet them, leaving Tudor Jones and Owen to talk between themselves.

"Listen to Methuselah," repeated Tudor Jones. "Well now, there's a thing."

"Isn't that the name of your parrot?" said Owen.

"Quite right boy. Quite right. And do you know how I came by that bird: that stinking, swearing bag of mouldy feathers? Well I'll tell you now. It come with my room that parrot did. One attic room complete with bed, table, chairs, carpet – and parrot. That's what I had to agree to rent off Old Mother Ryan. One room complete with parrot. Parrot named Methuselah, after the ancient old man in the Bible. Parrots live a long time Owen. They often live longer than them as looks after them."

He paused, and his voice rose with excitement as he continued. "But the most interesting thing about this Scrimshaw and that parrot is the name of the man who had the room before I did. That same man brought the parrot home with him to England. It was him who named it Methuselah. For twenty years that man lived in my room – when he was at home that is. But he wasn't at home very much. That was because he spent most of his time at sea. And the name of that pig-tailed old sea dog pickled in rum?" He paused then almost shouted the answer: "His name was Daniel Salt!"

Tudor Jones paused and stared at the creamy disc of ivory in his hand. "Listen to Methuselah, eh?" he said musingly. "Well, I been listening to Methuselah for the past five years, and he never made a jot of sense to me – screeching away in his corner like a rusty old saw. But now I'm starting to wonder if I've been listening right. Why is Old Mother Ryan so very particular about that parrot? And why do it have to live in my room? Why should a seafaring man like Salt leave his Scrimshaw here, of all the places to leave it? And how does this picture of the church fit in? We're going to have to listen to that bird more carefully Owen. I smell money somewhere. A lot of money."

No sooner were these words out of his mouth than there was a sudden commotion at the front of the shop and Adrian Bell ushered the two ladies out through the door amid squawks of protest. When he turned around his eyes were sparkling behind his spectacles and his cheeks flushed.

"I couldn't help but overhear your comments about the Scrimshaw, Mister Jones. It seems you can shed some light on this, this… Scrimshaw business."

Tudor Jones looked at him suspiciously then rubbed his chin and spoke to the ceiling as if he was looking for something.

"What business is that then?"

Adrian Bell's lips closed in a thin line and his eyes were suddenly cold as he thrust out his hand.

"My Scrimshaw, Mister Jones. If you please!"

Tudor Jones hesitated a moment, then handed back the mysterious object to the burly proprietor of the Odds and Ends Shop.

Adrian Bell looked at Owen, then he looked back at Tudor Jones.

"You were talking about money and about your parrot – name of Methuselah," he said. "I think we'd better have a bit of a chat, like. All three of us Welsh men together. Shall we go into my parlour?"

CHAPTER FOUR

A Fireside Partnership

With the air of a man who has made up his mind, Adrian Bell turned to the shop door and locked it, then hung up a sign informing the world that the Odds and Ends Shop was CLOSED FOR BUSINESS.

"Please follow me ," he said.

He led them through a curtain at the back of the shop into a parlour where a coal fire glowed and the setting sun lit up the pictures covering the walls. Adrian Bell evidently had a passion for ships. Brigs and luggers, galleons and sloops jostled for picture space. The snug little room was fragrant with the smell of coffee and Adrian Bell poured out three cups from a silver pot warming on a tripod by the fireside.

"Special treat for you here young man," he said, busy with cream and brown sugar. "Java coffee, all the way from the other side of the world. Why, bless my buttons, I was fifteen years old before I had my first cup of coffee. There you are now. Just take a sip and drink it very slowly."

Sitting down across the hearth from them, Adrian Bell drew the ivory disc from his pocket, holding it between thumb and forefinger.

"I suggest that we pool our knowledge of this affair and see if we can come to some understanding."

He sipped at his coffee and continued. "It seems that you

have a part of the answer to this… this riddle, and I have the puzzle itself. I mean this thing: the Scrimshaw."

There was a long silence as the two men looked at each other across the room. Owen, slurping at his coffee cup, felt warm and comfortable in the glow of the firelight as he watched the two of them thinking things through.

Tudor Jones looked steadily at the man opposite him. From his silver buckled shoes to the top of his big domed head, he was a gentleman of a type familiar to Tudor Jones. The sparkle in his eyes and the determined expression on the lined face marked him out quite clearly.

Tudor Jones finally leaned forward. "I propose a gentleman's agreement between fellow Welshmen. Whatever might come out of this in the way of … financial gain like, I suggest that we split it clean between us. What do you say, Mister Bell?"

"Between the three of us." Adrian Bell's voice was firm. "Agreed?"

"Agreed."

"Good. It seems only right. It was the boy brought you in here, and without him, neither of us would have known about the other one. There would have been nothing to link between the two of us and this… this delightful mystery."

His eyes sparkled as he continued, "Here I am, five years and more nursing this thing, and suddenly a boy comes flying in through the doors of my shop. He is as frightened as a snared rabbit, so in order to calm him down and make him forget his fear, I tell him a story about the first thing that comes to my hand: a slice from the tooth of a whale. Then just as I am telling him about the Scrimshaw, you come in. And you would have gone – just as suddenly as you arrived – but for the fact that the boy made me tell him what was written on the thing. And hearing what I said gave you a hint that you might know something of the matter.

There is the hand of Providence in our meeting. The boy should have his share of whatever comes of it. He certainly seems to be in need of a bit of good fortune. How did he come to be with you?"

Tudor Jones leaned forwards, spreading his bony hands to take in the warmth of the fire. He set out briefly the facts of Owen's arrival at his attic room window and what he knew of the boy's story.

The long day and the warm fire had combined with the fading light and the steady, murmuring voices to send Owen to sleep. With his chin on his chest and his empty cup in his lap, he snored softly as the two men probed at the mystery.

"Let's get down to it then," said Tudor Jones. "What do you know about this Scrimshaw and Bosun Salt?"

"Not a great deal." Adrian Bell leaned back in his chair and reached for a small velvet cap from the bookshelf beside his chair. "Not a great deal – but the little I knew was very interesting." He placed the hat carefully on his head. " For fifteen years Bosun Salt came in here with his scrimshaws, always with the same instructions. They were not for sale but for safe keeping, to be collected by another seaman named Abel Judd. Have you heard that name before?"

"Never."

"Well, Bosun Salt would come by every year or two and leave one of these things with me. Three months or six months later, Mister Judd would come in and pick it up. Once or twice he left a piece of his own for Mister Salt to collect. I gathered that both of them were sea-going men who seldom found themselves ashore in Bristol at the same time. It seems they used my shop as a means of exchanging information. As far as I could understand, their scrimshaws always contained some kind of coded message. What they meant was a complete mystery to me – as I'm sure they were supposed to be."

He rose to his feet and lit an oil lamp on the mantle piece, flooding the room with warm light as he continued in his dreamy, reflective voice.

"The last time Bosun Salt came in, I was surprised to see how sick he looked. He told me he had been wounded in a fight at sea with one of Napoleon's frigates – taken a musket ball in the lung. He had always been a hale and hearty sort of a man, but on that last visit you could see he was a dying one: pale and thin and coughing all the time. He knew he was just a step away from his coffin, no pun intended, and his instructions were different this time. He told me to keep this Scrimshaw for five years. If Abel Judd hadn't called for it in that time, it was mine to do with as I pleased. I can remember his poor crippled, voice. The air whistled in his shredded lungs as he spoke."

" 'I won't be seeing you again Bell,' he told me as he left. 'Not in this life anyway. And if Abel don't call in, he'll have gone where I'm bound and that thing's yours. I got no family,' he said 'and that there is my legacy.'

"I remember the bitter laugh he gave after the word 'legacy'. 'I'll never get it now,'" he said. 'I'll never get it now.' Then he coughed his way out into the street and he was gone. I never saw him again. Neither did I hear from Abel Judd. And that was over five years ago."

In the long silence that followed, the only sounds in the room were the gentle ticking of a grandfather clock and the stirring of a coal settling on the fire.

"Now for your side of the bargain," said Adrian Bell at last. "What do you know about Bosun Salt and his Scrimshaw?"

Tudor Jones pursed his lips for a moment.

"Old Mother Ryan," he said. "She's the woman owns the house where I got my room see. When I first moved in she was always going on about 'Poor Bosun Salt' and how he'd lived under her roof for twenty years with never a cross word between them. Never a cross word because he was hardly ever there and he paid her well. She told me as how he'd caught one of Boney's musket balls, even though he was a merchantman and not a Navy tar. She told me as how he'd coughed his lights out in my very room, she did. But the main thing was his parrot. I had to keep the thing in my room. She said as how Bosun Salt had left his little orphan with her so as she could keep him safe, and how it was a sacred trust. Sacred trust or not, she didn't want the old squawker down in her rooms, so it had to stay where it was. She said it felt at home there and wouldn't want to move. Methuselah, Salt called it, after the old chap in the Bible as was supposed to have lived for a thousand years. I've always thought the bird spoke nothing but rubbish, but maybe there's some sense to it somewhere if you know what it is you're listening out for."

Adrian Bell stroked his chin and stretched his legs before the fire, watching the light playing upon the buckles of his shoes.

"Two parts of the same puzzle," he said, thinking aloud. "The Scrimshaw was left with me and the parrot left with Old Mother Ryan. 'Listen to Methuselah' says the Scrimshaw, so what the parrot has to say and the picture of the church on the back of the scrimshaw are the key to the mystery."

Rising to his feet, he took the velvet cap from his head, put it back on the bookshelf, and placed a metal guard in front of the fire.

"I think we had better talk to your Old Mother Ryan and see what she can tell us before we start on the puzzle of what the bird has to say. A few bottles will probably help our business along." His voice smacked with relish as he pulled on an overcoat. "A nice drop of wine and a goose and apricot pie would make a very agreeable supper for us all, I think. Come along Mister Jones, if you will attend to our young friend there, I shall summon a coach to transport us to – who knows where?"

"Back to my rooms, is it?" said Tudor Jones. "I won't wake the boy up until the coach arrives Mister Bell. Let him grab a bit of sleep like. He's had a hard day of it"

"Just so, Mister Jones. Just so." And Adrian Bell vanished in search of a coach and horses.

CHAPTER FIVE

The Riddle of Martin Chapple

"Danz a bad boy! Put im in the scuppers!" The harsh screech of the parrot ripped across the room as they opened the door and went in.

Tudor Jones lit the oil lamp and as light filled the room, Adrian Bell began to set out the meal he had bought on the table.

"Can you make up a fire, Owen?" asked Tudor Jones. "I need to go and invite Old Mother Ryan up to supper."

"I know how to make up the fire," said Owen. "I done it loads of times, I have."

Tudor Jones clattered off down the stairs.

Rolling up half a dozen spills of paper and setting kindling sticks on top, Owen soon had a fire crackling in the grate as a range of appetising smells drifted across from the table.

Adrian Bell stood by the parrot's cage, stroking his finger against the wire.

"Who's a pretty boy then?" he said. "Pretty Polly."

The parrot scratched his beak with a scaly talon and

looked sly. It opened and closed its beak, pecked at a seed and sulked in silence.

Owen piped up, "No use talking to him Mister Bell. He only talks if you eggnore him. The more you eggnore him, the more he goes on, see. But when you talks to him, he just shuts up."

"Oh, really?" said Adrian Bell. "Know this parrot well, do you? And what else can you tell me about this bird you know so well?"

Owen was saved by the entry of Tudor Jones as the two men finished laying the table for supper.

Occupying the place of honour was a large pie with a shining golden crust. It was soon surrounded with bowls of pickles, cold potatoes and beetroot, a hot crusty loaf of bread and a yellow slab of butter. An array of odd plates and chipped glasses, knives and forks were set out on the table, with the final touch given by three gleaming green bottles.

"I think that should do it," said Tudor Jones. "It certainly looks appetising enough."

"It's a feast," said Adrian Bell. "A meal to solve a mystery." He crossed to the fire where he stood warming his hands behind him as he thought aloud.

"I wonder what will come of all this: scrimshaws and parrots and runaway climbing boys. Do you know, my new friends, you might be my salvation? Do you have any idea how many years I have been sat in that shop, waiting to have an adventure?"

"Will that Jem Noggins still be after me?" Owen asked.

"Don't worry about that," said Adrian Bell. "Mister Jones and I will be standing by you from now on. But while I think on it, it's probably best we try to find Jem Noggins and come to an agreement with him. He will need to be repaid whatever he gave to your mother, with a bit more for his trouble. It should only be a matter of a few guineas."

"But I haven't got a few guineas," put in Tudor Jones.

"I have," said Bell.

"I never meant to cause no trouble," said Owen. "It was just that…I never wanted to be a climbing boy, and…when my Pa died and Mam sent me away… I hated that horrible room with him getting drunk…And that chimbley, all full of soot. I couldn't breathe, see. And I was frightened of falling. It was horrible." His voice cracked on the edge of tears.

"It's all right Owen," said Tudor Jones hurriedly. "No need to worry, butty. You're with us now. And look at this feast we got in front of us."

"Quite right," said Adrian Bell. "Don't upset yourself now. Think about something else." His eyes lit up and he dangled the ivory disc in front of the boy. "Do you know what I think this is leading us towards? Treasure – that's what I think it is! This Scrimshaw and that parrot are the key to finding Treasure!"

"Pirate gold!" screeched the parrot. "Martin Chapple!"

"Do you hear that? Martin Chapple's pirate gold! We're on the track all right!" Adrian Bell rubbed his hands.

"But who is Martin Chapple?" Tudor Jones sounded mystified. "Old Mother Ryan don't know nothing about him. I've asked her before."

"Well I don't know, do I? It's all part of the mystery. The fun of any mystery lies in solving it. Perhaps Martin Chapple was shipmate of Bosun Salt's. It sounds like a sailor's name, don't you think? Just close your eyes and you can picture the scene: old Bosun Salt and his quartermaster Martin Chapple, the only survivors of a whole ship's company, drifting in an open boat after a shipwreck off the Dry Tortugas. The sun is blazing down like a brass hammer. The sharks are splashing in the water around the boat as Martin Chapple and Bosun Salt share between them the last piece of weevily ship's biscuit."

Adrian Bell got down onto one knee in front of the fire and held his hand to his forehead as if he was looking at something far away.

"Suddenly there is a line of dark blue on the horizon. 'Land!' croaks Bosun Salt, pointing a powder-burned finger towards the distant shore. 'Land, Martin! Land!' But the land comes too late for Martin Chapple. By the time the boat pulls into a palm – fringed lagoon, he is dying of yellowjack. Martin Chapple's last words are given in a painful whisper to Bosun Salt. He tries to tell him where his hoard of treasure is to be found. 'Come closer Dan,' he says. 'The treasure is hidden in…The treasure is hidden … in…"

"Stow that bilge!" said the parrot, in a voice of unmistakable scorn. "Put him in the scuppers!"

Adrian Bell rose to his feet, slightly red in the face. "Well, at any rate, that's how it might have happened. You know I

think that parrot needs to be taught some manners." He darted a hostile look towards the caged bird, which responded by opening its beak in a silent sneer of mockery.

Just then the door opened and Old Mother Ryan bustled in. She was transformed. Having been invited for dinner, she had dressed up for the occasion by throwing on a purple shawl decorated with green and yellow birds. Crammed onto her wedge-shaped head was a somewhat moth-eaten wig of red hair and a hat festooned with feathers. Decked out in this gaudy finery, she swayed slightly back on her heels and looked haughtily down her nose at everyone in the room.

With great dignity, she extended a limp hand the size of a mallet towards Adrian Bell and said, "Charmed, I'm sure. Very delighted to meet you, Dearie." A strong smell of gin wafted off her as she spoke.

After the introductions, Tudor Jones led them to the table and they set to work on the feast laid out before them. The goose and apricot pie in its rich pastry was soon reduced to a few crumbs. The pickles and the potatoes vanished. The green bottles passed backwards and forwards between the clinking glasses as the red wine ebbed and flowed.

Old Mother Ryan quickly thawed out towards the burly stranger who had provided all these good things. As she melted under the combined influence of the food, the wine and the fire, her tongue wagged freely.

"That parrot?" she answered Adrian Bell. "Poor Bosun Salt bought that parrot back with him, the trip before his last, may Saint Peter and Saint Paul have mercy on him! Didn't he just come walking into my washroom with the Thing sticking out of his overcoat pocket and swearing blue lights! The parrot I mean, not Bosun Salt."

Her voice grew harsh: "I thought it was a horrible thing

then, and I still do now, but poor Bosun Salt, he set great store by it, so he did."

"Thieving old witch!" shrieked the parrot.

"You shut yer beak!" Old Mother Ryan yelled at the bird, brandishing her fork in the air. "I wont have you talking to me like that in me own home, ye scrawny bag of vermin!"

Looking at the profile of Old Mother Ryan, with her feathered hat waving above her great curved nose, Owen was struck by a certain family resemblance between her and the parrot. The parrot responded to her tirade by raising a scaly claw to its beak and indulging in another of its silent sneers.

"You know, if it wasn't for the memory of poor Bosun Salt, I'd have thrown that thing in the river years ago," said the old woman, angrily. "He used to sit and talk to it for hours, so he did: teaching it swearing and abuse. He got very particular about it when he got back from that last trip – when he knew that he was dying. 'After I'm gone,' he says to me, 'you're to keep that bird up in my room and look after it like one of yer own.'"

She paused to fork down another piece of beetroot and swig at her glass before she continued.

"Well, to be honest, he never actually said to keep it in his own room. But I wouldn't be wanting it downstairs with me, would I now? Swearing and carrying on until the very air turned blue! So I just let out the room with the parrot in it as, as . . a sort of a sitting tenant. And you don't mind at all now, do you Mister Jones? Sure, I believe in respecting the wishes of the dead – especially when you're paid for it. Will you just top up me glass for me Dearie?"

"So Bosun Salt paid you to look after his parrot?" said Adrian Bell, pouring her another generous measure of wine.

"Oh that he did right enough," she replied. "Good gold

he paid me, to keep that bird as my lodger. It's a little odd, so it is. But Mister Jones here doesn't mind, and bird seed's cheap enough. Cheap and cheerful – like me! Cheep cheep, Birdie!"

With her last remark, she broke into a bray of laughter which caused her to choke on a piece of pickle. At this the parrot started cackling and sniggering horribly and it was some minutes before calm was restored and the talk could continue.

"Do you, by any chance, know of someone called Martin Chapple?" asked Adrian Bell

"Never in all my days."

"What about Abel Judd?" Bell murmured.

Old Mother Ryan froze in her seat. She turned on Adrian Bell a look filled with sudden hostility.

"And waddy you know of Abel Judd?" Her speech was now slurred. "Abel Judd was a pig!" She banged on the table with a great red fist. "It was Abel Judd told Bosun Salt I cheated him! Slander and libel! Twenty gold sovereigns! I never took them from what Bosun Salt gave me. And how was Abel Judd to know how much was given me? They was never ashore at the same time. Eighty was what Bosun Salt gave me! I never had any hundred sovereigns: with the roof falling down and the tradesmen threatening to put me in the workhouse. Abel Judd! Don't you mention his name again in this house! He's banned from here! Banned for life!"

With that, she drained her glass and tilted her head so far back that both she and her chair went down in a heap on the floor.

As she struggled to sit up, her hat was hanging over one eye and the red wig had slipped down over the other.

"I'm blinded!" she wailed. "It's the curse of Abel Judd! He's blinded me for his sovereigns, so he has!" Pushing her wig back, she discovered her sight restored and she struggled

up to a sitting position on the floor. "There we are, there we are," she slurred. "We mushn't quarrel now, musht we."

She held her empty wine glass up to Adrian Bell and simpered at him as one eye closed. "Jusht fill me glass up Dearie, like the darling boy you are," she said. Then her other eye closed and she sank gently back to lie on the floor. Almost immediately she started to snore.

Adrian Bell smiled as he picked up her fallen chair. "Well that was most instructive," he said. "It seems that once Bosun Salt learned he couldn't trust his landlady to pass things on to Abel Judd, he started to make use of me."

Tudor Jones took up the thread. "He couldn't trust Old Mother Ryan with his last message to his friend… so he gave half the message to his parrot and left the rest of it on the Scrimshaw with you."

Adrian Bell was hoarse with excitement. "Abel Judd would have known where to go after picking up the Scrimshaw. He would have known who Methuselah was and have found some way of getting the old woman to hand him over. It's my belief that Abel Judd and Bosun Salt passed one another information about various schemes and chances to make money that came their way over the years. If things turned out well, they would share whatever profits came of it. Once Mother Ryan started to take her own share from the money given to her by Bosun Salt to hand over to Judd, they hit on the idea of using scrimshaws left with me to communicate with one another."

The parrot croaked on cue. "Martin Chapple. Six steps from the parvis."

Tudor Jones frowned. "The trouble is that the bird makes no sense. Most of what he says is sailor talk about swabbing bilges and suchlike. No-one knows anything about this Martin Chapple; and what does six steps from the parvis mean? Or is he saying pelvis and not getting it right?"

Bell leaned forwards in his chair. "The parvis is an old word for a church porch. That would make good sense to Abel Judd, because the picture on the Scrimshaw is a picture of a church." Pulling the Scrimshaw from his pocket, he studied it intently in the lamplight. "So here we have a picture of a church, and a direction: take six steps from the church porch. But where is this church? It must be that Judd would have recognised it. Perhaps he and Salt had gone to a funeral there. Or a wedding. But how do we find it? How do we find this particular church?"

"It could be a chapel," said Owen.

Adrian Bell jumped to his feet. "Well done boy! That's it!" he cried. "Martin Chapple isn't a person at all! It's a place: Saint Martin's Chapel!"

"A neat trick," said Tudor Jones wonderingly. "A foolproof plan. The Scrimshaw showed Judd where to go and what to listen to, pointing him to Methuselah. And the parrot would tell him where to go once he got to the church. That's why Bosun Salt paid Old Mother Ryan to keep the parrot."

"There's money in this; a lot of money. I can feel it in my bones." Adrian Bell punched his fist softly into the palm of his other hand. "I knew that Scrimshaw was leading us somewhere. I just knew it."

"It's treasure!" said Owen. "And the Scrimshaw led us to it!"

Tudor Jones smiled. "Hold hard there boys. It hasn't led us anywhere yet. Nor will it until we find that church – and whatever it is that is six steps from the church porch."

Adrian Bell agreed. "Quite right. Quite right. Plenty of work still to be done. We can probably find St. Martin's Chapel in the lexicon of churches. Go round them all until we find one like the picture."

"First things first," said Tudor Jones. "This boy needs a bed. Then you can give me a hand getting the old woman downstairs. We'll call on you first thing in the morning."

In a daze of sleepy excitement, Owen lay down on the bed of cushions made up for him on the floor.

As the two men carried the old woman downstairs, his head was jumping with fragments of memories and images of what had happened to him since he had woken up that morning.

But it had been a long, long day. The last time he had slept had been in the reeking, shadow-haunted rooms of the drunken Chimney Sweep.

He was already fast asleep when Tudor Jones came back into the room, blew out the light, and shortly afterwards, added his own snores to those of the slumbering boy.

CHAPTER SIX

At The Grave of Briney Morgan

It was the best and longest sleep that Owen had ever had. The crowded hovel he had called had home was always filled with the noise of his family around him. They woke, rising to go to work before the first light of dawn. And with four children to a bed, squashed in head to toe, sleep was a restless, brief affair, snatched between kicks, squeals, groans and muffled threats. For the first time in his life, he had slept undisturbed for as long as he wanted. When he awoke, it was a luxury to lie back on his cushions, remembering all that had happened to him the day before…

The Chimney Sweep, dancing with rage in the street below as he made his escape along the roof tops; old Mother Ryan, scrubbing him clean in the steaming washroom; the mysterious Scrimshaw, turning between the fingers of Adrian Bell.

He laughed out loud at the memory of the parrot and the old woman squawking at each other across the dinner table. Then he remembered his mother giving him over to the chimney sweep, and he felt ashamed to be such a poor thing that even his own family didn't want him. But soon he was lost in dreams of treasure and riches as the busy flies buzzed against the ceiling and pigeons rustled on the ledge outside the window.

Then there was the sound of footsteps on the stairs, the doorknob rattled, and the bony face of Old Mother Ryan peered into the room. Her eyes were red and bleary under a mop cap.

"You're awake now then, are ye?" she said, stepping into the room. She was carrying a great armful of clothes which she dropped down beside Owen's nest of cushions. "I've been going through my oddments child, and I'm thinking you'll be needing more clothes. By the time I finished washing your poor rags, the only thing they was fit for is stuffing plumpers."

She put a hand to her forehead and groaned.

"Me head feels like the divil is dancing a jig in it. Them wicked men shouldn't of made me drink all of that wine, and me with the best part of a pint of gin inside me before I even come to the table. And now there's a great wagon – load of laundry to get done before tonight or I'll be ending in the workhouse. Don't ever be a laundry woman, boy. All you get is suds and sores. Ah, good morning to you Mister Jones. All right as for those as can lie in bed all day. Some of us have to work for our living, and a hard path of the sorrows it is we tread…"

And with that she was gone and the door closed behind her.

Tudor Jones climbed out of his bed and stepped into a pair of blue breeches. Pulling his night shirt over his head, he shambled over to the mirror hanging from a nail above the washstand. His hair was sticking up around his bald patch and he squinted sleepily at his reflection.

"Morning," he said, and proceeded to inspect his tongue

in the mirror. Then he poured some water from an earthenware jug into a cracked china bowl and proceeded to wash and shave, humming tunelessly to himself as the bright blade rasped across his skin.

Rummaging around in the pile of clothes that Old Mother Ryan had left, Owen was soon dressed in another assorted outfit, including a fine white shirt with the outline of a smoothing iron scorched into it.

It was while Tudor Jones was plastering his hair down with water that the sound of hurried footsteps was heard on the stairs and a knock on the door opened to reveal Adrian Bell. His eyes were bright with excitement.

"Saint Martin's Chapel! I think I've found it!"

Three hours later, a horse drawn carriage deposited the three of them deep in the rolling green heartland of Somerset.

Going through the Lexicon of Churches held in Bristol Cathedral, Adrian Bell had located St. Martin's Chapel in the sleepy country village of Clevedon.

Now they stood before it, watching their carriage pull away. The bustle of the city had given place to the peace of the countryside. The air was filled with the cries of the birds dipping and swinging through the blue bell of the sky and calling from the woods behind the church.

Adrian Bell looked at the Scrimshaw in his hand and at the old church in front of them. Shaded with ancient yew trees, it was the image of the one inscribed on the fragment of whale tooth – a plain, flat roofed Norman church

"This is it all right," he said. "It had to be really. Only Saint Martin's Chapel south of Gloucester."

Tudor Jones looked around carefully. He was carrying a long canvas bag that he quickly hid in the bushes beside the path leading up to the church.

"No-one around, far as I can see. Best get to it. Quick sharp."

The graveyard slumbered peacefully in the afternoon sunlight as they made their way to the church porch. Adrian Bell rested his carved walking stick on his shoulder as he peered at the notices on the oaken door.

"Good." He said. "The church has morning and evening services only, so the coast should be clear for a while yet. No doubt the parson is at this moment sitting down to a great platter of food at the expense of one of his flock. I hope we will have got what we came for and be down the road by the time he finishes his duff."

"Don't talk about duff," said Owen. "It reminds me of that Chimney Sweep."

"Don't you fret boy. Come on, 'Six steps from the parvis!'" squawked Tudor Jones.

They paced out six steps from the church porch. The path up to the church was made up of a number of big flat stones laid into the ground. Grass was growing in the space between them. Six steps from the church porch, a single flat slab of stone was set in the earth.

"Right. Let's have it up." Adrian Bell spoke quietly. "You take that side; I'll take this. Owen you take that corner. Now, work you fingers under it, and when I say 'lift', we'll lift together... Lift."

As the stone slab lifted, a scrabbling horde of wood lice dashed for cover. Beneath the rock was nothing but a flat expanse of moist brown clay, seamed with the tracks of the worms and centipedes that writhed and wriggled their way out of the sunlight.

"Just hold the stone on its side there," said Adrian Bell, unscrewing the ferrule from the tip of his walking stick to reveal a sharp metal point on the end of it. He pressed the pointed end deep into the moist earth. The stick slid in smoothly, meeting no obstruction. Again and again, he pushed down into the soft clay, probing beneath the surface for something solid. Then, with the ground full of holes, his questing stick finally met something; something not far beneath the surface: something that bent and caved in under the point of Bell's stick.

"Quick, Owen!" he hissed. "Get the shovel."

Owen ran back to the bag hidden in the bushes. He came back with a long handled pointed spade.

It was the work of a moment for Adrian Bell to thrust it into the soil and lever up a great sod of earth. There, in the middle of it, was a dented metal box.

Lifting the box free from the earth, Bell held it out in front of him, his eyes shining with excitement.

"My name is William Kidd, God's law's did I forbid
And most wickedly I did, as I sailed..."

Singing lustily, an unseen stranger was approaching.

While Tudor Jones and Owen frantically stamped the soil down and replaced the stone back on top of it, Adrian Bell ran with the spade and the box back to the bag lying in the bushes. They rocked the slab back in place and he rescrewed the brass ferrule onto his stick.

When the singing parson turned into his churchyard, he found two well dressed gentlemen and a boy lost in admiration of the beauty of the charming old church. Pleased and flattered, he showed them around some of the more interesting graves that lay at the rear of the church. One that he pointed out to them was of particular interest – the grave, he explained, of the only whaling man in his cemetery. The sailor had been buried ten years before, and his headstone inscribed with the words:

Here lie the mortal remains of Briney Morgan
Remembered as a good Shipmate
Now Safe in Harbour
In the Port of the Almighty

"His name was actually Bryn Morgan," the parson explained, "but his sailor friends who commissioned the headstone used the name they knew him by."

"So it was his funeral that Bosun Salt and Abel Judd must have attended…" said Tudor Jones, turning to his companions.

"Ahem, Ahem!" Adrian Bell coughed vigorously and pointed to a grave beside him.

"Oh, look at this. A tragic story if ever I saw one. This poor woman lost her husband and her babes all within the space of two years. Do you know anything of the circumstances, Parson Farrell?"

"Yes indeed," replied their guide. "As you say, a tragic tale… First it was the smallpox, then typhoid and diptheria. Here are four generations died within a week of each other from the Black Death…

"And here lie the remains of the great pamphleteer, Piers Madison McBride, a most original observer of the human condition…"

And so their wander through the quiet city of the dead continued, and Briney Morgan was left to sleep his long rest in the loam of the village churchyard.

When their cab returned, and they were leaving the churchyard, Parson Farrell was a little put out to see the big man reach down into the ferns and pull out a canvas bag.

A murmured reference to fowling and a half sovereign pressed into his palm relieved him of any lingering curiosity. He watched their carriage take them rolling back to the affairs of men, then turned once more to tend to his work of the Ages.

On their way back to Bristol, they stopped their cab to eat at The Star Inn. They sat at the table in a walled garden beneath the Failand Hills, bathed in Spring sunshine, eating wedges of fresh baked crusty bread, thick slabs of yellow cheese and sweet pickled onions. The two men were in great high spirits, toasting each other with brimming mugs of golden cider. They seemed to take it in turns to wink at Owen and repeat, "Say nothing. Dym Siarad."

At last their cab drew up back at Adrian Bell's shop. Climbing down from the coach, they made their way back in to his little parlour with its armada of ships lining the walls. There, once the lamps were lit, the long canvas bag was opened and the metal box brought forth into the light.

It opened easily under the blade of Bell's cold chisel. Inside was a leather bag with a sheaf of papers bound with tarred thread. Carefully, he lifted up the leather bag and poured out the contents onto a green cloth he had laid on the table.

Owen gasped.

A cascade of sparkling jewels rolled out onto the green cloth: bright rubies, glowing red in the lamplight; flashing sapphires and sea-green emeralds; white diamonds; purple amethysts; topaz and burning amber.

When Adrian Bell cut the string tying the sheaf of papers, a sheet of thinskin parchment fell out from between the pages. Bell spread the parchment open to reveal a crude map.

Then he smoothed out the papers, and began to read aloud.

CHAPTER SEVEN

Bosun Salt's Letter

"Dear Abel,

If you come this far and have got this message and this bit of booty, then you done all right. If it is not you what ends up reading this, then Old Nick must of done the same for you as he done for me, and whoever have dug up my box, I says good luck to them. I never had much luck in this world, and this last thing is enough to make a shark weep thinking about it. There ain't nothing for me now, only waiting to die, so I'm writing this to you Abel, to tell you what happened and to give you the chance to become rich. It would be a waste and a sin if all the gold and jewels as I had my hands on was just left buried. Nothing I can do to get it. My lungs is shot. But it may be as you can get it Abel, if you are able (hahahahaha!). If you do, I hope you'll call to mind how it were your old ship mate as give you your chance, and remember me in your prayers, as I remember you in mine.

After that last bit of business we finished, I got a berth as Bosun on the 'Mary Owen', a brig bound for Halifax, Nova Scotia, with a cargo of flannel, Madeira, salt and blankets. We sailed north about the top of Ireland and made a good clean crossing with fair winds all the way. Soon as we unloaded I signed off. The Master were a miser and a thief, charging the men for extra rum what he promised them, then drinking it all hisself. The pork and beef was rotten in their barrels, and the only bread we had was hard tack full of great fat weevils the size of slugs. Captain Kilshaw, the Master was called. He were a great sow-bellied walrus of a man, and I told the Agent about his shabby treatment of the crew as soon as I slipped my cable.

There was work a-plenty for a good seaman in Halifax, especially with Boney's ships trying to slip through to trade with the Yankees down in the United States. I shipped as Third Mate on the "Traveller", a Jamaica sloop carrying some Halifax finery for them woods people stuck down there in the howling wilderness.

Like most of the towns on the coast of Nova Scotia, Liverpool were little more than a gap in the forest, with a bit of a tidy anchorage. But it were making quite a name for itself with all the ships it were bringing in as prizes. What with wrecking and boarding, they was taking a fine old toll of shipping from Bonaparte and the Yankees – almost as good as a regular squadron of ships of the line.

We were unloading the cargo from Halifax when news come in of a big wreck, two hundred miles out on Sable Island. A heavy loaded French barque had run onto the sand bars off the lee shore of the island and was stranded helpless. Them Nova Scotia Bluenosers was all raring to get out there and share in the pickings of the prize before she broke up, and I were game for it too.

Now fix that place in your mind, Abel: Sable Island. 'Tis nothing but a long spit of sand in the shape of a hook, set down in the middle of the ocean and surrounded by sandbanks. Like a joke from the devil played on sailors. So many boats has been wrecked there, and sailors drowned or starved, that the Government put a Rescue Station on there at the start of the wars with Boney, complete with a platoon of Marines to keep off the wreckers.

Soon as we reached Sable Island, we reported in at the Rescue Station. Then we made our way round to the lee shore where the Frenchy lay fast on her side; her rigging gone from the jib to the mizzen and looking in pretty hard shape.

Three days we were busy with that barque, lugging the guts out of her before she smashed apart in the next heavy seas. The job were more or less finished by the fourth day, with the wind rising and the glass dropping. I left the men busy loading cargo and slipped ashore in the jolly boat to have a sniff about. A place like that you see, with so many wrecks so far from land: I had a notion as I might find something that would do me good.

I never seen anything like that island. The bones of dead men come to light with each strong wind that blows. The place is nothing but sand held down by a bit of marram grass, and with the wind shifting the dunes from one place to another all the time, the wonder is that the place don't blow away altogether. I walked for miles through them dunes, never out of the sound of the sea, and all the while I were walking, the wind was rising up and the sand blowing against me. Then on a sudden it sheered about and started to blow northwest. With that shift in the wind, the sand dunes started to move as if they was melting. I started to head for the shoreline, thinking to escape from the blasting sand and make my way back to the ship on firm going.

I was stumbling through those shifting dunes, half blinded by the blowing sand, when I came across a great

long pool of water. It was fresh water Abel! There must be a fresh water spring coming up from the sea bed, two hundred miles out from land! Queer thought ain't it? Anyhow, as I made my way along the side of the pool, I see something growing up by the head of it. Leastways it looked like it was growing. It was a hole in the sand, a little way up the side of a dune at the head of the pool, and it was getting bigger and bigger as the sand blew clear of it. I made my way up the dune towards it, and as I got closer I could see it was some kind of a doorway: a doorway made of two ship's timbers leaning against each other.

My boots was filled with sand and my legs were weak by the time I reached that doorway and pushed aside an old sheet of sailcloth to look inside. It was too dark to see anything much, but I could see there was some kind of a room, there under the sand dune. Now this were something like. Just the kind of thing I had in mind when I set out walking along that devil's spit of sand. The sailcloth was stiff and dry as old hardtack, and half buried in sand, but I managed to push it out the way enough to climb through and slide down a pile of sand into the room.

Out of the way of the wind, I hauled out tinder and a candle from my ditty bag and took a long look round. I was in some kind of a hut made out of ship's timbers and pieces of sail – just the sort of thing a castaway might have made before they put up that Rescue Station. The hut must of been buried by the shifting dunes, but it was still standing. Over in one corner of the room was a long mound of sand like the mound over a grave. It didn't take long to find out that it were a dead man under it, all shrunken and dried up. The dry sand had just sucked all of the water out of his body, and there he lay with his skin stretched out over his bones like old leather. I sniffed around a bit but found nothing more than a rusty old cutlass and a flintlock pistol. It was just a hut what some lost sailor had managed to scratch together out of bits and pieces of wreckage: a hut what had given him enough shelter from the wind and the cold for him to have time to starve to death. God rest his soul.

And now we comes to the nub of it. There were a great drift of sand over at one side of the hut, and when I run the cutlass into it, it was brought up short by something solid. I scraped away at the sand and soon I was bearing in on something interesting enough for the both of us Abel. It were a great seaman's chest, too big and heavy for me to drag clear of the sand to get a proper look at it. When I got the top of it free of sand, I see it was a brass bound oak chest with a nameplate on the lid. The nameplate was a bit pocked with sand and had that green stuff all over it, but after I give it a wipe I could read the name by the light of my candle. The name on that plate give both the man and his ship:

Captain Robert Culliford: "Resolution"

That's likely a name you remember Abel. I know I did. Whenever the talk in the fo'cusle turned to the subject of pirates, people always brought up the name of Captain Kidd. But the truth of it is that Kidd were so soft-hearted that his own men often had to threaten him with violence before he could be persuaded to launch an attack. The real chief of the pirates, a man who ran rings around Kidd, not once but twice, was Captain Robert Culliford.

Culliford knew Kidd well enough. He had served under him for some years, and ended up sailing off with one of Kidd's own prizes. Then Culliford set himself up on the island of Madagascar as a kind of king of all the rogues and cut-throats who used the island as a base for their pirate raids. After a few years of his rule, no man in Madagascar dared stand against him. A red-handed devil was Culliford: throw a man to the sharks as soon as kick him. He must of laughed up his sleeve when he seen Captain Kidd come sailing in to Madagascar with the richest prize of all, the "Quedda Merchant", a galleon what had been carrying the dowry from the King of Persia to the great Khan of India. Here was a chance for Culliford to rob the robber again. Once Kidd found out whose hands he had fallen into, it were an easy trick at the helm for Culliford to terrify Kidd into locking himself in his cabin. With Kidd out of the way, Culliford took the booty from the "Queddah Merchant" and added it to the great pile in the hold of his own ship – "Resolution". You might recall Abel, that Kidd lost heart after that and tried to give up pirating altogether. He went back to Boston, where he ended up dancing on the yard arm at Execution Dock. Culliford took the "Resolution" out of Madagascar, and was never seen again.

All of these old yarns from the fo'cusle come back to me in that buried hut beneath the sand on Sable Island, with that poor devil stretched out in his bones beside me. I was standing in front of the strongbox of Captain Robert Culliford, King of the pirates and the Master of the "Resolution"!

As I come to lift the lid, my mouth was near as dry as that of the poor devil down there on the sand. When I nailed my eyes on what was inside, I thought I were going to have a apoplexy. Gold moidores, doubloons and pieces of eight; emerald brooches, ropes of pearls; crowns and goblets crusted with rubies and diamonds. All of them a-twinkling and a-sparkling in the candle light, and my old heart flapping away like a sail in the roaring forties.

It was Culliford's treasure I were looking at, Abel. No doubt about it. And it were going to be Dan Salt's treasure before very much longer if I could lay my course to the wind. But as I sat there in the candle light warming myself beside all them riches, the problem tacking alongside of me was this: if I was to tell the officers at the government

Rescue Station what I had found, it would all be snapped up as Crown Treasure Trove, property of His Majesty King George. If I told the skipper of the Halifax sloop, he too might give it over to the Crown, or even take it for hisself. Whichever way it cut, Dan Salt was left with the lees in the scuttle butt. Well that weren't good enough for me Abel. Nor good enough for you neither, and I were thinking of you particular, shipmate. Fair sweating I was at the sight of all them sparklers and gold. My mind was racing round like a rat at the bottom of a biscuit barrel trying to figure a way to keep that booty without anyone else rigging in.

When my candle had nigh burned out, I loaded my pockets and ditty bag with as much as I could safely stow, then went outside to take my bearings. It was plain I had to leave the chest to bide where it lay, so I needed to know how to find the place again when I come back. But how was I supposed to map out the place, with all that sand flying about and nothing to take bearings on but sand dunes what shifted from one place to another like creeping slugs? But I were in luck, or maybe that castaway had built his poor hut there a-purpose, because twenty paces brought me up by the edge of the water at the head of the pool.

The pool is about two mile long, with grass growing in around the edge of the water. That pool is shaped like a kidney and is one of the landmarks for the map what is in with these papers. The hut is at the western head of it. I made my way from the pool back to the hut and pulled the sailcloth back over the doorway. Then I climbed up and pushed down a load of sand from the top of the dune until there were no more sign of it than footsteps on water. Then I walked due north, counting my paces. It were 856 paces to the shore where the dunes finished, but it might be more or less now. When I got to the shore, I looked for a mark, but all I could find was the ribs of a ship sticking up out of the sand half a mile west of me. I broke off the biggest spar as I could and hauled it back to the point I had marked where I come out of the dunes. Then I pushed the spar as deep as I could into the sand dune, carved my initials into it, and made haste back to my ship.

My plan was to sell off the jewels I had taken back in Halifax, then charter a skipper with a sloop to lay down to Sable Island and take off the booty at night. It were a simple enough plan, Abel, but it never come off. I got back aboard all right, and stowed away my jewels safe in the old sea chest with nobody any the wiser. The trouble come at the first dog watch.

It was the British man o' war, "Blonde", short of hands after fighting Yankee frigates. She had come by Sable Island to see if any men was handy to be pressed into His Majesty's Service. You know them press gangs as well as I do, Abel. There's many a poor Jack been hauled from a tavern by a bunch of redcoats and forced at the point of a pistol to follow the sea. The "Traveller" was easy pickings for the Marines what come aboard us. They took off a round dozen of us, including four Bluenosers who put up a fight and was hauled aboard unconscious for their trouble.

It stuck in my craw, I can tell you. There was me, secret and easy with the knowing of Culliford's treasure. Now, instead of laying course for a soft berth, I were stuck between decks in one of His Majesty's floating hell holes. No more control of my doings than a fly in a spider's web. With a full muster of hands, the "Blonde" shaped a course due southeast to join a squadron busy trading lives and cannon balls with some Frenchies across in the Azores.

A waste of good ships and men, Abel, and we was in among it all too soon: cannon and musket fire, smashing and screaming, and the decks slippery with blood. The jewels was still snug at the bottom of my sea chest, but they was no use to me when it come to dodging musket balls or keeping to the lee of a belching cannon. I got caught by the whip end of a blast of grapeshot and was lucky to stay alive to haul my carcase ashore at Hotwells Dock and back to Mother Ryan.

But I'm a dying man, Abel. I got no more kin than you have, and Mother Ryan's already had her share of what's mine and yourn. You been like a brother to me, saving my bones back there in Fiji when we was a-whaling. I want you to have that chest off Sable Island. I shaped the course with the Scrimshaw and the parrot to tell you where my bit of booty would be found, and I knew as you would remember that church in Clevedon where we buried poor old Briney. If you sell the jewels, they should give you the price of a ship to Nova Scotia. Then you can fit out a lugger and slip down there, quiet like. The map is the best I can do. Good luck on Sable Island and with all the rest of your life.

Look after Methuselah, Abel. He is only a young parrot and is likely to live past all of us. He likes peanuts and sunflower seeds and has been good as a tonic to me.

There's an end to it, Abel. Thank you for being my true friend and shipmate. A man could not have wished for better. For me it is a short trip now, running before the wind towards the gentle arms of Jesus, who I hope will show some mercy to a poor old sea dog shot fighting for his country. Pray for me and I will pray for you.

Your old shipmate,
Daniel Salt"

CHAPTER EIGHT

The Voyage of the "Caroline Louise"

Owen stood in the stern of a ship watching the crumbling cliffs of South Wales slip past as the islands of Flatholm and Steepholm receded in the distance. Things had moved fast in the two weeks since they had found the jewels and Bosun Salt's letter. The first thing that had been taken care of was the matter of Jem Noggins and Owen's mother.

When Adrian Bell first approached her, he found a frightened and angry woman. Jem Noggins had been round to see her, demanding back the three guineas he had given her in payment for Owen, and threatening to have her thrown in prison if she didn't pay him. As much of the money had already been spent on her debts, she was out of her mind with worry. With tears streaming down her face, she accused Bell of "robbing a lonely widow woman" and "press-ganging poor little Owen."

The twenty guineas that Adrian Bell pressed into her hand did a good deal to calm her down, as did the additional three guineas she was given to pay back Jem Noggins. And when Owen was set in front of her, healthy, clean and worried only about the anger of his Mam, she had thawed out altogether.

Over a dinner in The Llandoger Trow Inn, their plans to go to Canada were explained and she grew happy and excited about Owen's chance to see the world and better himself. With the money she had been given, she told them of her own plans to return with her family to Newport and set herself up in the laundry business. She sent Owen on his way with a light heart, freed from worries and sure of a welcome on his return.

Some of the jewels from the tin box had been easily exchanged for a large number of golden guineas, and with these they had booked a passage on the "Caroline Louise", a three-masted barque bound for Halifax, Nova Scotia. Now, with their luggage stowed and the rest of the jewels hidden in Adrian Bell's trunk, they were on their way. An escort of seagulls followed the ship, swooping and soaring in the sunlight and filling the air with their thin, sharp cries.

Turning his eyes away from the wheeling gulls, Owen noticed Tudor Jones looking with particular interest at a young woman standing by the ship's rail. She was sniffing and dabbing at her eyes with a tiny handkerchief. Then Adrian Bell tapped Owen on his shoulder.

"Come along Owen," he said. "Let's go and meet the Captain and leave Mister Jones to admire the view. Our skipper is an old friend of mine, and he particularly wants to meet you."

"Mister Jones is always saying women cause men nothing but trouble," said Owen as they walked along the deck. "So why is he so interested in them? He's always looking at them."

"Oh, I expect he's… He's probably studying them."

Inside the Captain's cabin, the light seemed dim at first.

Faded blue curtains framed a row of windows and the air smelled of tobacco, tar and hempen rope.

Sitting facing them across a desk strewn with charts, maps and navigation instruments was the ship's master. He had bushy grey hair, thick side-whiskers and a patch over his left eye. The left side of his face was blackened with powder burns. He looked up as they entered.

"Allow me to introduce Captain Cutler," said Adrian Bell.

"Ahoy there!" said Captain Cutler, rising to his feet. "What's your name young man?" He had a hearty voice, rich with the broad accent of Bristol.

"Owen Davies, sir," said Owen.

"Speak up lad," said the Captain, cupping his hand behind his right ear. "I've only got one ear. The other was bit off by a starving cannibal down in the Friendly Islands."

As Owen repeated his name, the Captain squinted at him through his bright, beady eye.

"Come closer boy," he said. "I can't see you too well in this light. I've only got one eye, as you can see. I lost the other one in a fight over cards in a grog shop in Portobello."

Having only the vaguest idea what he was talking about, Owen shuffled closer to his desk.

The Captain looked him over. "Right then lad," he said. "Where's your ticket?"

Owen rummaged in the pockets of his new jerkin and held out a handful of papers to him.

"I think the ticket's one of them, Sir," he said.

"Pass 'em on the other side, boy," said the Captain, raising an empty sleeve with a hook sticking out of it. "I've only got one hand. A cannon ball sliced the other off when I was shaking hands with Lord Nelson at the Battle of the Nile. Me and Lord Nelson both lost our hands at the same time."

The Captain glanced through the papers then passed them back to Owen.

"Come on then, young shaver," he said, "we'll take a stroll up on deck." He grabbed a crutch from the corner. "Don't walk too fast now. I've only got one leg. The other got taken off by a shark in the South China Sea."

Stumping up on deck with his peg leg, the Captain turned to look at Owen. His eye was twinkling and his mouth was twitching beneath his whiskers.

"Never been to sea before, have you lad?" he said. "Why, when I was your age, I was a year older. Been to the Sarcastic

Sea and back again. Hunting iceberg tigers. Just you wait 'til you see them lad: such a frightening sight that men have gone deaf just looking at them."

Owen blinked and swallowed but kept his gaze steady on the Captain's seamed ruin of a face.

The Captain suddenly burst out laughing. He laughed so hard he had to bend down and clutch his stomach and tears rolled from his good eye. Adrian Bell too was laughing, and Owen smiled uncertainly.

"Ah, Mister Bell!" said the Captain, wiping the tears from his cheek. "It gets better with every telling."

He ruffled Owen's hair with his hand. "But you're not afraid of iceberg tigers nor man-eating sharks, are you lad." His eye took the measure of the boy standing in front of him. "Now then Mister Bell," the Captain continued, "I've been looking at this charge of yours, this Owen Davies, giving him my hexamination, you might say. And I have this to tell you Sir, this young lad is oak! You mark my words Mister Bell, this is a boy what has got LATITUDE!"

"What do latitude mean?" asked Owen.

"It means you're sound, boy. Means you're a good 'un," said Adrian Bell.

They made their way towards the stern of the ship where they found Tudor Jones deep in conversation with the young woman who had been crying. Her companion had evidently cheered her up, as she turned towards them a lively face glowing with animation.

"Aye aye," said Captain Cutler, by way of a greeting. "I see you two have become acquainted. Now Miss, allow me to introduce you to my young shipmate here, Master Owen Davies. Now Master Davies, this is Miss Emily Bobbins, and I don't think she'll mind me telling you that she's on her way to Halifax, Nove Scotia to take up a position as a schoolteacher."

Owen smiled at her uncertainly.

"Hands, Owen," said Tudor Jones. "Show Miss Bobbins your good manners."

Owen squirmed and pushed out a hand like a limp fish. "Pleased to meet you, Miss."

Emily Bobbins shook his hand gently and lifted his face so she could look at him, smiling into his eyes.

"I'm pleased to meet you too, Owen." Her voice was gentle and soft and full of kindness, and her green eyes were warm as she smiled down at him.

"So you're off to Nova Scotia too," she said. "We're all having an adventure, so your friend Mister Jones tells me."

Another man was suddenly beside them. He lifted the young woman's hand and kissed it before she had time to snatch it back.

"Sir William Scammell at your service," he said. He pulled a perfumed handkerchief from his sleeve and wafted it daintily under his nose as he smirked at her through pursed lips. He was dressed in expensive clothes with a long pipe dangling from his mouth. His chin receded into a long neck. He ignored the rest of the group and stared boldly at the beautiful face in front of him.

Miss Bobbins wiped the back of her hand where he had kissed it on the fringe of the shawl she was wearing. Her green eyes flashed with anger.

"I don't care who you are, Sir," she said. "But I will

certainly thank you to keep your liberties to yourself. I do not permit complete strangers to come up and kiss my hand before it is offered, Sir or no Sir."

The man tittered, revealing a set of wooden teeth. The map of red veins running across his cheeks to his nose was evidence of a nightly bout with the bottle. "Oh come my pretty," he said. "Your country manners are amusing, but they do not apply to polite society. We have a long voyage in front of us, and you must let me get to know you better. I have a great deal to offer a young woman like you." The smell of strong drink and something unclean reeked from him as he reached out a hand to pinch the young woman's cheek.

Tudor Jones grabbed his wrist.

"You keep your hands to yourself, Mister. You heard the lady tell you as she didn't want none of your liberties."

The man's mouth curled as he snatched his wrist back.

"Keep your hands to yourself, you Welsh lout, or I'll have you horsewhipped and thrown into jail! I'm a knight of King George and a Justice of the Peace."

"Belay that now, Sir William," interjected a flustered Captain Cutler. "You're not on shore now. I'm the Master of this ship, and if anyone's going to be flogged or imprisoned, it'll be on my say so, not yours."

Sir William stared at Tudor Jones. "Shipboard trash, and Welsh at that!" he said scornfully. "Any woman who spends her time flirting with the likes of you scarcely deserves the name of a Lady."

Tudor Jones pushed his face close enough to smell the other's rum soaked breath. He reached up and grabbed him by the neck.

"See here Mister," he grated, "you might rule the roost on shore see, but on this ship you'd better speak to people proper or you'll find yourself with a broken neck!" And with a twist and a shove, he sent the aristocrat flying onto his back.

A chorus of laughter followed, for a number of the ship's crew had gathered around, sensing something happening.

Sir William climbed to his feet and glared around him. The men fell silent, for the look on his face spoke murder. He straightened his clothes.

"You insolent lout!" he hissed. "You will be sorry for this day. That much I promise you."

"Cut out of it Mister," returned Tudor Jones levelly. "Leave it alone before I shove them wooden teeth of yours so far down your throat, you'll end up with splinters in your breeches."

With an evil twist of his lips and a jerk of his head as though he meant to bite the other man, Sir William spun on his heel and walked away.

"Alright you men, get back to work!" Captain Cutler bawled. "Bosun! Reef the mainsail and haul in the jib. There's weather ahead." And with that he went stumping off, following the aristocrat to the front of the ship as the bosun's whistle shrilled.

"You've made a dangerous enemy, Tudor," said Adrian Bell. "Sir William Scammell looks to be a man with powerful connections."

"Thank you. Thank you so much. That was most kind of you." Emily Bobbins was breathless and her face suffused with colour. "What a dreadful man. And I'm afraid your friend is right, Mister Jones: your gallantry has made you a dangerous enemy."

Tudor Jones smiled at her. "It don't bother me, Miss," he said lightly, "as long as it's made me a friend of you. Is there any chance of you giving young Owen here a few lessons? He could do with learning to read and write."

The young woman lowered her face down to Owen's

level and looked at him seriously. "Would you like to learn to read and write, Owen?"

"I don't know if I can Miss," said Owen, thinking how he really liked her face. "But if you think I could learn schooling, I should be happy to give it a try."

The days moved on, and the final edges of coastline disappeared as they moved out past Ireland into the clear green water of the Atlantic Ocean. As the spring weather ripened towards summer, the ship moved steadily west towards the coast of North America. A wind blowing up from the south brought with it two days of increasingly uncomfortable heat, where the sea rolled in an oily swell and there was a sense of pressure, as though a great hand was pressing down on top of the sky.

The brassy heat of the afternoon found Owen dozing on deck amid a coil of ropes. His lessons over for the day, he lay with his head pillowed on the side of the coil, almost invisible as he drifted in and out of sleep. He could hear but not see Tudor Jones and Emily Bobbins speaking softly together by the rail of the poop deck. So Owen saw nothing of the fire that flashed from his friend's eyes nor the slow blush that ran over the lady's face as she allowed her hands to be fondled. All he heard was the quiet murmur of two voices: the man's voice deep and urgent, the woman's touched here and there with breathlessness. Nor did he see Sir William Scammell, watching them from behind the mast with eyes that burned with lust and envy.

The young woman spoke a few soft words to the man beside her, then turned and walked back amidships, where she vanished below deck. Tudor Jones turned from watching her graceful form to look placidly at the wake of the ship. The air was hot and clammy as he took his handkerchief from his pocket and wiped his face.

A sudden gust of wind canted the ship hard over and Tudor Jones, caught completely by surprise, fell onto the rail and tumbled over the side of the ship into the sea. His yelp of surprise stirred Owen from his slumber.

Lying in his nest of ropes, the first thing Owen saw was Sir William Scammell going past him carrying a bucket of fish offal that he emptied out into the water. The sight of Sir William doing such a thing was strange in itself. Then Owen remembered the sharks.

He and Adrian Bell had been watching the blue waters foaming behind in their wake one day when the cook had thrown a bucket of offal over the side. Summoned to the surface by the smell of food, two sharks had appeared, snapping and swirling amid the floating food. Buckets of waste from the galley were always standing on the deck as the cook filled one after another full of meat scraps and fish heads. It was usually one of the passing deck hands who emptied them over the side. What was Sir William doing with this menial work?

Owen jumped up and ran to the stern of the ship, just in time to see the head of Tudor Jones bobbing in the wake of the "Caroline Louise". The slick of blood and guts thrown over by Scammell was drifting towards him. Frantic for something to throw to the man in the water, Owen seized hold of an almost empty apple barrel.

Fear for his friend gave him strength as he pushed it across the deck and heaved it over the side of the ship as the "Caroline Louise" breasted the ocean swell. The barrel splashed into the water then bobbed upright and he ran forward with news of the disaster. Behind him, Sir William Scammell was busy emptying another bucket of offal into the sea.

"Mister Jones have fallen in the sea!" Owen shouted. "Help! Help!"

Captain Cutler put down his telescope and turned his one eye on Owen.

"Did you say 'Man overboard', lad?"

"Aye aye Sir. Mister Jones have fallen in the sea. Help him Captain…"

"Wear ship!" he was interrupted by a bellow from the Captain. "Man overboard! Stand by to launch the jolly boat."

Instantly the ship was alive with men swarming through the rigging and hauling on lines as the ship turned, flapping and groaning, onto a different tack. Captain Cutler stumped off to supervise the launching of the jolly boat as Owen rushed to the side of the ship to catch a glimpse of Tudor Jones struggling through the water towards the floating barrel. The white face and distant splashing were visible now and again as the waves rose and fell.

Owen remembered what Adrian Bell had told him about the sharks, savage creatures that moved through the sea eating anything that crossed their path. With their great crescent mouths lined with row upon row of teeth, they could easily bite a man in half. Many an unfortunate seamen had fallen overboard to perish, not by drowning, but in the merciless jaws of the sea hunters. He had seen their jaws on display in the taverns and wharves of Bristol, gaping wide enough to swallow a table. And now his friend was in the water where they lived, surrounded by the shark bait thrown overboard by the murderous Sir William Scammell.

The crew of the jolly boat was pulling away through the heaving sea as Captain Cutler came to stand beside him. Away on the far horizon, a solid bank of cloud had taken on a sinister tinge of dark green.

"Will the sharks get him Captain?" Owen asked, longing to be told that they would not and that his friend would soon be safe.

The Captain was silent as he scanned the sea with his telescope. Then, with a convulsion of movement, he whipped the telescope aside and bellowed across the water to the crew of the toiling jolly boat.

"Pull lively lads! There be sharks in the water!"

Owen's stomach turned to lead as the men in the boat redoubled their efforts. The distance between Tudor Jones and the upturned barrel was very little now, but in his mind's eye Owen could see the sleek grey shapes of the sharks streaking through the water, steadily closing in on the swimming man. He imagined the jaws gaping open as they swept towards their victim.

Then suddenly it was all too real. As the sea dipped and rolled, Owen caught a glimpse of a high dorsal fin hissing across the surface, leaving a thin white wake. It was closing in quickly, only yards away from the desperate swimmer.

But Tudor Jones was alongside the barrel and launched himself up from the water to fall headfirst inside. The barrel rocked crazily as the man tumbled into it, then spun

and reeled again as the shark hit it. For a few dreadful
seconds, it seemed that the barrel was going to roll over,
but it steadied itself as the shark swam around it in a tight
circle. Then the shark hit it again. It was as though it could

sense the meal inside if only the barrel could be tipped over. Again and again the shark's rubbery head pushed and banged against it, but the natural buoyancy of the barrel, weighed down by the man inside it, kept it floating upright in the water. Tudor Jones stayed motionless upside down, not daring to move, his elbows braced against the side of the barrel, knowing the horrible fate that awaited him if the barrel should roll over onto its side and take in water. The barrel rocked and spun but it remained upright. The solid oak planks with their iron hoops stood firm between the man and the questing jaws of the great sea hunter.

Then at last the jolly boat was alongside and a cutlass slash from one of the sailors persuaded the shark to try his luck elsewhere. Tudor Jones and the barrel were hoisted aboard and the men at the oars, now singing heartily, pulled back to the "Caroline Louise".

"Thank God for the man what threw over that barrel!" said Captain Cutler.

"It was me, it was." Owen spoke without thinking, overcome with relief at his friend's escape.

"You!" roared the Captain. "You did it? You saved that man's life you did! And you only eleven years old! Did you hear that Mister Bell? Miss Bobbins? This boy here saved your friend's life! What did I tell 'ee? This boy have got LATITUDE!"

Hugged by Adrian Bell and kissed by Emily Bobbins, Owen found himself blushing like a fool. When Tudor Jones finally stumbled back on board, pale and trembling but otherwise unhurt, Owen stood between Adrian Bell and Emily Bobbins feeling a sensation completely new to him – a brand new feeling of pride in being himself.

CHAPTER NINE

𝕿𝖍𝖊 𝕾𝖙𝖔𝖗𝖒

"I seen that Sir William emptying the cook's buckets into the sea right after Mister Jones fell in," said Owen.

They were sitting in the Captain's cabin. Tudor Jones, still pale and trembling, was wrapped around with warm blankets as he sipped a mug of hot rum toddy.

"A scurvy trick," muttered Captain Cutler, grinding his teeth together and polishing his hook on his sleeve.

"That's dreadful!" cried Emily Bobbins. Her eyes were warm with pity and her face pale with fright. "That horrible great shark coming at you! Ugh! It's a good job you could swim so well."

"I learned to swim when I was a boy in Porthcawl," said Tudor Jones, shivering violently as he spoke. "Mam said I was wasting my time. Just as well I did though, innit?"

"Aye. Many's the poor tar have sunk like a stone when he hit the water," Captain Cutler rumbled. "I should've sunk meself, in spite of me wooden leg. Most of us sailors can't swim. We prefers a quick death by drowning."

"So, are you saying Sir William Scammell deliberately set the sharks on me after I fell in?" Tudor Jones, shook his head in disbelief.

"It looks that way," murmured Adrian Bell. "I told you he was a dangerous enemy."

"I wondered why he was doing it," said Owen. "I heard a shout what woke me up, and the first thing I seen was Sir William emptying one of the cook's buckets over the side. I ran up to look for the sharks. Then I seen Mister Jones was in the sea and I threw in the apple barrel."

"Tried to murder me, did he! Men have been hanged for less!" said Tudor Jones. "That sneaking, sneering maniac! He should be put down like a mad dog, he should. Squashed like a poisonous spider!"

Adrian Bell gave a wan smile. "Have a bit of mercy on the animal kingdom, Tudor. Still, there's little doubt that he tried to kill you – and he deserves to be punished."

"Ease up there now, friends." The Captain waved his hook in the air. "You won't find a court on this ship or anywhere else that will convict him on the basis of what the boy says. Sir William is a knight of the Realm and a magistrate to boot, with powerful friends who will stand beside him. He broke no law by emptying a bucket over the side of the ship. We might have a good idea what he was up to, but none of us can prove it. Hold hard until we can see the course ahead."

Emily Bobbins stroked her friend's trembling hand. "But what if he should try it again?" she said. "He's a terrible man. What can we do?"

"Don't you worry about that," said Tudor Jones, his eyes lighting up as he looked at her anxious face. "I'll have my eyes open for that one from now on."

"But he set the sharks on you!" Owen protested. "You could have been killed!"

"Aye aye lad," Captain Cutler spoke gently. "And if it hadn't been for you, he likely would have been. That shark had man on his menu and no mistake. If it hadn't been for you and that apple barrel, Mister Jones would have been cold meat in that beast's belly right now."

There was a moment's silence. Tudor Jones paled and gulped at his mug of toddy as his forehead suddenly beaded with sweat and Emily grasped his hand tight.

Adrian Bell mused aloud. "Yes, the boy saved the day and no mistake. I told you Tudor: young Owen here is good luck."

"Latitude," rumbled the Captain. "I knew the boy had it. Knowed it from the moment I seen him."

Suddenly the door burst open and Sir William Scammell stood framed against a dark and threatening sky. As if on cue, a great peal of thunder ripped from the heavens.

"None the worse for your little swim then," he sneered. "I must confess that when I heard you had so foolishly fallen overboard, I was looking forward to a slightly less crowded quarterdeck. But I see you are none the worse for your ducking, so I suppose it's drinks all round." He bared his wooden teeth in a slack grin. "Saved from the jaws of death, no less! Well, it seems the sea has no use for you, any more than does the land. Where's the grog?"

Captain Cutler hoisted himself onto his crutch and rose to his full height.

"No grog for you here," he said, eyeing the man coldly. "And I'll thank you to take yourself out of my cabin."

Sir William Scammell's thin lips twisted into a sneer.

"You dare to talk to your betters like that, do you? Why, you're little more than a common tradesman. You had better mind your manners you old dotard ..."

"Stow that talk! I've told 'ee before. You might rule the roost on dry land, but I'm the Captain of this ship! I'm the King of this castle and I'll have you clapped in irons!"

" A king of shreds and tatters," scoffed Sir William. "A lord of planks and patches. You – a king? You're a one eyed old cripple is what you are!"

"Avast!" roared the Captain, his face purple with rage as he raised his iron hook in the air. "Get out of here, ye scurvy, bilge-mouthed lubber!"

Sir William paled and took a step backwards.

"You...you'll be sorry for this!" His voice was shrill. "I'll ...I'll tell King George about this."

A chorus of laughter erupted in the cabin, laughter that went on and on.

"Aye aye," said the Captain finally, wiping his eye with a grimy handkerchief. "You be sure and tell King George."

Sir William's face was white with impotent fury as he stood clenching his fists in the doorway.

"That's the way, my pretty boys. Go on and mock your King, you rebellious dogs! Mockery of the King is treason – a hanging matter. And remember that I am a baronet and a Justice of the Peace."

Tudor Jones rose to his feet, still draped in his blanket. He approached the other man until he was standing eyeball to eyeball with him.

"No-one is mocking the King, Mister," he grated. "It's you that we're mocking. And as for being anything to do with justice, I know you tried to kill me by setting the sharks on me. I might not be able to prove anything in a court of law, but I can certainly give you this!"

A solid fist rammed like a fence post into Sir William's scrawny stomach. With a whoosh of air, the aristocrat's wooden teeth shot out of his mouth and flew across the room to shatter against an oak beam. Sir William fell to his knees, clutching at his stomach. A succession of high-pitched hooting noises squeezed from between his pursed lips as he struggled to find some breath.

"Get out," said Tudor Jones, dragging the choking man to his feet. "And don't you come near me no more, Mister Scummy Scammell. You go and tell King George whatever

you like, Scummy, but if you come within spitting distance of me again, I'll have you over the side before you have time to fill your breeches."

And with that, he pitched the other man out headfirst onto the deck. Closing the door, he turned back into the room with a tight smile pale on his face.

"I feel a lot better for that," he said.

"Aye aye lad," said Captain Cutler heartily. "Come and sit you down now and we'll share a nice flagon of flip. That'll put the colour back in your cheeks."

The ship rolled as it caught a sudden gust of wind and Captain Cutler paused.

"On second thoughts," he said, reaching for his sea-cloak by the door, "I'd best go and check the rigging. It looks like we're in for a bit of weather. I'll leave you to make the flip, Miss Emily. Add a quarter pint of rum to a flagon of beer. Get it into him now. Do him good, so it will."

He stumped off to attend to the business of the ship, leaving Owen with Emily Bobbins and Adrian Bell to mix the flip in a large pewter jug and set about getting it into Tudor Jones.

Captain Cutler was quite right. As the level of the flip in the jug went down, so the colour returned to the cheeks of Tudor Jones and his trembling stopped. The little group was quite cheerful when the loaf-like head of the Bosun appeared around the door of the Captain's cabin.

"Beggin' yer pardon Miss, and the Capting's compliments to youse all, but would you go to your quarters right away before the storm hits. No telling how long the blow might last, and 'twill be a tricky business moving round once we're in it."

They made their way out onto the deck; Tudor Jones still firmly attached to his half-finished jug of flip. Above them, the sky had turned an ugly yellow grey and the sea was heaving uneasily. A menacing black squall was sweeping towards them from the south, pregnant with flickering lightning and rolling thunder. The air was filled with hoarse shouts and the sound of flapping canvas as the sails were furled and reefed and the ship steadied itself for the storm that was sweeping down on them like a sheet of darkness. Owen noticed the set faces of the seamen and the absence of their usual banter. There was a sense of heavy pressure in the air pushing down on them as they made their way down to their rooms between decks. The eyes of Emily Bobbins looked strained and frightened as she slipped into her tiny cabin. Even Adrian Bell, that calm and steady man, had deep frown lines etched onto his forehead.

Inside their small stateroom, Tudor Jones struggled into some dry clothes and threatened revenge on Sir William Scammell as Adrian Bell set about wedging Owen into his high-sided bunk with pillows and bolsters so that he wouldn't fall out. Then the storm hit them. As if it had been punched by a giant, the ship lurched sickeningly sideways and a great peal of thunder blasted down at them from the roiling clouds overhead.

With the movement of the ship growing ever more violent and alarming, the two men lay down in their own bunks. Facing one another across the room, they braced themselves against the rolling and pitching of the "Caroline Louise" as the ship staggered and reeled through the seas that grew more violent by the minute.

Time passed slowly. The noise of the wind grew louder and stronger until it was one continuous roar. This was joined by the sound of a torrent of rain drumming down onto the decks above. The storm held them fast in its toils as the ship was tossed and rolled like a mouse in the paws of a great cat. The little ship tilted back onto her beam ends to climb a rearing mountain of water; then rushed down an endless slope that seemed to lead to the very bottom of the ocean before beginning her climb over the next terrifying wall of maddened sea. On and on it went: the storm howling like some monstrous beast and the ship running helplessly before it. The noise alone suggested that at any moment the ship would burst apart in a fury of wind and waves.

Wedged securely in his bunk, Owen's fear of the storm slowly subsided, as the minutes turned into hours and still the ship stayed afloat. He found himself thinking of the island that awaited them somewhere across the tossing sea: an island grey and shrouded in mist, but at its heart was a wooden chest aglow with gold and jewels. He thought back to his family and the events that led him to this perilous point of time, and as he did so, he drifted effortlessly into the deep swells of sleep.

He was jolted from his slumbers by a terrific crash, then the ship heeled over and he was suddenly very afraid. Urgent shouting, followed by the noise of hammering could be heard above the tumult of the storm and Owen realised that he was alone in the room. He braced himself against the bunk to stop himself from falling out and looked around him. The cabin was moving in a most alarming way: the ceiling appeared to be trying to change places with the wall. A lump pressing against his back turned out to be the pewter jug that had held Tudor Jones's flip. How had it got there? And still the ship continued to heel over. The lamp in its gimbals threatened at any moment to crash against the ceiling and the wildly flickering light served only to show him the racing shadows of his own fear.

But at last the sickening fall of the ship stopped and she slowly pulled herself back upright. As the ceiling and the walls moved back into their proper place, the door of the cabin opened to admit Emily Bobbins. She tottered into the cabin and groped her way to the head of Owen's bunk.

"Are you all right Owen?" she said anxiously. "My, what a terrible storm this is! I thought I would come and keep you company. Your friends have gone on deck to see if they can lend a hand."

Owen groaned in distress. "I'm frightened, Miss Bobbins! Is the ship going to sink?"

"There now," she spoke soothingly as she stroked Owen's head. "Don't worry. It's only a storm. Ships are built to stand up to storms at sea. We're not going to sink."

But even as she spoke, the ship reeled once again, slammed almost onto its side as a great mountain of water burst over it.

"Heaven preserve us!" cried Emily, hugging Owen to her breast as the ship slowly righted herself once more.

Owen's eyes fixed upon the figure that suddenly appeared behind her.

In the wildly waving light of the cabin lamp, Sir William Scammell stood braced in the doorway, his face brooding and haggard as the shadows played across it.

Sensing his presence, Emily turned around and let out an involuntary gasp of fear.

"The ministering angel has come to comfort the little waif is it?" Scammell sneered in a voice thick with drink. "Well you can minister to me as well, my pretty. The boy is not the only one in need of your comforting arms."

With that he lurched across the cabin and grabbed the young woman around the waist, his lips nuzzling greedily at her neck.

"Stop it!" Emily Bobbins wailed. "Stop it, I beg you Sir William. I'm a good girl. Stop it, for Heaven's sake! Think about the boy!"

"Stop it?" echoed the drunken man. "A good girl? Why there's no such thing in nature! Every one of you is a trollop at heart!"

With that he grabbed her by the throat and pushed her up against Owen's bunk, his free hand pawing at her body as his tongue poked from his toothless, panting mouth.

Terrified by the sudden appearance of the man who had tried to kill Tudor Jones and who now seemed intent on murdering Miss Bobbins, Owen could think of only one thing to do. Reaching behind him, he grabbed hold of the heavy pewter flip jug and brought it down with all his strength onto the back of the horrible man's head.

Sir William Scammell staggered backwards, clutching at his broken scalp and his hand came away red with blood. He glared at Owen with eyes that glittered evil.

"You little guttersnipe!" he snarled. "You need to be taught some respect for your masters."

With one bound he was across the cabin and grabbed Owen by the throat. His fingers tightened on the boy's neck like the talons of a bird of prey.

Dimly aware that he was wetting his breeches, Owen choked and gagged, terrified at the murderous rage on the face of the man holding him. The lips of the toothless mouth were drawn back to the dribbling bare gums and the madman's eyes glowed red. As the walls of the cabin reeled about him, Owen heard, as if from a far distance, a voice crying, "Don't!"

Sobbing and terrified, Emily Bobbins cowered against the wall as she watched the drunken maniac tighten his death grip on the boy's throat. Grinding his gums together as he frothed at the mouth, he seemed to be grinning with glee as the boy's lips began to turn blue.

Desperate and furious, Emily sprang at him. Wrenching his head back with a handful of his scrawny hair, she raked at his eyes with her nails until he finally let go his hold on the boy and turned his fury upon her. From side to side of the cabin they lurched in a frenzied wrestling match, clawing and biting at each other as the ship reeled and rolled in the toils of the seas breaking over her. They grappled endlessly in the pitching lamplight, rearing and twisting whilst the wind and the sea mingled in a deafening roar that drowned completely the noise of their struggle. Emily was sobbing in fear and desperation; the man snarling with rage as they struck out with hands and feet to try to maim one another. It was a surprisingly equal contest: the woman young, fit and healthy; the man stronger and bigger but fuddled with drink and insane with lust and rage.

Time and again the ship reeled over so far that it seemed she would never recover, but each time she rose slowly back up out of the water to resume her battle with the sea. As the turmoil of the storm buffeted the ship, Emily suddenly found herself pinned against the wall with her throat clutched tight in Sir William's talons. The eyes glaring into hers were the eyes of a wild beast about to kill its prey. With a convulsive effort, Emily thrust her knee up between the man's legs and bent back one of the fingers wrenching at her throat so that his grip was broken. As she pushed him away from her, the ship rolled violently, pitching the madman backwards. His head cracked viciously against the corner of Owen's bunk and he fell to the floor where he lay without moving.

CHAPTER TEN

Landfall

"You'll have to put us ashore somewhere quiet, Captain." Adrian Bell spoke with decision. "We can do nothing about Sir William, but he will certainly want to do something about us."

"Aye, lad. No doubt about it." Captain Cutler ground his teeth together as he squinted up at the ceiling. "When we gets into Halifax, he'll have his fine friends come down on you and try to swing you all from the yardarm just for jolly. He won't let you be, that much is for sure. What with him being a knight and a Justice of the Peace, Scummy won't rest quiet, not until he's done you all the mischief he can."

"Fine sort of justice though, isn't it," said Tudor Jones bitterly. "Sir Scummy tries to murder three of us, and it's us who have to run and hide, as if we were the guilty ones."

Captain Cutler polished his hook with his sleeve. "Justice be a fine word," he said, "but it have precious little to do with the likes of us. Mister Bell there is on the right tack. I can put you ashore and then tell him you was all washed overboard in the storm. I'll make up some blarney about Miss Emily coming up on deck with the boy in her arms and getting carried away by the same gurt wave that washed you two out of the rigging. That way it will seem that there's no-one left alive to tell any tales on him, and he might leave it at that."

They were sitting in the Captain's cabin in the cold light of dawn. The storm had all but blown itself out, and away at the edge of the scudding grey sea was their first sight of the tufted, spiky horizon that was the eastern coast of the New World.

Captain Cutler banged on the table and bawled, "Butterby!"

The great bulk of the Bosun came shambling into the cabin, knuckling his forehead in a clumsy salute.

"Is that Scummy still unconscious, Butterby?" the Captain asked bluntly.

"Aye aye Sir," mumbled Butterby. "But I dunno how much longer he'll stay that way, Capting."

"Get some grog laced with laudanum down his neck," Captain Cutler told him. "Hold his nose and pour a pint down him. Don't let him wake up yet, whatever happens, or we'll all be run aground."

Bosun Butterby grinned. "Stand on me Capting," he said. "He'll not get past Butterby."

He left the cabin and a moment later Emily Bobbins stepped in. Her face was pale and marked with bruises, but her eyes were bright.

"He's getting better by the minute," she said. "His voice is a bit croaky, but other than that he seems all right. Can you give me one of your lemons Captain, to make a hot drink for his poor throat?"

"You're a Guardian Angel you are," said Tudor Jones, standing up beside her and placing an arm around her waist. "You know you saved that boy's life?"

"I know he saved mine," said Emily, pushing him gently away. "Have you got some lemons Captain?"

Captain Cutler speared a shrivelled lemon from the fruit bowl before him and offered it to her.

"Make him a nice hot toddy, Miss. He'll be needing his strength before the day's much older."

Emily darted a worried look. "What do you mean, Captain?"

"We're going to have to drop you ashore somewhere quiet, Miss. And do it today. While that there Scammell is still out to the world." Captain Cutler was uncomfortable, and his voice showed it.

Adrian Bell spoke urgently. "Think about it Miss Bobbins: If we go with him into Halifax, we'll have to tell the full story. Everything. Then it will be our word against his. He's a powerful man with serious friends. We can be sure of two things: he won't tell the truth; and he'll do all he can to destroy us. If we put ashore quietly and he thinks us dead, we may yet make it to safety, far away from him."

Tudor Jones spoke next. "The Captain is going to tell him we were lost in the storm," he said. "It won't be that far from the truth neither. I was never so frightened in my life. Worse than that shark bashing against my barrel."

" A bad storm it was for sure," said Captain Cutler. "A mad blow if ever I saw one. Cost me two good hands: poor Jonah Flanagan, washed clean out of the ratlines into a raving sea; and Matty Jones, taken from the foredeck by a great wave that jumped on us like a tiger and he was gone before we knew it. But some good might come of that storm if we can persuade Sir Scummy down there that you're washed overboard and gone forever."

"But can you be sure that your crew will support that story?" Emily's face was pale with worry. "And where will we go once we land ashore? We're supposed to go through the proper immigration process at Halifax. And what will happen to you Captain?"

The Captain smiled. "Bless you lass. Don't you worry about me. Once you people are out the way, he won't want

to make no make no trouble with me. Specially if I make it plain that I shan't say nothing about what happened or what might have happened before I found him unconscious in the boy's cabin. He has every reason to leave me well alone. As for the crew: most of 'em has been with me a fair while now and they'll do pretty much as I tells 'em. None of us wants to be tied up with courts and suchlike in Halifax. There's no money to be made lying idle in port. As for you and the so –called immigration authorities: this here is a big country. These Nova Scotia folk ain't what you would call pernickety about immigrants. People have been coming and going here pretty much as they please for nigh on two hundred years: Yankees; Frenchies; Hollanders – not to mention the Indians. I'll land you as best I can, then you must fend for yourself."

Tudor Jones looked nervous. "What about the Indians?" he said. "I mean, are they as fierce as people make out, cutting off scalps and what not?"

The Captain's laugh rumbled deep. "Nothing to fear from the Indians here," he said. "A peaceable bunch they are in this neck of the woods. Micmac they call themselves."

There was a tap on the door and Bosun Butterby came back in, his burly form seeming to fill the cabin.

"Excuse me gentlemen … and lady, begging yer pardon Miss. Permission to report Captain. That Sir William, he's out like a dead candle. He's stuffed so full of laudanum he thinks as he's a stone. He won't be stirring for a good twelve hours or more. I've tied him into his bunk and shuttered the porthole, just to be on the safe side, like."

"Aye. Good man. Well done Butterby." Captain Cutler nodded at him approvingly.

Emily turned and made for the door.

"I must get back to Owen," she said. "Thank you for the lemon Captain. We shall do whatever you say. I'm sure you know best."

As the door closed behind her, Captain Cutler rolled open a map and spread it across his desk. With a stubby forefinger, he traced out the coastline, mumbling to himself as he set out his plan.

"We want a place where there's enough settlers for you to be looked after, but not so many as will notice you much and start asking too many questions. If we sail up this river here for a stretch, we can drop you out of sight of any settlement but near enough for you to find one on your own."

His finger wandered over the chart then he tapped three times on the spot he selected. "We'll take you a little way up the Le Have river and put you ashore where no-one will see you land. Here's Lunenburg and the Le Have river just south west of us. With this wind blowing and the tide running with us, we should have you ashore about mid-day. Then we'll turn about smartish to catch the ebb and be well out to sea and on our way to Halifax when Sir Scummy comes back to hisself and starts to take an interest. You must pack what things you can and take only what you can carry. I shall drop off the rest of your baggage at Lunenburg on my way back from Halifax. No reason why anyone in Lunenburg should have heard anything of me or my ship. And if any awkward questions are asked, well, here's Mister Bell here claiming the stuff on behalf of his poor drowned brother."

Bell clasped his hands together and held them up his chin as he nodded thoughtfully.

"It sounds like an uncommonly good plan Captain, and we're all very grateful to you. You're quite right that it's much better for us to be dropped off quietly and vanish rather than land amid a great fuss in Halifax and face endless trouble with the law and Sir William's fancy friends."

"I just hope the boy will be alright," said Tudor Jones miserably. "I feel like it's all my fault. If I hadn't made Scammell so angry…"

"Stuff and nonsense!" exclaimed his Adrian Bell. "There are some people in this world who just set out to cause trouble and upset for people who are weaker than they are. It's how they get to feel they are strong. He's a man who will trample and destroy anyone he chooses to. We just happened to walk across his path."

"It still sticks in my craw," said Tudor Jones. "It's him who tried to murder us, but it's us what has to run away – as if we were the wrongdoers."

"Perhaps it's all for the best," murmured Adrian Bell. "A quiet landfall, away from the sight of those who might be a bit too busy about other people's business…"

"Ay, well, there we are," said the Captain, rising and straightening himself up. "We must make the best of what we can. We shall be making landfall within the next few hours. So pack up what you need and we shall make haste to be quit of one another before our nasty knight comes to his senses. Set the course Butterby. We must be up the Le Have river as the tide is making, ready to drop our passengers and turn the ship around the moment they are on dry land."

So it was that Owen came up on deck into a grey day to find they were moving slowly between the banks of a stately river lined with trees. The forest loomed all around them and the sharp scent of pine was like coming into the presence of someone solemn and grand. It was a landscape like none that Owen had ever seen before. There was precious little wilderness where he came from.

Then he found himself bustled into the arms of the Bosun and carried down into the jolly boat waiting alongside the ship. As they pulled away from the "Caroline Louise" towards the shore, the ship tacked about until she was facing back downriver towards the open sea. Crammed with his friends and their bundles of belongings in the little boat, Owen was astonished to see a dog-like head suddenly emerge from the water, turn its big black eyes towards him, and then vanish in a swirl of bubbles.

"That's a seal, that is Owen," said Adrian Bell quietly. "You'll be seeing a lot of new animals here."

The sky was overcast. The grey water of the river and the grey of the sky were separated by the wall of dark green trees. The world seemed drained of colour, vague and misty.

As the keel of the jolly boat grated onto the shingle of a bay at the river's edge, the little party disembarked. Scarcely a word was spoken as the bags and bundles were dumped ashore and the two seamen and the Bosun jumped back in

their boat and sculled away towards their ship. It seemed unreal to Owen: the lilting sudden firmness of the land beneath his feet; the sight of the tall ship poised for flight in the middle of the river; the jolly boat growing ever smaller in the listless haze of light. They stood beyond sight of any human habitation on the edge of the New World.

As the insects gathered about their heads, they watched the jolly boat being hoisted back on board and the ship getting under way. Captain Cutler stood in the stern with Butterby at his side, his arm raised in a silent farewell salute. The ship moved steadily off downstream until the white pyramid of her sails passed a bend in the river and was hidden from view by the ranks of dark green trees.

Emily Bobbins was the first to speak. "Ugh! These flies are biting. We must get into some shelter or a house before twilight – or the mosquitoes will eat us alive. Come on Owen, you can hold my hand and we can help each other along."

"True enough, Shipmates," said Tudor Jones. "We need to find a path of some kind. Got to get moving eh." Hefting a couple of canvas kit bags, he led the little group away from the river and into the forest.

In spite of the overcast sky, they were soon uncomfortably hot. The heavy woollen clothing they had bought for the sea voyage was too warm for the windless woods of the Canadian summer. The heat generated by the little group as they struggled through the undergrowth with their bags made them sweat. Their sweat attracted hordes of tiny biting blackflies that swarmed around their heads, adding to their discomfort. Big blue jays screamed above them as they made their uncertain way through the forest.

Although they were relieved to be back on dry land and away from Sir William Scammell, the dreary sky above them, the trees hemming them in and the swarms of biting insects whining around them combined to depress their spirits. Scratched by brambles and itching with sweat and insect bites, they moved slowly onwards under a darkening sky as the heat grew ever more oppressive and charged with the threat of another storm.

"Look out, Shipmates," Tudor Jones hissed suddenly, pointing up into a tree directly in their path.

A creature the size of a dog was sitting amid the lower branches. It was shapeless and menacing, rocking from side to side noiselessly. A mass of long spines covered its body, hanging below the branches on which it was sitting. No head or face of any description was visible: the creature seemed to be nothing but a squirming nest of very sharp spines.

The four of them stopped dead and stood looking uneasily at the strange animal. A minute passed and then another as the creature did nothing at all to respond to their presence.

"I don't know what it is, Shipmates," said Tudor Jones, "but I'm keeping well clear of it. Come on. We'll go round it."

Moving quietly away from the unknown menace in the tree, they made their way past it. Owen caught a glimpse of two bright, beady eyes staring out at him from a halo of black and white spines.

Several times they found themselves stuck in dense undergrowth and had to backtrack around the obstacles barring their way. They came across a narrow track of trampled down grass and shrubs that they followed for a time until it petered out and was lost amid the undergrowth. Looking for a way out of the forest, they turned and turned upon themselves until finally they found themselves standing in front of a tree where the same spiny creature sat motionless and menacing.

Adrian Bell wiped his streaming face with a sodden handkerchief. "We've been walking in a circle," he said grimly.

"We'll have to stick by the river," said Emily Bobbins. "If we just follow the river upstream, the Captain told us we would find some settlements. We could wander around in these woods until we drop dead or these insects eat us alive. Ugh! These flies are driving me mad."

The tiny blackflies were just as bad when they found their way back to the river. Trudging behind Emily Bobbins, Owen noted that Emily's hair was crawling with them. Weighed down as they were with their baggage, none of them were able to do much more than shake their heads, as horses do, to fend off the plague of insects buzzing about them. They struggled upstream as best they could, reluctant to leave the river, until they came at last to little headland. From there they could see across to the other side of the river for about a mile. There was a line where the trees ended and the fields were bright with ripening crops. A wooden house painted dark red sat in a clearing that sloped down to the edge of the water.

It was suddenly raining. Not rain of the drizzling kind of rain they knew from back home, but a torrent poured directly onto their heads, instantly soaking them. The fields and the farm vanished completely and the river frothed in the downpour.

Tudor Jones shouted above the din of the rain. "Come on. Keep going. If there's a farm on the other side of the river, we're bound to find one this side sooner or later."

They moved back into the woods where the trees were drumming under the downpour and the leaves coiled and hissed. There was some comfort in the fact that the flies had vanished with the first drop of rain and the cool water running over their faces relieved their hot, itching bites. The clammy oppressive atmosphere had gone. It was as though the deluge had started the forest breathing again. Pushing on through the trees, they were startled by a rat-like animal the size of a cat running across a clearing in front of them. As the creature paused for a moment to bare its yellow teeth and hiss, they saw four tiny kittens clinging onto the thin fur on its back.

Adrian Bell leaned against a tree and lifted his face to the rain, opening his mouth wide. He breathed out heavily.

"We must stop for a rest and have something to eat soon," he said. "I'm feeling my years – and poor Owen must be exhausted."

"I'm alright," said Owen. In truth he was feeling much better. The fresh air, the cool water and the exercise had done him a power of good, and as he was the one carrying the smallest bundle, he was the least tired. Too young to sweat, he had suffered less from the flies than the others. Then there was the relief he felt at getting away from the ship and Sir William Scammell. But as his friend spoke, he was aware of a distinctly empty feeling in his stomach.

"We must push on until we find shelter," Emily Bobbins was insistent. "Once the rain stops, the flies will be worse than ever, and when the mosquitoes come out, we'll be in serious trouble. People have gone mad with insects biting them in the woods."

"How did you come to know so much about mosquitoes and flies, Shipmate?" said Tudor Jones.

"When I was a girl we lived in the Forest of Dean. And can we leave off the 'Shipmates' now that we're off the ship…"

So they pushed on. The rain stopped; the trees dripped and the flies returned in force as Emily had predicted. The tormenting whine of the mosquitoes was already in the air when they finally staggered out of the trees into a field high with growing corn. The flies were left behind in the shade of the woods and above them the sky was washed clean of rain. The afternoon light glowed over the forest, the fields and the river. In a clearing below them, a wooden house showed smoke drifting from a stone chimney, and a fair-haired woman in a red pinafore was standing in the yard throwing feed out to some chickens.

CHAPTER ELEVEN

In the Woods of Nova Scotia

From the moment she caught sight of the little group coming towards her, the fair haired woman busied herself in making them welcome. Even as Adrian Bell was trying to explain what they were doing, wandering around in the woods, she was bustling them into the house and producing towels to dry them off and soothing ointment for their insect bites.

Inside, the house was cool and dark. The room they were in was walled with logs and filled with the tangy smell of wood smoke. The scent of pine was everywhere, for the whole house was made of pine logs, laid one on top of another to form four sturdy walls. A series of uprights driven into the ground kept the walls together, and the spaces between the walls were snugly filled with a mixture of mud and moss. The back roof had a longer slope than the front, with the eaves at the back reaching down almost to the ground and lost in shadow. A chimney of huge granite boulders dominated the centre of the downstairs room, effectively dividing it in two. A set of wooden steps led up to another level, used for sleeping and storage. Beneath the roof of logs, the ceiling was made of plaited straw, tightly woven to stop bugs falling down from the roof.

The woman set a pitcher of cider on the table and vanished with Emily into a part of the room partitioned off behind the great chimney as they set to changing into dry clothes. From the non-stop line of chatter coming from behind the chimney, it emerged that she was particularly glad to see Emily since she hardly saw another woman from one month to the next. They were just finishing changing when a sleepy-eyed toddler poked his head from behind the curtain at the back of the room to peer shyly at the newcomers.

"That there is Benejah," said the woman, coming from behind the partition. "My other boy, Joshua, he's about the same age as yourn, I guess. He's off in the woods with his dog, hunting squirrels."

Tudor Jones tucked his shirt into his breeches and looked across at Owen with his eyes shining.

"D'you hear that Owen?" he said. "You hear what the boys in this country do? They go out hunting in the woods. Or go off fishing. It's not poaching here, see. There's no gamekeepers nor lords saying everything belongs to them and you got to keep your hands off. This is a place for a boy to grow up! This is a sight better than being stuck up a Bristol chimney – or Buffin' and Codgering up and down Christmas Steps."

Thinking about the strange animals he had seen and still itching from a host of insect bites, Owen was not at all sure about the attractions of the woods, but he was happy to be under a roof and back on dry land. The violence of the storm at sea; the savage attack on him by the maddened Sir William; then the endless walk in the woods had left him feeling weak and uncertain about the future.

By the time an hour had gone by, they had been joined by the other boy, Joshua, and were busy devouring a meal of vegetable soup, brown bread, cheese and apples. Seated at a scrubbed wooden table in the middle of the big pine-scented room, Owen ate carefully, for his throat was still sore. Sitting next to him, the toddler Benejah kept up a constant stream of strange little sounds as he smeared food over his face or dropped it on the table, putting it anywhere, it seemed, except in his mouth. Beside him, a big, golden dog snapped at any scraps of food that fell onto the floor.

On the other side of the table, Joshua was concentrating on devouring his food. A lean, tanned boy with a pleasant open face, he occasionally lifted his eyes from the table to look at the newcomers with friendly curiosity, but he had little to say.

At first, the newcomers were hesitant, not wanting to talk too much or give too much away, but the woman's easy chatter and the relief generated by food, warmth and comfort, soon led them all to open up. In response to the questions put to her by her visitors, the story emerged of how the woman came to be living in this little farm on the edge of the forest.

Her name was Rebecca Caines, but she had been born Rebecca Hopkins. Her father had come over from West Wales as a British soldier to fight the French in Canada. After twelve years of soldiering, his reward was a grant of scrubby woodland in Nova Scotia – New Scotland. His efforts had then transformed the place into rich farmland and he had married the daughter of one of his old comrades in arms. They had gone on to prosper in a quiet way, raising a family and extending their plot of land. Rebecca was their youngest child, and she in turn had married a fisherman from Newfoundland named Danny Caines.

Rebecca and Danny Caines had bought some land at

the edge of the forest along the banks of the Le Have river. There, for the past eight years, they had worked to build their homestead. The wooden house nestling amid a patchwork of fields, surrounded by sombre stands of spruce, maple and birch, and bordered by the river running down to the sea, was the fruit of their efforts.

"But the money's always tight though," she told them. "There always seems to be more goin' out than there is comin' in. That's why my Danny is away. There's more money to be made farming the sea than there is working the land around here. Like many of our men, he's away fishing the Newfoundland cod banks for American dollars. Its good money, but I'm uneasy when he's away. The sea is a treacherous place for a man to make a living. And now here's the harvest to bring in, and no-one to help me and little Benjy but Joshua."

Her speech was English, plain enough to understand, but her accent was strange: a mixture of West Country and Irish and something foreign. Her voice was round and clear, nothing like the squawk of the fishwives along the Bristol wharves. A strong, confident women, with a ready smile and a sunburned face framed in a mane of hair the colour of straw, the visitors warmed to her open manner and easy talk.

First Emily Bobbins, then Adrian Bell told her something of their own story. Emily described how she had met up with the little group on the 'Caroline Louise' and started to teach Owen to read. Adrian Bell took up the story with an account of the terrible storm and the madness of Sir William Scammell that had forced them to land in secret.

Listening to Emily's description of the struggle in the cabin, Owen found himself blushing in response to a smile from Rebecca Caines and a look of admiration from Joshua sitting opposite him. Not a word was spoken of the treasure, and not a word came from Tudor Jones, who was seemingly lost in a dream as his eyes rested on the face of Emily Bobbins. Owen turned to look at the golden dog that lay gazing into the fire.

"So, as you can see," said Adrian Bell, "there are certain reasons for us to remain in this area for a while. At least until our ship has completed her business in Halifax and can drop off our luggage for us to pick up in Lunenburg."

Tudor Jones started out of his reverie.

"Perhaps we could stop with you, Mrs Caines, if you could put us up. Help you with the farm work and that," he said.

"We could help you with everything," said Emily. "We could help out in all sorts of ways."

"Well, my gosh! You can stay as long as you want if you don't mind helping out. Emily could have the upstairs bed in the back, and Owen can bunk in with Josh. You fellas can bed down in the barn. It'll be dry and warm enough until the end of the Fall when the cold sets in. I can't pay you, but I can surely feed you all."

Owen felt a hard kick on his leg under the table. Joshua, opposite him, was grinning furiously. Owen kicked him back, feeling his boot connect with shin. Joshua scrunched up his face but made no sound. They beamed happily at one another.

As the days moved on and the weeks turned into passing months, the newcomers found themselves tied up with the everyday work of farming in the New World. There were crops of barley and hay to be harvested as winter feed for the oxen. Other plantings would see the little family through the winter. Peas and beans, squashes and apples; potatoes and corn: all had to be picked and dried and stored or pickled.

They moved in an endless round of activity between the fields and the house; the house and the orchards; the barn and the forest. There were the livestock to be tended and endless old tree trunks to be uprooted to make the next Spring's ploughing easier. The work was hard enough in itself, but the intense and sweaty heat and the continuous attention of insects made it harder. Even so it was a fine time for the newcomers. It was work of a kind never known to them before, in a world filled with wild beauty. Elk, deer and bears abounded in the woods, along with many smaller wild animals. And gradually, they came to learn their names.

The spined creature that had frightened them in the tree was the harmless porcupine: harmless, that is, unless it was attacked. Then, its spiked tail would lash at the face of its attacker, leaving barbed and painful spines as a reminder not to bother it again. The animal that ran past them with kittens on its back was the 'possum, a creature as common as a rabbit in North America, and looking like nothing so much as a long, strong rat. Then there was the dainty black and white skunk, like a big squirrel, that visited the house every evening as dusk fell. Everyone left it well alone, including the dog. It was good for flushing out snakes, besides which, if it was alarmed, it would spray out the most rancid stench that would reek for weeks. Racoons, like fat kittens with furry spectacles and tails barred with rings of black fur, chattered and quarrelled in the trees at twilight. Brightly coloured birds dipped and swung through the sky. Yellowhammers, cedar waxwings and scarlet sentinels flittered about, feasting on the endless insects, and big honking geese and black and white loons made use of the river as a kind of aerial highway.

Early mornings and evenings grew crisp with cold as the weeks went by, but with none of the misty drizzle and damp of the old country. With the coming of the first frosts, the blackflies and mosquitoes died away, and as the Autumn ripened, the forest blazed with colour. Maples flamed in purple and red against the sombre green of the spruce and pine. Birch trees glowed in old gold as the sky turned an ever more brilliant blue and the river was a band of shining silver.

Working out of doors and eating plenty of good fresh food, Owen found himself enjoying his life as he never had before. The memory of his trials and troubles faded. Jem Noggins and the mad Sir William were a part of his past that he wanted to forget and of which he was somehow ashamed. He felt stronger and more in charge of himself as he grew to know the woods with Joshua and learned to read and write.

Rebecca Caines grew ever more worried. There had been no word of her husband since a Halifax fishing smack had blown into Lunenburg and reported seeing his boat 'The Dolphin' tossing in heavy seas off the coast of Newfoundland. Sitting around the fire of an evening, she told the newcomers what she knew of the dangers of fishing the Grand Banks for cod. The water was so cold that a man who fell in would freeze to death in minutes, assuming he could swim. Big sharks were always cruising around the fishing boats, ready to snap up whatever scraps were thrown overboard, including men. Few fishermen even bothered to learn to swim, reasoning that if they faced a choice between being eaten by sharks, freezing to death or immediate drowning, the last choice was the least troublesome.

The swirling mists and teeming waters gave life to tales that would chill the blood of the faint hearted. Great white sharks had been known to attack fishing boats, tearing the planking apart like a plough going through soil. There were stories of ships being hauled bodily under the water by giant squid; of whole crews found frozen to death aboard ships that had become floating coffins of ice. Unexpected storms blew beaten ships onto a shoreline studded with teeth of granite. Monstrous icebergs and sudden mists were a constant peril to the men who fished the wild Northern Ocean. Following the sea might be a profitable occupation for some, but it came with a considerable price of injury, fear and death.

There were dangers too in the woods. One afternoon Owen and Joshua were out picking blueberries and talking.

"There's more stars in the sky over here," said Owen, "and hardly any houses. In Bristol, there's houses everywhere: houses and chimneys as far as you can see. Like the forest, only it's houses and rooftops."

"A forest of houses," said Joshua. "I guess that would be something to see. Are there many animals there?"

"There's dogs and cats," said Owen. "Sometimes you see a dancing bear, but he's all chained up with a ring through his nose and some old drunk whacking him with a stick to make him jump around a bit. We got nothing like what you got here: elk and coons and that."

The boys paled and fell silent as they heard the sound of a heavy body crashing though the undergrowth, snapping branches is it came towards them.

Some days earlier, a blow fly had laid a brood of eggs in the ear of a brown bear as he lay asleep. Now the newly hatched maggots were eating through his ear drum into his brain. In his agony, he would kill anything that crossed his path, and the sound of their talking had turned his path towards the boys.

The looming hulk and the rank smell of the animal sent them running.

"Get out of here!" yelled Joshua. "It's a bear, and he ain't dancing!"

Even as he ran, Owen looked behind him. From out of the trees there came running a creature the size of a bull. Its face was contorted, with lips drawn back over great yellow teeth drooling long strings of saliva. The roar of its rage as it

caught sight of the fleeing boys sent a warm stream of fear running down Owen's legs.

Soaring over the ground in a flight of utter panic, the boys yelled their terror as the bear gained on them. Then, leaping over a fallen tree, Owen fell. Turning onto his back, he screamed at the mad brute that was suddenly rearing over him, towering above him as it roared out its pain and fury.

Time slowed down. Owen's nostrils were filled with the sick stench of the animal and he noticed the cloud of flies that swarmed around one side of the bear's head. Then the great drooling jaws came plunging down at him. As if in a dream, Owen saw a yelling Joshua hurl his basket of blueberries in the creature's face, distracting it for a moment so that it reared its head back and stood erect, bellowing its fury at Joshua and striking out at him with its yellow claws.

Then the sound changed to a strangled choking as a cluster of feathers suddenly appeared in the middle of the bear's throat. It raised its great arms towards its neck and two more arrows thudded into its chest. As it stood motionless for a long moment, another arrow took it in the eye. The bear fell backwards like a fallen tree. The mighty shoulders jerked and twitched and then were still.

Then Joshua was pulling Owen to his feet and the two boys stood looking down at the bear. A trail of horrible yellow slime ran from one ear, matting the creature's fur and crawling with flies. They turned to see their rescuers walking towards them: three brown-skinned men wearing feathers in their hair, with faces that were stern and solemn.

"Indians," hissed Joshua. "They sure saved our bacon!"

Still shocked and drenched from his sudden terror, Owen watched without speaking as the men approached them.

Their hair hung down on either side of their faces in long braids wrapped in fur. Their skin was dark brown and they wore beaded necklaces strung with porcupine quills across broad, hairless chests. Neither was there hair on their faces, which had wide cheekbones and dark, slightly slanting eyes. Each had a heavy woollen blanket draped over one shoulder, with a quill of arrows hanging from another. They wore leather breeches, tied below the knee. They each carried a wooden bow. The biggest of the three men had an enormous knife in a beaded sheath that hung from his belt. He came to a halt in front of the two boys and stood looking down at them.

He smelled strongly of wood smoke, sweat and old

leather, but it was a clean, healthy tang after the sick reek of the bear. He said something in a language neither boy understood. His voice was deep and serious.

"I'm Joshua Caines and this here is my friend, Owen Davies, from England," said Joshua. "D'you speak English?"

"Wales!" hissed Owen. "I'm from Wales, not England."

The big Indian squatted down in front of them, bringing his face on a level with their own.

"No English," he said, pointing to himself. "Meegha Magh."

"You a Micmac," said Joshua, nodding. "Don't speak English, I guess."

The Indian began to speak to them in his own language. He seemed very serious and solemn, pointing to the bear on the ground, to Joshua and then to the sky above them. Looking at his strong face and listening to the deep voice was strangely soothing to Owen, and the hammering of his heart began to ease.

The big man finally stood up straight again and pointing to himself and his companions he repeated, "Meegha Magh." Then he turned from the boys and started talking to the dead bear. He spoke to it at length and with great respect. The other two joined him and all three Indians addressed the bear in reverent tones, spreading their arms wide, then turning their faces to the sky.

"I guess they're praying for that old bear," said Joshua. "Looks to me like they're saying sorry for having killed it."

Owen recalled his glimpse of the maddened bear with its halo of flies and looked at the slime oozing from the dead beast's ear.

"I think they did it a favour," he said softly, still trembling. "I don't think the bear was enjoying its life very much just now."

"Well they sure did us a favour," said Joshua. "Mercy!

That was a close-run thing. If they hadn't of been there…"
His voice trailed off, and Owen noticed that he was
trembling too.

The Indians finally concluded their business with the
spirit of the dead bear and came round to dealing with the
body. The big Indian motioned the boys to sit down on the
fallen tree and the three men set to butchering the carcase.

The big man used his great knife to slit it open from the
neck to the groin, ignoring the purple and red innards that
came spilling from the body to lie steaming on the forest
floor. The other two sliced down the inside of each leg,
cutting through the skin until they joined up with the main
incision. Then the three of them worked expertly to peel
back the skin from the flesh in much the same way as a man
might pull off a sock. Once the skin had been rolled and
kneaded off the legs with the great sheathed claws in their
paws still attached, the rest of the skin was hauled upwards
until they reached the neck. Then the big knife severed the
head from the spine and the bear skin was spread out flat on
the ground, complete with head and claws. The massive
skinned body lay obscene and red beside it. Reaching an
arm into the gory mess, one of the squatting men pulled
out the liver and examined it carefully. He shook his head
decisively, evidently not pleased with what he saw, and he
said something to his companions.

The big Indian straightened up and wiped some of the
blood off his arms with a handful of leaves. He mimed eating
the flesh of the dead bear and getting very sick.
He spoke to his companions who turned the bearskin over
and began to scrape off some of the fat and membranes still
attached to it, seemingly undisturbed by the clouds of flies
that were gathering to feast on the carcase. Turning to the
boys, the big man motioned them to get up and head for
home, miming eating and sleeping.

Joshua jumped up to lead the way with Owen close beside him. Leaving his companions scraping away at the bear skin, the big Indian came behind them, moving as soundlessly as a shadow as he followed them between the trees. Past the tangles of undergrowth and poison ivy; around the dense clumps of brambles and nettles; through the thickets of bushes and the endless columns of trees, they made their way back towards the homestead.

At last, the three of them emerged from the forest onto the slope leading down to the farmhouse. In the clear sunlight of the late afternoon, they could see right down to the river. A battered looking ketch was riding at anchor. From the bow of the ketch, the graceful figure of a dolphin seemed about to leap forward into the water.

Joshua whooped his glee. "It's Pa!" he cried. "He's home!"

CHAPTER TWELVE

The 'Dolphin' is Commissioned

As they approached the farmhouse, the dog ran out and bounded around them, barking wildly at the smells of bear, blood and Indians. The noise brought everyone inside to the door, including a stranger who Owen guessed must be Joshua's Pa, returned from the sea. Joshua ran forwards to fling his arms around the man's neck, the two of them smiling with joy at each other.

Danny Caines was a solidly built man of about average height with light brown hair and a look about him that Owen recognised immediately: he was a Buffer and Codger, even if he was a bit young for the part. His skin was tanned and lined and his face shone with affection as he tousled his son's head.

Joshua couldn't get the words out fast enough. "A bear came after us, Pa! He was real mad. He come chasing after us when we was picking berries and we run like fire until Owen here falls over a dead tree. I thought he was a goner for sure. I threw my berries in the bear's face, but it didn't stop him none. He was about to start chomping down on us, when all of a sudden he upped and dropped dead! The Indians killed him Pa! Shot an arrow straight into his neck and then took him in the eye. He sure was a mean old bear, Pa! He would of killed us both for sure if it hadn't been for the Indians! They skinned him clean as a rabbit, Pa…"

"Well, hello to you too Josh," said his father easily. "Slow down there boy, or you'll meet yourself coming the other way. Seems like the first thing we've got to do is to thank this kind gentleman for saving the both of you." His voice was quiet and firm. He turned towards the Indian, then stretching out both his hands, he squeezed the man's muscled brown shoulders and smiled, looking directly into his eyes. "Thank you. Thank you my friend," he said softly.

The Indian's face cracked into an answering smile and he said something in his own tongue. His voice rolled deep, like a boulder in a cave. "Tankyu," he repeated.

Danny turned to face Owen and squatted down on his haunches so his face was level. "I guess you'll be Owen," he said. "I'm right pleased to make your acquaintance."

Shaking his hand, Owen noticed his palm was hard and calloused and that he smelled strongly of fish.

"I reckon we owe this gentleman a reward for saving the two of you, Owen. What do you think?"

In the excitement of the moment, without thinking, Owen blurted out, "We could give him one of the jewels from our treasure."

There was a long pause. Danny Caines got to his feet and gazed searchingly at the guests whom his wife had rescued from the wilderness.

The Indian, sensitive as an animal to the sudden change of mood, shifted uneasily from one foot to another and gazed back towards the forest.

"I don't think that a jewel would be much of a prize to

our friend when he's out there in the woods. He wants something he can use." Danny Caines ducked back into the shadow of the farmhouse and emerged a minute later with a sack of flour, a small keg of molasses, and a big, horn-handled knife. He showed the gifts one by one to the Indian as he placed them inside a gunny sack.

The Indian beamed and nodded as they were handed to him. "Tankyu," he repeated. He seemed especially delighted with the knife, which he hefted in his hand then stuck in his belt beside the knife he was wearing in a heavily beaded sheath. Taking the sack of flour and molasses, he spoke to them briefly in his own language then turned and walked back towards the brooding forest.

After watching his sturdy form move off into the trees, they turned to the business of cleaning themselves up and making ready for supper.

The lamp was lit and plates were set out as the dog sneaked in unnoticed and took up a hiding place under the table. Once everybody had taken their places and Danny had said Grace, the wooden plates were passed around and heaped with corn and squash, hot beetroot, rabbit stew, green beans and gravy. The buzz of conversation round the table ceased as they started eating and for some time the only sound was the noise of knives and spoons on plates.

Danny was the first to finish. He mopped up the last bit of gravy with a piece of bread then pushed his empty plate away and sighed with pleasure. "Sure is good to be back home again," he said. "You don't get to eat food like that on a cod-hauler." He looked around the table reflectively, noting how his guests kept their eyes fixed on their plates and seemed none too keen to meet his gaze. His wife looked up at him as she ate, arching her eyebrows in an unspoken question. "Nice to see you folks here too, and to see the family has had some company and help whilst I was away.

That was one long piece of fishing. Paid good though." In the brief silence that followed, he dropped his next words like stones into a pool. "What's this talk of Owen's about jewels and treasure?"

Three pairs of eyes swivelled towards him. Adrian Bell, Tudor Jones and Owen Davies looked uncertainly at the man sitting at the head of the table. The eyes of Emily Bobbins, Rebecca Caines and Joshua were bright with curiousity. Ignoring them all, little Benejah was busy scraping the food around and around on his plate, with the dog snatching at each morsel as it fell to the floor.

Adrian Bell pursed his lips and frowned. His long forefinger drummed on the table.

Tudor Jones was the first to speak. "I think we should tell our friends now," he said. "We was always going to do it sooner or later anyway. We can't do anything without help from somebody, can we?"

"What do you say, Owen?" said Adrian Bell. "It's as much your secret as ours."

"I'd be glad to tell them all." Owen spoke without hesitation. "They deserve a reward, don't they? All the help they give us. Joshua came back to fight the bear and saved my life. He could have been killed, couldn't he?"

Adrian Bell took a deep breath before he began to speak.

"I don't know what we would have done without your wife, Mister Caines," he said. "We have come to trust and rely on her completely. And as her husband, we must behave the same way to you." He paused. "As far as we can make it out," he said, "this business with jewels and treasure started with two sailors who used to leave messages for one another at my shop in Bristol." He pulled the Scrimshaw from his pocket and placed it on the table. "And one day, one of them left this."

So it was that the story which had first unfolded amid

the bustling streets of Bristol and moved on to the peaceful West Country graveyard was told again in the farmhouse on the edge of the silver river in the New World. As Adrian Bell set forth the tale, shadows shifted in the firelight and the lamp was lit. Little Benejah and the dog both fell asleep, and the eyes of the listeners grew bright with excitement.

When he got to the part where they opened the tin box found at the grave of Briney Morgan, Adrian Bell drew out from beneath his shirt a leather pouch and placed it on the table . As he lifted it gently, a small cascade of rubies and emeralds, opals and diamonds rolled out to lie shining in the lamplight. In the stunned silence that followed, he went on to tell them of Bosun Salt's letter and the story of Robert Culliford's treasure, cached in secret on Sable Island.

"It didn't take the sale of more than a dozen of them pretties to cover all the costs of our journey out here," Tudor Jones chipped in. "Still plenty left over, see. But we thought we'd need to use the rest of it to hire a ship and a trusty type of crew to take us to the island and get the treasure off of it."

"Trusty type of crew?" said Danny Caines." A sniff of pirate treasure and trust don't sit easy together. There's few would stop at cutting your throat for the chance to grab it for their own."

"That's where you come in," said Adrian Bell. "You must know some good men, having a ship of your own. I put my faith in your good heart, and that of your good lady, Mister Caines."

Danny Caines smiled grimly. "Faith seems to have brought you a long way, so far," he said. "I admire you going after it, but how you thought you would bring the treasure off the island beats me, even if you managed to find it."

"We can find it alright, if only we can get there," Tudor Jones cut in. "We've got a map. That's why we've been waiting for you so long, see. We were grateful to Rebecca for all her help, and the more we saw of her, the more we felt sure we could trust her. And if we could trust her, we were hopeful that we might also trust you, and you might be the man to help us with your boat…"

"Ship," said Danny Caines shortly. "She's a ship, not a boat. A boat is something you might row around with oars. That there ketch of mine is a ship."

"And here was me thinking we were staying to help Rebecca with the harvest until her husband returned," Emily Bobbins put in angrily. "And now the truth comes out that all the time you were thinking of nothing but how to get your hands on a pile of stolen treasure! And you kept it from me as if I wasn't to be trusted. Keeping it a secret all to yourselves! All of you! At least I thought better of you, Tudor Jones!"

That young man flushed as he looked at her with the eyes of a beggar. "Don't be like that Emily," he pleaded. "I wanted to tell you all the time. I really did. It was just that we thought we had better wait until we could come to it all together, like."

"Indeed, indeed," said Adrian Bell hastily. "I can tell you honestly that our young friend here wanted to let you in on our secret even when we were back on the ship with that wretched Sir William Scammell. It was me insisted that you should be kept in the dark until the right moment arrived. For your own safety as much as anything. Imagine if Sir William had got a whiff of the treasure. I felt that the fewer the people who knew about it, the better for all of us…er, I mean… everyone concerned."

There was an uncomfortable moment of silence.

Owen was upset that Emily should think he had let her down. "I would've told you, Miss Emily," he said, "but they said it would only put you in danger. We wasn't trying to keep you out of it, honest. Whenever we spoke about it, Mr Jones always said he wouldn't give nothing for no treasure if it meant he had to keep it from you. You saved my life Miss Emily. I wouldn't never do nothing against you. You can have it all, for all I care!" He was almost crying.

Emily's anger evaporated as she looked at her downcast friends. "Of course. I'm just a bit shocked, I suppose. I'm sorry. You'll have to forgive me. All of you."

Tudor Jones spoke quickly. "The boy speaks for me too, Emily," he said. "We all owe one another. That boy saved me from the sharks just as sure as you saved him from Sir William: curse his wooden teeth. I hope he gets woodworm in his jaw."

Danny Caines leaned forwards across the table. "Tell me about this Sir William," he said. "Who is he, and what is he to you?"

The story of the drunken aristocrat's evil behaviour on the "Caroline Louise" was soon told: his efforts to set the sharks on Tudor Jones; the murderous violence of his attacks on Emily and Owen during the storm; and their fears that had caused them all to be landed in secret so that they might escape further harm at his hands.

Danny Caines whistled softly. "I don't want to alarm you folks," he said, "but when we were landing our catch in Lunenburg, there was a high and mighty Englishman called Sir William strutting around the harbour in company with a bunch of redcoats. I didn't take much notice, being in a hurry to unload and get home. The thing that struck me about him was the fact that he had wooden teeth."

Emily Bobbins went white. "That dreadful man!" she said. "And he's here, you say? Right nearby. My goodness, we should get away immediately. If he hears that we are with you…"

"No need to upset yourself," said Adrian Bell quickly.

"There's nothing to worry about yet. If Captain Cutler kept his word – and we have no reason to think he didn't – Sir William thinks all of us are long drowned. There's no reason in the world for him to come looking for us."

"What if he learns about the baggage that was left for us?" said Emily fearfully. "What if he finds out that a Welshman called Bell was in Lunenberg with Rebecca to collect that luggage?"

Remembering his visit to Lunenberg three weeks earlier, Bell's face dropped. "Well, perhaps we should be leaving soon," he said. "Yes. We should definitely go."

"It might not even be him," said Tudor Jones, but his voice lacked conviction. "It might be someone else with wooden teeth."

"We can check it out," said Danny, "but I'm pretty sure this fella is your man. Not too many Sir Williams with wooden teeth to be found in these parts."

"Why is he here, of all places?" mused Tudor Jones. "He has the whole of the New World to roam in, and he ends up a few miles down the river from us in Lunenburg."

"As for what he's doing here," said Danny Caines, " that's simple. There's always redcoats snooping about between the ports and harbours of Nova Scotia. The smuggling trade between Canada and the States is something King George would like to put a cap on. If your man with the wooden teeth was going to be the King's man in Nova Scotia, he would be attached to the garrison in Halifax. It's the redcoats are the rulers here."

"But he's not in Halifax: he's in Lunenburg," said Emily.

"He'll be out on patrol," replied Danny. "I would guess he's with a foot patrol of the South Shore. Probably spend a few days in Lunenburg before heading down to Liverpool and Shelborne. All we have to do is sit tight here and they'll move on."

"I don't like it," said Emily. "The thought of that man being near us gives me the shudders. I just wish we could sail off in that boat of yours, Captain Caines."

"Ship," said Danny with a smile. "The "Dolphin is a ship. And I'm Danny to my friends, Miss Emily. So where would you sail off to in my ship?"

Emily replied without hesitation. "I would go straight to Sable Island and bring off that treasure before the Winter is upon us. I would rather the business of finding the treasure was done with before we decide what to do next. And as for Sir William Scammell, if he is here, in this vicinity, then I should prefer to be somewhere else."

"So you're with Mister Bell," said Danny. "That's two for going. What about you, Mister Jones?"

"I just been waiting to get on a boat, I mean a ship, and set foot on that Island ever since we found the jewels," came the reply. "We've all been waiting for you, see. It seemed like Providence when we turned up on Mistress Rebecca's doorstep and then found that you were the Captain of a ship. And now that we've met you, I'd be glad for you to take us, sooner rather than later if you please. I know that Sir William Scumbucket would like nothing better than to see me swinging from a rope's end. Take us out to find that treasure, and it's fair shares all round."

Danny Caines looked across at his wife. "So there's three for it. What do you say Becky? Shall I ship out with them to Sable Island and go on a search for treasure? Or shall I bide and sit tight with my own treasures right here?"

Rebecca Caines gave a wan smile. "As for that," she said, "you know what you will do and it isn't for me to tell you. But this I will say: the waiting gets terrible hard here alone with you out after the cod. I don't know how I would have got through these past months without the company of these good folks. I'd surely like to help them; and I'd like for you to have enough money not to need to go out for fish again. If helping them out means an end to your risking drowning on the Grand Banks, then I would say that was a pretty good bargain."

"We could be there and back within a week or so. And best to do it right away before the snow comes," mused Danny Caines. "We'll be cutting it fine with the weather whatever happens. If we take on some more stores tomorrow, I could line up Snow Parker and Sylvanus Hopkins. With those two, and Ken Ralph to crew, we could be out on the tide the day after tomorrow."

"Now we're coming to it!" Adrian Bell was rubbing his hands together, his eyes shining. "The day after tomorrow! Are your crew men you can trust?"

Danny Caines looked at him across the table. "As for that," he said, "It's hard to say who can be trusted when it comes to a heap of treasure. Can I trust you, I wonder? Men go mad around gold and jewels, as I've heard tell. But if it's a fair share of rich pickings that's on offer, then that might do for me and my crew. I'll go into Lunenburg tomorrow."

CHAPTER THIRTEEN

Leaving Lunenberg

Waving goodbye to Rebecca, Josh and little Ben was a mournful business for Owen. They had given him his first taste of family life since he had left his home to go with Jem Noggins, and he was sad to be leaving it behind. He had seen another way of living in the Nova Scotia homestead across the ocean. Unafraid of the wilderness and the isolation, the family busied themselves tending the farm and looking after their beasts whilst Danny scoured the cold northern seas for fish. It was a hard life, as hard in its way as that of the people toiling in the factories and mines of Great Britain, but there was a cleanness to it, and a pride in standing alone.

As the "Dolphin" sailed downstream, the waving figures dwindled behind him and the farm shrank to a little clearing hemmed in by the endless trees. Then came the bend in the river and there was only the forest and the flocks of wild birds.

They dropped anchor in the middle of Lunenberg harbour shortly after mid-day and Danny Caines sculled off in the "Dolphin's" jolly boat, having given strict instructions for everyone to stay below decks and out of sight.

After the past months of increasing security, the future was filled again with dangers and uncertainty. The possibility of Scammell learning that a Welshman called Bell, in the company of Rebecca Caines, had collected luggage from a harbour official in Lunenberg, could not be discounted. As the little group talked it over, the more likely it seemed. Their fears grew as the afternoon dragged by like a headache.

A boat filled with armed redcoats, with Danny Caines shackled between them, heading towards the "Dolphin" and commanded by Sir William Scammell, was the image haunting them all.

Owen tried to think of something else, but that brought little comfort. He found himself missing Joshua, left behind to be "the man of the house", as Danny put it. He missed his friend, and as he thought about it, he missed Rebecca too, and the farmhouse, the golden dog, and Ben – and the woods he had wandered in with such a sense of freedom.

Watching from the galley porthole of the "Dolphin" as the first shades of dusk dimmed the sky over Lunenberg, Owen was struck by how different the town looked compared to those of old England. He was used to buildings made of brick and grey stone. Here, everything was made of wood: from the great warehouses fronting onto the water to the rows of brightly painted homes behind them and the church spires that jutted above the trees and the rooftops: all made of wood. As the sky darkened to cobalt blue and the lights winked on behind the windows of tavern and home, Owen longed to explore the beckoning town, but the danger of meeting Sir William kept them all prisoner. They waited.

The burning red of the maple leaves rearing among the rooftops of Lunenberg was fading to a glimmer when Adrian Bell finally announced, "Here he comes."

With his distinctive green knitted cap pulled down to one side, Danny Caines was pulling powerfully on his oars as he skimmed across the water in the light of the sinking sun. There was no sign of pursuit. No boatload of armed redcoats. The wake of Danny's jolly boat was the only sign of disturbance on the placid surface of the bay. Soon he bumped alongside the "Dolphin" and climbed aboard. Then his feet drummed on the steps of the companion-way and he came through to join them. His face told them that something was badly wrong.

"Come and lend me a hand, quickly," he said, pulling Tudor Jones to his feet. "It's Scammell. I've had to shanghai him. We must get him below before he's missed in Lunenberg."

The pair of them disappeared back up on deck. They returned after a few minutes, carrying a large sack between them. Dumping it down, Danny untied the strings binding the top of the sack and pulled it back to reveal a horribly familiar face. The man's eyes were closed and his mouth was covered with a rough gag, but there was no mistaking who it was. Sir William Scammell was back with them once again. He reeked of sherry and was obviously unconscious.

Pulling the sack away from him, Danny emptied Sir William out onto the floor of the cabin where he lay snoring and muttering. His hands and feet were tied together; his uniform stained and befouled.

"What happened?" said Adrian Bell. His voice sounded bleak and wintry. "Why did you have to bring him here of all places?"

"It was that or kill him," said Danny. "He knew about Becky and you coming into town for that luggage. It was only a matter of time before he went out to the farm – and I couldn't risk leaving him behind to make trouble while I was away. Give me a hand to get him down into the hold. I'll give you the full story when the vittles are stowed and we're on course to Sable Island."

Danny glanced out of the porthole. "Look lively now! Unless I'm much mistaken, that's our lighter on its way out to us, and if they catch sight of Scammell, that's our game up before it starts! Give me a hand to get him stowed away below."

Three hours later, under a bright moon, the "Dolphin" was nosing her way out into the Atlantic, complete with a supply of ship's stores and the addition of three extra crew members. They had come out to the ship on the lighter, the supply boat laden with barrels, crates and boxes which were swung aboard in the last of the fading light. With the extra three hands to help, they made haste to stow the supplies and ready the ship to leave harbour on the falling tide.

The lights of Lunenberg vanished behind a last headland and then there was only the dark tufted coastline of forest against the night sky. They were back at sea once more and the crew moved smoothly about their business as they headed for deep water.

Of the new men who came aboard, one was the Captain's Mate, Ken Ralph: a burly man in middle age with grey hair hanging below his woollen sailor's cap. His round face was roughened by weather and there was a deep cleft in his chin. With his powerful shoulders and thick bull neck, he was a picture of strength and resolve. Working beside him, Snow Parker was a lean, hawk-faced young man, a young man who had a mane of white hair that hung down to his shoulders. With his thin lips and hooked nose, he had the profile of an Indian warrior, but his eyes were a startling shade of blue. The final one of the trio, Sylvanus Hopkins, was a trim, sprightly man in his early thirties, yet whose face was deeply creased and lined like that of a much older man. All three had crewed with Danny Caines in the teeming water of the Cod Banks many times before.

With the sails set and the crew going about their business

on deck, Danny settled beside the stove in the cabin to tell them what had happened to him in Lunenberg.

"I was pretty sure that two of the men I was looking for would be found in The Mermaid Inn, and that's where I headed as soon as I landed ashore. Even that early in the afternoon, the bar of The Mermaid was fuggy with pipe smoke and I couldn't hardly see when I first walked in. The usual crowd were working hard on drowning their sorrows. A couple of the crews from the two Halifax ships in harbour were racing cockroaches. At another table, a group of Yankees were making a great racket with their dominoes. The doxy booths where certain ladies entertained their gentlemen were doing brisk business behind closed doors and the fishwives were busy squawking and gossiping over their gin toddy.

"The two men I was looking for were sitting down next to the fire. Both of them were puffing away easy on corn cob pipes with their legs stretched out and pots of beer brimming in front of them. They looked mighty comfortable. One of them was Sylvanus Hopkins and the other was Snow Parker.

"He's called Snow on account of that head of snowy hair he carries around. You'll be thinking he's a young man to have such a head on him, and you wouldn't be wrong. His hair has been that colour since he first shipped aboard a whaler as a boy of sixteen. Six months into the voyage, she was sunk with all hands by a maddened sperm whale in the Java Sea. For three days and three nights Parker clung on to a floating spar in the warm seas you get down in the blue water of the tropics. As the nights fell, the ocean turned luminous, as if it was lit from below, and he could see the great fish devouring their prey in the water below his feet. But the sharks glided past beneath and about him, leaving him unharmed. As the sun burned his head during the scorching days, he expected with every second to feel the clamp of great jaws close upon him and drag him under. For three long days and eternal nights he stood his fear and suffering.

"Snow finally washed up on the muddy shores of some island where the natives took pity on him and helped him to find his way back to the world. When they dragged him from the water, his skin was wrinkled and tough like pickled beef, but he had absorbed enough water through it to prevent him dying of thirst. His hair had turned white though, like you see it now, and he came back to Lunenberg as "Snow" Parker, vowing he would never go a-whaling again. But he's still game for the cod banks, and a fine ship-mate he is for our little caper.

"Sitting beside him in "The Mermaid Inn", roasting his hands in front of the fire, was Sylvanus Hopkins, another who could tell a tale of Trial by Sea but who chooses not to. If we need someone who can keep a secret, Hopkins is the man for us. The story clings to him that he's a man who has eaten human flesh.

"It must be nigh on ten years ago when Hopkins, along with the rest of the ship's crew, took to the long boats when they ran aground on an unmarked reef one night in the Indian Ocean. Adrift for weeks on end, the two long boats got separated in a storm and each gave the other up for lost. A convict hauler, bound for Botany Bay finally picked one of them up. All of the shipwrecked men were alive but in a terrible state. One of them died within an hour of being taken aboard. Three days later, the same ship came across the other long boat and picked up Sylvanus Hopkins.

"All of the men with him were alive, and in much better condition than those in the first boat. But the cabin boy was missing. Their story was that the boy had gone mad with thirst and jumped over the side: that the sharks had got to him before they could fish him out. But the contrast between the crew in Hopkins boat and the starving scarecrows in the other one told a different story. The suspicion lingered that it was no shark that ate the cabin boy. Rumour put it about that he had been killed and his body divided up among the men in his boat according to the ancient 'Custom of the Sea'. No-one enquired too deeply, but many in Lunernberg still look askance at Sylvanus Hopkins. In all the years I've been sailing with him, he's never spoken of it. But he's the right sort of sailor for a job like this: handy, reliable and silent as the grave.

Danny Caines paused and poured himself a mug of water.

"So the next thing is, I'm sitting with them over a jug of toddy, whispering out the course for Sable Island and getting them ready to come on board. You can rest easy Mister Bell. No-one was paying us any mind. The Mermaid is a pretty hard place to hear yourself speak betimes, never mind listen to what other people are saying.

"I had pretty well finished setting out my stall when I saw one of the doxy booths open and out comes a Redcoat Officer, much the worse for the wear. He walks, well more like he staggers, across the bar and outside to the necessary.

"Then the landlord, Little Clem, comes bustling over to us all of a sweat. He tells me the Redcoat is the officer who was in earlier asking about a family, name of Caines, recently in town with a Welshman, name of Bell. Little Clem says he told him nothing, but he reckoned that when the Redcoat sobered up, he'd be taking up the question once again. All this whispered out in as much time as it takes to tell, then Clem bustles back to his bar to mind his drinks.

"When the redcoat came lurching back into the bar, the

first thing he did was to trip over a flagstone and fall headfirst into Hagstench, one of the fish wives selling whelks and crab claws. So the pair of them go crashing to the floor. Hagstench shrieks and the redcoat curses and the whole room erupts with laughter at the sight of the pair of them flailing around among a mess of mussels and crabs, oil and vinegar. The Redcoat was slipping and sliding as he tried to regain his feet, only to be pulled down again by Hagstench as she tried to pull herself upright.

"Little Clem goes fussing to the rescue of the officer and pulled him to his feet. As the Redcoat sets to brushing himself down, Hagstench, still sitting on the floor, holds something up to him.

"Is these yours dearie?" she says, clicking them open and shut. It was a set of wooden teeth.

"Everyone is laughing as the redcoat crams the teeth back into his mouth and tries to face down the general hilarity.

"Mutineers and miscreants!" Danny put on Scammell's nasal English voice. "I'll smoke the lot of you out! You're nothing but a damned colonial rabble!"

"Arrest Cameron for mutiny, General!" a voice calls out. "He won't stand his round!"

"Another shouts out, "Take Smoking Gunn first Major! He's always miscreantin' – and it smells something awful.'"

"Arrest Hagstench Captain!" another cry goes up. "She miscreanted with Gunn last week and nearly squashed him flat!"

"The redcoat officer steps over to our little group, where Hopkins is helpless with laughter. "Do you know who I am?" he shouts.

"He's so drunk, he's forgot his own name!" someone yells.

"Then the Redcoat draws out his sword from its scabbard and the laughter dies away.

"All except for the boy called the Mazeling. He's the half-witted boy Clem keeps to help him with the pots. The Mazeling just sat there with his mouth open and a kind of dead laughter falling out of his mouth in lumps.

"The Redcoat steps over to the boy and pricks his face with his sabre. The boy's laughter dies off as the point of the sword under his nose forces him to his feet.

"I am Captain Sir William Scammell," the Redcoat announces to the room in general. "I am an officer of His Majesty King George. Mocking an officer of the King is treason. I'll have you remember that. So there's enough of your damned colonial impudence!"

Danny paused and looked at the ring of faces around him in the cabin of the "Dolphin". He took a drink from his mug and continued.

"So that's how I made certain of who he was and now I had to find a way to get him off our case. I didn't want him making trouble for Becky while I was away. Nor did I want to leave him to start chasing us with his crew if he got a whiff of the treasure."

"But what will we do with him?" said Emily. "He'll be furious when he comes round."

"I could sell him on to a Yankee whaler. They can always use another hand and could care less about his red coat and the commission of King George. They're sometimes gone for three years at a time, way across in the Pacific Ocean. No telling what might happen to him out there." Danny Caines mused.

"But I'm getting ahead of myself. As little Clem comes over to sooth Sir William down and rescue the Mazeling, I set the tone for the rest of us by piping up, "I'm sincerely sorry, Captain. I'm afraid that none of us here was aware of your rank or importance. Would you care to sit down and join us in a drink? I am Captain Gilbert, Sir, at your service, Sir."

Hopkins strikes up alongside of me. "No harm meant, Sir," he says. "Captain Gilbert speaks for all of us Sir. No-one would have chaffed you if they had known who you was, Your Worship."

Snow Parker joins in from my other side: "I'm with Captain Gilbert, Sir. No-one would have dreamed of making fun of a member of the nobility, Your Honour."

Danny sniffed and chuckled to himself.

"So Scammell takes our expressions of respect as genuine and allows me to buy him a drink. I persuade him to join the party at our table and set to plying him with more drink.

I had to work out a plan to take him out of action. The only thing that came to mind was the old British press gang trick: get a man blind drunk then drag him aboard and set sail. So I sat and chatted with him, filling him with flattery and lies. A regular charmer he was, with a fine opinion of himself that was only matched by his contempt for everybody else. When he was well on the way to being as soused as a pickled herring, I tipped the wink to Hopkins and Parker while I nipped out to gather in Ken Ralph and round up the necessaries.

"I found Ralph at home and gave him the story and a list of the provisions he needed to get on board. There was never a doubt that Ken would be coming with us. He's as true a sailor as ever sniffed a pilchard, and I've been in his debt since he pulled me out of the Dancing Sand up on the coast of Cape Breton."

"Dancing sand?" said Tudor Jones.

Danny Caines explained briefly. "On some shores, you get a continuous disturbance of the sand under the sea caused by conflicting currents. A man might set foot on such sand without knowing and then be sucked under beyond all help. It was while I was up there, putting some repairs to the "Dolphin" that I found myself trapped. But let me get back to my story. In fact there's not a lot more to tell.

"Having got hold of a sack and an empty sherry barrel from my chandler, I cart it up to the "Mermaid" and wait behind the woodhouse. When Snow Parker comes out for a visit to the head, I tip him the wink and he joins me. So when Sir William comes staggering out to empty his bladder, we tap him on the head, sack him up, put him in the barrel and cart him down to the harbour. He won't have been missed until the evening roll call, and they won't start looking for him seriously until tomorrow morning. So now you can see why we had to leave port in a hurry, with Sir

William stowed in the hold. He's a poor cargo, but someone has to carry him."

Emily Bobbins sighed and pulled Owen to her side.

"Don't be frightened of old Sir William," she said. "He can do us no harm in the hold. And just think: we're finally on our way to Sable Island!"

Danny Caines looked at the little group around him. "Way I see it, we've done all we can do. Right now, he's safe out of the way and we can keep an eye on him. The only other option was kill him, and there's no way I'm going to be a killer. That would make me worse than him. You people should get to your bunks and get some sleep now. It's been a long day. You can worry about tomorrow when it gets here."

"That sounds good to me," said Tudor Jones, yawning. "Let's get to bed and think about tomorrow in the morning."

CHAPTER FOURTEEN

Sable Island

"What the devil d'you think you're playing at?" huffed Sir William Scammell, brought up blinking from the hold to stand in the light of day. His eyes were red and his wig hung crookedly over one ear. His uniform was stained and foul after a night spent in the hold, the usual inhabitants of which were dead fish.

On one side of him was Sylvanus Hopkins, and on the other stood Snow Parker. Scammell pulled himself erect and stuck one hand on his hip as he stared down his nose at the man facing him. "Do you realise that you have abducted a personal friend of His Majesty, King George?"

"Never mind King George. Do you remember me?" Danny asked.

"You. You're Gilbert. What do you mean by kidnapping an Officer of the King in this outrageous fashion? You'll swing for it Sir, unless you take me back ashore this instant. Hung from the yard arm over Halifax Harbour as a warning for other colonial rebels!"

He suddenly changed tack and his voice took on a more reasonable tone. "If you take me back immediately, I promise there will be no further reprisals. What on earth can you be thinking of man? This is utter madness! You're behaving like Americans!"

"Reprisals is what it would have been if I had left you behind," said Danny, easily. "And don't be threatening me, mister. You should know better than to threaten a Captain on the deck of his own ship. Besides, I have done you a considerable favour. You have been busy looking for a certain party, I believe. Well now you've found them. Let me introduce you to the rest of my crew."

Adrian Bell was the first to step out of the cuddy onto the deck, followed by Tudor Jones and Emily, with Owen carrying up the rear.

Scammell's pale face took on a yellow tinge as they stood in line before him. His eyes bulged and he swallowed like a man trying hard not to be sick. He opened his mouth, but no words came out.

"Last time we met," said Emily Bobbins, "you were trying to kill us. You tried to rape me, then you tried to strangle little Owen here."

There was a silence. They looked at him and he looked at them.

His eyes shifted and he took in the boundless sea surrounding them and the far away coast, low on the horizon. His wooden teeth fell forwards and he caught them with his tongue and sucked them back in. His face took on a hunted look. He seemed to physically shrink in front of their eyes as the swagger leaked out of him. His hands dropped to his sides and he hung his head like a child awaiting a scolding.

"I see you have me at a disadvantage," he said, his voice sounding small and pathetic. "I am alone and defenceless. I can only ask your forgiveness and I throw myself on the mercy of the court."

"Which is a sight more mercy than you would have shown us," said Tudor Jones, looking grimly at the bedraggled wreck of a man standing in front of them.

"Throw myself on the mercy of the court?" Danny Caines echoed. "Now there's a pretty phrase! Where have I heard that before?"

"He has been a magistrate, I believe," said Adrian Bell. "It is the usual custom of magistrates in England to invite those who stand before them to plead guilty and throw themselves on the mercy of the court. Judge Jeffries most famously established this practice. It turned out that his ideas of mercy included hanging, imprisonment, transportation and flogging of any poor soul unfortunate enough to appear before him. The mercy of the court was conspicuous by its absence. No doubt Sir William was a magistrate of the Judge Jeffries mode."

"Not so Sir. Upon my word," Scammell kept his eyes fixed on the deck. "I was always a merciful man at the Assizes."

"Like a mouthful of fish bones," said Danny Caines, "that's a difficult thing to swallow. But let us look at your situation directly. On the evidence of my companions, you are guilty of malice and attempted murder. On the evidence of my own eyes, you are guilty of tyrannical abuse of your authority. You are a menace and a bully. On a ship, Sir, the Captain is the judge and jury, and you are sentenced herewith to serve before the mast on account of your crimes against these good people here with me today. You can think yourself lucky."

His voice turned brisk. "My First Mate, Mister Ralph will show you the ropes, and you can sling your hammock alongside the others. If you pull your weight with no foolishness, you'll live to strut and swagger again yet. Any nonsense mind, and you're over the side, or I'll sell you to the first Yankee whaler we come across as is outward bound."

Scammell lifted his eyes and attempted a fawning smile.

"You can stand on me, Sir. I'll give you no trouble. May I ask where we are bound, Sir?"

"No, Sir, you may not, Sir." Danny Caines fixed him sternly with his eye. "You are to be told nothing about our business other than how to tie a knot and where to reef a sail, to learn fore from aft and to jump sharp when you are told to. Now get below and put on some decent clothes. I'll have no Marines on this ship Sir, nor no damned lobster backs neither."

"Yes Sir," was the muttered reply, and with his face still averted from the little group in front of him, the abject man was led below.

The land was a distant smudge on the horizon and the sky was heavy with clouds as the "Dolphin" cleaved through the waves. Before the morning was finished, the first squall of snow had passed over them, and Sir William Scammell was to be seen shivering on the fore deck under the watchful eye of Ken Ralph as he attempted to master the art of sewing the heavy canvas sails.

Ken Ralph busied himself with instructing his new deckhand. He showed a surprising dexterity as he set to work with the needle and thread, a skill which was completely lacking in the new recruit. He joined the little group in the cuddy to take his lunch, where he showed himself to be a quietly spoken, good humoured man with a very low opinion of the ship's latest recruit.

"About as much use as a jellyfish in a jolly boat," he said. "Us will have to stow him below if us hits dirty weather. And there's some coming up, make no doubt of it."

"It's a bad time to be sailing in these waters," Danny explained. "You get the tail end of the hurricanes up from the tropics blowing out around this time of year. They bring all kinds of freak weather with them. And coming down out of the north are ice storms and stray ice floes. Then there are the waters around Sable Island itself, as treacherous as any you could find. One minute you're in fifty feet of water, and suddenly you've run aground. It's the sand dunes under the water: the waves just keep moving them around so there's never a reliable chart. The graveyard of the Atlantic they call it. There have been more ships wrecked off Sable Island than any other place in the world."

"Including Culliford's ship, 'Resolution'," murmured Adrian Bell.

Tudor Jones slapped his thigh. "And now we're nearly there," he said, his eyes gleaming. "It's been a long journey from Bristol, Adrian. And now we're almost in sight of it!"

"There's a sight of things we haven't sorted yet," said Danny Caines grimly. "We don't know where to land, nor whether we can find the strong box – if it's there to be found. It's a murderous place I'm telling you…"

"Oh, I'm sure we will survive, Captain," said Emily Bobbins with a smile. "This is not the time for despondency. You'll have poor little Owen worried at this rate. We are committed to this course now, so let us set about it with a good heart."

Danny Caines looked at her and smiled. "You are quite right, Miss Bobbins," he said. "Who ever it was said women were the weaker sex got it altogether wrong."

For two days the "Dolphin" ran before the wind as the weather grew steadily colder.

Proving himself to be as useless as Ken Ralph predicted, Sir William Scammell – now christened "Scummy" by the seamen – was set to work sewing up five big knapsacks out of canvas. Reasoning that they would be unable to carry the big trunk described in Bosun Salt's letter, Danny Caines set him to making the sacks that they would pack the treasure in for transport back to the ship: one for each member of the boarding party.

Owen busied himself about the ship, sometimes lending a hand in the galley where Snow Parker kept his endlessly bubbling pot of stew. This was a dish which he never finished, but just kept adding extra bits to: oats, fish, beef jerky, pork belly, a head of cabbage, salt pork, potatoes, celery, carrots – and more fish. The flavour varied from meal to meal. Owen also helped out with the fishing line that Tudor Jones kept running from the stern, which brought in a fine succession of cod, halibut and sea bass to add to the pot. As he practiced tying knots under the guidance of Sylvanus Hopkins, Owen tried to put from his mind the thought that his teacher might be a hardened cannibal, now patiently teaching knots to a youngster about the same age as the one he was supposed to have eaten. The time passed quickly enough anyway.

At the end of the third day, the "Dolphin" heaved to in the darkness. They could hear the distant boom of pounding surf, and Danny Caines declared he would go no further until he could see.

"That's the noise of Sable Island," he declared. "If we're near enough to hear it, we're near enough to be wrecked. We'll bide here and wait for the dawn. Once it's properly light, we'll creep in as close as we can and sail along the shore, looking for that marker."

As the dawn broke, the first sight of their destination was of a low line of dunes humped up above the grey sea and fringed around with a cloud of surf. It seemed no more than a mile wide.

"It's not a very big island," Tudor Jones commented to Ken Ralph, standing beside him in the cold morning light.

"That's because us is looking at it end on," he explained. "Like looking down on the top of a man's head, and thinking that's how big he is."

When the ship turned onto a tack heading due east, the

perspective of the land changed quickly. It was a long spit of sand stretching across the horizon for miles, bounded by a line of booming, tumbling water. The Atlantic rollers, suddenly faced with a steeply shelving wall of sand, reared up with tremendous power to smash onto the shore. Each wave was yellow with tons of sand. The "Dolphin" stood off well clear of the island and the thundering surf, moving uneasily along the line of the shore. From the prow of the ship, Snow Parker dropped a weighted rope into the murky grey water, knotted and tied with bits of rag and leather to show the depth of the sea beneath the ship.

He called the length out to Danny Caines at the helm in an endless singsong chant: "Ooohhh, here's three strips and a little white rag…" The dripping line was hauled up and cast out again."Ooohhh, here's three strips and little red rag. ..Ooohhh…"

As the island passed by their port side, the hopelessness of the plan outlined by Danny Caines became increasingly obvious. The clouds of spray along the coastline prevented any clear view of the shore, and they could get no closer to the island for fear of running aground. Bringing the ship right around the island and back to the westernmost tip on its southern flank, they found a freak of the wind and the tide at work.

The bulk of the island was acting as a windbreak to create a kind of a lagoon of calmer water where the waves were less angry than the great rollers booming up against the rest of the shoreline. Danny Caines decided to sail in a little closer to enable them to land the jolly boat in this relatively quiet water. Amid the clamour of the thundering surf, running under topsails and jib, the "Dolphin" nosed in towards Sable Island.

Swinging the weighted rope into the water again and again, Snow Parker called out the depth of the water beneath them, no longer singing it out, but using a shorter way: "By the mark six. By the deep five."

The ship groped her way forward, guided by the long finger of the leadsman probing down into the water below him. Again and again the measured line was dropped into the water, and the depth called back to Danny at the wheel. The voice was reassuringly monotonous, calling its repetitive message above the needling cries of the seagulls and the rumble of the surf.

"By the deep three...By thunder! Hard a starboard!" yelled Snow Parker. "We're drawing less than three fathoms!"

Danny Caines hauled frantically at the helm, but it was too late. Even as the "Dolphin" swung to the helm, her keel ground into the bank of sand beneath her and the ship lurched to a standstill. Deprived of motion, she immediately succumbed to the wind and the tide and canted over onto one side.

"Reef the sails!" shouted Danny as he ran towards the shrouds and scrambled up the ratlines. "Get every stitch of canvas off her!"

The seamen swarmed into the rigging and the next few minutes were a frenzy of activity as they struggled to clew up the sails and prevent the wind from pushing them over any further. Finally, with the last topsail furled tight, they were all standing together on the slanting deck looking at the choppy grey waves washing against the prow.

Danny Caines looked grim. "We'll have to kedge her off. We can't wait for the tide to float us free. If the wind freshens any more, she'll be over. The tide is still making – just, but it will turn within the hour. And if we're caught here on the ebb, it will break her back."

That was when Owen learned about kedging. It consisted of rowing out and dropping one of the anchors in deep water, then using the winch and capstan to pull the ship free into deeper water.

Leaving only Ken Ralph with Emily and Owen to man the capstan, Danny Caines and the other seamen, along with Adrian Bell and Tudor Jones, took to the ship's jolly boat. They rowed into place under the anchor at the stern of the ship, and Ken Ralph carefully lowered the heavy anchor down into their boat.

For a moment Owen thought the anchor was going to sink them, as once they had taken the full weight of the great lump of metal, there were no more than six inches of the gunwales proud of the water.

With the anchor cable trailing behind, the men heaved at the oars and the jolly boat rowed out into deep water, looking for a place they could drop the anchor.

It was while their attention was concentrated entirely on trying to save the "Dolphin" that Scammell made his move. Taking advantage of the moment, he slipped over the side of the ship. Careful to keep the bulk of the "Dolphin" between himself and the jolly boat, he swam and waded through the shallow sea towards the shore. By the time his moving figure caught the corner of Owen's eye, he was almost ashore.

With Ken Ralph busy feeding out the anchor line to the kedging party, Emily and Owen watched Scammell splashing through the water. He took a few steps more, then he stopped. His chest rose up out of the water and he was standing.

He had got away from them, and with the "Dolphin" still stuck on a sandbar and with everybody busy trying to save their ship, there was precious little they could do about it. He turned to face back towards the ship. He started waving and yelling, his voice thin in the distance amid the tumble of the surf.

There was a chorus of shouting from the jolly boat as on a count of three, the great anchor was heaved overboard. Then the kedging party quickly turned and rowed back towards the "Dolphin".

Freed from the business of feeding out the cable, Ken Ralph finally looked round and took in the situation with Sir William at a glance. Emily and Owen watched as Scammell yelled and waved his arms above his head.

"He's mocking us I fear," said Emily. "He must know we can do little to catch him now."

Ken Ralph peered through his telescope and his lips tightened.

"No Ma'am," he said grimly. "Us can't catch him now. Nor never will."

"Why don't he just go ashore," said Owen "instead of standing there shouting and waving?"

"He's not shouting, boy. He's screaming," said Ken Ralph hoarsely. "Not waving, but drowning. He's stuck fast in dancing sand!"

Even as they watched, Scammell was visibly sinking. The water reached up his chest and then his shoulders were barely above the water. The treacherous sandbank beneath him was trembling with the vibration of the great waves battering the island where the colliding currents met. The dancing sand was sucking him under. Millions of grains of quicksand were flowing around his legs, pulling him down relentlessly into the maw of the hungry tide. His shoulders disappeared and there was only his head above the water, his mouth opening and closing. His thin wailing cries mingled with the stark screams of the wheeling gulls, the thundering surf, and the wind whistling through the ratlines of the "Dolphin".

Emily turned away, her face white with horror. Owen watched with Ken Ralph as the cries choked to an end and the last trace of Sir William Scammell vanished beneath the cold, grey sea.

"There was nothing we could do," Ken Ralph spoke grimly. "We couldn't get to him, and it was him who put himself into it. I guess that's a friend King George will have to do without."

As they climbed back aboard the "Dolphin", there was precious little grieving when Danny Caines and the rest of the kedging party learned what had happened. Indeed there was no time for anything other than saving the ship.

All that Danny could think of was that the tide was running at its height and it was about to turn. If the "Dolphin" was to be floated free, it had to happen immediately.

Urged on by their worried Captain, everyone gathered around the capstan and began to heave it around, bending to the bars together and hauling the anchor line taut to winch the "Dolphin" free of the sandbank. Slower and slower the capstan turned as the anchor line grew ever more taut and they heaved and pushed at the bars, gasping and groaning.

"Heave hearty!" shouted Danny. "Heave hearty and rally!"

The iron pawls clicked slowly round and the capstan turned again.

Looking aft, Owen saw that the great rope cable seemed stretched to half its original width. Beads of water were jumping off it as he felt the ship begin to move.

Danny's voice was hoarse with the effort of pushing. "She's moving!" he cried. "One more heave now! Heee – eve!"

A wave washed under them and the clicking of the pawls came faster. The stern of the "Dolphin" turned and floated free as the ship eased upright. Then with a final heave at the capstan, the prow grated clear of the sandbank and the "Dolphin" was pulling her way back out to deep water.

"We're off!" cried Danny, and all broke out a chorus of ragged cheers as the "Dolphin" moved steadily backwards, away from the toils of the menacing sands.

Half an hour later they were all sitting in the cuddy drinking steaming cups of strong, sweet tea. The "Dolphin" was riding easy at anchor and they were hatching their plans for the next step.

"The only safe water around Sable Island is rain," said Ken Ralph. "Us had a narrow miss there Captain."

"We'll stay anchored here," said Danny decisively. "The only way I want to sail from this spot is on a direct line away from Sable Island. The place is a very graveyard for ships. It makes me shudder to think how near we were to losing her altogether."

"Well, we lost Sir William, anyway," said Tudor Jones with some satisfaction.

"True enough. But t'was a horrible way to go," said Ken Ralph.

Danny Caines wasted no time on Sir William Scammell. "Never mind that useless bit of flotsam, Ken," he said. "Here's what I want you to do. You will stay on board with Snow and Sylvanus to look after the ship. We'll take the jolly boat in – Snow Parker, you can drop us off ashore. Then the three of you will stay aboard here and keep an eye out until we get back. We're going to have to go along the island on foot, so we may be gone for some time. If any other ship comes by, tell them you've landed a water party. But there's not much likelihood of anyone else hailing you. This is not a popular place for ships to visit by choice. Any questions?"

"Aye. What about shares?" piped up Sylvanus Hopkins. "We haven't decided on shares yet."

"We'll decide on that when we've got something to

share," said Danny Caines briskly. "You know I'll see you boys all right. I always do don't I?"

"We haven't fished no treasure out before," said Snow Parker stubbornly. "What's fair shares for us?"

"Let's leave it be boys." The deep voice of Ken Ralph rumbled out. "No sense in starting to argue about nothing. And nothing is what us got right now. Let's leave it till us can see what we're talking about. Agreed?"

"Agreed." said Hopkins after a pause.

"Aye aye. Have it your way," said Snow Parker with a shrug.

So it was that under a darkening sky the colour of slate, the jolly boat pulled the landing party across the mile of choppy, grey sea to landfall. Paddling ashore through the shallows, Owen could feel the sand pulling at his feet, and he shuddered at the memory of Sir William's horrible death. He couldn't get out of the water fast enough. Even on dry land, the ground beneath his feet vibrated with the crashing thunder of the great waves pounding. The little group moved off as an icy wind came scything in from the north, lifting the sand in clouds from the dunes of Sable Island.

CHAPTER FIFTEEN

Smoakey hutt

Owen narrowed his eyes against the sand blowing into his face as the landing party trudged across the northern tip of Sable Island and headed south along the shoreline. To their left, the endless procession of great Atlantic rollers came powering in, each of them yellow with tons of sand. To their right lay the low humps of the dunes, one behind another as the little group moved down the shore through a world of sand, wind and rolling tides.

Pausing at a point between two dunes, where a little valley gave some semblance of shelter from the wind and the stinging sand, Adrian Bell gathered his friends around him as he smoothed out a piece of thinskin parchment on the sand. Owen recognised the map he had last seen spread out on the green baize table at the back of the Odds and Ends shop. Outlined in fading ink, the map of Sable Island looked like a reaping hook. In the middle of the hook, a kidney shaped area was shaded in and marked "water". A cross was scrawled towards one end of the pool. An arrow pointed the direction north.

"Now that we are actually on the island," said Bell, "and have sailed pretty well around it, let's see if we can make a little more sense of this map. What does it mean to you, Captain Caines?"

Danny Caines pointed to the tip of the island. "We're anchored just north of here," he said. "This is where we ran aground." His finger ran along the cutting edge of the hook. "This here is the southern shore we're tramping along right now." He traced his finger along to the shaded area and stopped. "If this map is anywhere near accurate, we should find that pool of water no more than about three miles from where we're standing. It looks pretty straightforward from here. That's a fair sized body of fresh water. Finding this hut will be the tricky bit."

They moved off briskly enough, for they were carrying nothing but half empty knapsacks, and walking at a fast pace was one way to keep warm in the cutting wind. For the next half hour they made good progress along the hard packed sand at the edge of the tideline. Tudor Jones and Danny Caines were striding out in front, whilst Emily Bobbins and Adrian Bell paced along behind, with Owen between them. It seemed to be getting colder with each passing minute. The sky was dark with menace as great wavering plumes of sand blew from the crests of the dunes.

"What I don't understand," said Emily Bobbins, raising her voice to be heard above the wind, the waves and the wheeling gulls, "is why the island doesn't blow away completely."

Adrian Bell turned towards her. "I beg your pardon, my dear." he shouted. "I didn't hear you properly. Are you warm enough?"

"I'm perfectly fine," she yelled back. "I was just thinking that with all the wind and the waves washing everything away, why doesn't the island simply vanish into the sea?"

"A good question," he shouted, shielding his eyes. "The island has no reefs to protect it; no stones to hold it down; no mountains to root it to the sea bottom." He stopped and gestured about him. "Yet here we stand, on dry land in the middle of this mighty ocean. The wind and the tide – the same forces that are wearing it down and blowing it away – are at the same time renewing it. The sand carried away is replaced by the sand that washes in. A spring of fresh water, bubbling up from the sea bed, keeps the sand in place around it. In this way, the forces of nature keep the island eternally poised between existence and non existence. This must be one of the strangest places on Earth…"

Then the storm that had been threatening shrieked in upon them with a ferocious flail of ice. The wind, blasting down from the polar ice cap, had caught a heavy shower of rain as it fell, chilling it to just above freezing point. The moment the rain touched anything and stopped moving, the wind froze it solid. This was the ice storm that now blew across Sable Island. Within seconds, they were all being coated in a sheath of frozen fire.

"Hide in the sand!" Danny Caines shouted at them, as he turned to run up the shallow hill into the dunes.

Shocked and half blinded by the sudden onslaught of ice, the others staggered after him and burrowed frantically into the sand. Copying Danny Caines, they lay on their backs with their woollen caps over their faces, wriggling like worms into the sand to seek shelter from the freezing needles of the rain. Scooping armfuls of sand over their bodies, they were quickly resting in a row of shallow graves amid the dunes, protected by the sand from the ice storm raging over them.

For almost an hour, the freezing rain kept them buried. The sand they had scooped over themselves coated quickly with ice and stopped them from getting ever wetter or colder.

Owen's lips nearly froze from keeping his mouth clear to breathe, but apart from that, the heavy woollen clothes that Adrian Bell and Rebecca Caines had bought for them on their trip into Lunenberg weeks earlier kept them from any serious harm. Their thick trousers and felt-lined boots kept out all but the worst of the cold, and when they finally broke free from their frozen moulds, none of them were much the worse for wear.

The wind had died down and the ice tinkled around them in shards as they stood up. The dark veil of rain was blowing away to the east, leaving the sky almost clear to the west, where the sun was sinking through a fleece of clouds towards the horizon. The dunes were sheathed over with ice so that the island looked as though it was made of glass, reflecting the evening light from every rolling crest of sand. After the previous chaos of the ice storm, it seemed strangely still and beautiful. As they moved back towards the shoreline, the surface beneath their feet crackled and bounced as the ice took their weight on the sand below.

The firm ground along the shore was a-glitter with a billion splintered shards where the blowing spindrift caught in the storm had frozen over. The ice crunched beneath their feet like eggshells as they turned and headed east, casting long shadows before them in the red light of the sunset. The crying of the gulls died down as the birds took to their nests, and the little group walked along the trembling sand to the rhythm of the booming surf.

It had something of the strangeness of a dream: wandering the shore of a desolate island in a vast ocean, searching for a sign from the distant past. The wind shifted and lost its bitter edge as the evening moved into twilight and the crystal shards melted into the sand.

Pacing along the shoreline, they searched for the landmark described by Daniel Salt: the bit of wreckage he had upended by a dune beyond the reach of the tide; a visible sign such as a man might leave on purpose. There were odds and ends of ship's timbers by the score, but nothing that looked like Daniel Salt's sign. The hummocks of sand squatted along the shoreline, like giant creatures waiting to drink. As each passed by without pause or comment, Owen's hopes dwindled. In the years since the Bosun's landing on Sable Island, anything might have happened to the marker he had left behind to guide him back to the hut.

But Danny Caines and Tudor Jones finally stopped. Drawing nearer, Owen could see it clearly. Mid way between the high tide line and the shelving sand of the dune beyond it, a bleached spar of timber was leaning backwards out of the sand, its top buried in the dune behind it. Encased in its dripping sheath of ice, it glittered like a silver arrow pointing back inland.

"This could be it!" said Tudor Jones, turning towards the others, his eyes bright with excitement. "Clear as a sign post to Swansea."

Adrian Bell agreed: "This might be it! If it is Bosun Salt's sign, we should go inland from here. We take eight hundred and fifty paces due south, according to his reckoning. That should bring us to the big freshwater lake he described."

"Does it have anything carved in it?" asked Owen. "Didn't Bosun Salt say he carved his initials on it?"

"Good boy Owen. He did too. Let's have a look then," Tudor Jones peered along the bleached spar then exclaimed, "Here it is." Carved into the salt white wood was a clear DS.

"Let's give it a go then," said Danny Caines. "We've walked a good three miles, and this is the likeliest thing we've seen. We haven't got long before the light goes completely, so let's move fast while we can still see."

Turning their backs on the thundering tide, they climbed up into the dunes and headed inland. Following Danny Caines, they took a straight course up and over the hummocks, the ice on the sand turning to slush beneath their feet.

It was hard going: climbing the succession of steep sided sandhills; sinking up to their knees in places, they panted and puffed their way up one dune and down another. Soon all of them were sweating inside their heavy clothes, but a rising tide of excitement gripped them.

Away to the east, the cobalt blue of the sky faded in the gathering darkness of the night. To the west of them, the sun dipped below the horizon, leaving only a purple glow on the clouds towering above it. Then they breasted the top of yet another dune, and there below them, a rippling lake of dark water reflected the tones of the evening sky. Upwards of half a mile wide, this had to be the lake shown on Daniel Salt's map. Danny Caines and Tudor Jones were soon down at the water's edge, questing along the bank. Moving diagonally down the slope behind them, the others were almost at the bottom of the dune when Owen's foot caught in something and he fell headlong.

Adrian Bell knelt down to look more closely at whatever it was had tripped Owen. Then he started to scoop away the sand around it. "Over here!" he shouted. "I think we've found something."

A piece of wood jutting up out of the sand had tripped Owen. A piece of canvas was attached to it. It was anchored to something down beneath the sand.

Their lanterns were soon lit and they started to dig, scooping the sand backwards like dogs digging for bones as the stars gathered above them. Their labours gradually revealed a rough screen of sailcloth nailed to a wooden frame. Impatiently pulling at what appeared to be a makeshift door, Tudor Jones wrenched the rotten canvas apart and held up his lantern. A thick wooden beam was on a level with his eyes. Carved roughly into the wood were the words "Smoakey Hutt". Behind the wooden beam was a dark space of nothing. More sand was scooped away until the space was big enough to enter. Ducking down low, Tudor Jones stepped sideways over the remains of the canvas door and went in, the rest crowding in behind him.

Inside it was like a cave within a sand dune. Rough wooden uprights had been draped over with canvas to form a primitive shelter, and as it had been built against the side of the sand dune, the dune had simply drifted over it. The structure was still standing, though the canvas sagged beneath the weight of sand covering it. Sand was everywhere:

erupting under the canvas walls and partly covering the mummified yellow corpse that lay stretched out on one side of the hut. On the other side, a wooden chest bound with strips of green brass gaped open, half buried under the mound of sand that had cascaded in from the wall. Kneeling down before it, Tudor Jones swept the sand aside. His mouth dropped open. Beside Owen, Emily gasped softly.

Winking and beaming in the yellow light of the lanterns, a host of jewels of all shapes and colours nestled amid a bed of silver and gold.

"Well I'll be damned!" said Danny Caines softly.

"Hell's teeth . .!" murmured Adrian Bell, falling to his knees at the side of Tudor Jones, brushing and blowing more of the sand away.

A great ruby strung with diamonds lay atop the glistening pile. It was mounted between the gaping jaws of a golden serpent with eyes of brilliant sapphire.

Lifting it reverently, Adrian Bell held the heavy necklace up in the lamplight, shaking it free of sand. Beautiful and barbaric, the massive ruby in its golden mount was strung on a chain of small golden skulls with diamonds for their eyes and teeth of inlaid silver.

"The Red Empress!" Adrian Bell's voice was a strangled croak. "I never dreamed to find it here. This necklace was worn by the high priestesses of Shiva, the Hindu god of destruction. It has not been seen for a hundred years and more."

"How d'you know about it?" asked Tudor Jones. His eyes had gone glazed and were as round as marbles.

"Buying and selling old curiosities, one takes an interest in reading about certain treasures. You might say that it feeds the imagination."

Tudor Jones lifted the necklace from Adrian Bell's outstretched fingers and brandished it in the air. "No more sniffing around for odds and sods," he shouted triumphantly, his voice was oddly harsh and dry. "No more grovelling to the quality. We're set for life now Emily, and this can be your wedding present!"

Emily Bobbins shrank away from him. "That thing?" she said. "It's horrible. I don't want it anywhere near me."

Tudor Jones's face changed. His lips tightened. "If you don't want it, I'll have it." he said.

"Just hold on there fella," said Danny Caines. "Let's decide who gets what when we come to divide it back at the ship."

Tudor Jones turned towards him. "Who are you to say what's what? Eh boyo? Who found the map what brought us here? This is between the three of us. We'll decide who gets what and what you get."

"Which three of us did you have in mind?" Bell's voice was cold.

"You, me and Emily, of course," said Tudor Jones, his voice grating.

"And what about the boy?" asked Adrian Bell.

"The boy don't count here. He can have some of mine."

"Oh no," said Bell. "You don't think I'm senile do you? You and the girl walk away with two thirds between you? The devil you will! We'll split it half and half."

Danny Caines had turned white with fury. "So you're planning on throwing me just the cod cheeks are you? You limey peckerheads! You think you can just toss a few scraps to me and my crew and keep the rest between you?"

"We'll see you all right Captain," said Bell. "No-one promised you a percentage."

"Don't come the high hand with me, you maggotty old goat!" roared Danny Caines. "We agreed equal shares! If you try and cut me short, I'll take it all — and leave you here to rot with the seagulls!"

"Stop it!" cried Emily desperately. "Stop it! There's more than enough for everyone!"

Tudor Jones's face was contorted into an ugly sneer and his eyes glittered.

Throwing the necklace back into the chest, he dropped into a wrestler's crouch and began to circle Danny Caines. "You think you're going to ship this lot without me on board, you got just one little problem butty," he grated. "You're going to have to kill me first." He pulled a knife from his belt.

"Problem?" snarled Danny Caines. "That's not a problem."

The lamplight flickered and guttered as shadows shifted in the darkness. The boom of the distant surf beat like a drum as the shouting voices filled the cave in the sand. Looking at their faces, contorted with anger and greed, Owen could scarcely believe they were the same people he thought he had come to know.

Their dream of riches had ended in this sordid nightmare: a battered hut of rotten canvas and driftwood, with a shrivelled corpse lying obscenely on the floor as people who had once been friends fought over the great chest containing the riches of the Earth.

On top of the strongbox of 'Resolution', the great ruby in its necklace of gold and diamonds lay coiled. In the wavering light of the oil lamp, the red stone flickered with a life of its own. As Owen stared at it, the shouting voices grew faint. Like a lump of living fire, the ruby glowed and blinked, deep within its luminous depths, seeming to grow and grow until Owen could see nothing else.

From the heart of the flaming stone, a face appeared. It was the face of a bearded man with long black ringlets of hair reaching down to his shoulders. He was pointing at Owen and laughing, showing yellow teeth between glistening wet lips. Watching the sunburned face twist with cruel laughter, it came to Owen that he was looking at Culliford – the pirate.

Then the face changed to that of another man. He was not looking at Owen, but at something above him. His weak face was hopeless and lost, his eyes bulging with fear. He was mumbling something to himself as his head was surrounded by a dangling hangman's noose. Kidd – the pirate dupe.

The ruby blinked again, and the dark face of a woman peered out. She was wearing a crimson turban studded with jewels and she was smiling a cruel smile that chilled Owen's heart. She held before her a golden goblet filled with blood, then lifted it and drained it to the dregs. She pouted, and from between her stained lips, a red jewel appeared. Taking it in her hand, she held it out towards Owen. The jewel shone and glittered wetly, but beneath the surface it was filled with flames. And amid the flames was a coiling serpent.

The faces in the stone fused with the shouting voices surrounding Owen:. Like a sleeper in the grip of a nightmare, Owen watched as Danny Caines drew his great sheath knife and slashed at Tudor Jones, with Adrian Bell holding Emily back as she tried to stop them.

The stone called its foul breath of temptation to Owen. The stone was at the heart of this evil!

Leaping past the struggling men, Owen snatched up the necklace from the chest and ran for the door. Squirming past Bell's outreaching arm, he ducked outside and stumbled through the sand towards the lake. His mind was jumping with visions of the host of people whose lives had been ruined by the Red Empress. Dragged from the depths of the Earth where it had lain since the world was formed, the great ruby had been brought into the sunlight only to cast darkness into the human soul. Carrying within it a flame like a coal from Hell, how fitting that it should be surrounded with skulls! Owen hated the thing. Even as he felt a hand grab at his ankle, his arm was arching over his head and the horrible necklace soared high into the air. Like a comet trailing stars, it flew across the glittering sky, curving slowly down until it vanished beneath the rippling waters of the black lake.

Owen lay in the sand and listened to the lapping of the lake and the distant drumming of the surf.

Behind him, Danny Caines groaned, then let go of his ankle and got to his feet, shaking his head as if to clear it.

"Are you all right, Owen?" called Emily Bobbins.

The others straggled out from the darkness of the hut and stood outside blinking, like sleepers awakened from a dream.

"Good Heavens!" Adrian Bell's voice was filled with wonder. "Just look at the sky!"

Above them, the night was alive with light. A million stars beamed an endless river of radiance. Playing across them, like the notes of some magical music, a succession of luminous colours flowed over the sky. Purple and violet, green and blue, the colours fanned from side to side, advancing and retreating across the star-filled sky. They watched for what seemed like an age, awed by the ribbons of cold fire rippling and dancing across the face of the infinite universe that showed itself above them.

It was Danny Caines who broke the silence. "The Northern Lights," he said. "First time I've seen them this year. I guess they make diamonds seem like pretty small beer. I have to say sorry to you all about what happened back there. I guess we just went a little crazy."

"I don't what come over me," said Tudor Jones. "I don't like to think of it. Like being drunk or something. I'm sorry to all of you – especially you, Danny."

"It's not the first time men have gone mad over treasure,"

said Emily. "Thank God you have come to your senses."

Adrian Bell's voice was urgent. "Amen to that. Now listen. It nearly ended in murder back in there. I was as mad with greed as everyone else. We can only break the curse that hangs over this treasure if we share it out fairly amongst all of us. God knows there's enough there for all of us. But unless we agree on equal shares, we will fight each other until it ends in death. Let this be the way of it: We land with the treasure in Boston or New York, and I will turn my hand to changing it all into cash. But we must trust one another. Captain Caines, if you can land us down in the United States, I swear to you that each of us – including Ken Ralph and your friends – shall take an equal share of what I raise. Are we agreed?"

Tudor Jones nodded his agreement and offered his hand to Danny Caines. "It's fine by me Danny. I'm sorry."

Danny smiled and shook him by the hand. "Sounds good to me," he said. "But first we got to load it up and haul it out."

Making their way back from the lake into the dark squalor of "Smoakey Hutt", they began to empty the strongbox of the "Resolution".

Emily and Owen held up the lamps and watched as the others crammed into the knapsacks handfuls of pearls and golden moidores, bracelets and brooches; diadems crusted with sapphires and rubies; an endless cascade of gold and silver rings set with shining jewels; figurines of solid gold; agates and amethyst.

All of the glamorous riches seemed out of place in the rank little hovel buried in sand whose only occupant was a disgusting mummified corpse.

As his friends collected the treasure, Owen moved over to scoop some sand over the withered body lying on the floor; to cover the pirate who had died beside his great hoard of the riches of the Earth. Kneeling down to his task, he saw something. Almost hidden beneath the rotten sailcloth of the dead man's pillow was a box. As he pulled the box from under the man's head, Owen was startled when the skull rolled away from the neck and lay grinning at him. Putting the box to one side, Owen heaped sand over the body and the skull until they could be seen no more.

Then he picked up the box and took it over to show it to Emily. Together they looked at it in the lamplight.

The box was inlaid with silver and gold. Wonderful birds spread their wings across its lid, with eyes of emerald and lapis lazuli. Emily lifted the lid. Inside it was moulded into little compartments covered in purple velvet. Ink bottles made of ivory and carved into the form of tiny monkeys sat beside pens of ebony with nibs of gold. An elegant book lay at the centre of the box, faced in red leather and bearing the same design of soaring birds that featured on the lid.

Her eyes shining with pleasure at the sight of this beautiful writing set, Emily lifted back the cover of the book and turned back a gold – edged sheet of paper. Written at the top of the page in a flowing bold hand were the words: "The Wreck of Resolution" by Robert Culliford.

"Listen everyone!" cried Emily. "This book – it's Robert Culliford's story. It must tell us how the treasure came to be here."

His knapsack bulging and his face fairly twitching with excitement, Adrian Bell came over to stand beside her.

"Read it out," said Tudor Jones, looking up from the remains of the treasure.

"Yeah. Read it out to us while we finish packing the rest of this pile away." said Danny.

Taking the book out of its box, and with Adrian Bell holding the light behind her, Emily began to read out loud the story of the long dead pirate.

CHAPTER SIXTEEN

The Wreck of 'Resolution'

30th November, 1765. Sable Island

It was a whale that sank 'Resolution'. After robbing the dupe William Kidd, we sailed from Madagascar in late August, aiming for Charleston in the Carolinas. The hold was fairly splitting with jewels, gold and silver, and our spirits were high as we weathered the Cape and made our way north. It seemed we were making a charmed passage, with following winds and easy seas. Seemed is the word.

We were near a hundred miles north of the Bahama Islands, on a night filled with mist and the sounds of whales calling all around us, when one of the whales attacked us. The first we knew of it was a great thud on the hull, then the splintering of wood and a mighty tumult in the water at the stern. A whale had come up from the water beneath us, ramming the hull so severely that we immediately began to take water. Then the creature set about shattering the rudder. We had to man the pumps continually after that.

When the morning came, the whales had vanished – all but one.

Looking through the telescope, I could see she was an enormous sperm whale, with her great head covered in old scars. I believe she must have been a mother cow that had seen her calf killed by whalers. She probably thought we were a spouter – a whaling ship – which was why she went for us. For whatever the reason, she just stayed with us, all that day long, and for many a weary day after, if we had but known the future.

We fixed the leaking hull and mended the rudder as best we could, but no sooner were we back on board and under way again than the beast came back and smashed the rudder once more. It happened again and again. And she was clever: she wouldn't come at us across the water so that we could get a shot at her with a cannon or a musket. She came straight up from underneath the ship, smashed the rudder to splinters, and went straight back down again. Then she would surface a mile or so away and roll around hissing and blowing like a she-devil. She was with us as the night fell, and it was with a sense of dread that we saw her still in the days that followed.

Scuppered and haunted we were by that whale: without a rudder, struggling to stay afloat, scarce able to keep abreast of the wind. She would never leave us alone, but came back again and again as we drifted at the mercy of the wind and tried to put right the damage she inflicted on the ship.

The final time we attempted to fix the rudder, Swampy Hope and Cribb were down in the jolly boat when up comes the whale and tips it over. It lifted the boat clean out of the water, dropping them both in the sea, then smashed the boat to splinters as she fell on it and dived back down. Hope sank like a stone and Cribb was splashing towards the rope was thrown him when the two sharks that had been following us hit him. After that, nobody would leave the ship to go onto the water.

The days passed and we drifted north and eastwards, away from the sea lanes, unable to tack or make our way. And the whale, floating out of the range of our guns, followed the 'Resolution' like a witch's curse.

There was a man with us who had served aboard a whaler: Benjamin Douane, a Nova Scotia 'Blue Noser' as they liked to style themselves. 'Fingers' Douane the men called him, on account of the fact that he had lost three of his fingers a-whaling. Like many another before him, he came to be a pirate after his ship was seized by the Brethren, and he took to the life at the point of a cutlass.

He was ashamed of serving as a buccaneer, and I liked him for it. I took him on as my personal bodyguard, so all he ever had to do was watch my back. Douane it was who saved me from the pike of a mad Lascar when we took Kidd's treasure; just as it was Douane who turned aside the cutlass of Slaver Scarret at the great fight in Hangman's Bay. Douane said he never knew a whale to behave in such a knowing fashion. Though he tried his hand as a harpooner to rid us of it, he got no chance at a clean stroke. Under and up it came, then down and beyond, and never a sight of its flanks until it was well beyond our reach. He called it an enchanted whale. I called it a cursed one.

Day followed day and we saw no other ships, the sea as empty as a beggar's plate. The men grew steadily more terrified of the creature, looking on it as if it was some sort of supernatural being come to have vengeance on them for all their wickedness. As we drifted north, the weather grew colder and the days shorter, yet still we met no other ship. Day by day we were driven further back out into the North Atlantic – and away from any home or harbour.

The men began to die. We had shipped with water and food a-plenty for the voyage we had planned, but not for one like this. The water turned foul in the casks and the salt pork had to be rationed to a single ounce per man, twice a day. One of the biscuit barrels we broke open was filled with nothing but crumbs and great fat weevils that tasted disgusting, even when they were fried. Argue Lewis took the scurvy and died raving of pig's kidneys and sailing the Blue Nile. Murphy and Davies stabbed each other to death, fighting over a piece of mouldy cheese the size of one of my buttons. Big Mo dropped dead with the effort of working the pumps. Killing work it was, just to stay afloat.

There were no more than a dozen of us left alive when she finally did for us. It happened in the afternoon, just after we had finished burying William Fox. No more than a minute after we had dropped him over the side, the whale came up at us like a battering ram. The moment she hit us, I knew it was all over with the ship. We scarce had time to bring up the big chest and put it in our one remaining boat before the 'Resolution' was awash beneath our feet. With the strongbox in the boat, there was room for no more than seven. I had to pistol Morris and Henderson to prevent them from swamping us all as they tried to clamber on board. They turned over and sank – along with all the gold and silver plate in the holds of 'Resolution'.

Then we were sitting in that little boat all alone in an empty ocean, looking around to see if that whale was going to come back and tip us over. Apart from swords, the only weapons we had on board were my pistols, and I could see them having little effect on the huge creature that had been tormenting us with such intensity of purpose. We waited a long time, keeping still as we could in that little rocking boat, and the sea seemed vast and full of fear. A great bubble erupted in the water, but it was only the last breath of the sunken 'Resolution' as the air was squeezed out of her. Big Conrad started to say his prayers, and the Creole, Ishmael, joined him.

We dipped and swung as the waves took us, with only a hand on the tiller to keep the jolly boat running with the wind. The oars lay shipped at the bottom of the boat. We made neither noise nor movement. It was as if we were trying to hide – as indeed we were: trying to hide in the middle of the open sea. The sky overhead was grey; the ocean empty and calm. The waves lapped against us and we lay there on the swell. Not a man was moving.

Then, not ten feet from the side of the boat, the surface of the sea bulged, heaved and rolled apart as the whale pulled up out of the water and settled herself beside us, big as a ship turned belly up. Her breath spouted out in a great whoosh of mist and she lay still, looking at us, with that big eye just above her mouth. Five times the length of our boat, the colossal body stretched out in the water behind her. Her eye was on a level with mine and the top of her head was far out of my reach, even if I had been standing. I knew that just a twitch of her tail could send the lot of us plunging down to join Morris and Henderson and the rest of the crew of 'Resolution'. And I felt she knew that too. All that lay between us and a horrible death in the wastes of the sea were the thin planks of the jolly boat. I wanted to bury my head as the whale stared across at me. I felt as if she was reading my mind. She lay there in the water, looming over us with that big, bright eye, puffing and blowing while Ishmael and Conrad went on with their prayers and the rest of us sat still and quiet. The water from her spouting fell over us like warm rain and her smell came drifting across in waves of fishy steam, like a pan of boiling cod.

Never was I so close to a whale, nor felt so many questions jangling in my mind. I sat there transfixed by that black liquid eye that seemed to gaze into my very soul. The breaths drew gently in and out of her like waves breaking on a beach. Quite still she lay beside us: watching us; inspecting us; making up her mind. The grey sky began to clear and I saw a frigate bird come climbing up from the west. Soaring and wheeling, the bird circled to become a speck, until it vanished. And still the whale watched and we sat waiting.

Then, with a final whoosh of air, the whale lowered her head beneath the water and dived. Her giant body seemed to slide past our boat forever as the rest of her followed her head straight down into the depths. Her tail flukes finally lifted high into air, like a great cross in the sky, and she was gone. We still sat there quietly for a while, thinking she might come charging back out of the water to send us down to Davey Jones' Locker. Nothing happened. Conrad and Ishmael were still babbling away giving thanks as I began to take stock. Seven of us were in the boat, with a cask of water and a keg of salt pork between us, and the nearest land, by my reckoning, five hundred miles to the west.

Four of the men died. We were in poor shape anyway for a tussle with the sea, what with starving for days on end, and the men worn out working at the pumps. At the end of the first week, Ishmael and Yankee Jack went over the side, raving about some island they could see, full of trees and fruit and flowing streams. We watched them trying to reach it until the sharks got them. Samuel Delisser took a chill and died of the fever that came on him, in spite of all anyone could do. After we dropped his body over the side, Bilski, the Pole, for all his giant strength, simply lost heart. He refused to take his turn at the oars and just sat looking at nothing. The next morning we found him lying on his back

stone dead, still wearing that same blank look on his face.

The day after he died, we found dry land. Douane was the one who saw it first, just after noon: an island on the horizon two hundred miles before we should have reached any land at all by my reckoning. Dry land did I call it? It was like a trick from the Devil played on sailors. But we didn't know it for what it was until we were upon it.

We reached it the following morning and rowed along the coast, looking for a place to land. A great long spit of sand it was, boiling with clouds of surf. All we could see were sand dunes, mile after mile of them, rising in the middle of the island to about one hundred and fifty feet. There were no trees as far as we could see, but grass in plenty, so we thought there must be animals and water in there somewhere. Thought was the word.

We must have pulled for some twenty miles along that line of surf, looking for a way in. In the end, too tired to keep searching for something that may not exist, we simply found a place where the tide was less violent and took our chance, streaming in through a great cauldron of surf to finally beach on the shore.

We found water not far from where we landed – a great pool of it. A bit brackish, but drinkable enough, and there was plenty of it. We hauled the strongbox over to the pool, so as to keep an eye on it, then we set to building a shelter beside the water. There were bits of shipwrecked timbers dotted along the shore, and a whole topsail, half buried in a dune, that furnished us with canvas. So there we were, two days after landing, in our little canvas hut in the sand dunes: me, Big Conrad and Benjamin Douane – and a chest of jewels and gold rich enough to buy a palace and land for each of us.

It was the Blue Noser, Benjamin Douane, who told us where we were: Sable Island – French for Island of Sand.

He'd heard of the place from other Nova Scotia sailors –
who avoided it like the plague. By the time we had
finished walking over it, he knew it could be none other
than Sable Island, for there was no other like it in the
world. It was a desert set down in the middle of the sea, a
sort of place where a man might burn in summer and
freeze in winter. And starve from season through season as
far as I could see.

From one end to the other of this cursed place, there is
no scrap of food to be found. The gulls have picked
everything as clean as a skull in an ant heap. There are no
birds' eggs, no animals, no plants. There is only sand and
marram grass and pools of water. Along the whole length of
the island, the ground shudders and shakes as the great waves
smash against the shore. I find myself shuddering too – at
the thought that I might spend the rest of my days in this
desolate place.

8th December, 1765

The days pass and never a ship comes nigh. No fishes jump
to our hooks nor birds to our snares. One night we lit a
bonfire on the shoreline, but no ship came by. The only sails
we ever saw but once were away off just above the horizon,
and vanished before we could so much as light a stick. The
white foam breaks over the countless sand bars stretching
out from the island, showing why no ship comes near this
dreadful spot. At night we sit in our hut made of shipwrecks,
burning shipwreck wood and choking on shipwreck smoke.
The island is a very graveyard of ships. Hunger chews on
me like a shark, and I can do nothing but sit and write this
diary of the damned. Douane has carved a name for this
wonderful home of ours on the spar above the door. He calls
it 'Smoakey Hutt'.

I might wish he had called it something different, for it seems to me that it reeks of the smoke of the burning pit, and the water at our door is there only to prolong our agony as we die of starvation. The weather grows daily colder and the wind is like a knife. At times all we can do is sit in the hut to escape being choked by the storm of sand that blows around us night and day.

16th December, 1795

Douane and Conrad have taken the jolly boat and gone. We finished the last scraps of our salted meat two days ago, and yesterday we agreed there was nothing else to do but try to reach for the shore of the mainland. At the western tip of the island the sea is relatively calm, and we hauled the jolly boat along the sand to set it in the water where it would have least danger of capsizing. They pulled away lustily enough and drew clear of the surf, and I watched them until I could no longer see for the tears in my eyes. They might be the last of my fellow men I shall ever see. I told Douane to take Conrad and go for help. But I would not go with them. I could not risk losing all the jewels and gold by putting it back to sea in a cockleshell boat. Nor would I leave it for somebody else to find. The strongbox weighs me down and manacles me to this cursed place with the fetters of King Midas. I am helpless to leave it.

I trust the Blue Noser, Douane, and I know that if he lives, Douane will come back for me, because that is the nature of the man. Just as Conrad will come back because he said he would. A pair of good men they are. With a keg of water and a fishing line, the two of them rowed off towards Nova Scotia. Soon it will be Christmas. No snow as yet, but bitter cold.

God knows when – 1796

My tale is almost done. I used the last of my powder a week ago to shoot a seagull – a mouthful of stringy burnt meat. Yet today I might have shot a seal and feasted for a month! Ha ha ha. A number of them were playing in the water, but I was too weak to go after them. I found the carcase of a seal pup washed up on the shore, and that has kept me going through these last days. But now I have nothing left at all. It is fearfully cold. No fishes bite.

End of time – God Knows!

I see the eye of the whale gazing at me even as I write. Like the eye of a prophet. I swear that creature knew where she was bringing us. I see the image of her tail raised like a cross against the sky. Every moment I am awake drags past me like a knife on a slate, and my sleep is filled with spiders. All my escapes from death seem like missed opportunities. I have given my life to misery and pain. I have scabbed my soul and rubbed crime into its sores. Smoakey Hutt is hell. And yet I fear to die for all eternity. I am arrived in hell.

New Dawn!

I am redeemed! I am redeemed! I am going to see the whale! She is spouting all around the island! I feel her eye upon me! She is the Christ Whale!

I can hear the seals barking in the water!

The dead men killed by Culliford shall rise up through the sea. It was not I who killed them. I am cleansed! I am made anew! The Christ Whale is my salvation! I shall be born a Dolphin or a Seal, my soul washed clean as a bleached bone in the sunlight! The sea is washing through me like a river of rain! The sun rings out like a church bell on the Holy Sabbath! Oh! My book shall be my pillow when I lie down with the Lamb!"

There was a long silence as Emily finished reading from the book.

"That's the end of it," she said.

Above the distant roar of the tumbling surf, a faint honking noise had grown steadily louder, and the pool outside the hut was suddenly alive with the splashing of geese landing in the water. Cronking their signals to one another, they were barely settled before they took off with a great flapping and fuss to head for the far end of the pool as Danny Caines and Tudor Jones stepped from the cave in the sand.

"He said there was no life here. No food. No birds." Emily Bobbins sounded mystified as she and Owen followed them from the cave out into the night.

"For him, it seems, there was nothing," said Bell thoughtfully. "This was his place of suffering. But he is done with it now. And so are we. We will arise and go now, and leave the poor man to his long rest."

Danny Caines and Tudor Jones came out to stand beside them. A few strong pulls at the canvas and wooden supports of the hut sent the dune collapsing in on top of it. The grave of Robert Culliford was ready made.

"We will not leave him without a prayer," said Emily firmly.

"Dear Lord, have pity on the poor creature lying before you here. That he was bad, we know. That he did wicked things, we know. Yet we would ask you to forgive him, as we ask you to forgive us all. What do we have but a few short years and a handful of dreams? What is any one of us but a poor thing in your sight, oh Lord? Yet of your mercy we ask you not to turn your back on Robert Culliford, nor

184

on Sir William Scammell. In the name of Jesus Christ, our Lord, we will say the Lord's Prayer."

The familiar words were murmured by all of them together, standing there on the sand, as the Northern Lights rippled their glowing colours across the star-filled sky.

The geese at the far end of the pool honked softly as the flock bedded down for the night. The wind had died and the world seemed quiet around them as the waves of the pool lapped gently against the sand.

Turning away, with knapsacks crammed full, the group from the "Dolphin" started back across the dunes, towards the distant thunder of the sea.

CHAPTER SEVENTEEN

The Long Way West

A patchy, freezing mist hung over Boston Harbor as the "Dolphin" made her way in from the Atlantic swell under a sky sullen with snow. Six days out from Sable Island, the ketch turned into the safe haven of the United States of America with her precious cargo stowed below hatches. Though they had seen other ships, none had interfered with them, the weather had stayed cold but calm, and the last leg of their voyage had passed peacefully. Moving up the roadstead between the tall-masted ships, sea-worn brigs and grubby fishing smacks, they finally anchored alongside a sinister black whaler.

None of them had ever seen a ship like it. All of her sides above the deck were studded with the ivory teeth of the sperm whale. Her rigging was bound to pegs and blocks of sea – ivory. Her figurehead, an Indian chief burned black with the suns of four oceans, was draped with ivory pendants. Even the tiller was carved from the lower jawbone of a whale.

"That there is a Nantucket whaler," said Danny. "Ain't she something?"

He explained his choice of their strange mooring companion as they prepared to go ashore. "That claw-footed old spouter, decked out like a cannibal chief will draw all eyes upon her. No-one will even look at us, moored down in her shadow. If and when the Customs men finally come on board, our goods will be safe in the bank. They're looking for contraband cargo – not knapsacks filled with…"

"Ahem. Ahem. Quite so." Adrian Bell cut in. "Let us just get ashore with no more ado. This is too much for me, I have to tell you. I shan't be easy until we have it safe in the bank. My heart is all a-tremble at the thought of losing what we have to some rummaging Customs man. The sooner we've got it ashore, the sooner my mind will stop tormenting me."

Picking up the loaded knapsacks they had brought from Sable Island, the little group slipped over the side of the "Dolphin" into the jolly boat, leaving only Ken Ralph behind to keep watch until their return. The cold mist rolled across the water and the barbarous black ship loomed above them as they pulled away.

A bearded, brown-faced man, buttoned up to the chin in heavy pilot cloth leaned over the rail and gazed gravely down at them from under a wide brimmed black hat.

"He looks more like a parson than a whaling man," Tudor Jones said quietly.

"If you were a whale, I guess you wouldn't like his sermons too much," said Snow Parker as they passed beneath the prow of the black ship. "That preacher would give a whole new meaning to the words from the Bible, 'wailing and gnashing of teeth.'"

Sylvanus Hopkins guffawed. "Very good Mister Parker," he said. "I must remember that one. Wailing and whaling. Yes. Next time I have a party, I must remember to ask you along. A story of Whales and a story from Wales – where our Welsh shipmates is from."

They continued to gibe at each other, but Owen was lost in looking at that ship. It seemed strangely familiar, reminding him of the story of the Scrimshaw and the killing of the whale, told to him by Adrian Bell so long ago in Bristol. That menacing black ship looked like nothing so much as the lethal, studded club of some monstrous race of savages, murdering their way across the great shroud of the sea.

"Wales and whalers," murmured Adrian Bell sitting beside him. "How fitting that we should find that ship beside us at our journey's end. All of our adventures began with a single slice of a sperm whale's tooth. Robert Culliford's log describes how a sperm whale forced him towards Sable Island then sunk his ship. We hold Culliford's treasure through a sperm whale; and now we are landing it in the shadow of our ebony friend over there – a black ship dedicated to the destruction of the entire species. Whales and whalers: puny mankind and the great leviathan – a massacre across all the oceans of the globe. What a terrible story is in there somewhere."

The sharp cries of the gulls lanced though the mist and the oars creaked in the rowlocks as they made their way between the ships at anchor and finally tied up to a rusted stanchion in the wall beneath a flight of stone steps. The sea slapped against the wall, not the clear, clean sea of the past ten days, but a muddy swell crusted with bits of wood and rope, corks and floating garbage. Owen's feet touched firm ground for the first time since leaving Nova Scotia, and glad he was to be ashore. Clinging to the iron handrail, they stumbled up stones that were slippery with weed until all were arrived on the dockside and they stopped to look about them.

The harbour was busy with people going about their business, but none of them, it seemed, had the slightest interest in the group from the "Dolphin". A throng of people from every port in the world seemed to have business in Boston on that misty winter morning.

A bearded African wrapped in a brown cloak passed in front of them, in company with a giant in a turban whose golden ear-rings and silk pantaloons seemed strangely at odds with his heavy blue stevedore's jacket. Men from Arabia and India mingled with those from China and the Americas. Two soldiers in uniform wandered along the wharf, lost in their own conversation. A hawk-faced man with an ivory stump on his leg brushed past them, followed by a tall brown man carrying a harpoon, his face covered in square tattoos and his head plucked clean of hair apart from a scalp-knot twisted up on his forehead.

The group from the "Dolphin" made their way across the ice-slicked cobbles and out through the harbour gates without challenge, and were instantly lost among the people crowding the busy streets of Boston.

They finally stopped in front of the biggest, most impressive bank in the business district of the town.

Inside, the central banking hall was like a church, with

great vaulted ceilings and stained glass windows and the kind of hushed quiet usually found in churches. A host of clerks sat scribbling behind their desks or counted out money for customers. Big, solid-looking doors with brass plates on them opened off from the central chamber, and equally big, solid-looking men with long rifles stood on guard at both ends of the hall.

Danny Caines and Sylvanus Hopkins were sent off in search of a lawyer to bring back with them to the bank. Tudor Jones and Snow Parker set out to find a jeweller.

For a brief few minutes, Emily and Owen were left in charge of a small pile of knapsacks – all of them, in fact, except the one that Adrian Bell took in with him to see the Bank Manager in his office behind the biggest brass plate and the most solid-looking door.

When the Bank Manager came out from behind his door, he looked dazed. The rest of the knapsacks were carried through into his office and Adrian Bell, Emily and Owen were sat down in front of a blazing fire. They were served tea and hot chocolate while Adrian Bell told the outline of their story. A great load seemed to fall from Bell's shoulders as he described their adventures. The lines in his face appeared to smooth out and he looked across at Owen again and again, smiling and winking as he caught the boy's eye whenever Owen happened to feature in the story.

Sitting beside him, Emily smiled and squeezed his hand, and Owen looked at those bulging knapsacks and felt more safe and secure than he had ever felt before in his life.

In due course, Danny Caines and Sylvanus Hopkins arrived with their lawyer, closely followed by Tudor Jones and Snow Parker with the jeweller. Then all sat down around a big mahogany table to set about the business of their meeting.

"We have agreed the procedure then," said Adrian Bell.

"I will describe each piece; Mister Faulkner, the jeweller will pronounce the estimated value; Mister Wainwright, the lawyer will write it down, and Mister Saunders, the Bank Manager will take delivery of each item as agreed. Shall we begin?"

His eyes sparkling behind his half-moon spectacles, Adrian Bell took the first item from his knapsack and laid it on the table. "Item one," he said: "One emerald necklace. Three large stones set with diamonds in a rope chain of pure gold. Pearl inlaid clasp."

The jeweller examined it carefully. "Say, fifteen hundred dollars," he said.

The lawyer's quill scratched over the heavy vellum paper under his hand and they moved on to the next item. At the end of an hour, half of the contents of the first knapsack had been noted and valued. Rubies and diamonds, amethysts and pearls, rings, bracelets and necklaces lay scattered across the gleaming mahogany table, glowing in the light of the oil lamps burning on the walls. The Bank Manager, Saunders, was sweating and smiling; Mr Faulkner the jeweller was wide-eyed and astonished; and Lawyer Wainwright, as dry and dusty as a legal paper, looked as bitter as if he had swallowed a lemon, irritated, no doubt, to see such vast riches revealed and yet to have agreed his fee beforehand. They took a break to eat some cold pie and chicken that was brought in for their lunch, and then they went back to it again.

It took the whole of that day and most of the next to note down and value each of the items they had brought back with them from Sable Island. But the business finally came to an end, and the Bank Manager, the Jeweller and Lawyer Wainwright duly signed and witnessed the paper which said that the Bank had taken the whole of their hoard into its safe-keeping.

Adrian Bell was authorised to let the Bank arrange the sale of the valuables for cash that would be paid into a joint account to be divided equally between the eight members of the group on the "Dolphin".

"We must all be patient now," said Adrian Bell. "It will take time to turn that pile into cash. You must trust me and I shall make sure that each one of us gets his note of credit for an equal share as soon as the last sale is completed. Mister Saunders has received precise instructions, and his bank will act on behalf of us all."

"And here is a thousand dollars advance to each of you on the account," said a beaming Mr Saunders, handing out wads of American dollar bills. "You are very rich indeed, my friends, and the Bank is entirely at your service."

They walked out of that place with nothing but empty knapsacks. The great hoard of jewels had been traded in for promises written on paper. A sparse whisper of snow blew hither and thither in the cold wind and Owen felt as if he was in a dream.

"It's funny when you think about it," said Tudor Jones. "We go to all that trouble to get hold of that amazing treasure; then as soon as we've got our hands on it, we can't wait to be rid of it and turn it into pieces of paper."

"That's true enough," said Danny Caines. "Paper money seems somehow safer. Doesn't carry all that weight of pain and sorrow with it."

"You can turn paper into almost anything," said Sylvanus Hopkins. "And I'm going to turn some of mine into a slap up meal. What are you eating Snow Parker?"

"Why, I'm going to have a rib of beef with bacon and squash and horseradish sauce, hot beetroot and roast potatoes…"

"…A roast goose and a half dozen bottles of claret," chimed in Tudor Jones.

"Champagne for me, I think," said Emily, "and a Dover Sole on a bed of asparagus."

"A full English breakfast, twice," murmured Adrian Bell.

"...And a dish of plum duff and brandy sauce," Snow Parker went on.

"And I'll have some duff," said Owen.

"And so will I, and Danny Caines is paying!" shouted Sylvanus Hopkins.

Danny stood there and grinned at them all. His face was alight with happiness and his eyes sparkled. "You got it folks," he said. "We'll go and collect Ken Ralph, then away to the "Hope and Anchor" and the finest food in Boston!"

The finest food in Boston – it seemed like the finest food in the world to Owen. The little band feasted that night on dishes served from silver platters as the wine flowed and stories were swapped around the table far into the night. It was an evening warm with happiness and relief and it seemed to go on for a very long time.

Owen was fast asleep long before it ended and he woke the next morning to a strange sense of emptiness and sadness that their adventure had come to an end.

It hadn't come to an end of course – but he wasn't to know that. It was just another turn of the page. But it felt like the end, especially when it came time to say goodbye to Danny Caines and his crew, who were leaving them to return to their families in time for Christmas.

As they said their farewells on the dockside, Danny cupped Owen's chin so the boy was looking up into his friend's weather beaten face.

"Don't you worry fella," said Danny. "We'll be seeing you again. You and that son of mine will meet up one of these days and talk about your times in Nova Scotia. When you get to wherever it is you're going, you just write. We'll be sure and write back. And we'll be travelling too. Don't forget, we're all rich now. Rich folks can travel where they want to. We'll be seeing you again."

In spite of his comforting words, a lump stuck in Owen's throat as he watched the "Dolphin" leave the harbour and turn her head towards the North. Emily dabbed at her eyes with a handkerchief and sniffed, then held his hand tightly.

As they walked over the ice-sheathed cobbles, it started to snow in earnest: thick, heavy flakes that fell in an ever – increasing swarm, whirling about them so they could hardly see. By the time they arrived back at the snug wooden house they had rented, a shell of snow coated them from head to foot – and it felt like Winter in Owen's heart.

But his spirits lifted as the days moved on towards Christmas. The snow fell and then froze; then it snowed and froze some more, so that by Christmas Eve, the streets of the city were buried under more than a foot of ice. The shoes of people and horses alike lost their grip on the treacherous surface, and whooping boys went sliding and skidding up and down the side streets. The roads were thronged with people and animals whose clouds of breath seemed to add to the freezing mist, and icicles hung on the end of every nose without a muffler. Dead turkeys and geese, chickens and ducks, rabbits and game birds hung in frigid lines outside the butcher shops, where men in blood-stained aprons chopped and carved, wrapped and joked with an endless procession of customers. Coming out of shops, balancing a great pile of parcels and packages, ladies dumped their loads into their waiting wagons then dived off in search of still more things to buy. It was almost like being back in Bristol, only colder.

Towards twilight, as Owen and Emily made their way home laden with presents and food, it started to snow again, big whirling flakes that quickly coated every twig, every house, every fence post and branch with a feathery white coat. Back in their warm wooden house, Owen sat by the window in the firelight and watched the whirling dance of the snow that came down endlessly though the night.

On Christmas morning the world outside was muffled with whiteness. Even the deep ruts left by the heavy wooden wagons were rounded over with clean snow. The tracks of a small animal traced across the street to the Christmas tree standing in the garden opposite. Bright with decorations, apples hung from branches bent with their weight of snow, lemons and oranges and strings of coloured berries and beads. A blue jay hopped from branch to branch, pecking in a leisurely fashion at the fruit and berries, sending miniature avalanches running from the tree onto the ground beneath. A gaunt black cat jumped out from where it had been hiding under the tree and shivered its coat free of snow before heading off purposefully towards the kitchen door. Even as Owen watched, the snow began to fall again.

All day long it snowed, and their great Christmas feast and the presents they unwrapped stayed forever tumbled up in Owen's memory with the warm firelight and nuts and dates and oranges, all glowing vivid and clear against a backdrop of falling snow.

Owen never forgot that day, nor what happened at the end of it, when Tudor Jones stood in front of the fire with a twinkling glass of Port in his hand and announced that he and Emily were going to head out West, to buy a house and some land, and settle in the United States.

"There's a different world out there," he said, his eyes bright with excitement. "In England, and even in Wales, its nothing but work and drudge and raise your cap to your master. In this country, any man can be his own master if he has good luck and the courage to persevere. And away out beyond these settled regions is a wild land of prairies and mountains and Indians! It's an adventure waiting to be explored. No more Bristol nor Cardiff for me: no Scammells and Lords, nor Buffers and Codgers neither. We've done with all that. We're going to make an adventure of our lives, ain't we Shipmate?"

Standing beside him with her arm linked through his, Emily smiled at him. "I think our lives are an adventure anyway," she said. "And I thought we agreed to stop the Shipmating."

Looking at Tudor Jones nuzzling gently against Emily's hair, Owen suddenly remembered that other man he had seen pushing his face against her on that storm-tossed night in the cabin of the 'Caroline Louise'.

"Adventures are a bit frightening sometimes, aren't they?" said Owen.

Emily's eyes shone as she looked at him. "That's why they're adventures, Owen," she said. "Do you want to join us and share our adventure? You are more than welcome, if you want to come with us."

"Ahem." Adrian Bell coughed and rose to his feet. "This is very good news. Very interesting news. I too have some interesting news." He paused to blow his nose vigorously and to wipe his spectacles with a handkerchief. "Life as an adventure indeed. There's an interesting idea. Ever since this young man came flying in through my shop doorway, my life has turned completely upside down. But I…Well, it seems I have got somewhat used to this rambling about and wandering in company with our young friend here." He patted Owen's shoulder. "I know you young people have your own lives to live, and no doubt your own children to look after in the future. Ahem. So, in view of all that, I have decided to take it upon myself to look after the boy."

Adrian Bell's kindly face looked down at Owen in the firelight and he continued: "I have written to my solicitors, instructing them to sell my business and property in London and to pass the capital raised on it to Owen's mother. I have also written a letter to her that I should like to read to you. I would be grateful for your judgement of whether it strikes the right tone."

Tudor Jones was smiling broadly. "Buffers and Codgers," he said. "I can always pick 'em. Go on then, Mister Bell, read it out to us."

"Ahem," he began. "My Dear Mrs Davies,
Since last we met, a great deal of good fortune has come our way, good fortune for which your son Owen has been largely responsible. He is a boy in whom you should take great pride. By the time this letter reaches you, my attorneys should have arranged for you to receive a substantial sum of money. This money is yours to spend as you wish. I invite you to use it to purchase passage on a ship for you and the rest of your family, so that you may all join us here in the United States. My bank in Boston, whose address is on this letter, will direct you where to find us. Should you decide to join us, you will find that both Owen and I are in a position to give you all the support you require.

We intend to travel: to explore this country until we find a place where we wish to settle. Whatever you may decide, Madam, you may be assured that I shall look after Owen as if he were my own son. I must express the warm hope that Owen's mother, his brothers and sisters might join us in this country, but we neither of us wish to return to England, or indeed to Wales. I would repeat that the money you receive is yours to do with as you wish. It is my dear hope, Mrs Davies, that you may one day do me the honour of visiting us.

Yours sincerely,
Adrian Bell."

"That's a real Buffers and Codgers letter, that is!" cried Tudor Jones, wringing him by the hand.

The Buffer in question passed the letter over to Owen. "What do you think Owen? Will you sign that letter along with me?"

Owen didn't need to think about it. From the quiet conversations they had had when the two of them were alone, the old fellow knew exactly what the boy was hoping for, and he had put it all in that letter. His smile said it all and the next thing he knew Emily Bobbins was hugging him and ruffling his hair.

"So we are all going to be explorers! That's splendid news," she said. "I'm so glad. Our happy band can all go together. I was dreading saying goodbye to you. And now you can sign your own name and we can keep up with our reading and writing lessons."

"We'll be getting married after the New Year," said Tudor Jones. "We can leave soon after that and go and see what's what in the Land of the Free."

But as Adrian Bell had predicted, it took a good deal of time to dispose of all the treasure and turn it into hard cash. It was a while before the last diamond was disposed of and the last dollar deposited in their joint bank account. Then, true to the promise made on Sable Island, the money was divided into eight equal parts between all who had made the journey. Even divided by eight, it was a fabulous sum that each of them owned.

As part of their shares, both Tudor Jones and Adrian Bell had offered to let Emily have a choice of some jewels as a wedding gift, but she had steadfastly refused the offer. No-one else wanted to keep any of them either. It was as though they felt the treasure to be tainted by the blood and suffering attached to it. But the dollar bank notes were crisp and new and backed by the solid gold reserves of the Boston Bank of Credit and Commerce. The day finally came when the money orders were sent off to their friends in Nova Scotia, and soon afterwards a stagecoach carried the little band of travellers along the broad highway leading out of the prosperous city of Boston, Massachusetts.

The trees were sprouting fresh greenery and the spring air was filled with birdsong as they made their way south. This was a different world to the spruce and tufted fir of the Nova Scotia forests. It was beautiful, mellow country. The sparkling lakes and winding rivers, the shady woods and the fertile plains unrolled before them like a vision of the Promised Land. But the cities were different and they somehow depressed their spirits so that they moved on with each new day. The little towns, with their painted wooden houses, looked pretty and appealing, but the people seemed cold and suspicious of strangers.

The Spring ripened into summer as they travelled on through the eastern United States. Reaching the broad Potomac River, they turned westwards, following the path of the setting sun. Crossing the Allegheny Mountains, they moved through Virginia and Ohio to the bustling city of Cincinnati. Then they found themselves caught up with other travellers, many of them driving great wagons pulled by oxen and teams of horses. They were headed for St Louis and the empty, open lands that lay beyond it to the west. Every night brought them new surroundings and a different crop of stories from their companions. A restless current seemed to be driving them all ever westwards; and Owen and Emily, Adrian Bell and Tudor Jones were borne along in the migrating tide towards the setting sun.

Then they reached the Missouri River and a little town beside it that dreamed amid the summer dust.

The wide and muddy river was dotted with wooded islands, and beyond the river, as far as the eye could see, an endless plain of waving golden grass lost itself in the blue haze of summer. The town was like many another they had passed through, but it was different. The river made it different. The river, with its traffic of paddleboats and rafts, and its beckoning islands covered with cottonwood trees made this a special place. Suddenly all of them were tired of travelling. What was the purpose of travelling on if you had arrived at where you wanted to be? They wanted to be there, right there in that town, and that is where they decided to stay.

While Emily Bobbins and Tudor Jones were out looking for a house and Adrian Bell was off dealing with lawyers and money, Owen took off by himself to explore.

It was a long time since he had been on his own. He wandered along the side of the river and took it all in. Just across the water, a stand of cottonwoods cast a pool of green shade where the cows stood sleepily, nodding their heads and twitching their tails at flies. Scores of small birds called to each other along the banks of the river. A big catfish jumped out of the water and fell back. Ropes of weed rippled in the current and a distant paddle steamer vanished round a bend in the river, leaving the echo of its whistle behind it. Woods on both sides of the river beckoned for the future.

Leaving the river behind him, Owen wandered along through the quiet little town and thought about how different it all was to the world he had left behind in Bristol. The tree-shaded houses, each one resting comfortably in its own plot of land, were a far cry from the crowded city and the two-roomed homes he had known. In place of the din of the traffic and the cries of hawkers and fishwives, there was only the rasp of the saws in the lumber yard, the chirping of the crickets and the bright calls of the birds dipping among the river shallows.

The teeming highways and alleys of Bristol with their host of unsavoury smells had given way to these quiet streets filled with the odour of flowers and the drowsy murmur of the bees at work among them. The town dozed through the long summer afternoon. The world of chimneys, factories and mines was just a distant memory.

A yellow dog trotting down the street towards him suddenly stopped and sat down in the dust, nuzzling in its coat for fleas.

Turning a corner, Owen saw a cluster of children grouped around two older boys who stood leaning against a barrel. Just behind them, another one was busy painting a high wooden fence with a long handled brush. Owen wandered over towards them.

One of the older boys had a laughing, freckled face under a tattered straw hat, and the pockets of his blue dungarees were bulging. The other was skinny and dressed in old trousers too big for him, held up with one suspender: a deeply tanned boy with dirty yellow hair and brilliant green eyes who sucked on an empty corn cob pipe. Owen saw him nudge the other one and they both turned to look at him.

Standing there in his new clothes fresh from the stores of Boston, Owen must have looked a strange, city kind of a creature to them. But he had hardly spoken to another boy since leaving Joshua Caines back in Canada, and he was hungry for his own kind of company.

Owen looked at them and they looked at him. Owen was stumped for a moment, then he knew exactly the right thing to say. He had something in his pocket. He had a story for them.

"Have you ever seen a whale's tooth?" he said. "I can show you one if you like. It's got a picture carved on it. The picture shows how people hunt whales out there on the ocean."

The boy with the pipe took it from his mouth and

smiled like a happy dog, showing strong yellow teeth.

The freckled boy took a step towards him and held out his hand. "Say, you ain't from around these parts are you? I can tell by the way you talk." He gestured across to the boy with the pipe. "This here is my pal, Huck Finn, and my name's Tom Sawyer. What's yourn? Show me that there whale's tooth and I might just let you take a turn to paint my fence."

Which is where Owen's story ends, and another, much better one begins.

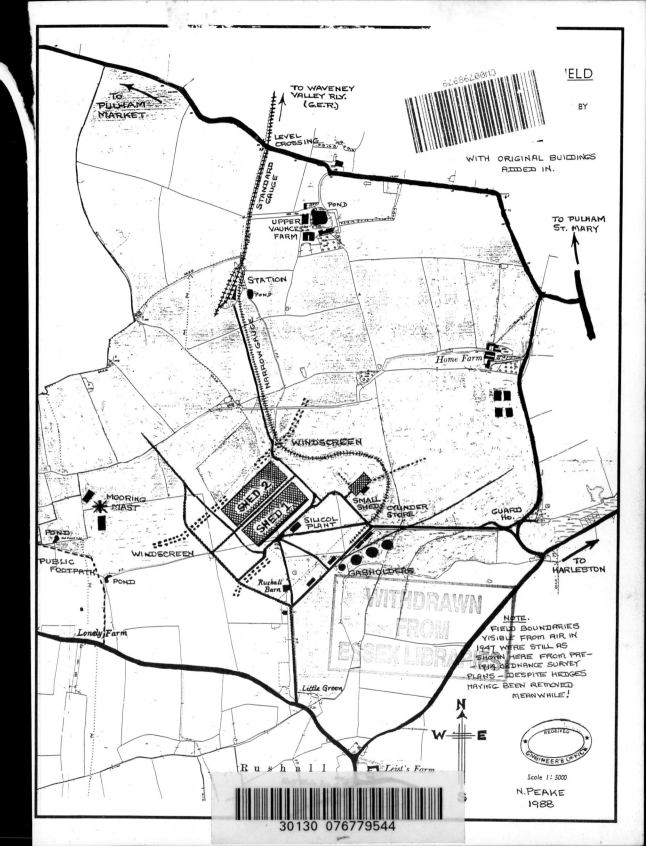

'ELD

BY

WITH ORIGINAL BUILDINGS
ADDED IN.

TO WAVENEY
VALLEY RLY.
(G.E.R.)

TO
PULHAM
MARKET

LEVEL
CROSSING

STANDARD GAUGE

UPPER
VAUNCES
FARM

POND

TO PULHAM
St. MARY

STATION

POND

NARROW GAUGE

Home Farm

WINDSCREEN

SHED 2

SHED 1

MOORING
MAST

SMALL
SHED
CYLINDER
STORE

GUARD
Ho.

SILICOL
PLANT

POND

WINDSCREEN

PUBLIC
FOOTPATH

POND

GASHOLDERS

TO
HARLESTON

Rushall
Barn

Lonely Farm

NOTE.
FIELD BOUNDARIES
VISIBLE FROM AIR IN
1947 WERE STILL AS
SHOWN HERE FROM PRE-
1914 ORDNANCE SURVEY
PLANS — DESPITE HEDGES
HAVING BEEN REMOVED
MEANWHILE!

Little Green

N
W E
S

Rushall

Leist's Farm

RECEIVED
ENGINEER'S OFFICE

Scale 1: 5000

N.PEAKE
1988

PULHAM PIGS

Overleaf: Members of the crew of the R.34 read a newspaper account of their transatlantic flight after their arrival at Pulham on 13th July, 1919. The only uniform seems to be the heavy knitted guernsey.   *George Swain*

PULHAM PIGS

The History of an Airship Station

by

GORDON KINSEY

TERENCE DALTON LIMITED
LAVENHAM . SUFFOLK
1988

Published by
TERENCE DALTON LIMITED

ISBN 0 86138 050 9

Text photoset in 10/12pt Baskerville

Printed in Great Britain at
The Lavenham Press Limited, Lavenham, Suffolk

Contents

THEY MARK OUR PASSAGE AS A RACE OF MEN
EARTH WILL NOT SEE SUCH SHIPS AS THESE AGAIN
Cutty Sark, Greenwich

Foreword

MAN-CARRYING flight today is shared by the fixed wing aeroplane and the rotary winged helicopter, and these two hold pride of place in the world of air transport as they move from one great achievement to another, speed and passenger-carrying capability forging ahead unceasingly.

We must not, however, forget that the airship contributed in no small measure to this conquest of the skies, even if today the mammoths of yesteryear are regarded by many with disfavour and tragic memory. It is true that their history is marred and scarred by disaster and failure, but there were triumphs also to record, often achieved in the face of almost impossible odds.

Airship operations were totally different from those of the aeroplane—no serious watch needed to be kept on the airspeed of the craft as, unlike the aeroplane whose lifting planes require forward speed to sustain lift, the airship could stop its engines and float. Engine failure was not the source of anxiety it was in winged and rotor-bladed craft. With the larger crew that the big rigid airships carried, watches were kept as on board ship, with alternating periods of off-duty and duty. One could also indulge in the luxury of a walk along the internal catwalk within the gigantic hull of the rigid airship, where with upwards of 880 feet to utilise this could be quite a stretch. Engines were contained within power cars which enabled the engineers to operate their charges in comparative comfort and if necessary to carry out in-flight repairs.

Slow perhaps, but graceful indeed, the airship was one of the more spectacular of man's endeavours to rise above his earth-bound environment. Now reports are seen from time to time in newspapers and magazines which give hope for the return of the airship, not in its past form, often fragile and almost totally at the mercy of the elements, but as the result of new technology, with helium now employed as the lifting element. Sustained by this non-flammable gas, the new generation of airships will, it is visualised, carry out operations in the heavy-lift cargo field where speed will not be the all-consuming factor.

This book is not about the history of the airship, as many authors have already covered this subject, but about the day-to-day life and achievements of a famous airship station and the men and women who were its lifeblood.

Acknowledgements

THIS BOOK would not have been possible but for very many people and organisations who have assisted me by their generous gifts of valuable information. All are worthy of individual thanks and notes were space available, but within these limits I must record my thanks to the individuals and groups listed alphabetically.

Mrs Anna Aldrich, Harleston; Mr Roger Aldrich, Hemel Hempstead; the late Mr R. B. Aldrich, Harleston; Dr Ian C. Allen, Thorpeness; Mr J. M. Bruce, Hendon; Mrs V. K. Bailey, Little Shelford; Mr F. D. Charity, Briston; Mr Peter Claydon, Felixstowe; Mr W. F. Cobb, Barnham Broom; Mr Charles Cutting, Pulham; Mr George Cook, Driffield; Mr M. S. Denny, Harleston; Mr Geoffrey Easto, Ipswich; the Reverend G. R. Epps, Pulham Market; Mr H. Fairhead, Langley; Mrs I. H. Finlayson, Seaford; Mr C. E. John Gaze, Palgrave; Mr J. W. Gosling, Framlingham; Mr G. Greenwood, Lincoln; Mr J. Hadlow, Melton; Mr I. L. Hawkins, Bacton; Mr R. J. R. Hayward, Mildenhall; Mr W. Herring, Pulham; Mr and Mrs Ken Leighton, Ipswich; Mr Stuart Leslie, Scarborough; Mr W. K. MacKenzie, OBE, Leamington Spa; the Reverend C. Mather, Hunstanton; Dr D. W. Moyes, Oxted; Mrs M. R. Payne, Starston; Mr Norman Peake, Norwich; Mrs Judith Rabsey, Norwich; Mrs D. Read, Pulham St Mary; Mrs J. V. Riseborough, Aldeby; Mrs J. Rushen, Tivetshall St Mary; Mr Geoffrey Soar, Holbrook; Mr John Spiers, Diss; the Reverend S. Spiking, Dickleburgh; Mrs Mavis Streeter, Caythorpe, Lincolnshire; Mrs E. Taylor, Pulham St Mary; Flight Lieutenant S. E. Thorn, Wroxham; Mrs D. Trouw, Horning; Mr John Venmore-Rowland, Leiston; Mr Ivan Underwood, Diss; Mr K. Wheeler, Wymondham.

Organisations which contributed material and photographs included Anglia Television, Norwich; Airship Industries Limited, London and Cardington; British Broadcasting Corporation, Norwich; British Aerospace, London; British Industrial Gases Limited, Waltham Abbey; Depwade District Council, Long Stratton; *East Anglian Daily Times* and its associated newspapers, Ipswich; *Eastern Daily Press*, Norwich; Ipswich and District Historical Transport Society and its ever-helpful members, Ipswich; Ipswich Public Library and its staff; Martlesham Heath Aviation Historic Society, Martlesham Heath; Ministry of Defence (Air), London; Norfolk and Suffolk Aviation Museum, Flixton; Radio Orwell, Ipswich; Royal Aeronautical Society, London; Royal Air Force Museum,

Hendon; Shorts, Walkers Studios Limited, Scarborough; 100th Bomb Group Association (UK), Thorpe Abbotts; the East Anglian Film Archive.

My very special thanks to Dr P. D. Rawlence, of Pulham St Mary, who conducted my wife and myself on a wonderful tour of his ex-patients from whom he was able in a truly professional manner to coax startling tales of the station up on the hill; to Mr and Mrs Duncan West, who entertained us in their picturesque farmhouse, steeped in nostalgia, set on the site of the air station and from where all the features remaining were shown to us with a great spirit of enthusiasm; and to Mr C. E. "Holly" Hall, who has produced another eye-catching jacket for this book.

Assisting again with unstinting patience with the prolonged research required to reveal the true secrets of this long-departed air station was my wife, Margaret, to whom I give my deepest gratitude and heartfelt thanks. She is a source of measureless counsel and advice, especially in checking and cross-checking manuscripts and the seemingly endless list of items for indexing. Many thanks also to Mr Robert Malster, the publishers' editor, for his always willing help and guidance, and to my publishers and their staff for their co-operation, quiet counsel and excellent workmanship.

Gordon Kinsey
Roundwood Road
Ipswich
Suffolk, 1988

CHAPTER ONE

Coastal Airship Station

PULHAM Air Station or, to give it its official title, No 2 Coastal Airship Station was commissioned during February, 1916, but it was not until 31st August that it received its first Coastal airship and settled down to the serious business of sending out airships of the non-rigid type on patrols over the southern North Sea.

The discomfort suffered by the crews of these aircraft was almost beyond imagination. The early Sea Scout type of non-rigid airship employed on these long patrols, carried out in all weathers, had only an aeroplane fuselage with open cockpits for the crew slung beneath the gasbag and there was little or no protection from the elements for the pilot and observer.

Among the first airships to arrive at Pulham were several small coastal airships which had been intended for despatch to Mudros on the Aegean island of Lemnos, but with the collapse of the Dardanelles campaign and the evacuation of allied troops from Gallipoli these aircraft belonging to No 3 Airship Wing of the Royal Naval Air Service went to Pulham instead. Other sections of the same wing took up residence at stations along the East and South coasts of England.

Perhaps it was one of these early non-rigid airships, or possibly one of the kite balloons also based at Pulham for experimental work, that prompted the chance remark uttered one day by a local man as he looked up at the fat envelope of the lighter-than-air craft floating above him: "Thet luk loike a gret ol' pig!" It was natural for the Norfolk people, with their farming background, to give the airships the nickname of Pulham Pigs; it was a name that stuck, and is even today remembered in the region.

Although Pulham became operational only in 1916, the story of the air station goes back much further. It was in 1912 that Mr Clement Gaze, then head of the family firm of Thomas William Gaze and Son, surveyors and land agents, of Diss, was appointed by the Board of Admiralty to acquire a group of farms at Pulham.

"In brief, his somewhat short instructions were that no one must know the actual buyer," says Mr C. E. John Gaze, of Palgrave, the son of Mr Clement Gaze.

The R.33 on the Pulham mast about 1920. In the background can be seen the two big airship sheds, with the windscreens intended to protect airships from crosswinds as they were moved into or out of the sheds.   *Mrs V. K. Bailey*

1

"Possession was needed by the Board of Admiralty. They set no financial limits, but secrecy was paramount, and in consequence it was leaked that my mother, who came from a Shropshire hunting family, wanted the land in order to establish racing stables."

Mr Gaze delved into his company's extensive records to ensure complete accuracy of the details of the acquisition of the land by the Admiralty. One of these documents, dated 4th September, 1913, shows that one parcel of land required for the establishment of the air station was Home Farm, Pulham St Mary the Virgin, which was owned by Christ's Hospital and occupied by Mr Herbert Owles; this farm brought the owners an annual rent of £230. Mr Owles was also the tenant of the adjacent Brick Kiln Farm, comprising a mere 36 acres, for which he paid an annual rent of £40 to the trustees of Mrs C. Mason. The third farm needed by the Admiralty was Upper Vaunces Farm, owned by Christ's Hospital and farmed by Mr Thomas Lincoln, who paid yearly dues of £178 for the 204 acres.

Lengthy negotiations were conducted by Mr Clement Gaze with Mr J. W. Stone, Surveyor of Lands in the Lands and Coast Guard Branch of the

Pulham in its setting. Redrawn from an Ordnance Survey map published in 1914.

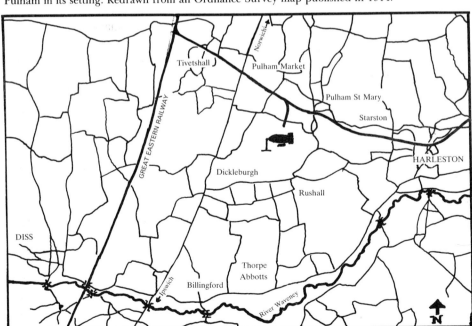

Admiralty, and with the owners of the land, much of the day-to-day work being carried out behind closed doors and in the greatest secrecy; it was essential that nobody should know the identity of the would-be purchasers. However discreet the negotiations, older residents of the area recall that rumours were rife as to the intended purpose of the buildings which eventually went up on the site, and the story in greatest favour was that it was to be a base for aeroplanes or airships.

Although he was actually a civil servant employed in the Admiralty, Mr Stone is remembered as "Admiral Stone". Was his non-existent rank a nickname given to a rather pompous civil servant by the staff of Gaze's office, one wonders.

After a great deal of discussion asking prices of £11,000 for Upper Vaunces Farm and of £800 for Home Farm were put forward. "I understand that it was not too difficult to get the first two farms, but the price became sticky for the remainder—and the circulated tale did sound a little bit thin," Mr John Gaze says. "However, the whole 500-odd acres was eventually acquired and the Admiralty started to clear the site. It was ready for work to begin by August, 1914." The asking price for the two farms owned by Christ's Hospital seems to have been rather high; all three farms were in due course acquired by the Admiralty for a total of £11,300. The tenants were given twelve months to clear all their crops and vacate the land, being given compensation for the enforced move.

All the land bought for the air station was in the parishes of Pulham St Mary the Virgin and Rushall, on the north side of the valley of the River Waveney, which meanders betwixt Norfolk and Suffolk, its course marking the county boundary for many twisting miles. Pulham Mary, as it is known locally, has a sister village of Pulham St Mary Magdalene, more usually referred to as Pulham Market, only a short distance away to the west nor'west.

At the time of the compilation of Domesday Book this was one of the most densely populated areas of England, but by the twentieth century it was something of a backwater, the population of Pulham Market being little more than a thousand and of its sister parish a mere 700 or so. The district was well known to the military of many centuries ago; there is strong evidence of Roman occupation, with the ageless track of Stone Street at Pulham and the major arterial route built by them to service their station at Burgh Castle passing through the nearby village of Ditchingham.

In this corner of East Anglia, traversed by narrow lanes which skirt odd-shaped fields, many sites have unusual names such as "Hangman's Acre", a piece of land amounting to some seven acres owned in medieval times by the Lord's hangman, and a prominent landscape feature are the large common pastures or greens, two surviving examples being Pulham North Green and Tivetshall Common. A curiosity also were the small parcels of land given to local residents by the Lord of the Manor and known as "Cornage"; in return for this land the recipients of cornage were obliged to blow a horn to announce the

The construction team, including Mr Victor Dunton Easto, pose outside one of the former farm buildings on the airfield site in 1914. Stout clothing, heavy boots and leather buskins were necessary because of conditions on the windswept plateau. *Mr Geoffrey Easto*

opening of the manor court, for which duty they also received fourpence and a meal.

Surrounded by this fascinating patchwork of agricultural history is Pulham Market, which consists of colour-washed cottages grouped around the village green beside which are the two "locals", the *Falcon* and the *Crown*. Their bar parlours often resound to the soft Norfolk drawl as older residents regale their audiences and visitors with tales of the "goings on" up at the old air station. The picturesque village church, dedicated to St Mary Magdalene, overlooks this tranquil scene; its neighbouring place of worship, St Mary the Virgin, rises above the trees just along the valley at Pulham St Mary. The latter church is set high up on a bluff and looks out towards the south on to the plateau, fairly elevated by East Anglian standards, where the air station was located. Trees lining the street shade buildings of great antiquity which include the remains of a Guild chapel dating back to 1401. A room built by William Pennoyer in 1670 is still part of the village school.

The villages were served at one time by the Waveney Valley line of the Great Eastern Railway, later to be part of the London and North Eastern Railway and later still part of British Railways. Both villages boasted stations with goods facilities. Improvements to the area's roads and the advent of motor road transport and public road services brought about the demise of this railway line in the nineteen-sixties.

Local labour was engaged mainly in agricultural pursuits, but over the period covered by this book many people found employment, both full-time and part-time, at the air station, and it is largely in the words of this now rapidly diminishing group of older men and women that the history of the station is told.

One of those with memories of the station is Mr Geoffrey Easto, of Ipswich, whose father, Mr Victor Dunton Easto, was an Inspector of Works employed on the construction of the station.

He told me that he was appointed there out of the blue. Arriving late one evening, he began to make inquiries about Pulham and about possible places where he could stay. There were many rumours and stories of spies and queer goings-on in Norfolk in those wartime days, and having eventually found a roof for the night he was about to get into bed when he received a visitor, the robust village constable. Fortunately my father was able to identify himself fairly quickly and thereafter the two men became very good friends, often joking about their introduction.

My mother and I eventually moved into a cottage in the village. I can just remember being scared by the noise of an airship's engines, but I am told that this fear completely disappeared after I had been taken into one of the sheds and allowed to explore the gondola of a "Pulham Pig".

That experience obviously made a deep impression on me, for some time later I was discovered in a rather grubby state in the village blacksmith's shop banging away at a piece of scrap metal. When my mother said that I must not be a nuisance, the blacksmith replied "He's enjoying himself—he just told me that he's making an airship to go up and see where the thunder and lightning come from." Just over twenty years later I joined the Meteorological branch of the Royal Air Force.

Little now remains of the once-busy establishment that Mr Easto's father helped to construct. All that is to be seen is a few broken buildings with unglazed casements and doors creaking in the wind, three massive concrete foundations where the gigantic airship sheds stood, and an open area of flatness where growing crops and tall grasses sway and sing in summer zephyrs and winter gales.

5

CHAPTER TWO

From Acorns

FIRST buildings to be used by the new occupiers of the site at Pulham were the main farm buildings of Upper Vaunces Farm, and these were soon joined by other buildings erected by the main contractors, Smith of Burwell.

Very soon the contractors' workmen were joined by men of the Air Construction Corps who were responsible for the erection of some small airship sheds for housing the little non-rigids which were to be stationed at Pulham. Small as they were, these sheds became a landmark on the plateau overlooking the Waveney Valley. They became even more prominent as hedges were grubbed out when work started on levelling the surface of the airfield; ditches were filled in, hollows filled and hummocks flattened. Fences were erected to enclose all the newly acquired land, and the appropriate warning notices were posted around the perimeter.

In order to make a suitable working area for the airships, 216 acres were levelled and laid down to grass by local farmers under contract to the Admiralty in addition to the considerable area of the airfield itself. Their Lordships, more used to dealing with the victualling of battleships and the bunkering of destroyers and gunboats, were by no means at a loss when dealing with such agricultural matters; they specified that the grass seed, to be obtained from Suttons of Reading, should be sown at a rate of 40 lb to the acre[1]. The 8,640 lb required cost £208 6s 6d and the cost of sowing it was £28 5s. Land surplus to the requirements of the Admiralty was rented to various local farmers and the grass surfaces of the station itself were made available for grazing, a licence being granted to the West family, who incidentally in 1985 still farmed the site.

Being a Royal Naval Air Station, the establishment at Pulham was run on naval lines and all the officers and men stationed there held naval ranks. Naval uniform was worn, but the flying crews had of necessity to wear flying clothes, some of it of Royal Flying Corps origin, which owed nothing to naval tradition.

The Royal Naval Air Service was formed on 23rd June, 1914, but the history of naval flying dates back to 1908 when a decision was made to go ahead with the construction of an airship for naval use. Word had been coming through from the Continent that both the Germans and Italians were making good progress with the development of large rigid airships which might prove useful for military purposes.

Chief advocate of the use of airships for naval operations was the Director of

Naval Ordnance, Captain R. H. S. Bacon, DSO, and it was he who proposed that this type of craft should be built. He was supported by Admiral Sir John Fisher and by the Board of Admiralty, and in January, 1909, the Imperial Defence Committee reluctantly agreed to have a figure of £35,000 put into the 1909–10 Naval Estimates for the design and construction of a naval rigid airship.

A rigid airship had an internal structure of light alloy girders or reinforced plywood members; the material used in His Majesty's Airship No 1 was duralumin[2]. Housed within this structure, which consisted of radial rings forming the main frames with longitudinals spaced around their circumference, were the numerous gasbags containing the lifting gas, hydrogen; each gasbag had its own automatic gas valve to vent hydrogen as it expanded with increasing altitude or with the sun's heat, and also a manually operated manoeuvring valve. In between the wire-braced main frames were intermediate frames, not braced but supporting the longitudinal members. This complicated structure was covered with a heavy doped fabric laced to the framework.

A contract was awarded to Vickers on 7th May, 1909, and work proceeded on His Majesty's Airship No 1, a vessel which was named the *Mayfly* because it

The Sea Scout Zero S.S.Z.3 being handled by ground crews in front of the Pulham sheds on a snowy day in 1918. There is a wooden non-rigid airship shed to the north of No 2 rigid shed. Radial lines on the bows of the airship are strengthening ribs to reinforce that part of the envelope. *Stuart Leslie collection*

was designed to alight on and take off from the water. The name was taken up by the popular press to emphasise the many delays experienced during the process of design and construction. Some at least of these delays were caused by the fact that the airship proved to be grossly overweight. Launched from a floating hangar at Barrow-in-Furness on 22nd May, 1911, the airship was moored out for a few days and successfully rode out a gale with winds gusting up to 45 mph. Last-minute alterations aimed at reducing weight and enabling the airship to take off included the removal of the main keel that stiffened the vessel. Emerging from its shed on 24th September, 1911, in preparation for its maiden flight, the airship broke its back; thus ended the life of the first rigid airship to be constructed outside Germany.

All further development of rigid airships was abandoned by the Admiralty; the faith of both Admiralty and Government was further shaken by several accidents which occurred to rigid airships abroad. In 1910 "Jackie" Fisher was replaced as First Sea Lord by Admiral of the Fleet Sir Arthur Knyvet Wilson, who was no lover of the new-fangled flying machines; and the recommendation of Rear-Admiral Sir Doveton Sturdee, who was in charge of the inquiry into the loss of HMA No 1, that the monster should not be repaired reinforced the view that airships were not worthy of further consideration.

Only Germany appeared to be making progress under the inspired guidance of Count Zeppelin, and that country held the undisputed lead in the design and construction of rigid airships in the years leading up to the outbreak of war in 1914. This naturally caused a great deal of uneasiness in military circles in Britain, and in 1912 the Committee of Imperial Defence sent Captain Murray Sueter and Mr Mervyn O'Gorman, chief engineer at the Royal Aircraft Factory at Farnborough, on a visit to the Continent to study airship development[3]. At Fühlsbüttel the duo were taken aloft in the *Viktoria Luise*, Count Zeppelin's latest airship and one of a number operated by DELAG, the German airship transport company; they and other passengers were taken on a five-and-a-half-hour flight over Hamburg, the Bay of Lübeck and the Elbe, and they were most impressed. Their reports did not, however, impress the Committee of Imperial Defence, whose somewhat feeble excuse for refusing to countenance the construction of a further naval airship was that there were no naval personnel capable of operating such a craft.

Captain Sueter's persistence did eventually break down the resistance of the Committee of Imperial Defence, aided by Rear Admiral Sir John Jellicoe, who in 1908 had become Third Sea Lord under Fisher and was later Second Sea Lord. The purchase of two airships for the Naval Wing was authorised; first choice was a Zeppelin, but the German government imposed an embargo on the building of rigid airships for foreign customers, though allowing Britain to acquire a Parseval non-rigid. A semi-rigid was also ordered from the Italians, but on the outbreak of war this craft was ordered into service with the Italian army.

The non-rigid airship is very different from the bigger rigid with its complicated framing; it is merely an aerodynamically profiled balloon envelope employing the gas and air within the envelope to maintain its shape. This is essential both for control and also to reduce air resistance to the craft's forward passage through the air. Gas in the envelope is at greater pressure than that of the atmosphere surrounding the outside of the envelope, and this pressure within is automatically regulated by valves which allow gas to escape should the internal pressure increase beyond safe limits. If gas pressure within the envelope is high at ground level, decreasing atmospheric pressure as the airship rises will allow the gas to expand; gas will be vented off through the automatic valves, and this loss of gas would become critical as the airship descends because outside pressure impinging on the outer face of the envelope would cause it to lose its shape and become aerodynamically unstable.

To overcome this, separate compartments or ballonets are built into the interior of the envelope, and these are filled with air. As the gas expands, air is allowed to escape from the ballonets so that the expanding gas replaces the internal volume previously occupied by air. When the envelope is pressurised by the gas alone the craft is said to be at its "pressure height". The reverse procedure is carried out as the craft descends, air being forced into the ballonets as gas pressure decreases so as to maintain the designed profile of the envelope.

Semi-rigids are similar in all respects to non-rigids except that they have a rigid keel running along the bottom of the envelope. This keel allows a lower gas pressure to be used, as the profile of the envelope is better maintained; the keel carries the suspended weights of the control car and other appendages. In the semi-rigid the gas is usually contained in gasbags, giving the crew better control over the trim of the craft.

On the establishment of the Royal Naval Air Service in July, 1914, this force was charged with the operation of all British lighter-than-air craft. At the outbreak of war in the following month the British airship strength comprised the German Parseval 18, which served as HMA No 4, a French Astra-Torres, HMA No 3, and the former Willows No 4, which was HMA No 2. Also on the strength were the diminutive non-rigids *Beta II* (No 17), *Delta* (No 19), *Eta* (No 20) and *Gamma* (No 18), former army airships which were put on to coastal reconnaissance and training duties. All these craft had done very little flying, and their crews were inexperienced.

Although sceptical at first as to the usefulness of these craft, the Admiralty soon gained confidence in them and began to appreciate their potential usefulness. The first coastal patrol was carried out by the RNAS on 10th August, 1914, and when the British army crossed the English Channel to take up positions in western France the two naval airships HMA No 3 and HMA No 4 escorted the ships and carried out anti-submarine patrols.

Development work on a new rigid airship, HMA No 9, had begun in 1913, but all was not to prove plain sailing. In December, 1914, Mr Winston Churchill—who had taken over as First Lord of the Admiralty in 1911 and remained in that post until 1915—stated that they were not in favour of spending more money on airships; he preferred to develop the use of heavier-than-air craft. Three months after his statement all work on the new rigid airship was stopped. Churchill later said "Had I had my way no airships would have been built during the war except the little blimps for teasing submarines."

At the outbreak of war the only two establishments connected with airships were Farnborough in Hampshire, which had two small sheds, and Kingsnorth on the Isle of Grain, west of the mouth of the Medway, in Kent, with similar accommodation. Farnborough had been the base of No 1 Company (Airship,

The Army airship *Gamma*, which became No 18 when transferred to the Royal Naval Air Service at Pulham. The gondola is slung very low.

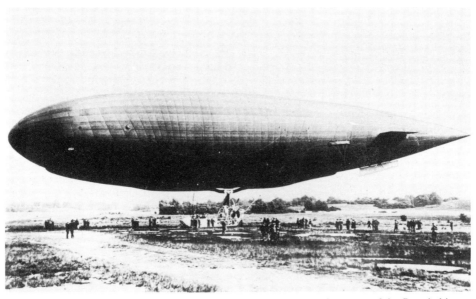

The German-built Parseval non-rigid airship which became No 4 and was one of the first airships to be stationed at Pulham. The gondola is of a particularly primitive design.   *Stuart Leslie collection*

Balloon and Kite) of the Air Battalion of the Royal Engineers when that unit came into being on 1st April, 1911, under the command of an officer seconded from the Essex Regiment, Captain E. M. Maitland. To begin with No 1 Company's equipment consisted of the Farnborough-built non-rigids *Beta* and *Gamma*, and after the unit became No 1 (Airship) Squadron of the Royal Flying Corps on 13th April, 1912, it received the redesigned and rebuilt non-rigid *Delta*.

The Naval Wing of the Royal Flying Corps had only one airship, the non-rigid Willows No 2, which was used solely for training purposes. When the Royal Naval Air Service was formed out of the Naval Wing a number of stations were being prepared, and the first Royal Naval Air Station to become operational was that at Capel, near Dover; by midsummer, 1915, further stations at Polegate, near Eastbourne in Sussex, on the island of Anglesey and at Luce Bay in south-west Scotland were ready for service.

These stations were well placed to protect shipping in the English Channel, in the Irish Sea and off the Scottish coast, but further stations were needed along the East Coast to cover the North Sea, a vital sphere of operations in any war with Germany. Big new stations were therefore planned at Longside, near Peterhead in the north-east of Scotland; at East Fortune, near Edinburgh; at

Howden, in Yorkshire not far from Selby; and at Pulham. These East Coast stations were all to be equipped with large sheds for the housing of rigid airships as well as facilities for operating the little non-rigids.

So it was that during 1915 work on the construction of the Pulham Air Station neared completion and an advance party of RNAS personnel moved in to make all the necessary arrangements for the reception of No 3 Airship Wing. To begin with there were no more than a hundred men on the station, but as the weeks went by the population gradually increased until at the end of the war there were more than three thousand servicemen and women on the station.

Another Parseval non-rigid, built in Britain to the German design, joined the RNAS in 1917 as HMA No 5. She was given an enclosed cabin and there were other improvements on the original design, but she still appears very crude by later standards.   *Stuart Leslie collection*

CHAPTER THREE

Attack and Defence

WHEN man first took to the skies the possibility of using aircraft for offensive purposes was regarded as quite improper. At the 44th annual meeting of the Aeronautical Society held on 10th September, 1909, Colonel F. G. Stone of the Royal Artillery read a paper entitled "Limitations of Aerial Bombardment by International Law" in which he explained that bombing was prohibited by international law except as a method of breaking down the resistance of defended towns or destroying the enemy's war materials.

These rules were to be changed soon after the outbreak of war in 1914. Count Ferdinand von Zeppelin, a former Prussian cavalry officer and a man with the determination to overcome opposition and disaster, persuaded the German government that the airship was potentially a great weapon of destruction and one that the German army and navy might develop with great advantage. It was as well for Britain that when hostilities began neither service was prepared for an onslaught of the kind envisaged by von Zeppelin.

The first Zeppelin raid on Britain occurred on the night of 19th January, 1915, when L-3 carried out an attack on the undefended town of Great Yarmouth, dropping eight 110 lb high explosive bombs in a line across the built-up area and on the South Denes. The two people killed in the attack were the first British citizens to die in an air raid.

Later the same night L-4 dropped bombs on King's Lynn, killing a woman and a child. That raid by L-3 and L-4 was the first of many directed against Britain during the First World War.

Air defence of the Pulham station when it became operational in 1916 was partially in the hands of No 38 Squadron of the Royal Flying Corps, formed at nearby Thetford on 1st April, 1916, as a Home Defence unit equipped with the slow B.E.2c biplane, the standard night fighter of the period. The squadron continued in this role, participating in attempts to counter a number of Zeppelin raids on the Eastern Counties, until moving to France as a night bomber squadron in May, 1918.

Hans Fritz, the commanding officer of L-3 when it attacked Great Yarmouth, seems to have been unaware of the existence of the Royal Naval Air Station on the South Denes as his bombs fell wide of the hangars and other installations. And it seems likely that other airship commanders who flew on raids against Norfolk and Suffolk were equally unaware of the existence of the station at Pulham, although they passed right over the station in the darkness during their somewhat erratic wanderings.

An attack on East Anglia was made on 13th April, 1915, when L-5, commanded by Kapitän-leutnant Aloys Böcker, bombed Lowestoft, little more than twenty miles to the east of Pulham, setting fire to a timber yard. Another raider, L-7 commanded by Kapitän-leutnant Werner Petersen, crossed the Norfolk coast the same night and made its way over the darkened countryside, but it failed to find a target and took its bombs home.

More raids took place during May, when Zeppelins dropped their missiles on Bury St Edmunds, and then in June it was the turn of Ipswich, some

A B.E.2e, the standard night fighter employed to intercept raiding Zeppelins. *Stuart Leslie collection*

twenty-seven miles south of Pulham. The warm summer nights meant that the Zeppelins arrived later so as to avoid being seen in the evening twilight, and on the night of 9th–10th August, 1915, the L-11 under the command of Oberleutnant-zur-See Horst Freiherr von Buttlar flew along the coast off Lowestoft, jettisoning his bombs in the water before making for home. Two nights later Oberleutnant-zur-See Fridrich Wenke in L-10 dropped his bombs on Harwich while von Buttlar, again in L-11, attempted to cross the Norfolk coast but was driven back by a violent thunderstorm raging in the area[4].

Becoming quite a frequent visitor, von Buttlar was over East Anglia again on the night of 13th–14th October and bombed villages in South Norfolk. Perhaps he was looking for Pulham with the intention of disrupting the work then going on at the air station.

For the most part these early air raids met with little or no opposition either from defending fighters or from anti-aircraft artillery. Pulham escaped again on the night of 31st March, 1916, when a Zeppelin passed over the station without its crew detecting the possible target beneath them; instead they dropped twelve bombs in the Stowmarket area. No doubt the commander of the Zeppelin, Kapitän-leutnant Heinrich Mathy, knew of the New Explosives Company's guncotton works on the outskirts of Stowmarket and had made this his target, but the bombs missed; a direct hit on one of the buildings could have brought untold destruction to the area. An anti-aircraft battery opened up on the L-13 as it began its bombing run, and two of the Zeppelin's gas cells were damaged by the shells; a message pad picked up in the Stowmarket area the following day, apparently blown overboard before it reached the telegraphist who was to have transmitted the signal, bore the information that the Zeppelin had been hit by anti-aircraft fire and was having to return to base.

The operations of the big German naval Zeppelins were very different from those of the little airships stationed at Pulham in the early days of the station. Those early days are recalled by Mr F. D. Charity, of Briston in North Norfolk, who joined the Royal Naval Air Service in 1916 and was drafted to Pulham in June of that year.

> In those days the Air Station had only just started operations on a large scale and there were still only a few sheds and a large wooden structure which had been erected by Messrs Hippersons, builders, of Norwich. It housed a Sea Scout non-rigid airship and three other small craft named *Beta*, *Gamma* and *Delta* which had been previously operated by the Royal Engineers. The commanding officer was Colonel E. M. Maitland, later killed in the R.38 when it crashed into the Humber.

Things that go bump in the night—the crater made by a Zeppelin bomb which fell in open country not far from Pulham, with a member of the RNAS helping to give scale to the hole.

The first "pig" that I can recall was one of the Coastal Patrol type, and it was followed by several others, the C.17, C.26, C.27 and the first of the North Sea type. The second ship of this later type ran into trouble on its way to Pulham and came down at Stowmarket, apparently because a batch of petrol tanks came adrift from their rigging which suspended them each side of the two outside sections of the envelope.

Airships using the Air Station during the First World War ranged from the single-engined Sea Scout (S.S.) to the slightly larger S.S. Zero and then the much larger twin-engined Coastal or C. Their duties embraced coastal patrols, escort duties for convoys and anti-submarine searches. As many of these duties called for very slow forward speeds in order to keep in formation with their charges below, or hanging silently over a U-boat sighting, this type of aircraft was ideally suited for the task. On the debit side the majority of these airship types were very susceptible to winds of almost any strength and their crews often experienced long and anxious hours as they battled against strong winds when returning to base with rapidly overheating engines and even more rapidly dwindling amounts of fuel in the tanks.

First into service was the Sea Scout, production of which had been delayed because it would appear that all the firms who were capable of working with fabric were engaged on aeroplane construction and none was prepared to switch to airship fabric work. Eventually a raincoat manufacturer and a furniture-making company joined forces and production of the airship components got under way. As a matter of expediency, conventional aeroplane fuselages of several types were brought into service as control cars for the blimps; all used Renault or Rolls-Royce motors.

The blimps were difficult to manoeuvre and prone to mechanical trouble as they had been designed and built to a budget price, and the aircraft fuselages which were used for control cars were not really suitable for the task. The Renault 60 hp air-cooled motor, which had been designed for faster movement through the air to cool its cylinders, developed cracked cylinder heads due to the continuous overheating and the British manufactured magnetos fitted to these engines were a never-ending source of trouble. Breakdowns and subsequent drifting were the rule rather than the exception, and even if the crew were able to effect repairs to the engine, one of the crew then had to clamber outboard and stand on a narrow skid as he attempted to start the engine by swinging the heavy propeller—not the most enviable of tasks when carried out several hundred feet over the North Sea.

The envelopes of the earlier non-rigids were small, only 143 feet long and with a maximum diameter of 27 feet, giving a volume of 60,000 cubic feet. A tubular sleeve suspended beneath the envelope in the airscrew's slipstream directed air up into the ballonet to maintain the designed shape of the envelope.

As a result of experience gained with the Sea Scouts a further type, the S.S. Zero, was developed with a slightly larger envelope having a maximum diameter

The Army airship *Beta*, which became No 17 when transferred to the RNAS and was employed at Pulham mainly on training duties.

of 30 feet and a volume of 70,500 cubic feet. One of the main improvements was the substitution of a specially designed control car for the aeroplane fuselage of the earlier type, giving greater comfort for the crew, who were also given increased confidence by the knowledge that the design of the control car incorporated boat-like qualities so that in the event of a forced landing at sea their chances of survival were greatly enhanced. The S.S. Zero also had a simplified tail unit with two horizontal tailplanes and a single underslung fin and rudder instead of the two fins above and below the envelope of the Sea Scout.

Further development resulted in the Sea Scout Twin (S.S.T.) powered by two 75 hp Rolls-Royce engines mounted on an outrigger gantry above the control car, which accommodated a crew of four. This type had a length of 165 feet and a maximum diameter of 35 feet, with a volume of 100,000 cubic feet. The provision of twin engines produced only a marginal improvement in performance, the forward speed being increased by no more than 1 mph, but the extra power unit did give crews a much greater sense of security; engine failure had resulted in the loss of several of the single-engined airships and their crews.

Although this variant of the Sea Scout was developed during 1916 it did not enter service until the following year, as did another development of the Sea

Scout, the S.S.P., which was similar in many respects to the original S.S. but had a better performance.

Many of the lessons learnt from the operations of the earlier types and from their many shortcomings were incorporated in the Coastal or C class, which had a length of 195 feet and a maximum diameter of 37 feet. The volume was 170,000 cubic feet. A much larger control car, which had skids for landing purposes, was fitted to the Coastal. Mounted on the car were two 150 hp Sunbeam water-cooled motors, two 100 hp Berliet Ford or two 200 hp Renault motors. In spite of the variation in power all these power plants gave the C class an approximate range of 545 miles and a duration of eleven hours at full speed or fifteen hours at three-quarter speed; in the case of the Sunbeams the maximum speed in still air was 47 mph.

A crew of five were carried in open cockpits, seating being in line astern with the coxswain in the front seat, followed by the pilot, the observer, the wireless operator and, last of all, the engineer. Two water-cooled Vickers machine-guns were fitted as defensive armament.

Further modifications to the design resulted in the C star type, of which ten were built. Envelope dimensions continued to increase, the first three of the type being 207 feet long and the rest ten feet longer. Diameter of all this class was 49 feet, and the volume around 210,000 cubic feet. The power car of these airships contained a 360 hp Fiat and a 110 hp Berliet Ford engine, both of these being water cooled.

The first of another new type, the N.S.1, arrived at Pulham Air Station on 8th April, 1917, to conduct operational trials which revealed a number of minor defects, most of which were rectified without too much trouble. This, the North Sea type, was the last non-rigid to be developed during the First World War, a total of sixteen being built.

The North Sea type was designed and built at the Royal Naval Air Station at Kingsnorth, across the Medway from the dockyard at Chatham, with the intention of producing an airship suitable for long patrols over the North Sea in co-operation with naval surface ships. Initial orders for the type were for six craft. The original order was dated January, 1916, and N.S.1 took to the air for its maiden flight on 1st January, 1917.

The specification was quite ambitious for the period, the requirement being a craft of fairly large dimensions which would have a twenty-hour duration at a speed of 55 mph. The North Sea type had a trilobe envelope—that is, looked at head-on the envelope had the appearance of a clover leaf, with two lobes at the bottom and one at the top—with a length of 262 feet and a gas capacity of 360,000 cubic feet. The lifting gas was, of course, hydrogen.

The envelope was of the French Astra-Torres design, with many of the rigging lines housed within the envelope. This had the twin advantages of keeping the rigging lines out of the weather and reducing aerodynamic drag,

A marvel of improvisation, the Sea Scout non-rigids proved most successful and gave rise to a number of variants including, above, the S.S.P. or pusher type, designed by Lieutenant F. M. Rope and Warrant Officer Righton. Below is the original Sea Scout with twin engines, S.S.E.2, designed at the Royal Naval Air Station at Mullion in Cornwall and hence known as the Mullion Twin.

Both Stuart Leslie collection

while also allowing the control car to be slung close beneath the envelope, thus keeping drag to a minimum. In an emergency the top lobe could be rapidly deflated by means of two ripping lines operated from the control car.

To maintain the aerodynamic shape, in the two bottom lobes there were six ballonets with a total capacity of 120,000 cubic feet built into the lower part of these lobes; air was blown into these through internal tubing, the air being admitted to the ballonets through crab-pot non-return valves. These ballonets occupied some 35.5 per cent of the total internal volume of the envelope. To blow air into the six ballonets retractable scoops were lowered into the slipstream of the propellers.

Early craft of the North Sea type carried their fuel in light alloy tanks attached to the outside of the envelope in the cleft formed by the top and bottom lobes. Operational experience, however, proved that this arrangement was unsatisfactory due to the long pipes necessary to convey the fuel from the tanks to the engines being susceptible to fracture due to the changing shape of the envelope. Modifications were carried out and the fuel tanks slung on the internal rigging within the envelope, from where shorter, more rigid fuel lines ran down to a header tank above the engines.

Aerodynamic control was achieved by two large vertical fins mounted on top of and underneath the rear of the envelope, a rudder being attached to the rear of the lower fin to give directional control. At 90 degrees to the vertical fins were mounted the tailplanes carrying the two elevators. All the stabilising and control surfaces were of orthodox wooden frame construction with fabric covering. Kingposts extended from these structures to support external bracing wires to give extra stiffness and prevent warping.

Accommodation for the crew of ten was in the control car, closely suspended beneath the fore part of the envelope. Constructed of steel tubing, cross braced with steel wires, the structure, 35 feet long by 6 feet high, was covered with light alloy sheeting, plywood and doped fabric. Large windows in the front and sides of the car and a series of portholes in the aft section made this structure light and airy, and provided the crew with the most spacious and comfortable accommodation provided for airship crews up to that time.

The flying controls were housed in the forward part of the car, as well as the air and gas valve controls, the telegraphs to indicate to the engineers the revolutions required and the voicepipes which allowed communication among the crew members. In true naval tradition the steering wheel was a replica of a ship's wheel; a similar wheel situated on the side of the car operated the elevator for height control. These positions were manned by the Chief Coxswain and the Height Coxswain. From this section of the car ran lines, guided over pulleys and through fairleads, to the valves in the ballonets and gas portions of the envelope. There were six air and four gas valves. These valves, although normally manually operated from the control car to discharge gas, were also automatically operated if design pressures were exceeded in the ballonets or envelope. Other control lines actuated the water ballast valves and allowed this essential commodity to be discharged as height requirements dictated.

Behind the forward section of the car was the navigation cabin, equipped with chart table, navigation instruments, signalling equipment and all the paraphernalia required to guide the airship on its course. Side by side with the navigator's compartment was the Wireless Telegraphy Room, where the duty operator transmitted and received wireless messages to and from base, other airships and surface ships. Adjacent to and behind these two operational sections was the cabin where the off-duty watch slept; the crew maintained a two-watch system of five men per watch. Electric lighting in the control and power cars was provided by dynamos and batteries which also powered the signalling and wireless equipment.

Aft of the tapered-off rear end of the control car were the mechanics' car and the two engines, the two cars being separated by a few feet and linked by a wooden gangway with wire handrails and, usually, canvas sides. The designers stated that the reason for the gap was that it helped to decrease vibration and noise in the navigation, W/T and sleeping sections. Mounted outboard in parallel were the two 250 hp Rolls-Royce Eagle water-cooled engines driving four-bladed wooden pusher airscrews through a complicated transmission system of

The N.S.7, a representative of the final class of non-rigid airship, the North Sea type. The enclosed cabin and motor compartment provided much better working conditions for the crew. N.S.7 was the last non-rigid to serve with the Royal Air Force. *Mr Roger Aldrich*

A North Sea non-rigid returns to Pulham at the end of a patrol over the North Sea looking out for U-boats and floating mines. The crew are probably relieved to see the Pulham sheds.   *Mrs M. Martin*

gearing and independent shafts. Various other engines were used of Rolls-Royce and Fiat design and these ranged from 250 hp to 300 hp. Situated between the engines was the engineers' car where the crew members responsible for the power plants and their maintenance in flight were housed. It also contained the engineers' end of the speed indicators from the control car telegraphs for engine speeds. Stowed in odd corners were the various tools needed for in-flight maintenance. Of paramount importance was the electric soldering iron, in almost constant use for radiator and pipeline repairs; unlike the aeroplane, the airship could do its own repairs while aloft.

Large inflated airbags located beneath the control and power cars served the dual purpose of cushioning the effect of a heavy landing and providing buoyancy in the event of a landing on the sea.

A vertical canvas tube containing a rope ladder gave access from the control car to a gun position on the top surface of the upper lobe of the envelope. From this position a Lewis gun could be used against enemy aircraft, other guns being deployed from the windows of the control car. Some of the type carried additional armament on a mounting beneath the engines for downward defence. Up to 800 lb of bombs were carried as the occasion demanded in racks below the control car and these were released by wire lines and toggles.

During their early days the North Sea type ran into a few snags, mostly arising from the airscrew transmission. The first of the transmission defects manifested itself during a long-range endurance test carried out from Pulham by N.S.1 on 5th June, 1917; all went well for sixteen long hours, and then a universal joint broke, leaving the N.S.1 to limp slowly home to Pulham on one engine.

Repaired, N.S.1 set out again on 26th June and recorded a flight of 49 hours 22 minutes, during which time 1,536 miles were covered and only minor faults cropped up. The engines consumed 730 gallons of petrol and 24 gallons of oil during the flight. On the following day the second ship of the type, the N.S.2, left Kingsnorth for a trial flight out towards Pulham and back, but the airship lost lift through loss of gas and was wrecked when it attempted to land in a field on the outskirts of Stowmarket[5]. It did eventually reach its destination, as a salvage party from Pulham picked up the remains of the ship and took them home.

The arrival back at base of the non-rigids was not always a straightforward operation, as in many cases something would have gone wrong during the flight and although the ship had succeeded in crossing the coast it could not always reach Pulham. Returning partially disabled, a "Pig" might be forced to alight in a field, sometimes some considerable distance from its base, and local residents would turn out in force, dropping their tools both in the field and workshop to go to the assistance of the usually exhausted crew. Holding on to the trail ropes which hung from the sides of the envelope, the volunteers would restrain and guide the ship as it floated along over hedge and ditch back towards the station. Bumps and bruises, aching limbs and torn clothing were the order of the day, but there was never a lack of helpers for the task when the call went out for assistance.

The Pulham trials of the N.S.1 proceeded, with various modifications being made to the ever-troublesome transmission system. The conclusion of these trials was that the type had been brought into service before it had been proved and that further more prolonged trials would have to be carried out. The cure was eventually found when in 1918 the Rolls-Royce engines and the complicated, many-jointed airscrew transmission arrangement were replaced by Fiat engines driving the airscrews direct.

Later in the year the North Sea ships were moved up to Scotland to operate over the northern North Sea as information had been received that German U-boats were active in this vicinity and the N.S. type with its longer range was suitable for this long-range patrol work. Sixteen were built and several served right up to the time of the Armistice. Post war they were used for mine detection patrols and minesweeping experiments, and one, N.S.14, was sent to the USA for evaluation. One achievement post war was a flight by N.S.11 of 101 hours and 4,000 miles. Last non-rigid to serve with the Royal Air Force was N.S.7.

CHAPTER FOUR

Fully Fledged

WITH the dawn of the year 1917 Pulham Air Station was emerging as a major establishment, with experiments in parachute development and in cinematography being carried out as a sideline to the normal airship development work.

The commanding officer at this time was Colonel E. M. Maitland, an officer who had already shown great devotion to the airship cause. Listened to by all those in authority because of his deep knowledge of balloons and airships, he was also greatly respected by those who served under him and it was no surprise that later in 1917 he was appointed Superintendent of Airships at the Admiralty, with the new rank of air commodore.

Edward Maitland had seen service with the Essex Regiment in the Boer War and was still serving with that regiment when he took up ballooning. He was one of three men who in 1908 covered a record-breaking 1,117 miles in a balloon, flying from the Crystal Palace in London to Mateki Derevni in Russia. He was subsequently appointed to the Air Battalion and on the formation of the Royal Flying Corps became commanding officer of No 1 (Airship) Squadron. When all airships were taken over by the Royal Navy he transferred to the RNAS and found himself in Belgium in command of the *Beta* and some captive balloons employed on artillery spotting duties. In 1915 he took command of the Kite Balloon Training Station at Roehampton in Surrey, and two years later was appointed to Pulham.

Officers and men of the Air Construction Corps billeted in Pulham Market were at this time employed on levelling the ground for the erection of a large shed for rigid airships. The actual erection of the shed was carried out by civilian engineering contractors, and when they had finished their work the new shed was painted in a camouflage scheme designed by Flight Lieutenant Wheelwright, who in pre-war days had been an artist.

Posted to Pulham from Blandford in Dorset in June, 1917, was Mr G. Greenwood, of Lincoln, who recalls that the air station seemed at the time to be "a sort of mixed establishment with men in both navy blue and khaki uniforms",

A head-on view of the trilobe envelope of a Coastal non-rigid airship, introduced in 1916. Thirty-five of this class were built.   *Stuart Leslie collection* although officially it was a Royal Naval Air Station. "About this time the War Office was forming a unit of the Royal Flying Corps composed of skilled engineers, electricians, bricklayers and joiners, all of whom would be employed in the construction of airfields," he says. "It was named the Air Construction Service, or ACS. Pulham appeared to be a drafting station from which skilled men were sent to airfields under construction. Our commanding officer was Captain Haines, and I also remember a Lieutenant Jacks and a Chief Petty Officer Crooks."

The station had also become the headquarters of the Parachute Experimental Staff, who were testing somewhat rudimentary parachutes as a means of escaping from disabled airships and kite balloons. Nobody had yet thought of jumping from a moving aeroplane, it being deemed more practicable to attempt to land a crashing aeroplane, provided it was not on fire, than to launch oneself into space with only a silken umbrella to provide a dubious measure of safety. Moreover, the cumbersome parachute in use in 1917 could hardly be stowed in the restricted cockpit of an aeroplane, though it was possible to find space for it in the slightly more roomy gondola of an airship.

Experimental drops were usually made from an altitude of 200 feet, the canopy deployment and rate of descent being closely observed and recorded. If to modern eyes this altitude might seem rather low, it should be explained that this was well before the era of the free-fall parachute. The canopy was carried in a container attached to the airship gondola or the kite balloon basket, the weight of the falling airman dragging the silken canopy from the container; it deployed almost as soon as it had left its housing, if all went according to plan. Colonel Maitland, who had earlier been the first man to parachute from an airship, himself made a successful parachute descent from the C.17 on 13th February, 1917, when the airship was flying at an altitude of 1,000 feet over the station, the whole proceedings being recorded by both still and cine photography from an escorting airship, the C.27. He landed safely.

Later in the year a number of naval officers were treated to a full-scale demonstration by the Pulham unit, a number of dummies being dropped by parachute for the edification of Rear-Admiral Everett, Commodore Sir Reginald Tyrwhitt, in command of Harwich Force, and Commodore A. A. Ellison, in command at Lowestoft.

Pulham's first rigid airship, HMA No 9, arrived during April, 1917. It had already become a white elephant due to a very long constructional period which made it almost obsolete before it was completed[6]. The original design had been started late in 1914 by Vickers but the war diverted funds to what were deemed more urgent projects. Work was taken up again a year later and proceeded in an on-off manner, the craft eventually being launched during November, 1916. No 9 suffered from changes of policy and design alterations; even when it was partially constructed the design of the keel was changed. One of the features of

No 9 was that the structure was much more robust than that of the German Zeppelins, as the Admiralty envisaged that this craft would in the main be handled and flown by inexperienced officers and men and therefore would come in for more punishment and damage than might be expected from operational crews.

Even the power units were changed by a quirk of fate. Originally No 9 was to have been driven by four German-designed Maybach petrol engines built by the Wolseley Company under licence from Vickers giving 180 hp, but in September, 1916, the Zeppelin L-33 had been forced down at Little Wigborough in Essex. The wreckage was examined minutely and great interest was taken in the L-33's undamaged Maybach engines which were of an improved

The enclosed cabin of HMA No 5, one of the British-built Parsevals, which entered service in 1917, although ordered from Vickers long before. This photograph, taken on 22nd December, 1917, shows very well the uniform of the RNAS ground crew and the leather coats of the airshipmen.
Norman Peake

design and gave 240 hp. After detailed examination at the Airship Testing Station at Kingsnorth, an engine was sent to Vickers to be installed in No 9 in place of two of the smaller engines. It was thought at the time that this engine had been developed for high altitude work and as No 9 was intended for low altitude operations the engine was re-workcd for this type of running. This involved removing the pistons and shortening them to lower the compression ratio. The designers need not have bothered, as this engine was a low altitude one all the time!

The first British naval airship of rigid configuration to fly, HMA No 9 had left her makers' shed for the first time on 16th November, 1916, but ran into trouble from the outset; part of the control car bottom surface was damaged as it left the shed. When this damage was repaired it emerged again, only for the discovery to be made that it was incapable of lifting the contract weight. The Admiralty refused to accept it. It was at this time that in order to reduce weight, Vickers changed the No 9's gasbags for lighter ones and mounted the

The first British rigid airship to fly, HMA No 9 was resident at Pulham from April, 1917, until she was broken up in June, 1918. She was employed at Pulham on experimental work.   *Mr Roger Aldrich*

ex-Zeppelin motor in place of the two smaller ones. In this state the airship was accepted for service on 4th April, 1917, and flown to Howden Airship Station in Yorkshire and later to Pulham. At the Norfolk station a specially drafted landing party of 1,000 men arrived to carry out the landing of the station's first rigid airship.

One of No 9's tasks, all of which were of an experimental nature, was to be moored out on to drogues in the nearby Wash to test over-water mooring techniques. She was brought down to about 350 feet to windward of a mooring buoy. A sea anchor or drogue was lowered from the ship's nose into the water, and as the ship drifted astern past the buoy a launch attached the drogue (which, by then, contained about two tons of seawater) to the buoy using a rope some 500 feet long. The ship then rode high on the single rope, while the drogue remained too heavy to lift. Sideswings produced by changes in wind direction, so dangerous in most mooring experiments, were largely damped out by the drogue dragging through the water—which it did on an arc about 500 feet radius, with the buoy as centre. No 9 was also moored out at Pulham to evaluate open anchoring systems. While engaged on these menial jobs the airship suffered quite a considerable amount of superficial damage, due to handling in and out of the shed. This procedure was often carried out with the airship's bow hawser tethered to a winch mounted on the rear of a heavy tractor or an ex-Army tank whose delicacy of manoeuvring was not all that could be desired. After being shedded at Pulham on 29th October, 1917, the unfortunate craft remained there until June, 1918, when after a comparatively short flying life of 198 hours it was broken up and struck off charge on the 28th of that month.

Part of No 9 remained at Pulham for some time as the Commanding Officer had twenty feet of the airship's bow cut off intact and erected as a proboscian bandstand and rose trellis.

In passing it is interesting to note that a man who was to be one of Britain's great aircraft designers, Barnes Wallis, was involved with the design of No 9. One disconcerting fact regarding No 9 was that the craft entered service four years after commencement of design, while at this time the Germans were producing comparable craft on a ten-week schedule from keel-laying to acceptance flight.

Extended operational trials continued with one of the North Sea ships, and an endurance flight of 49½ hours was achieved. One unusual feature of this design was that the twelve petrol tanks were located outside the tri-lobe envelope and as it became necessary for fuel to be switched from one tank to another for trimming purposes one of the engineers had to climb up from the control car on · to the top of the envelope lobe to turn the appropriate taps, not a very enviable task during the hours of darkness over the North Sea. Later models had the petrol tanks slung inside the envelope and there was a facility for making these switching operations from the control car.

In the early days of the air station hydrogen for the airships was brought to the station in large cylinders, but early in 1916 a gas-producing plant was constructed on the eastern side of the station. Early in the war portable silicol plants capable of producing 2,500 cubic feet of hydrogen per hour were supplied to airship stations, and later the Admiralty replaced these with larger fixed silicol plants yielding up to 10,000 cubic feet per hour.

These silicol plants, which are illustrated and described in the *Admiralty Hydrogen Manual* produced in January, 1916, involved the use of caustic soda and produced a poisonous sludge which had to be disposed of on site. The present farmer, Mr Duncan West, says that to this day nothing will grow on that part of the site on which the waste material was dumped.

The gas was stored in three large and one medium-sized gas holders on the other side of the road. There were also two small tanks to hold gas alongside the plant, which was housed in a tight group of brick buildings with asbestos-clad roofs. A network of pipes ran from the gas plant by way of a valve house and a control and pump house to filling points near the sheds, and it was here that the airships received their supplies of lifting gas.

The silicol plants had to be used with considerable care as if the process was not properly controlled there was a danger of explosion. Such an explosion occurred in the Pulham plant on 14th April, 1917, at midday. Two men were blown through the side of the gas house; one of them, Lieutenant Wildmass, was killed and the other, a rating, died later. The gas officer, Lieutenant Mitten, was badly shocked when he was covered with caustic soda and a civilian workman was badly burned. Also injured were Lieutenant Bevington and Lieutenant Pollett, who with the other casualties were taken to a military hospital in Norwich.

The *Admiralty Hydrogen Manual*, as revised in October, 1916, and November, 1918, contains an illustration of a hydrogen installation which might be that at Pulham. This manual also describes the steam-iron process for the production of hydrogen which by 1918 was operating at all large airship stations, including Pulham, which had a steam-iron plant capable of producing 14,000 cubic feet per hour.

Pulham also had a plant producing hydrogen by the expensive and somewhat limited electrolytic process, in which water was broken down into hydrogen and oxygen by using an electric current. The considerable amount of electrical current required was provided by diesel-powered generators housed in a large brick building on the opposite side of the road to the gas plant. Water was provided from a deep well adjacent to the plant. The well and the pumping plant were later used by Depwade Rural District Council for providing a public

An aerial view of Pulham showing the station gas plant and No 1 Shed. Beyond this shed can be seen the concrete floor of the second shed, moved to Cardington in 1928. *Mr Roger Aldrich*

Coastal airship C.17 which was shot down over the southern North Sea in April, 1917, by German seaplanes flying from Zeebrugge. The crew of five all perished.   *Mr Roger Aldrich*

supply, and now, fully modernised, still function as part of the Anglian Water Authority's network.

The same week that saw the explosion in the Pulham gas plant also saw the loss of one of Pulham's non-rigid airships, the C.17, with all its crew while on patrol. A wireless message was received from the C.17 at 09.30, then nothing more was heard until a fishing boat reported that an airship had been seen to come down in flames off the North Foreland.

Later the German radio reported that an airship had been shot down off Nieuport, Belgium, by German fighter floatplanes from the seaplane base at Zeebrugge in the face of intense defensive machine-gun fire from the airship. Those lost with the C.17 were Flight Sub-Lieutenant E. G. C. Jackson, the pilot; Chief Petty Officer Chivers, coxswain; Assistant Paymaster H. Warlters, observer; L. M. Farquhar, engineer; and A. M. Munro, wireless operator.

After the loss of the C.17 patrolling airships were ordered to obtain their position by wireless every hour when out of sight of land. This procedure assisted the airship's navigation, but it also made life a good deal easier for the pilots of German fighter floatplanes operating from Belgian bases; instead of having to search for their prey they were able to fly direct to its approximate position in order to make their attacks[7].

These floatplanes became quite adventurous during this period. Two of them attacked the 2,784 gross ton steamer *Gena*, a vessel which had been built at Whitby in 1893, off the Suffolk coast on 1st May, 1917. One was shot down by the *Gena's* defensive guns but the other launched a torpedo which hit the ship, causing severe damage. The *Gena* managed to limp towards shallow water, where it sank without loss of life. It was fortunate that no Pulham blimp was in the vicinity at the time of this attack as it would have been no match for the marauding aircraft.

Nevertheless, airship patrols continued in all but the very worst of weather in spite of all kinds of mechanical troubles manifesting themselves. One of the commonest problems was broken petrol pipes caused by vibration; the engineer was usually able to carry out a makeshift repair. Another common problem was the shearing of the magneto drive. Vibration was the cause of many breakdowns,

A Brandenburg two-seater fighter seaplane of the type which shot down the C.17. The example shown was captured and used by the RNAS for evaluation purposes. *Mrs Pomeroy*

including faults with the radiator, which was a vital part of the power plant. Propeller bolts were apt to work loose; when this happened the engine would be stopped and an engineer would have to climb out to tighten the bolts, a perilous task that called for agility of a high order. Self-starters were unknown at that time and in order to get the engine working again the propeller had to be turned, first of all to suck fuel into the cylinders and then to get the engine firing. For this operation the engineer on his precarious perch needed the assistance of another member of the crew on the hand starter magneto; when the engine fired the engineer had very quickly to get out of the way of the swiftly turning propeller blades.

Without an engine the airship was merely a free balloon, at the mercy of the wind, so the efficient functioning of the power plant was absolutely necessary for the well being of both ship and crew. In December, 1917, two of Pulham's Coastal airships were lost, one of them through enemy action and the other through running out of fuel.

Three Brandenburg floatplanes from the Zeebrugge seaplane base were responsible for the loss of C.27 on 11th December, 1917, with all her crew of five. The battle was all over in two minutes, the airship being shot down in flames by Oberleutnant Friedrich Christiansen. Among those lost was the airship captain, Flight Sub-Lieutenant Dixon.

The car of Sea Scout S.S.41, showing the flexible pipes bringing fuel from the petrol tanks which proved so vulnerable. The air scoop supplying air to the ballonets is also clearly seen.   *Norman Peake*

34

The Coastal airship C.27 falling in flames after being shot down by Oberleutnant Friedrich Christiansen.   *Norman Peake*

Next day another Pulham airship, the C.26, captained by Flight Sub-Lieutenant Kilburn, carried out an extensive search of the area in which the C.27 had been lost, but neither wreckage nor any survivor was found. At the conclusion of the search Kilburn turned the airship for home, but he had reckoned without the very stiff westerly breeze. Fuel consumption was soon giving cause for concern, and before land had been sighted the tanks ran dry. Drifting before the wind, the helpless airship was blown back across the North Sea and over the Dutch coast. The crew eventually brought it down at Eesmess in Holland, where they were interned for the remainder of the war.

As a result of the loss of the C.17, C.26 and C.27 it was decided to discontinue the coastal airship patrols off the East Anglian coastline. Operations from Pulham were restricted to patrols by rigid airships, with the recently arrived HMA No 23 playing the major role.

The first of the "23 class", No 23 had arrived at Pulham on 15th September, 1917, her construction by Vickers having been somewhat protracted owing to the difficulties encountered during construction. She looked very much like her predecessor, HMA No 9; the hull was almost identical except that it contained an extra bay amidships which increased the gas capacity from the 866,000 cubic feet of No 9 to 942,000 cubic feet. Power was increased to 1,000 hp, but the engines of the new airship were found to be two tons heavier than their estimated weight.

After initial trials it was found that No 23 was overweight. Once again the Zeppelin L-33 came to the rescue, one of her wing power cars being used to replace the original engines of No 23. Other modifications were also made to No 23 before she took up residence at Pulham, where she was employed mainly in a training role.

One of the highlights of No 23's career came when she established a flight duration record of 40 hours 8 minutes. That record was bettered, however, by another ship of the "23 class", R.26, while flying from Howden in Yorkshire on 4th–5th June, 1918, though only by 32 minutes. Also dogged by faults, the R.26 arrived at Pulham late in her days to be used mainly for mooring experiments, her bows being strengthened for these trials.

Almost from her commissioning the R.26 seemed doomed for the breaker's hammer, and she did not serve very long at Pulham. She was struck off charge on 10th March, 1919.

The handling of these unwieldy rigid airships on the airfield required very large numbers of people, and many Norfolk men remember helping to hold

Built by Vickers at Barrow-in-Furness, HMA No 23 spent much of her life at Pulham and took part in some spectacular experimental work. She was not the most successful of the rigid airships, being overweight and underpowered.   *Mr Roger Aldrich*

A RNAS ground handling party with an early winch car seen beneath the belly of a non-rigid. Like all naval vessels the airship wears the Union Jack as well as the White Ensign, not visible in this picture. *Mr Roger Aldrich*

down the airships and walk them in and out of the sheds. As many as 350 to 400 people were sometimes needed; fortunately there seemed to be no shortage of volunteers in those days. All too often the unwieldy craft seemed to have a mind of its own as it was walked slowly across the airfield towards the shed by a numerous landing party, the slightest puff of wind causing it to leap upwards forty or fifty feet. Members of the handling party would of necessity cling desperately to the trailing ropes hanging from the airship's side as they were jerked as much as fifteen feet off the ground. Sometimes they hung on until the airship dropped and their feet touched the ground again, at other times they let go and fell back to earth; broken limbs were not unknown on such occasions.

Handling the airships on the ground was a job for hefty men, but at Pulham there was also a seemingly large number of women looking after the needs of the airships as well as those of their crews. There were vast areas of balloon fabric to be kept in good repair, and this was a job the women did superbly well. The mechanical side of the airship servicing was not beyond their capabilities and several women were employed as engineers; reports of their work show them to have been extremely efficient and most reliable.

In addition to those who were employed on the maintenance of the airships themselves there were the ladies who performed the task of messengers, riding their bicycles around the station in all weather, and others who served as cleaners, cooks, gardeners and clerks. Many of these ladies wore a cumbersome uniform comprising a long flowing dress with either a white or a black collar, depending on rank, lace-up boots and a large broad-brimmed felt hat—not the most glamorous of outfits. The inside jobs were carried out while dressed in a variety of garments according to the work involved.

Women engineers pose as they ascend a ladder to work on the engines of a rigid airship, the R.36, at Pulham. The size of the airscrew can be judged by comparison with the women on the ladder.
Mr T. L. Dodman

CHAPTER FIVE

Experimental Work

B IRTH of the Royal Air Force on 1st April, 1918, brought a degree of confusion to Pulham as the Royal Naval Air Service and the Royal Flying Corps were merged into a new service. Naval officers and Army officers alike found themselves wearing a new uniform and acquiring new ranks; naval flight lieutenants and flight sub-lieutenants became captains and lieutenants.

The technical organisation of the airship service remained under the control of the Superintendent of Airships at the Admiralty, Air Commodore Maitland, however. And airship stations such as Pulham continued to be designated Royal Naval Air Stations, despite the visible change from the dark blue of the naval uniform to the pale blue of the junior service which became evident as personnel acquired their new uniforms.

Experiments were carried out at Pulham during 1918 and 1919 into various methods of mooring out airships, both rigid and non-rigid. The background to these trials is described by Captain J. A. Sinclair in his book *Airships in Peace and War*, published in 1934:

> In this country we made the first serious attempt at mooring an airship so far back as 1911, in which year the Naval airship No. 1, commonly known as the *Mayfly*, was launched at Cavendish Dock, Barrow-in-Furness. This experiment did not last long owing to the ship becoming a complete wreck while handling her out of the shed. Shortly after this the Army Airship Section attempted the mooring of the *Delta* and the *Gamma* at Farnborough. It was during these experiments that the mooring mast was first introduced. Experiments were also carried out with these two ships and with the *Beta* on Salisbury Plain.
>
> When, just before hostilities broke out, all airships were handed over to the Navy, Commander Usborne turned his attention to the problem of mooring. He introduced a new system, that came to be known as the Usborne system, which was a big advance on anything attempted up to that time. The *Parseval* airship No. 4 was tried out on this system with most promising results. Commander Usborne was unfortunately killed in an airship accident in 1915. After his death the experiments in mooring were dropped for a while.
>
> The problem was taken up again by Commodore Masterman at Barrow. Experiments were carried out with various types of masts and a small non-rigid airship. At the same time experiments were begun with a similar type of ship and mast at Kingsnorth, under Group Captain Cave-Brown-Cave. The British airship service, which up to this time had been operating non-rigids, was now turning its attention to rigid airships, and a proposal was put forward to erect a mast at Pulham, the airship experimental station, with the object of testing mast mooring for rigid aircraft.

All mooring experiments were then transferred to Pulham, where an exhaustive series of experiments of various types of mooring was carried out, with both rigid and non-rigid ships.

The object of some of the exercises carried out at Pulham was that airship stations with sheds were rather far apart, and patrols might more conveniently start or finish at an intermediate point, provided the airship could be safely secured. This could be done if means could be found to detach the car rapidly so that the inflated envelope could be held down, belly on the ground, with sandbags. Additional "eta patches" were cemented along the envelope for the "bagging-down" ropes; once these ropes were holding the gasbag so that the car supports were slack, the car was released by specially designed slips and wheeled away on a bogey-trolley. The envelope could then be bagged down tightly to the ground in the lee of a belt of trees, or even in a forest clearing. At Pulham, with a practised team of eight men, it was found that a ship bagged down in this way

Below: The Sea Scout Zero S.S.Z.3 taking part in mooring trials on a snow-covered Pulham airfield. With extended handling ropes dangling fore and aft, she is moored by a single wire to a winch truck; four Eta patches have been attached to the side of the envelope to take one of the three bridles attaching the airship to the mooring wire—an arrangement similar to that employed on barrage balloons twenty years later. *Stuart Leslie collection*

Opposite: The semi-circular yoke of the Masterman mast is clearly seen in this view of S.S.36 at Pulham in September, 1918. A flexible canvas pipe allows the ship to be gassed while on the mast. *Stuart Leslie collection*

Opposite below: Three Sea Scout non-rigids moored out at Pulham on 4th September, 1918, using different types of experimental mooring. On the left is the Masterman mast with its yoke; S.S.14a in the middle of the picture appears to be moored by a single wire similar to that used by S.S.Z.3 in the photograph below; and on the right another Sea Scout is moored to a later type of mast. S.S.14a was originally S.S.13. *Stuart Leslie collection*

could be made operationally airborne in fourteen minutes and securely bagged down again within ten minutes of landing.

A second method, for rigids, was also tried out at Pulham. This required merely very securely anchored rings, set in an equilateral triangle 800 feet apart on the ground; from there, ropes were attached to the mooring cone in the ship's nose so that it could ride high on the pyramid of wires kept taught by its own lift, and yet still be able to swing with the wind like a weathercock. The R.9 was moored in this way for four days at Pulham, but the girders converging at the nose proved insufficiently strong to cope with the lateral thrust resulting from a sudden gusting change of wind direction; several of the girders sheered, bringing the experiment to an end for the time being.

The R.26, with her nose specially strengthened for that purpose, was afterwards successfully moored at Pulham in the same way. She remained on this mooring for ten days, but was destroyed when a heavy snowfall brought her crashing to the ground. Later, however, this same system was used to moor the R.34 at Mineola, Long Island, after her transatlantic flight in July, 1919, neither shed nor mooring mast being available at the American station.

Apart from the difficulty of disembarking crew, refuelling and revictualling, etc., this method required continual monitoring of the ballast and gas valves in order to keep the ship horizontal. Of course, this same problem also occurred at the mooring mast. Much later, with the R.100, but not at Pulham, it was partly overcome by keeping the ship light, but held down horizontally towards the tail by one or more heavy cricket-pitch rollers. As she swung at the mast, these would roll around on a circular path across the grass field.

Attempts to use this method with the S.S.29 at Pulham were not very successful, and it was deemed unsuitable for non-rigids.

The reorganisation of the service which resulted from the formation of the Royal Air Force led to the departure of Wing Captain E. A. Masterman, who as trials officer at Pulham had been in charge of the mooring experiments. With the rank of brigadier general he took over the Army's Scottish Command, his place as trials pilot at Pulham being taken by Wing Commander W. C. Hicks, an officer who was to continue in the airship service after the war.

One of the more secure pieces of equipment was the Masterman mast, named after its inventor. This was a comparatively short lattice mast terminating at the top in a vertical semi-circular yoke; at the outer ends of the yoke were attachments which engaged with mooring points on either side of the ship's bow section. The mast was rigged with wire guys so that it was held rigidly in its upright position. When moored to the mast the airship was able to rotate so that it was always head to wind. A discomforting feature of this system was the need for the crew to climb a rope ladder to gain access to the ship's gondola; but an advantage was that the system incorporated a flexible hose, allowing the ship to be supplied with gas while moored to the mast.

The R.26 on a three-wire mooring at Pulham in the winter of 1918–19 after she had been strengthened by the addition of diagonal wiring between frames two and three. She lay to this mooring for more than a week, but on the tenth day it rained and she absorbed two tons of water; then snow fell, and she came down to the ground, rolling around like a stranded whale. On the afternoon of 9th February, 1919, the snow melted; her cars were cut off and R.26 rose again to float through the night. Considerable structural damage had been suffered, however, and on 24th February it was decided to scrap her.   *Stuart Leslie collection*

The Masterman mast was purely experimental and did not enter regular service. Nor did another Pulham-designed mast which was similar in design and construction but lacked the yoke at the top; trials were carried out with this mast during 1918.

These experiments did eventually lead to the construction of a successful mooring mast which allowed the large rigid airships to moor directly to the mast without the intercession of a large ground handling party. This 120-foot mast was erected in 1919 in the centre of the airfield and during the nineteen-twenties was much used by the big rigids which set out to pioneer the civil use of airships. Unlike the later mooring mast at Cardington, the world's first giant cantilever mooring mast, with its lift to carry crewmen and passengers to the masthead, the Pulham mast had to be ascended by an exposed ladder on the outside of the lattice structure. Climbing such a ladder needed strong nerves as well as strong arms and legs, but such work came naturally to naval men who might have begun their service by climbing the rigging of a training brig.

Moving a big rigid from the mast into the shed still required a large handling party, though mechnical aid was enlisted even in this operation. No 23 was moved about the airfield with the aid of a tank of the very early type that had served in France when such "landships" were first introduced. This machine had been put into service at the air station pulling and pushing the massive doors of the airship sheds, and eventually it was fitted with a short steel mooring mast to which the airship could be secured. With the airship's bow attached to the mast the juggernaut would roar slowly along towards the shed; its power, supplied by a petrol engine, was adequate to the job but its manoeuvrability did leave much to be desired, and when it came to taking the airship into the shed it was left to the ground handling party to walk her in. Out on the airfield the tank's tracks

The early tank which was used at Pulham for opening and closing the hangar doors and for manoeuvring airships on the airfield.

Mr L. S. Smith

enabled it to travel over the softer stretches of ground when it was necessary to fetch one of the rigids into the shed area.

This machine supplemented the large steam traction engine equipped with a steam winch at the rear end which was used to handle airships on the ground and to manipulate the shed doors; the dangers of employing a steam engine to handle airships filled with inflammable hydrogen had to be accepted by the powers-that-be, but at least the traction engine's chimney was fitted with a spark arrester. In fairness it has to be stated that no accident ever did occur when using these two fearsome machines.

During 1917 and 1918 Pulham became more and more involved in experimental work, not all the activity being directed towards the development of mooring techniques. Major G. H. Scott, who had been involved with airships since the beginning of the war, was the chief experimental officer. He had begun his service as commander of HMA No 4, the German Parseval, and had gone on to command HMA No 9, the first rigid to enter service. He was destined to become captain of the R.34 and to command her on her pioneering transatlantic flights. As Assistant Director of Airship Development, Flying, he flew in R.100 on her successful crossings of the Atlantic in August, 1930, and was in the R.101 on what was to have been the first airship flight to India; he died when she crashed at Beauvais, in northern France.

The station staff grew with the drafting in of several non-flying officers who were engaged in engineering work in connection with the experiments carried on at Pulham. These included trials of defensive armaments for airships with HMA No 23 in the role of workhorse. One of the trials involved a 2-pdr quick-firing gun mounted in the upper gun position on top of No 23's hull; the gunner fired this weapon into the wide grassy expanse of the airfield as the airship cruised around the station at low altitude—the range rules must have been honoured more in the breach than in the observance. Conducting these trials was a young man from Vickers, Barnes Neville Wallis, who had learnt his trade under H. G. Pratt in Vickers' London office; he had worked on the design of HMA No 9 and the "23 class", and later in life was to win fame for his development of geodetic construction and the bouncing bomb. None of the shells fired into the grass was ever recovered, so it must be concluded that they ricocheted around the surrounding countryside instead of burying themselves in the Pulham turf.

Whatever the dangers posed by our own airships and their armament, it was the German Zeppelins that continued to strike fear into the hearts of the civilian

The Pulham tank prepares to move HMA No 23 across the airfield, aided by a very large ground handling party. By the time of this picture, probably taken in 1919, the tank had been fitted with a short mooring mast. *Stuart Leslie collection*

population in Britain. People living in the Pulham area heard the sound of German motors on the night of 12th–13th April, 1918, when the L-62 commanded by Hauptmann Kuno Manger circled over the area, dropping a few bombs in open countryside, when on his way to the industrial Midlands. There was good reason to fear the Zeppelins, because L-62 carried three 300kg bombs, fourteen 100kg bombs and twenty incendiary bombs, a load which could cause extensive damage and considerable loss of life when dropped on a town such as Coventry, which was Manger's target on this occasion. On his way home Manger circled high above the Norfolk landscape in a successful effort to elude fighter aircraft which were lying in wait for him; he crossed the coast near Great Yarmouth and reached his North German base in safety.

After the departure of No 38 Squadron from Thetford for duty in France other Home Defence squadrons were allocated for the protection of the air

An F.E.2b fighter of the kind which equipped No 51 Squadron.
Stuart Leslie collection

station at Pulham. These were No 75 Squadron, whose headquarters and B and C Flights were at Elmswell and whose A flight was at Hadleigh, and No 51 Squadron, which had its headquarters and C Flight at Narborough in the north-west of Norfolk, its A flight at Mattishall and its B Flight at Tydd St Mary, near Wisbech. No 75 Squadron was equipped with Avro 504 biplanes, a type which was better known as a training machine than as a fighter, and No 51 had the F.E. 2b pusher biplane.

The last Zeppelin raid on Britain occurred on 5th August, 1918, when the newly constructed L-70, commanded by Kapitän-leutnant Johann von Lossnitzer and with the chief of the German Naval Zeppelin Division, Fregattenkapitän Peter Strasser, on board, approached the Norfolk coast in company with a number of other naval airships. Unknown to the raider's crew a de Havilland D.H.4 from Great Yarmouth air station flown by Major Egbert Cadbury with Captain Robert Leckie as his gunner was cautiously stalking the Zeppelin. Cadbury manoeuvred into position so that Leckie could fire into the giant airship; in a few seconds the raider was ablaze from stem to stern, its red-hot remains plunging into the North Sea[8]. All the twenty-two crew members of the L-70 perished in the flames.

During four years of war the Zeppelins had made fifty-one raids on Great Britain, dropping 196 tons of bombs and killing 557 people and injuring another 1,358. The Zeppelin had developed rapidly during its operational life until the latest types introduced in 1918 could carry five tons of bombs and had a defensive armament of up to ten machine guns; perhaps most important of all, they could climb to altitudes in excess of 17,000 feet. Yet the loss of the L-70 showed that even the most magnificent of airships carrying 20 mm machine-cannon as well as lighter weapons was vulnerable to surprise attack by fighter aeroplanes using explosive and incendiary ammunition.

So it was that much thought was given at this time to the possibility of airships carrying their own defence in the form of fighter aircraft that could be released to fight off attacking aeroplanes. Officers from Pulham discussed the matter with technical officers from the Royal Naval Air Station at Great Yarmouth, who no doubt remembered an earlier ill-fated attempt to combine an airship and a heavier-than-air craft.

The earlier experiments, which had ended with the deaths of Squadron Commander W.P. de Courcy Ireland and Wing Commander N.F. Usborne, had been aimed at finding a means of attacking Zeppelins, which were able to climb much faster than the fighters which sought to destroy them. The officers concerned slung a complete B.E.2c fighter under the envelope of a Sea Scout airship, the idea being that until the aeroplane was released the combination should be handled as an airship; when the pilot was in a position to attack he would release the B.E.2c from the envelope and it would be handled as a normal fighter aircraft.

Now the idea was to give an airship its own fighter defence, and No 212 Squadron at Great Yarmouth was to be involved with carrying out the necessary research[9]. A system of trapeze and release gear was to be attached to the belly of the airship, and a corresponding set of engaging gear was to be fitted to the upper mainplane of a fighter. When the necessary equipment had been constructed the trapeze was fitted to the underside of HMA No 23 and a Sopwith Camel single-seat fighter was equipped with the engaging gear; a weighted dummy pilot was strapped into the Camel's cockpit, and all was ready for the initial tests—it is significant that this time there was to be no danger of the pilot being killed as a result of a malfunction of the release apparatus, as had happened in 1916.

The Camel was attached to the trapeze and the engine started; a control wire led from the throttle into the airship's control room so that the Camel's rotary engine could be revved as it left the trapeze in order to give the little aircraft flying speed. It might otherwise have stalled as it left the mother ship,

Opposite above: The attachment beneath the belly of HMA No 23 for the upper mainplane of a Sopwith Camel. The struts holding the attachment appear fragile. *Stuart Leslie collection*

Above: A camel attached to HMA No 23 awaiting takeoff from Pulham for the release trials. The power car with its outriggers carrying swivelling airscrews is well seen in this view.
Mr T. L. Dodman

Opposite below: Sopwith Camel D6635, one of a batch built by Boulton and Paul Limited at Norwich, waits on the airfield at Pulham to be attached to HMA No 23, which is being walked across the field by a host of ground handlers.
Stuart Leslie collection

although the controls had been set to give the aircraft a natural glide once it had been released.

After the system had been given extensive testing on the ground No 23 took off one day in June, 1918, with the Camel hanging from the trapeze and flew to a sparsely populated area not far from Pulham. The Camel's motor was speeded up, the release gear actuated, and the fighter dropped gently from beneath its carrier and made a powered glide down to a soft landing in a large field. The system worked satisfactorily.

The first man to be released from an airship in this way was Lieutenant R. E. Keys, DFC, of No 212 Squadron. In another Camel he successfully accomplished release from No 23, started his motor and circled around the airship before landing safely at Pulham. The airship was commanded at the time of this experiment by Flight Lieutenant G. M. Thomas, DFC.

Experiments with the aircraft release gear continued for some time. On 6th November No 23 carried out another "aircraft carrier" experiment, this time with a pair of Sopwith Camels of the type known as Ship Camels because they had been modified for naval work. They had again come from Great Yarmouth. The two aircraft were attached to a slightly modified release apparatus mounted beneath No 23's hull, both of them piloted by officers from No 212 Squadron. Each of the aircraft was released in its turn, and both flew down to land at Pulham.

While the two Camels were being borne aloft by No 23 an airship of a type not seen before at Pulham was circling around awaiting its chance to land at the air station. This was S.R.1, the designation standing for semi-rigid, that is, an airship with an envelope similar to that of a non-rigid but with a keel. It arrived at Pulham at 13.30 but was obliged to wait for more than an hour while No 23 dropped her "chicks" and did not land until 14.40.

The S.R.1 had been built in Italy and had been purchased by the British Government with the intention of gaining experience with this type of airship. A British crew had been sent by troopship to France and thence by rail to Italy to deliver the new airship to her base at Pulham. The delivery crew comprised:

Captain	Captain G. F. Meager
Chief Officer	Captain T. B. Williams
Coxswain	Chief Petty Officer G. F. Clarke
First Engineer	Chief Petty Officer R. G. Owen
Second Engineer	Petty Officer A. Leach
Third Engineer	Petty Officer R. Tomlins
First Wireless Op.	Leading Mechanic B. Bocking
Second Wireless Op.	Air Mechanic R. J. Rook
Italian passenger	Lieutenant di Rossi

When the party arrived at the Italian airship works at Ciampino, near Rome, the airship had not been completed, so members of the delivery crew filled in the time with a spell of sightseeing. When at last the new airship was ready for trials two officers arrived from England to oversee the trials; they were Major R. Cochrane, who in the Second World War as Air Chief Marshal Sir Ralph Cochrane was to win fame as the author of the famous dam-busting raids carried out by No 617 Squadron, and Flight Lieutenant Michael Rope, a leading airship design technician who was later to be lost in the R.101.

Inspections and trials were satisfactorily accomplished, and after a few minor modifications had been carried out all was ready for the trip to England; but the start was delayed by unfavourable weather conditions. Eventually S.R.1 left Ciampino at 4.25 pm, Central European Time, on 28th October, 1918, to fly

The S.R.1 arriving at the end of her eventful delivery flight from Italy. She spent almost her entire active life at Pulham.   *Norman Peake*

across the South of France, up through the middle of France and then across the English Channel to the airship station at Kingsnorth in Kent[10].

It was by no means beyond the bounds of possibility that French troops would mistake the S.R.1 for a Zeppelin and would open fire, so special precautions had to be taken to ensure the semi-rigid's safe passage over French territory. The likelihood of a hostile reception from French soldiers was by no means the only peril of that flight; there was also the lashing wind and rain which seemed to accompany the airship on its flight, and the temperamental running of one of the motors, which needed almost constant attention to keep it functioning.

The fracturing of an oil line was just one incident among several that created danger for the delivery crew. Hot dirty oil spurted from the fracture and ran all over the floor of the control car as the engineers worked frantically to repair the pipe, leaving the floor like a skating rink; the crew had to take great precautions to avoid anybody falling overboard.

When passing over Chauffailles part of the exhaust manifold of the midships engine above the control car burnt through, crashing down on to the petrol tanks immediately below. The red-hot manifold lay in close proximity to hundreds of gallons of high-octane aviation fuel and beneath almost half a million cubic feet of equally inflammable hydrogen. Realising their danger, Captain Williams and Petty Officer Leach leapt up a ladder and pushed the burning mass overboard, at the same time brushing out glowing sparks with their hands.

By contrast the next day's misadventure seemed to present little danger. Captain Williams was manning the elevator controls in the height coxswain's position as the airship flew slowly along at low altitude in near-blind conditions, the clouds reaching almost down to ground level. Looking out from the side of the control car, Captain Williams was watching intently as the airship made a gentle descent so the navigator could check its position. Suddenly a small hillock loomed up through the murk, and on top of the hillock was a brown and white cow. Captain Williams stared at the cow, and the cow seemed to stare at Captain Williams, who wondered which of them was the more startled by the unexpected confrontation.

In spite of such vicissitudes the S.R.1 crossed the Channel and made a safe landing at Kingsnorth, where a pause was made for the weary crew to rest and for the airship to be overhauled. Then, on 6th November, the S.R.1 left for her new home at Pulham, her crew joined by a Colonel Cunningham, a senior airship officer. Even on this relatively short trip it proved difficult to keep all three motors running together, but the crew were by then well aware of the shortcomings of the power units and of the action needed to get them running again when they faltered.

Every member of the S.R.1 delivery crew was decorated after the flight from Italy. The Italian Government awarded the Croix de Guerre to Captain Meager, who was the first airship officer to receive such an award, and Captain Williams received the Air Force Cross.

The S.R.1 was airborne on the day after its arrival, making a local flight to give some senior airship officers an insight into its handling capabilities, and it was aloft again on 7th December when it carried out an extensive flight over the North Sea with a party of naval officers and boffins who were engaged on secret work in the anti-submarine field.

One result of the arrival of S.R.1 was that Pulham acquired an airshipman as adjutant, for Captain Williams, who had had accountancy training before joining the service, was put in charge of the station's administration.

Not all Pulham's airships were by any means as new as S.R.1. One of the early blimps which had made its flight trials at Vickers' works at Barrow during

1915 was modified at Pulham in 1918. This was HMA No 6, a Parseval airship which, like its sister ship HMA No 7, had a length of 312 feet, a diameter of 51 feet and a volume of 364,000 cubic feet. Old as she was, No 6 continued to perform a useful role as a coastal patrol craft and was used for mine-spotting duties.

Another Pulham blimp, N.S.11, created an endurance record by remaining aloft for 61 hours 30 minutes during the course of a long-range mine-spotting patrol. Delivered in September, 1918, she was one of the last of the non-rigids to enter service.

Two days before the signing of the Armistice one of the Pulham airships was given a part in the Lord Mayor's Show in London, the R.26 flying low over the route of the procession. It was the first time that such a duty had been carried out by the Royal Air Force—and the last.

With the ending of hostilities there came an easing of tension, but the work of the air station went on just the same. On 20th November, 1918, two of the

HMA No 23 which besides the aircraft release experiments carried out armament trials at Pulham under the watchful eye of Barnes Wallis. Modifications visible here include the installation of wheels under the forward car, a re-covered front section and various armament installations.   *Vickers*

Pulham airships, HMA No 23 and S.R.1, were detailed to proceed to the South Cutler buoy off the Suffolk coast to escort surrendered German U-boats into Harwich harbour. Destroyers and cruisers of Tyrwhitt's Harwich Force

Surrendered U-boats moored in the River Stour after being brought into Harwich harbour escorted by the Royal Navy and two Pulham airships.
Mrs M. Martin

shepherded twenty U-boats towards the Harwich approaches as the two airships and flying boats from Felixstowe air station flew overhead, and as they sailed into the harbour they passed the Felixstowe base from which flying boats of the War Flight[11] had day by day set out on patrols over their transit routes to seek them out and if possible destroy them. The two Pulham airships were able to maintain the same speed as the submarines as, with the White Ensign above the German naval ensign, they made their way into port. With the airships keeping watch from above and the escorting ships keeping an eye on them below the U-boats moored four deep in the River Stour off Parkeston Quay; these moorings were known for some time afterwards as "Submarine Avenue". After completing their duties the two airships received a signal from the officer in charge of the escort that their job had been well done; dipping their bows in salute, they turned and flew back to Pulham in line astern.

With the arrival of peace a question mark hung over the future of the airship service. HMA No 9, Britain's first flyable rigid airship, had already been scrapped by the end of the war and others were soon to go, but construction of some rigid airships was allowed to go ahead. The spring of 1919 was not an easy time for the staff at Pulham as the workload had become very light, as it had at most stations, and the men found themselves put to all manner of menial tasks in order to keep their minds off such things as demobilisation.

Not that the situation in "Civvy Street" gave much comfort to those who were soon to leave the service. Unemployment was already a problem and there was industrial unrest which further complicated the situation for men facing "demob". Those who were first out were getting the available jobs, and it seemed that there would be no work for those who were being retained in the service until later.

Quite suddenly one day in March the smouldering tinder burst into flame. Having been to dinner, the men refused to return to work and instead mustered outside the Officers' Mess, voicing their misgivings that while the Navy and the Army were well ahead in releasing men back to civilian life the Air Force appeared to be dragging its heels.

The commanding officer took no chances. Arms were issued to the senior non-commissioned officers and a party of Royal Marines and Military Police was drafted in to assist in maintaining discipline. Fortunately the situation cooled down and order was eventually restored without there being a need for drastic measures.

The first of the new rigid airships whose construction had been allowed to go ahead at the end of the war, the R.33, arrived at Pulham in March, 1919. Longest lived of all British rigid airships, the R.33 had been built by Armstrong Whitworth at their Barlow Works about three miles south-west of Selby, in Yorkshire, on the estate of industrialist Lord Landsborough. Manufacture of components for R.33 and her sister R.34 had begun as long ago as the summer of 1917 but actual construction of R.33 in a shed some 700 feet in length, 150 feet wide and 100 feet tall did not begin until the following year.

Both R.33 and R.34 bore a very marked resemblance to the German Zeppelin L-33, though the similarity in numbering was mere coincidence. They did indeed owe a great deal to the design of the Zeppelin, for British designers and engineers had made the most of the opportunity presented by the forcing down of the L-33 at Great Wigborough, Essex, on the night of 23rd/24th September, 1916. The L-33, commanded by Kapitän-leutnant Aloys Böcker, had been participating in a raid on London when it was damaged by anti-aircraft fire and then intercepted by a night fighter flown by Lieutenant A. de B. Brandon, whose fire failed to ignite the hydrogen in the gasbags but did so much damage both to gasbags and to fuel tanks that the Zeppelin was forced to descend. The crew attempted to destroy their airship after landing but there was little hydrogen left to burn, and it was only doped fabric that flared up when they fired signal flares into the ship.

The light alloy framework, although buckled in places, was virtually intact and the motors were undamaged, although the wooden airscrews had splintered when they struck the ground. A tented camp quickly grew up alongside the wreckage to house a team of investigators who recorded every feature of the "R-type" Zeppelin. The work took nearly five months and resulted in the publication of the secret CB1265; the drawings and information contained in that document enabled British airship designers to produce the R.33 and R.34.

The R.33 was launched at Selby on 6th March, 1919, just eight days ahead of her sister ship which was being built by William Beardmore Ltd at their Inchinnan Works on the Clyde. Semi-streamlined fore and aft, with a parallel midships section, the R.33 had a long control car well forward and ahead of the leading power cars. This forward car appeared at first glance to be a complete structure, but on closer inspection it was seen actually to be two separate units with a small gap in between, a construction designed to prevent vibration from the forward engine, housed in the rear section of the car, from being transmitted to the control car with its instruments. Two more power cars suspended in the wing positions amidships each contained a single engine while the after power car, on the centreline, housed two engines geared to a single 19-foot diameter propeller; those in the forward and midships power cars turned 16-foot two-bladed wooden propellers. All five engines were 275 hp Sunbeam Maori water-cooled petrol units.

The power cars showed advanced design features which included two gearboxes for each engine, enabling the engines to be started and run up without the propellers rotating. Sufficient fuel was carried for eighty-eight hours' engine running, but to increase the range it was possible to use only three of the five engines, giving the craft a speed of 40 knots at a petrol consumption of one gallon a mile. The main petrol tanks were in the hull, fuel flowing from them by gravity to header tanks in the power cars, this arrangement giving a smoother and more precise fuel supply than the older arrangement of direct gravity feed.

The forward power cars contained radiators to which the air supply was regulated by movable shutters. The rear power car still had the old form of installation in which the radiator was moved bodily up and down into and out of the airflow to regulate the temperature; the connection between radiator and engine was made by flexible pipes.

The light alloy girder structure of the hull, 643 feet long and 78 feet in diameter, comprised twenty main frames and thirteen main longitudinals, but as there were intermediate stringers between each pair of main longitudinal members the outer surface of the hull appeared to have twenty-six sides. Nineteen gasbags gave the R.33 a disposable lift of almost 26 tons, obtained from 1,950,000 cubic feet of hydrogen, but 15½ tons was taken up by fuel and ballast; in order to assist with emergency lift a ton of water ballast was carried in bow and

Pulham Air Station about 1919, seen from the shed roof. The nose cone of HMA No 9 can be seen outside Station Headquarters, where it was erected by the commanding officer when she was broken up.   *Mr Roger Aldrich*

stern containers, and this could be rapidly dumped by use of controls from the control car. Modern equipment included electricity generating gear backed up by racks of batteries, long-range radio equipment and direction-finding sets for navigation.

The R.34, whose maiden flight was made on 14th March, 1919, differed only slightly from her sister. Slight damage was incurred during the initial four-hour flight which preceded delivery to East Fortune air station near Edinburgh, and repairs had to be made before a sixty-one-hour flight was undertaken over the Baltic in preparation for a proposed transatlantic flight. During one of her preparatory flights over the North Sea the R.34 ran into a gale; heading into the wind with all her motors running at full power the airship had a forward airspeed of 40 knots, but she was in fact being blown backwards for more than eight hours.

Almost as soon as she arrived at Pulham the £350,000 R.33 was in action. During the period from 18th June, 1919, to 14th October, 1920, she made twenty-three flights totalling no less than 337 hours. One of her tasks during 1919 was flying over London and other cities publicising the sale of the Government's Victory Bonds; one flight from Pulham to South Wales and back is recorded as having taken twenty-five hours. On 2nd July, 1919, as the R.34 took off from East Fortune at the start of her transatlantic flight the R.33 left Pulham with the S.R.1 to show off to the public by flying over the route of the Peace Procession in London; the big rigid trailed a very large banner advertising Victory Bonds.

The flight over the Peace Procession might well have ended with more publicity than was intended, for while over central London the S.R.1 suffered a malfunction which deprived it entirely of engine power[12]. The crew, by now well used to the erratic performance of the motors, carried out urgent repairs as the airship floated motionless above the cheering crowds along the route of the procession. While thus deprived of power the S.R.1 was caught in turbulence and shot up into the clouds close to where the R.33 was also cruising, but by good fortune control was eventually restored without further problems. The engines were restarted and the airship returned to its Norfolk base after a ten-hour flight, the crowds in the London streets having remained totally unaware of the drama played out above their heads.

One wonders how much they had heard of the performance given by a military band playing away on the gun platform on top of the R.33's hull. Unfortunately the band would have been out of sight of those directly beneath the airship, and one supposes that the strains of their music as well, perhaps, as their sheet music would have been borne away by the slipstream.

On another occasion during July the R.33 undertook a lengthy flight which took her over Sheffield, Bradford, Manchester, Liverpool, North Wales, the Isle of Man and the Irish coast, with the band again performing from the upper gun position as the airship hovered above the major cities. Flying time for this trip was thirty-one hours. The motors of the semi-rigid fortunately behaved themselves when the S.R.1 made a twenty-five-hour cruise distributing Victory Bond leaflets over South Wales and the West Country on 6th/7th July; she returned to her base just as darkness was falling on the 7th, her crew doubtless

Parachute trials being conducted with a Coastal, possibly at Pulham. The cranes to be seen in the background might be employed in the erection of the first rigid shed.
Norman Peake

much relieved that they would not have to spend another uncomfortable night on board.

After having carried out a considerable amount of experimental work HMA No 23 was shedded during the spring of 1919 so that a new strengthened bow section could be fitted. This was needed for further trials with the three-wire mooring system. As it turned out these trials were of short duration, and the first of the "23 class" rigids was broken up at Pulham in September that same year. Never capable of operational service, HMA No 23 had nevertheless done a great deal of hard work and had taken considerable punishment in the course of mooring trials and the airborne aeroplane release experiments, all of which might have been extremely valuable if airship development had been allowed to continue unhampered.

It was not only the rigids that took part in experimental and development work, for in June, 1919, a twin-engined Sea Scout under the command of Captain Meager demonstrated the airship's ability to loiter by remaining

Major G. H. Scott seen in the window of the R.34's control car as she landed at Pulham after her flight to the United States and back. The smile of triumph was well deserved. *George Swain*

airborne for 52 hours 15 minutes; it was a considerable achievement for so small a craft.

The parachute trials carried out at Pulham culminated in the parachute being made a standard part of the airship's equipment at about this time. The parachutes supplied for airship crews were still not of the later self-contained type but were stowed away in containers with a static line to release the canopy. Crews were encouraged to make practice jumps with this equipment, and it is recorded that on 9th August, 1919, Sergeant Lee dropped from the S.R.1 when it was flying at 2,000 feet; he reached the ground safely after a four-minute twenty-second descent. That was one of the last occasions on which the S.R.1, by then something of a veteran, was airborne; when the parachute operations were concluded the semi-rigid was shedded and deflated to join the rest of the non-rigids which had all been decommissioned.

It was a gala occasion when the R.34 arrived at Pulham for the first time on Sunday, 13th July, 1919, at the end of her double crossing of the North Atlantic[13]. She had flown from East Fortune to Mineola, New York, a distance of 3,130 miles, in 108 hours 12 minutes, using up 4,900 gallons of fuel on the way. There was an official crew of thirty for the Atlantic crossing, plus two pigeons, a kitten and a stowaway, Aircraftman Second Class William Ballantyne. Disappointed at not being included in the R.34's official crew for the pioneering flight, Ballantyne had climbed aboard the ship and hidden himself in the hull; he was not discovered until the airship was well out over the Atlantic. Officially the young airman was in disgrace; he was not allowed to make the return flight in R.34 but was sent home by sea, yet Brigadier-General Maitland, who had been in command at Pulham in 1917 and had since risen to become the senior officer of the British airship service, merely reprimanded him and did not take further disciplinary action, realizing the bitter disappointment the young airman had suffered when not selected for the transatlantic flight. Billy Ballantyne later trained as a pilot and was eventually commissioned.

Leaving the United States of America on 10th July, the R.34 made good time eastbound and while over Ireland received orders to proceed to Pulham; she arrived over Pulham on the Sunday morning seventy-five hours and two minutes after leaving Mineola.

A great crowd of pressmen and photographers watched as Major G. H. Scott brought her down at 6.56 am. A large number of local residents and

The elevators are hard down to correct a slightly nose-up attitude as the R.34 arrives at Pulham after her Atlantic crossing.

servicemen from Norwich and East Harling had been assembled to assist with the landing, and the station band was in attendance to provide appropriate martial music as the R.34 circled the station twice before coming in slowly so that the landing party could pick up the trailing ropes.

The R.34 was in fact the second aircraft to make a non-stop crossing of the Atlantic from west to east, as Alcock and Brown had managed to coax their Vickers Vimy twin-engined biplane from Newfoundland to Ireland on 14th June, though they had been unable to reach their destination and had finished up in an Irish peat bog; Alcock and Brown were both knighted for their achievement and received the Britannia Trophy and a prize of £10,000 from the *Daily Mail*. In stark contrast, just one OBE, four Air Force Crosses and six Air Force Medals were awarded to members of the airship's crew; all that the lower ranks received to commemorate the voyage were silver propelling pencils which were presented to them by members of the New York Fire Department on their arrival in America. The R.34's rather low-key arrival at Pulham caused several voices to be raised in protest at the somewhat shabby treatment of its crew by officialdom.

Left: R.34 is eased into Pulham's No 1 shed by a large handling party after her flight from America. *George Swain*

Right: The R.34 safely shedded alongside her sister ship R.33. *Dr P. Rawlence*

The R.34 did not remain long at Pulham but was moved to Cardington for a major refit and then sent to the operational base at Howden in Yorkshire to perform general training duties. While engaged in these duties she was destroyed in an accident, fortunately without loss of life, on 28th January, 1921.

July, 1919, was a month of both triumph and tragedy for Pulham air station; just ten days after the arrival from America of the R.34 one of the station's airships was lost with all hands. It was the N.S.11, which had earlier created an endurance record while on a long-range patrol over the North Sea. Flying along the North Norfolk coast in thundery conditions while on a circular flight from Pulham to Kingsnorth, the N.S.11 was struck by lightning shortly after passing over Cley; the crew of eight all died as the non-rigid plunged down in flames. Among those lost with the N.S.11 were her commanding officer, Captain Warneford, and her first officer, Captain Elliott, both of them well-liked and much-respected Pulham officers.

While the R.33 and R.34 were being constructed by Armstrong Whitworth and Beardmore two other airships to a different design were being built by Short Brothers at their Shortstown Works at Cardington in Bedfordshire[14]. The design of these two rigids, R.31 and R.32, had been formulated by a team comprising men from the Corps of Naval Constructors and civilian employees of Short Brothers, making full use of information and drawings which had come from the Schutte-Lanz works at Mannheim; they are said to have been brought to this country by a Swiss employee of Schutte-Lanz, a Herr Muller, who had also brought with him a new wonder glue called "Kaltleim" which was used to produce lightweight plywood girders such as those used in R.31 and her sister.

Second of the "31 class", the R.32 made her maiden flight on 3rd September, 1919, and arrived at Pulham only three days later. Her appearance immediately aroused comment, for instead of the usual cars suspended beneath the hull the "31 class" had a streamlined control car formed into the bottom surface of the hull, a configuration which had many advantages over the earlier arrangement. A generator provided electric lighting, there was electric starting for the engines, and the R.32 was equipped with a telephone system giving communication between the various working sections of the ship. With a gas capacity of 1,500,000 cubic feet, the R.32 had disposable lift of 16½ tons and was 615 feet long, with a maximum diameter of 65½ feet. Originally powered by six engines, she went into service with five, giving a total of 1,500 hp and a speed of 57 knots.

Originally commissioned into the Royal Navy, R.32 was decommissioned during October when the Royal Air Force took over all airship operations and was then seconded to the National Physical Laboratory to carry out experimental work on manoeuvring procedures. This work, carried out from Pulham, involved the R.32 making tight turns while flying at various angles and at different speeds; readings were taken at various positions in the hull to record the stresses imposed by the manoeuvres. One of the intriguing features of the R.32's construction was that the wooden structure was slightly flexible; crewmen standing at opposite ends of a catwalk within the hull disappeared from each other's sight when the craft made a tight turn.

Certain troubles manifested themselves during her early flights, mainly in the petrol transfer systems. When malfunctions occurred a great deal of manpower was employed at the hand pumps to transfer the vital fuel to the engines. In spite of such tribulations the R.32 proved to be quite successful and was well liked both by its crew and by the American airshipmen who came to the United Kingdom to train in preparation for taking over the R.38, which was then under construction at Cardington and was sold to America as the ZR-2.

During September, 1919, the British Government staged a "Britain's Power in the Air" campaign and Pulham staged demonstration flights as part of the campaign. The R.32 and R.33 were despatched to Amsterdam where the 1919 Aircraft Exhibition was being held. The two ships must have made an impressive sight as they flew in line astern over the flat landscape of North Holland on 11th September and circled the city of Amsterdam before dropping a message in a parachute-borne container addressed to the officer in charge of the exhibition.

For this flight a number of beds had been installed in the two craft and a chef was carried to provide a five-course dinner for a number of guest passengers, in order to demonstrate that the airship had great possibilities in the realm of civil aviation. Very soon the Air Ministry, confident that a great future lay ahead for the commercial airship, would put forward proposals for an airship service to India, a scheme which promoted great discussion but came to naught when the Treasury refused to fund the scheme, for which £844,000 would have been needed over two years.

From Amsterdam the two airships turned south along the coasts of Holland and Belgium, then turned to overfly Brussels and Antwerp and then the battlefields of Flanders. They returned to Pulham after a twenty-two-hour flight during which a ship's newspaper was published, copies being distributed to the pressmen who had been invited on the flight.

In spite of such operations the autumn of 1919 was a time of some confusion within the airship service. On 25th September it was decreed that all Direct Entry officers should be demobilized immediately; this order was rescinded a day or two later, and then brought into force again within a few weeks. As a result of this order many of the officers who had flown the Pulham airships in fair weather and foul broke their connection with the Norfolk air station and with lighter-than-air craft in general.

It was perhaps ironic that General Sir Hugh Trenchard, later as Marshal of the Royal Air Force Lord Trenchard to be recognised as the Father of the Royal Air Force, chose September to inspect the Pulham station. "Boom" Trenchard, as he was known because of his very deep, resonant voice, examined the rigid airship sheds and spent some time "talking shop" with the airship crews who had been assembled for his inspection.

CHAPTER SIX

Post-war Heyday

GENERAL flying at airship stations had been suspended since the Autumn of 1919 and many of the wartime stations had closed down, but Pulham survived as the Airship Experimental Station. It was still able to put one craft into the air, the experimental Sea Scout S.S.E.3, and this ship made several experimental flights during the Spring of 1920.

Many of the experienced airship officers and other ranks had left the service, and those who remained, like Captain Williams, had vastly different jobs from those which they had been trained for and had previously carried out. Captain Williams had been transferred to the Accounts Branch and in this capacity was responsible for the accounts of several RAF stations in the area, as well as for their pay arrangements.

Make do and mend maintenance work was the order of the day, and even this was carried out at a leisurely pace.

A sound not unfamiliar to Pulham and Norfolk was heard again on 22nd June, 1920, when the first of two Zeppelins which had been handed over to the British Government as War Reparations arrived at the air station. This was the L-64. It was followed to the Norfolk base on 30th June by its sister craft L-71. Reluctantly handed over by the German Navy, the two Zeppelins were flown to Pulham from their North German bases by their former crews. On arrival at their new home they were put into the rigid sheds.

The L-64 and L-71 were both representatives of the very latest types of Zeppelin to enter service with the German naval airship service. The L-71 was an "X-type" Zeppelin with a volume as built of 2,195,800 cubic feet, but after a few flights she had been shedded and a new section had been spliced into the hull which lengthened it from 693 feet to 743 feet; the modification also increased the capacity to 2,418,700 cubic feet. Diameter of the hull was 78 feet. The L-64 was very much like her sister as she had been before lengthening.

Commissioned on 10th August, 1918, after making her maiden flight on 29th July, the L-71 had only a brief service life; she made only eight flights before being de-commissioned on 9th November with the other units of the Naval airship service.

With the lower ranks of the German Navy in a mutinous state, the airship officers were segregated from their ground crews at the North German airship stations some days before the Armistice. On 9th November the officers were ordered back to their bases and with the ground crews were instructed to deflate their ships and leave them suspended from the roofs of the airship sheds, as was normal procedure for large rigid airships. When the lifting gas was valved off the weight of the ships was taken by large slings in the form of loops which suspended them from the roof, preventing them subsiding on to the control and power cars.

The crews who flew the Zeppelins remained loyal to their crumbling country in spite of defeat. At the same time that their waterborne comrades were scuttling their vessels in Scapa Flow, they stealthily entered the silent sheds at Nordholz and Wittmundhavn on 23rd June, 1919, released the straps which held the craft and allowed them to crash down on to the hangar floors; irreparable damage was done to them which prevented the craft being handed over to the victorious Allies. At Alhorn air station, however, no action was taken by the crews and the L-64 and L-71 remained intact to be handed over to the victors.

One witness of the L-71's arrival at Pulham remembered the Zeppelin alighting on English soil:

> I was in charge of the landing party at Pulham when L-71 came in and I don't think I ever saw such a fine exhibition of airmanship and control as the crew of the Zeppelin gave. I was simply astounded at the way the ship's commander, Kapitänleutnant Heine, brought the ship to the hangar area. He had one hand on the engine telegraphs to the various power cars mounted beneath the ship and the other hand out of the opened control car window as he manoeuvred the ship practically into the shed before he dropped a single handling line. It certainly did not require more than fifty men to get him into the shed and there were, I think, some five hundred men standing by for the task[15].

Several other local residents who were on the station at the time remember the resentment displayed by the German crews as they handed over their craft to the British authorities; it was a bitter pill for any serviceman to swallow. The *Eastern Daily Press* for 2nd July, 1920, reported the event:

> The great German airship L-71 which had been handed over to the British Government arrived at Pulham on Thursday, visiting Norwich and other parts of Norfolk before effecting a landing. It is surely the limit of irony that this splendid yet terrible creation which was designed and built for the bombing of New York should be led captive into England and that her officers and men, under the surveillance of three British officers, should suffer the indignity of piloting her across the North Sea to the aerodrome at Pulham in Norfolk.

With the First World War now over, thought was turned to aviation in its peacetime role of connecting the British Isles with Europe and the Empire. During 1919 the first international air service was inaugurated between London and Paris, and this was later expanded to link the major European capitals. June of that year saw John William Alcock and Arthur Whitten Brown cross the North Atlantic and the R.34 make the double crossing to America and back. Many raised their eyebrows at the R.34's performance; its average speed of

The L-71 arriving at Pulham in 1920. In spite of a certain amount of secrecy ahead of her arrival Norwich photographer George Swain was on hand to record the Zeppelin's arrival at the Norfolk base.   *George Swain*

35 mph for the trans-ocean crossings was only 6 mph faster than the fastest ocean liner on that route.

Disciples of the airship pointed out to the advocates of the aeroplane that passengers in the airships would be able to walk about above the clouds and gaze down at the passing scene below, and for the ship enthusiasts it was further pointed out that the airship eliminated all the discomforts of sea sickness. Perhaps airsickness had not been thought of at the time! One school of thought put forward the large rigid airship as the ideal form of transport, and the airship lobby went to great lengths to publicise its capabilities of endurance, load lifting, city-to-city travel from suburban terminals and the provision of a new style of comfort for the passengers. Unfortunately there was neither finance nor sufficiently advanced design technology available at this time to provide these new craft; the ex-military airships would have to fill the gap until such time as new craft became available.

This state of affairs was accepted by the Government and by the Royal Air Force. The latter was not particularly keen on the Airship Scheme because of a lack both of men to operate the craft and of accommodation for them. What is interesting is that at this time information was being circulated that all help possible both with craft and associated equipment would be given to any airship-operating organisation in the commercial field, as long as it had Government approval. This was, of course, linked with the twin requirements that the organisations were economically viable and their plans technically feasible.

Thus it came to pass that the Air Council, who had taken over control of airships and airship operations from the Admiralty during April, 1919, registered two large RAF rigid airships as civil aircraft in 1920 to carry out limited programmes in the commercial field. The first to be civilianised for this purpose was R.33, which for this transitional period was fitted out with sleeping accommodation within the hull; cooking facilities were also provided so that an airborne chef could relieve the passengers' pangs of hunger. The R.33 carried the civil identification insignia G-FAAG on the hull sides and the large international "G" for Great Britain on the fins. In this guise she arrived at Pulham, which was handed over in 1920 to the Controller-General of Civil Aviation as an experimental establishment, and began experimental work mainly in the mooring sphere. The National Physical Laboratory was still conducting trials on large rigid airships and R.33/G-FAAG participated in this work.

The second airship to take part in this scheme was to be the R.36, which in 1920 was still building.

Most significant of the development work carried out at Pulham was undoubtedly that on mooring techniques, and in particular on mast mooring. A lattice mast was constructed by Vickers with the intention that it should be erected at Barrow-in-Furness, but in May, 1918, the decision was made to erect it at Pulham. A comparatively short tower, 120 feet high, was capped by a mooring attachment which allowed the moored craft to swing through a full 360 degrees so that it would face into the wind at all times. A fundamental advantage of the new system was that only a dozen or so men were needed to secure the craft instead of the large ground handling party required earlier; this was of particular importance during a period of austerity and financial restrictions.

As the new mast was basically a prototype it had no lift to enable the ship's crew or passengers to reach the top in comfort. Instead they had to climb the many steps up the outside of the tower to reach the rotating cap at the top. Entry to the ship was gained by means of a circular platform encircling the cap, from which one clambered up a sloping gangway with canvas sides to reach the entrance door in the forward hull section of the airship. Stout hearts were needed just to gain access to the ship.

HMA No 24, second ship of the "23 class", was flown from Howden to Pulham on 31st May, 1918, with the intention that she should be used for mast mooring trials, but it was not until March, 1919, that the mast was set up at Pulham. No 24 was fitted with a modified nose cone, a bow-coupling winch and additional ballast tanks and her midships gondola was removed before the trials could begin.

She was moored to the mast for the first time on 11th June, remaining on the mast until 30th June. She was taken from the mast for inspection and minor modifications, but was back on the mast from 1st September to 15th October and

again from 7th November until mid-December. In these experiments the mooring cable was attached to the mast while the ship was on the ground, and no "yaw guys" were used to steady her nose as she approached the masthead. Two men remained on duty in the control car and one below during her sojourn on the mast so that water ballast could be taken aboard by hose if she became light and began to "ride up" and gas could be fed in if she became too heavy for a discharge of ballast to be beneficial. During her total of sixty-two days on the mast, in all weathers, she coped with wind speeds of 45 mph without trouble.

While at Pulham No 24 tested a system involving the use of ropes to guide the craft down; this was not found to be satisfactory, though it did lead to the development of a more functional system some time later. HMA No 24 was deleted before the end of the year, and it was left to R.33 and R.36 to carry on the mooring trials at Pulham in the nineteen-twenties.

The revolving masthead was later fitted with an attachment designed at Cardington. Named the Bedford-Pulham mooring attachment, it comprised an elaborate arrangement of cables intended to facilitate the linking of an airship to the tower. One ran from a winch at the base of the tower through an attachment at the top of the tower and then out at a downward angle to another attachment

70

Left: The R.33 in her new guise as a civil airship, bearing the registration G-FAAG, flies slowly over her base at Pulham, one of her crew standing erect in the upper gun position on top of the hull. In the shed is the damaged R.36. Clearly seen in this view is the windscreen, part of which is parallel to the line of the shed; the outer part is set at an angle.

Mr Roger Aldrich

Right: The man who was Pulham, Major George Herbert Scott. After being chief experimental officer at Pulham he became commanding officer in 1920.

Mr Roger Aldrich

set in a large concrete square on the airfield some distance from the tower. At this end was a quick-coupling device.

Airships equipped to use this mooring arrangement carried a similar cable and coupling attachment in their bow section. To moor, the airship slowly approached the concrete square at low altitude and in line with the cable running up to the top of the tower. The airship's cable and coupling attachment was lowered and a member of the ground crew, positioned adjacent to the concrete square and lower attachment, prepared to receive the cable. Great caution had to be exercised at this juncture as the airship's passage through the air had generated considerable static electricity which would earth itself as soon as the cable was close to the ground. To save himself from a hefty shock the ground crew member had to ensure that the cable had touched the ground before he attempted to retrieve it.

When all was safe, the airship's cable was attached to the ground cable and the cable was then gradually wound up towards the top of the tower. Eventually the nose of the airship reached the mooring attachment on the tower top and was fastened securely to the tower. As the top of the tower revolved it allowed the airship to ride into the wind or "weathercock", in airship terminology.

Built by Vickers in 1917, HMA No 24 finished her life at Pulham carrying out mast mooring trials on the new mast built in 1919.   *Vickers*

Advantages of this system were that the airship could be moored aloft by day or night. A craft could take up moorings in wind speeds of up to 35 knots.

The new mast was used a great deal and over several months some fifty successful moorings were made by R.33 under the supervision of Captain Williams; this involved 171 hours' flying. One surprising fact which emerged from these trials was that craft could be brought up to the mast and attached in very bad weather conditions; one report stated that the R.33 was successfully moored when the wind was gusting at 80 mph. The R.33's stint on the Pulham mast proved that the mast design was sound and efficient and that a great step forward had been taken in the ground handling of large rigid airships. Many local residents recall the impressive sight of the R.33 riding at the mast at night, with floodlights shining on her silver-coated hull; the lights on board gave the impression of an ocean liner lying in dock.

During her many days on the mast the R.33 proved that neither rain nor dry snow posed a problem, but following the destruction of R.26 it was recognised that wet snow certainly did. Captain F. M. Thomas at Pulham devised snow-clearing gear which consisted of an endless wire atop the ship between frames 7 and 34 which dragged lengths of two-and-a-half-inch hemp rope fore and aft along the ship's cover.

On 3rd June, 1921, a heavy rain squall forced the tail of the ship to the ground, despite release of ballast. It was thought to be the dynamic pressure of the raindrops rather than their actual weight that did this. Fortunately, the tail-fin was submerged in a pond on that occasion and the airship escaped damage.

During May, 1920, the R.33 flew north from Pulham to Howden Air Station in Yorkshire to carry out an unusual experiment with a fighter aircraft which had been fitted with an experimental fuel tank designed neither to leak nor to explode if the plane crashed. A Sopwith Camel—there seemed to be a surplus of this type for use as test pieces—was suspended beneath the R.33 by its release gear and together they left the Howden station to fly to an open and sparsely populated stretch of countryside on the North Yorkshire Moors. When all was ready the Camel's rotary engine was started up and the pilotless fighter slipped from the release gear to make a powered descent. It crashed into an area of moorland, but did not catch fire. Whether the failure to catch fire was due to the leakproof fuel tank seems to be unknown; no concrete conclusion seems to have been drawn from the experiment as to whether the new tank was successful or not, and the experiment was not repeated.

At this time Pulham Air Station came under the command of Major G. H.

The crew of the R.33 climb the mooring mast to reach their ship.
Ted Stupple

73

Scott, who had been chief experimental officer at Pulham towards the end of the First World War. Major Scott became the proud holder of British Airship Pilot's licence No A1 (First Class), dated 4th February, 1921, though he had in fact been flying airships since 1914 as a naval and then as an RAF officer. He was known in the service for two characteristics, determination and alleged hamfistedness. In spite of the latter, which resulted from a number of misfortunes with the rather delicate airships of wartime days, he was very highly regarded in the airship service and was indeed numbered among the "Big Three" of that service, the others being Wing Commander R. B. B. Colmore and Lieutenant-Colonel V. C. Richmond.

On 20th September, 1920, the Air Ministry ordered that all work on airships should cease, but the run-down took another twelve months to implement. This order did not apply to the R.38, being prepared at Cardington by Short Brothers for sale to the Americans at a price of £500,000.

At this time R.33 was badly needing an overhaul, but as the two surrendered Zeppelins were occupying a large proportion of the shed facilities at Pulham it was decided to fly her up to Howden Air Station, where she stayed until 2nd February, 1921.

January, 1921, was a very bleak time for British lighter-than-air craft as the Royal Air Force Airship Scheme was disbanded due to lack of funds, and the craft would have a future only if they could be utilised for commercial purposes. After the hustle and bustle of active wartime flying many of the crews who had left to take up their new occupations in "civvy street" became discontented with their lot in the new world, and sought again the more active life back with the Forces. One such gentleman was Captain T. B. Williams, AFC, who returned to the former scene of his activities during 1921, when in a civilian capacity he was appointed Civil Airship Officer by the Controller General of Civil Aviation. Only the second person to hold this post, Captain Williams played a prominent part in the experimental work at Pulham; Major Scott had been the first Civil Airship Officer.

The R.33's experimental work did not proceed without incident. During the spring of 1921 there occurred an accident which might have been attended with tragic consequences and which doubtless helped to give the R.33 her reputation of being a lucky ship. A rigger who was engaged on a task high up in the envelope slipped and fell; in his descent he ripped open one of the gasbags in the stern. His fall was arrested by the bottom structure of the hull, and the airman was not hurt, and only slightly affected by the escaping hydrogen.

However, the loss of lift resulting from the deflation of the gasbag caused the stern to drop, and a ton of water ballast had to be released from the stern tanks so that trim was restored, and the ship returned slowly to its Pulham base.

A few days later on 17th March, 1921, after repairs had been made, a rudder jammed while the R.33 was carrying out a flight over Essex. The ship was forced to circle for an hour or so over the Thames Estuary while the riggers struggled to free the obstinate control surface.

Varied tasks undertaken by this craft included after-dark flights over South London and Surrey to view from the air the new airport lighting system at Croydon and assisting the police with road traffic problems during Epsom and Ascot race weeks. To avoid the ship having to return to its Norfolk base each night while engaged on these duties, the R.33 moored up to a wooden mast at Croydon on the nights of 14th and 15th July, 1921. This was the only occasion that this little-known airship mooring site was used; it is assumed that pilots of airliners using the then-new airport for London objected to its presence so near to the airfield.

When the R.33 was airborne there was always excitement in the neighbouring villages. Lorries from the air station picked up willing villagers who would be needed to assist with the ground handling when the "local resident" came home. When local help was required villagers were notified by posted notices, if time allowed, but in more urgent cases a lorry would tour the villages surrounding the air station and a bugler would sound a call to let all and sundry know of the need for their assistance. Gathering at specified pick-up points, the volunteers were then conveyed to their place of duty, while those living closer to the station made their way there on foot. There was never any lack of volunteers for this job, and manning the trailing handling ropes became almost second nature to many Norfolk people as they walked the airships in or out of the sheds and to and from the mooring mast. Good control by the ground handling parties was essential for the safe passage of the huge craft on their low passage across the field; when low down they were out of their true element and were subject to any fickle breeze that tended to swing them off their intended course. The military authorities often praised the good work carried out by the local ground crews.

On 2nd April, 1921, the day after her launching, the new airship R.36 arrived at Pulham at 5.52 pm and was safely moored after being walked across the field to the mast by the ground handling party. Besides her crew she carried several distinguished passengers, including the Director of Research at the Air Ministry, Air Commodore Robert Brooke-Popham. The captain for this flight was Flight Lieutenant A. H. Wann.

The R.36 had been constructed by Beardmore Limited at their Inchinnan Works on the Clyde in Scotland. She belonged to the lengthened "Class 33" type, which in turn had been derived from the Zeppelin L-48 which had been brought down at Theberton in Suffolk. Building had commenced before the end of the First World War, but at the cessation of hostilities the work had slowed down almost to a standstill. When construction was resumed orders were received for the airship to be completed as a civil craft; she bore the civil aircraft registration G-FAAF.

The new craft was 675 feet long and had a maximum diameter amidships of

78½ feet, the 2,101,000 cubic feet capacity giving a disposable lift of 32 tons. The modified construction also gave the R.36 a maximum loaded altitude of 17,000 feet.

Power arrangements were unusual. The Zeppelin came into the picture yet again; the two forward power cars, each fitted with a Maybach IVa engine of 260 hp, had been removed from the L-71 which was being dismantled at Pulham. One snag was that these German motors were high-compression engines and could not be run at full throttle below 6,000 feet. The other power units were three Sunbeam Cossack engines of 350 hp each, housed in the rear power cars.

A distinguishing feature of the R.36 was the long control car and cabin, some 131 feet in length, directly attached to the underside of the hull. The ship was fitted with mast mooring gear. The crew comprised four officers, two coxswains, two wireless operators, seven riggers and thirteen mechanics and there was accommodation for fifty passengers. After the civilianisation had been carried out the craft's disposable lift had been reduced to 16 tons, which did not give a large enough margin for the overseas duties for which the new ship was intended.

The fact that passenger accommodation had been incorporated in the design while the ship was under construction made the R.36 the first true British civil airship. Although accommodation was not lavish, it did comprise two saloons with folding tables and wicker chairs; sleep was catered for with a series of two-berth cabins. An all-electric galley could provide hot meals during flight. All these facilities were contained in the single long car under the hull.

Three days after the R.36/G-FAAF had arrived at Pulham she set out on an extensive cross-country flight. While she was flying at 6,000 feet in turbulent conditions in the Bristol area the upper vertical fin and starboard horizontal stabilizer failed and buckled due to the pounding they were given by gusty winds. As a result, the R.36's bow dropped and the ship dived down to 3,000 feet. Immediate reaction by the captain, Major Scott, restored equilibrium; he ordered the crew to move aft to bring more weight into that area, shut down the engines to slow the ship down, and dropped water ballast from the forward tanks. This returned the ship to horizontal trim, and then it was decided that as all appeared to be correct they would proceed very, very slowly back to Pulham. The ship managed to gain altitude and was flying at 4,300 feet.

Before they set course for home, two of the riggers clambered out on to the crumpled tailplane and secured the threshing torn fabric and twisted metal framework so that it would not foul the remaining operative rudder and elevator. It was a heroic act on the part of the two crewmen, who had to make foot- and handholds in the tail surfaces and locate the metal structure beneath the taut fabric in order to get out to the damaged part to secure it. At the same time they would not know if the structure beneath them was still capable of carrying their weight and that it would not at any moment fold and hurl them

Some of the forty Members of Parliament who flew in the R.36 on 17th June, 1921, seen at Pulham before setting out. In the middle of the group is Brigadier-General Lord Thomson.   *George Swain*

into space. Of course they had lines holding them to the ship, but it was little consolation to know that if you fell you would be dangling beneath the ship with only a fifty-fifty chance of being pulled back to safety.

For the remainder of the flight horizontal trim was maintained by the crew moving along the keel in the hull as directed in order to bring weight to bear where it was required at the time. Arriving back over Pulham after dark, the R.36 was gently lowered to the ground where it was safely taken over by the ground handling crews, who held it down in preparation for shedding. Before she could be taken in, however, sister ship R.33 had to be taken out from the

The R.36 lying at the Pulham mooring mast not long after her arrival at the station in April, 1921. She was badly damaged when returning to Pulham on 21st June, 1921, and although repairs were made she never flew again. The steam traction engine used for towing airships around the field can be seen at the left.

George Swain

shed and put on the mast, so that the damaged R.36 could be housed in its place. The rest of the space in the sheds was occupied by the two partly dismantled Zeppelins L-64 and L-71.

Doubtless the passengers on this curtailed demonstration flight, who included a number of Air Ministry officials, were not greatly impressed with this performance. The incident must have increased their desire to hand over airship operations to private commerce.

The aeronautical journals of the day, in spite of the incident, gave the R.36 a favourable write-up, but went on at great length to point out that they regarded it as an experimental airship. They were not entirely sold on the idea of an ex-naval airship becoming a successful commercial craft.

On 14th June, 1921, the repaired R.36 was airborne again at 6.30 am on a fine Summer's morning; her passengers for the day were a group of Fleet Street journalists. The purpose of the flight was to demonstrate how this type of craft would co-operate with the police in controlling road traffic; there was plenty of that about as it was Ascot Race Week. The impressions of the airborne reporters reached their offices in good time as the despatches were dropped from the ship on to Croydon Airport as the R.36 passed low over it. One major criticism from the passengers was that the flight lasted twelve hours, during which time they were neither fed nor watered; and to many of them the ban on smoking was an almost insufferable curse.

Complaints of a technical nature were recorded regarding the considerable amount of noise from the wing power cars, which were located outboard from the rear of the cabin. Once again all deplored the fact that they had to climb the numerous steps to the top of the tower in order to enter the ship, and clamber down them again on their return. The latter was quite frightening, as the R.36

did not arrive back home until 11 pm, and the landing had to be made with the aid of searchlights; passengers had to descend the tower steps in the dark.

Three days later R.36 was abroad on another demonstration flight, this time with forty Members of Parliament. Course was set from Pulham round the East Anglian coastline and then back to the mast at Cardington, this being more convenient for the Honourable Members to regain the comparative safety of the House; it had a lift.

Luck ran out for the R.36 on 21st June, 1921. She had returned to Pulham after a local flight, the approach was easy as it was an almost windless day and there was no hint of trouble in store. The ship's mooring wire had been lowered and connected to the masthead line — and then things went wrong.

Somehow the wire fouled the winch at the foot of the tower, overturning it. The ship overran the tower, coming to a shuddering stop as the cable became taut; the wire sang as it vibrated under the sudden strain. The ship's bows were pulled sharply downwards by the taut wire; the strain proved too much for the airship's structure, the bow section collapsed and Numbers 1 and 2 gasbags were holed. The situation was worsened by the loss of lift forward as the gasbags deflated.

The wire held, and the crippled ship was eventually hauled down safely by the ground crew, but there was no hope of mooring the ship to the mast because of the damage that had been done. To make matters worse the weather began to deteriorate, and it was clearly imperative that the R.36 should be shedded as soon as possible to prevent her receiving further damage. The loss of lift in the forward section was making her unmanageable.

What was to be done? Some thought was given to flying the R.36 slowly to Howden, but this was considered altogether too hazardous. The only answer to

Left: The R.36 on the Pulham mast. The narrow gauge railway which ran across the air station can be seen at right.
Mr Roger Aldrich

Right: The damaged R.36 rests in the shed after the accident of 21st June, 1921. The remains of the L-64 are heaped on the shed floor. *Mr Roger Aldrich*

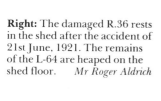

the problem seemed to be to take the craft into one of the sheds, but both were occupied.

In the light of all the facts, an on-the-spot decision was made to scrap the Zeppelin L-64 which resided in one of the Pulham sheds. Problem piled on problem as the ex-German craft refused to move from her berth in the shed. In desperation a cable was passed through the centre of the ship and a tractor was hitched to one end of the cable, but when forward gear was engaged the tractor proved unequal to the task; the Zeppelin remained immovable.

Major Scott, who was in charge of the operation, decided that stronger measures were needed. The Zeppelin was lowered to the shed floor and chopped up with saws and axes; the pieces were dragged out of the shed by the sweating workers. Mrs Scott and other officers' wives played an active part in the proceedings by keeping the working parties supplied with food and hot drinks.

Thus ended the life of one of Germany's super-Zeppelins which had been intended to drop its load of destruction on the cities of England and America but had ended its days under the axes and saws of its former enemy.

When space was available at about 2 am the R.36 was moved towards the shed, handled by a party of about 170 men. Nature had not finished with the intruder into its element yet. The increasing wind meant that the airship had to be taken to the far end of the shed and sheltered for a while behind one of the massive windbreaks which stood at the entrance to the shed. The damaged ship was gradually eased into the shed until almost 300 feet of its length was accommodated and lashed down to rings in the floor. Under the increasing strain on the exposed hull outside the shed one of the anchor attachments in the hull failed and the fragile structure was smashed into the door entry; extensive damage resulted in the midships section. Further failure of attachments allowed more damage to result, and it was not until 7 am that the battered R.36 was secured.

Flight Lieutenant Irwin stepped out from the control car and broke down when he saw the damage to the ship.

The mishap was caused by the attachment wire forming a large loop which engaged on an obstacle on the ground. When the wire became taut it caused the forward emergency ballast tank, which was full at the time, to rupture; and as the weight was released, the R.36's bow rose sharply. This in turn caused the collapse of the bow section. The Court of Inquiry into the incident gave a tongue-in-cheek verdict that it had happened because of lack of suitable equipment; some of the gear used was of the home-made variety and not really up to the job.

This was to be the last movement of the massive R.36. Although she was repaired, she remained in the shed until 1926, when a decision was made to break her up. A scheme to rebuild the craft to carry out tropical trials was not implemented.

Post-war depression had taken a tight grip and severe economic measures were the order of the day; no one was really surprised when the Air Ministry announced that as soon as Short Brothers had completed the R.38, to be sold to America, they would abandon airships. On 28th June, 1921, just a week after the accident to the R.36, the news was given in the House of Commons that, owing to the state of the economy at the time, all Government airship operations would cease and that airships R.33, R.36, R.37 and R.80 and the remaining ex-German Zeppelin L-71 would be given free to any operator who could fulfil the Government conditions; at the same time it was announced that if no suitable offer had been made by 1st August, 1921, the airships would be disposed of. In actual fact, although no offer was made, the craft were not scrapped but remained in store.

All the same, the R.33 was to have her moment of glory the following month when she made a dramatic appearance at the Royal Air Force Pageant at Hendon. On 21st July, 1921, Londoners in their thousands made their way to the famous airfield on the north-western perimeter of the Metropolis to see all the stars of the service, both men and machines, displayed for their delight. The Pulham airship lurked off-stage behind a phosphorous cloud laid by a Handley-Page bomber, bursting through the cloud on cue to the admiration of the watching multitude.

On 30th July full-power trials were carried out and a speed of 52 knots was recorded. This was 5 knots slower than the German LZ-33.

Unfortunately the R.33's appearance at Hendon was almost her swan-song; her public appearance over, she flew on 18th August to Cardington, where she was shedded three weeks later. After being deflated she was lowered in the shed and stored. It seemed only a matter of time before her girders and frames would swell the heaps of light alloy girders and corrugated sheets in the local scrap dealer's yard. Fortunately no such decision was taken, and the R.33 lay in the shed at Cardington and gathered dust for the next three years.

Meanwhile the R.38 was slowly taking shape at Cardington. She had been ordered from Short Brothers in September, 1918, but the work proceeded in an on-off fashion, just as it had done with so many British airship projects. The Admiralty decided to take over Shorts' works at Cardington but to leave the manufacturers in charge of the site in order to build commercial airships, and then in January, 1919, the R.38 order was cancelled and Cardington was nationalised under the Defence of the Realm Act, Short Brothers being paid a mere £40,000 compensation for loss of contract and loss of the premises at Shortstown, as the Cardington establishment had become known; Cardington became the Royal Airship Works[16].

It was at this time that it came to the ears of the Air Ministry that the Americans badly wanted a large rigid airship so as to gain experience in this field, one which they had not previously entered. The R.38 was offered to them and contracts were exchanged in October, 1919. The whole process of building the ship started up again and facilities were offered to the Americans to train their airship crews in the United Kingdom on British ships; much of the training was carried out at Cardington and Pulham.

The R.38, or ZR-2 as she was to be known to the US Navy, was built to a new and untried design, aimed at producing a high-altitude airship with a high speed. Almost as soon as she flew it became obvious that strength had been sacrificed to achieve lightness and so enable her to reach the designed altitude. When she first flew from Cardington on 23rd June, 1921, under the command of Flight Lieutenant J. E. M. Pritchard a number of faults came to light, and others were found in later trials.

On her delivery flight to Howden the R.38 went into a steep dive; it was afterwards found that two of the girders had failed under load, and the ship had to be grounded at Howden for repairs.

On 23rd August, 1921, the R.38 left Howden for Pulham under the command of Flight Lieutenant A. H. Wann, a very experienced airship officer. It was a fine summer's day, and the coastline was shrouded in a dense sea fog resulting from the warm moist air off the land being cooled over the cold North Sea; the swirling banks of fog quickly advanced into the coastal strip of East Anglia, and when the R.38 arrived over Pulham nothing could be seen of the air station. It was impossible for the airship to land and moor for the night, as had been intended, so the airship's commander decided to fly out over the sea and to cruise around off the Suffolk coast during the night.

When daylight returned the R.38 was set on course for Pulham, passing over Thorpeness in the early morning sunlight. As they approached Pulham it was evident from their vantage point high up that conditions had not improved, and as they had used up considerable quantities of fuel while cruising over the sea during the hours of darkness it would be prudent to abort the visit to Pulham and return to Howden. The journey need not be a waste of time; on the way north the commander decided to carry out some high-speed trials which were part of the flight programme. During one of these spurts a top speed of 68 mph was recorded, and this speed was sustained for a quarter of an hour.

There was disappointment on board the R.38, because one of the passengers was Commander L. A. H. Maxfield of the United States Navy, the commander-designate of the R.38/ZR-2, who had intended to inspect the Pulham mooring mast, which had been put at his disposal for training purposes.

Midday passed and the R.38 was nearing its Yorkshire base. As things were going so well, her commander elected to carry out another part of the programme which included yawing manoeuvres at a height of 2,500 feet. To accomplish this move the craft was worked up to high speed and then the rudder was moved hard over from one side to the other, which put a very heavy stress on the ship's hull.

Those flying in the R.38 as she began her tight turns above the Humber had no idea of the danger those manoeuvres put them in. Nor had the people on the ground whose eyes were attracted to the airship as she passed over the town of Hull.

Quite suddenly disaster struck. At 5.37 pm the R.38 broke in half. Moments later there were two explosions, and the blazing wreckage of the forepart fell into the Humber, taking with it most of the forty-nine people who had been aboard; only five survived in the tail section, which did not catch fire.

Among the dead were Air Commodore Maitland, the father of British airships, and Mr C. I. R. Campbell, the airship's designer. Flight Lieutenant Wann, the ship's commander, was among the survivors, but he was too seriously injured to give evidence at the inquiry into the airship's loss. Only one of the seventeen American airshipmen on board survived.

One witness of the disaster afterwards recorded his memories of what happened:

> I had just stepped out of the building where I worked when my attention was attracted by the airship's great bulk, roughly a couple of thousand feet up, shining dull silver in the sunlight. Within seconds, and before I had time to appreciate the great wonder above me, I was horrified to see a small blood-red flame appear high towards the upper surface and approximately at a third of its length.
> Grim disaster followed at once. Fire spread crackling audibly and fiercely in all directions like some ravenous beast savaging its prey. Simultaneously the giant's back

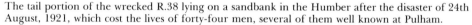

The tail portion of the wrecked R.38 lying on a sandbank in the Humber after the disaster of 24th August, 1921, which cost the lives of forty-four men, several of them well known at Pulham.

broke and whilst the two unequal parts of the hull scissored downwards there issued from the blazing cleavage, with tremendous violence, a fantastic belch of flaming crimson gas.

The roaring inferno, a gigantic inverted vee of fire, went down behind close-by horizontal housetops and by the grace of God fell in the River Humber. After a pause, tense and quiet, fuel tanks exploded in the water and thousands of shattered window panes crashed out on to the pavements.

Others recalled that as they watched the ship change course it also changed shape, and almost resembled a balloon as the envelope rose up at both ends before the explosions occurred.

It would appear that the R.38 was flying in a south-easterly direction at an altitude of 2,500 feet and a speed of 54 knots when the structure failed between midship frames Numbers 9 and 10 during a tight turn. Electrical cables in the envelope were severed, causing sparks which ignited the fuel gushing out from the ruptured tanks, leading to two large explosions which partially destroyed the fore section of the airship. Two of the survivors came down with the stern

The memorial in Spring Bank West cemetery at Kingston-upon-Hull to the men of the R.38 who died in the disaster. On the opposite page is a panel listing the names of the British airmen who died. A similar panel on the other side bears the names of the American victims. *Robert Malster*

portion and landed on a sandbank in the river; one of the dead parachuted from the stricken craft and descended into the blazing wreckage.

A memorial stands to this day in the cemetery on Spring Bank West in

Kingston-upon-Hull commemorating the disaster and the dead. It is interesting to note that the American servicemen stationed in this area during the Second World War regularly laid wreaths on the memorial on the anniversary date of the disaster.

Captain Williams, acting in his role of Mooring Officer at Pulham, was on duty at the top of the 120-foot Pulham mast awaiting the arrival of the R.38 when he received a message to come down and see Major Scott. On reaching ground level Scott broke the news of the disaster to him.

A formal RAF Court of Inquiry reported on 5th September and then a sub-committee of the Accident Report Committee investigated the cause of the accident. They concluded it had been caused by structural weakness accentuated by very high control forces. The constructors were cleared from all blame and it was found that the design and construction requirements had been fully in accordance with specification requirements. It was also stated that the Short Brothers-built ship was in fact stronger than the comparable Zeppelin L-71, but the latter was not capable of being manoeuvred as sharply and was therefore protected from such high stresses.

The disaster brought about the cancellation of several projects for British commercial airships that were in future programmes. Nothing further was done until 1924, when a Labour Government sanctioned experiments to look into the prospects of commercial airship operations.

Most shapely of the British rigid airships, the R.80 had a good turn of speed but was too small to play any role in the proposed civil airship programme. *Vickers*

After this tragic incident there was concern .in high places regarding the safety of large rigid airships, and an Airship Stressing Panel was instituted so that designers would be under an obligation to design and build future ships to higher safety factors. It was ironic that the voice which had pleaded for more rigid rules in the design and stressing of large airships was stilled when Mr C. I. R. Campbell of the Royal Airship Works at Cardington perished in the disaster.

Just a few days before the R.38 met with disaster another rigid airship, the R.80, arrived at Pulham. She had been used as a training ship for the R.38/ZR-2's American crew, and much of her 73 hours' flying time had been spent in this way. Designed by Vickers' visionary Barnes Wallis and constructed by the same company, the R.80 was the best looking of all the British rigids. Of streamlined appearance, she had the look of speed about her; even the control car suspended beneath the hull was a departure from the glasshouse variety and resembled more the cockpit section of a modern airliner.

The R.80's arrival at Pulham on 20th August was not a particularly colourful affair. The only passengers were the commanding officer's livestock, which had been air-lifted from Howden Air Station; besides the domestic pets themselves, the R.80 delivered their hutches and the necessary fodder.

With four German-designed Wolseley-Maybach 240 hp engines, the R.80 had a top speed of 60 mph and was undoubtedly an efficient ship, but she was too small to fit in with the proposed commercial airship programme. After several months of indecision she was tested to destruction in the Pulham shed and was eventually dismantled in 1925; her main contribution to the development of airship design was in the structural strength and stress fields.

It was hoped that one of the greatest drawbacks to airship development, the necessity of using inflammable hydrogen as the lifting gas, would become a thing of the past when in December, 1921, the world's first helium-filled dirigible, the United States C-7, flew for the first time. Hope was short lived, however, as the American Administration placed an embargo on the export of helium and the rest of the world was forced to struggle on with hydrogen as the lifting medium.

In Britain the Admiralty had lost interest in airships, and the Air Ministry found them rather an embarrassment; they agreed to let the Airship Service lapse. The Secretary of State for Air, Mr Winston Churchill, never an advocate of the airship, initialled the proposal and added the words "and the sooner the better".

Manufacturers such as Short Brothers and Vickers still hoped to find a future for airships for commercial operation and worked on new designs for ambitious craft with accommodation for fifty to a hundred passengers and ranges of up to 6,000 miles in still air.

What appeared to be a concrete proposal was put forward on 22nd March, 1922, by Commander (later Sir) Dennistoun Burney. This gentleman, who was an associate of Vickers, had the backing of that company and also of the giant Shell Petroleum Company for his Imperial Airship Scheme; the two companies could provide the finance for the scheme — it was lack of capital that had caused the failure of other such schemes.

In order to put the scheme into effect a new company, the Airship Guarantee Company, was formed with £4 million nominal capital and backing from the governments of the United Kingdom, Australia and India. It was visualised that these three countries would be linked by the new service. All airships and equipment and the manufacturing facilities at Cardington and Howden were to be made available to the new company.

At the outset the prospects seemed rosy, but there followed a period of indecision. Then official policy changed with the replacement of Lloyd George's Coalition government by the Conservatives in October, 1922. Discussions on the various issues seemed almost endless and it was the middle of the following year before the scheme was accepted in principle.

On 10th July, 1923, the sub-committee of the National and Imperial Defence Committee headed by Sir Samuel Hoare issued its report on the financial aspects of the scheme for the development of a commercial airship service. The sub-committee recommended that a commercial airship service should be established between the United Kingdom and India, that new airships should be constructed to operate on that route, that all existing airships should be transferred to the operating company and that the airship stations at Pulham and Cardington should be leased to the company.

It was too late. Before the contract could be signed the Conservative Government resigned, to be replaced by the first Labour Government which came into office in January, 1924. The Airship Guarantee Company was back at square one, and the discussions began again. Then in May, 1924, the Prime Minister, Mr Ramsay MacDonald, announced that the Burney Scheme had been thrown out on the grounds that it gave the company a complete monopoly in the British airship field, and that was not in line with Government policies. At the same time the Government did state that they intended to carry on the airship development programme, and that it was authorizing work to be resumed on the reconditioning of existing experimental airships for this work.

Under the new arrangement the Air Ministry came back on to the scene. It was to be responsible for the airship experimental programme and for the construction and maintenance of bases along the intended routes. To operate the service the Air Ministry was to design and build a large passenger-carrying airship of five million cubic feet capacity; and the Airship Guarantee Company was to be given the opportunity to design and construct a second airship which would operate alongside the Air Ministry's ship on the Imperial Airship Service. The contract for the latter craft was signed with the Vickers-Burney company on 1st November, 1924.

Thus were conceived the last two big rigid airships to be constructed in Britain during the late Twenties, the R.100 designed by Barnes Wallis and built by Vickers at Howden and the R.101 designed by a Cardington team and built at the Bedfordshire base. Neither of them would ever visit Pulham.

CHAPTER SEVEN

Tested and Tried

THE GREAT doors of the Cardington shed were cranked back on 2nd April, 1925, to allow the reconditioned R.33 to be brought out. For more than four years she had lain in the berth vacated by the unfortunate R.38, her companion in the shed being the incomplete R.37, soon to be scrapped to allow for the enlargement of the shed.

The R.33 emerged from the hangar like some huge moth emerging from its chrysalis. The RAF roundels and the red, white and blue tail stripes had disappeared, and the large black registration letters G-FAAG alone adorned the hull. During her reconditioning following her four-year lay-up new gas cells of a modified design had been installed, and the motors had been modified. Not much else had been changed. For a few days, as if spreading and drying her wings, she sunned herself on the mooring mast and made a few local flights in the Bedford area.

The crew as well as the airship had been civilianised. Although still dressed in their naval-style white roll-neck sweaters and blue serge trousers, the crew were no longer service personnel but now enjoyed civilian status; but the officers and the chief coxswain were still serving members of the RAF. It was altogether a confusing situation, for the airship was still Air Ministry property in spite of her civil registration; the Civil Certificate of Airworthiness which had been issued listed the Air Council as the legal owner.

The details of this Certificate of Airworthiness were interesting:

(1) The minimum crew shall comprise One Officer, Five Riggers, and Seven Engineers.
(2) The Sunbeam Maori engines give 220 hp at 1,800 rpm (ground level) using 15 gallons per hour of petrol and 1.25 gallons per hour of oil.
(3) The minimum quantity of ballast carried shall be three tons, of which one ton of fuel may be considered as jettisonable ballast.
(4) The maximum static ceiling is rated as 11,000 feet.
(5) Gross Lift is 59.9 Tons and Disposable Lift 24 Tons (Useful Lift).
(6) The maximum range at 52½ knots is estimated at 2,750 miles in 52 hours.
(7) The maximum range at 40 knots is estimated at 4,000 miles in 100 hours.
(8) Electrical power for main lighting is 80 volts DC.
(9) 14 Volts DC is provided for bomb-release gear and secondary lights.

No explanation seems to have been given of why a civil airship required bomb-release gear.

When all was considered well the R.33 left Cardington under the command of Flight Lieutenant Carmichael Irwin and with Group Captain Fellowes as the Air Ministry observer for the base that she knew so well, Pulham. She had a crew of thirty-four and the loaded weight at takeoff was 33,970 lb. The flight to Pulham lasted four hours forty-five minutes and was considered such a success that Air Marshal John Salmond sent a congratulatory telegram to Group Captain Fellowes which awaited him on arrival at Pulham:

> Please congratulate all on successful flight of R.33 today. This important event definitely ends the inactive stage of British airships and will I trust be the forerunner of steady further progress.

First task of the R.33 at Pulham was to carry out a series of pressure plotting tests in conjunction with the National Physical Laboratory, whose technicians came on board to superintend the experiments. The tests involved the fitting of manometers — instruments used to measure gas pressure — and sensing devices to the outer hull of the airship; these were connected by electrical circuits to instruments on a panel in the gondola which recorded the pressures being encountered on the hull surface. Readings of the laminar flow, as it is now designated, were needed to give the designers an idea of the pressures set up at varying speeds and angles of attack.

These experiments provided the technicians with a great deal of basic data to be used in conjunction with the study of scale models employed in wind tunnel tests. Such data were essential in the design of the new giant airships R.100 and R.101.

The first flight of the R.33 while engaged on this work lasted thirteen hours. On board for this flight were all the top men in the airship world, including Lieutenant-Colonel V. C. Richmond, Assistant Director of Airship Development (Technical), and his technical assistant, Squadron Leader F. M. Rope, Major Scott, now Assistant Director of Airship Development (Flying), and Flight Lieutenant R. S. Booth, who was to be the captain of the R.101.

Records of this flight show that the R.33 flew over Suffolk, passing over Ipswich and Felixstowe and then setting course along the Essex coast to Shoeburyness, across the River Thames and over Kent to Croydon. Turning north, the airship passed over London and arrived back at Pulham at five in the morning to find thick fog shrouding the Norfolk countryside. She had to cruise around above the fog for several hours, and it was midday before she was able to moor up at Pulham.

Within little more than a fortnight of her arrival at the Norfolk base the R.33 was to have an adventure which would not only enhance her reputation as a lucky ship but would prove that airships were not necessarily as disaster-prone as it seemed from the record of other ships.

During the night of 16th/17th April the wind, which had been blowing gently enough during the evening, increased to gale force. Towards dawn there were gusts of up to 50 mph, mostly from a westerly direction. Moored to the Pulham high mast, the veteran R.33 weathercocked from side to side as the shuddering gusts tore at the fragile, drumming fabric of her envelope.

Only an "anchor watch" was on board; when the ship was moored out part of the crew performed watch-keeping duties, ensuring that all was well on board as the ship rode above the flatness of the Pulham airfield. The night watch who had ridden out the dark hours in the bucking craft were relieved by an NCO and eighteen civilian airshipmen under the command of thirty-year-old Flight Lieutenant R. S. Booth as the new day dawned.

The men coming on watch set about their task right away, ensuring that the ship was still secure and that no damage had occurred during the night. One of them, Ted Stupple, was instructed to check the security of the bolts attaching the swivel bollard on top of the mast. He stood with one foot on the mooring mast top and the other on the nose of the airship as he struggled against the wind, a hundred and twenty feet above the ground, to reach the bolts with his wrench.

Just as he placed his wrench on one of the bolts the R.33 gave a particularly vicious swing, putting an intolerable strain on the mooring arm. As the arm gave

The R.33 landing at Pulham after her thirteen-hour flight which took her over Essex, Kent and London in April, 1925. The ground handling party has the trail ropes in hand.

East Anglian Film Archive

Safely down and in the hands of the ground handling party, the damaged R.33 waits to be walked towards the shed. The flight that had begun as an emergency had ended as a triumph; it was hailed by Major G. H. Scott as one of the greatest achievements of an airship.

Dr P. Rawlence

R 33 arriving home at Pulham
after her mishap during the gale
of april 16/25

way the airship was torn from the mast, at the mercy of the gale-force wind. Ted Stupple instinctively threw himself backwards on to the tiny circular balcony which surrounded the mast top.

Drifting away from the mooring mast, streaming water ballast from her bow ballast tanks, the R.33 narrowly missed the doors of the airship shed. No 1 gasbag was punctured, and there was a danger that the fractured light alloy girders in the ship's broken bow section might puncture No 2 gasbag as they threshed about in the gusts, causing the nose to fall further. The collapse of the girders as a result of the damage sustained when the ship was torn away from the mast caused the bow section to fold inwards, forming a hollow into which the wind and rain beat with relentless force, pushing the bow down still further. Only the release of water ballast from the bow tanks saved the ship as she was blown rapidly backwards.

As the airship gained height the Maori engines were started up one by one and the drifting ship was brought under control. Flight Lieutenant Booth and his coxswain, G. W. "Sky" Hunt, had to assess the damage; to do so they ascended to the upper forward gun platform, from which they crawled forward as far as they could.

It was found possible to prevent damage to the remaining gas cells by rigging the deflated No 1 gasbag and the flapping envelope fabric as a shield. All kinds of equipment were jettisoned from the forward section in order to help return the ship to an even keel.

As soon as the plight of the R.33 was realized attempts were made to calculate the ship's drift and urgent wireless messages were sent to the appropriate authorities. The fishery protection sloop HMS *Godetia*, under the command of Commander F. W. D. Trigg, was ordered to make ready for sea in great haste and was despatched from Lowestoft to render assistance should the airship be forced down into the troubled waters of the North Sea. The local lifeboat was also called out under Coxswain Arthur Spurgeon; using sail as well as motor power to drive the lifeboat through the rough seas, Coxswain Spurgeon did his utmost to keep the airship in sight. The lifeboat was continually swamped by the waves and the airship was only partially visible through the driving rain and scud. When the weather worsened the boat had to reduce speed and was quite unable to keep up with the drifting airship; the R.33 disappeared into a rainsquall near the Holm Sand as the lifeboatmen reluctantly turned their boat round and headed back to Lowestoft.

With her engines running the R.33 was able to keep head to wind, but not to make headway against the gale. As she drifted out over the North Sea her wireless operator, Mr S. T. Keeley, transmitted messages each fifteen minutes both to report on the ship's condition and so that the ship's position could be fixed using the powerful wireless equipment at Pulham, the station at Croydon and the Dutch station at Waalhavn. Pulham was able to inform the R.33's commander of the latest meteorological reports so that he could plan his return course.

Five hours after the ship had broken away from the Pulham mast Flight Lieutenant Booth reported that he was able to arrest the ship's drift, but still the weather was forcing her nearer to the Continent. At 3.45 pm she was forty-four miles north-east of the Dutch port of Ymuiden. Offers of help were received by the airship's commander from both the Dutch and German governments, who

Flight Lieutenant R. S. Booth, who had charge of the R.33 during her unplanned flight across the North Sea and back to Pulham in April, 1925.

Dr P. Rawlence

were prepared to put landing crews at his disposal. Politely he declined their offers.

At one stage the airship came dangerously low and there were fears that she might crash into the sea. Flight Lieutenant Booth gave orders that everything portable and surplus to immediate requirements should be thrown overboard, and fire extinguishers, hammocks, parachutes and spare clothing all found a new home at the bottom of the North Sea. The R.33's luck was in, for the rain stopped and she was able to regain the height she had lost.

During the late afternoon Flight Lieutenant Booth received instructions to head on to a northerly course in the hope of finding a more favourable weather "window" that would allow the craft to make a slow passage home. The wind continued to lash the airship, however, and still she drifted downwind towards the Dutch coast. At 6 pm she was only ten miles from Ymuiden; at 8.25 pm she had been driven over the Dutch coast and was ten miles the other side of Ymuiden. The good news was that height had been gained and the R.33 was up to almost 9,000 feet.

With the drift apparently continuing Pulham transmitted a message that it would be advisable for the R.33 to proceed to Cologne, where the German authorities had a landing party standing by to bring the ship down safely. The Dutch authorities at the same time mounted a full emergency operation, putting ground crews at Soesterberg and Dekody on full alert to receive the stricken ship if she arrived at either of these airfields. The Dutch Navy also responded and had a tug and two torpedo boats ready at the naval base of Den Helder to make a dash to the rescue if necessary.

Such assistance was not needed. Late in the evening the R.33 came to a hover with her engines running, and she maintained her position off the Dutch coast until 5 am next day. Thanking the various authorities by wireless for their offers of help, the R.33 transmitted to Pulham the signal "Returning to England". Then began a long, slow flight back across the North Sea.

Eight hours later, after a tremendous struggle against the wind, the damaged airship with her crumpled, flattened bows crossed the Suffolk coast at Covehithe. Shining in the weak, watery sunlight, the R.33 was greeted by crowds of wellwishers lining the shore.

As news of the airship's return spread reporters and photographers from practically all the country's newspapers converged on Pulham; every hotel in Diss, Harleston and for miles around suddenly filled with people awaiting the crippled airship's arrival.

At ten minutes to two in the afternoon the R.33 appeared over Pulham. The great hollow on top of the nose bore testimony to the ordeal she had been through.

There was no shortage of volunteers to man the trail ropes as the ship was eased down towards the ground. There was no hope of bringing her to the mooring mast in her damaged state and the ground handling parties, under the control of Flight Lieutenant H. C. Irwin, had to walk the R.33 towards the shed, where she was safely berthed alongside the damaged R.36 later in the afternoon. When the triumphant but desperately tired crew disembarked they were overwhelmed by the interest generated by their exploit.

Pulham's commanding officer, Major Scott, described the safe return flight of the R.33 as one of the greatest achievements of an airship. For the part they

Undeafeated, the R.33 returns to Pulham after her North Sea wanderings. Her crumpled bows bear witness to the damage caused when she was torn away from the mooring mast. *Mr John Spiers*

Almost there! The damaged R.33 is walked towards the shed by a landing party made up largely of local people who had gathered to welcome "their" airship home. *Dr P. Rawlence*

had played in that achievement the entire crew were later presented with watches by King George V, and the coxswain, Flight Sergeant "Sky" Hunt, was awarded the Air Force Medal; it was typical of him that he always insisted that he had only received the award on behalf of the crew as a whole. Flight Sergeant Hunt died in the wreck of the R.101 little more than five years later, having gone back into the wreckage to try to save members of the crew.

The crew of the R.33 when she broke adrift were Flight Lieutenant R. S. Booth, Flight Sergeant G. W. Hunt, Messrs C. S. Oliver, G. E. Long, L. H. Rowe, R. W. Moyes, J. Walkinshaw, G. Watts, G. V. Bell, L. H. Moncrieff, R. W. Dick, J. E. Scott, S. T. Keeley, G. N. Potter, S. E. Scott, N. G. Mann, L. H. King, W. R. Gent, Z. Little and J. F. Ramp.

A new nose section, designed by the Design and Drawing Office staff at the Royal Airship Works at Cardington, was constructed at Pulham and spliced into the hull in place of the original nose during October, 1925; it was specially strengthened for mooring experimental work.

The airfield at this time of airship activity was very much a self-contained township, as Mr R. W. Moyes, now of Oxted, Surrey, recalls:

Hundreds of huts were provided as housing quarters for airmen and also for the carpenters, electricians, plumbers and mechanics. Nearby was the gas plant, which had been rebuilt from the time when it blew up.

Every year the landing ground produced wonderful crops of beautiful mushrooms which were gathered by the villagers. The myriad rabbits which infested the area were trapped, skinned and sold by a gipsy-type character whose name I cannot remember. He also cured the skins and from these he made gloves, muffs and hats which sold readily, for the winters of Norfolk can be very cold. There was a time, however, when the demand for the finished goods outstripped the supply of rabbits and then there was a great outcry from miles around at the mysterious disappearance of the local cats.

There was intense local interest in events at the air station, and considerable pride in the achievements of the R.33. Mrs D. Read of Pulham recalls that Mr S. Rice Cattermole, the Pulham St Mary baker, marked the airship's exploit in 1925 by having a painting made of the R.33 which was printed on the flour bags sold in his shop. Beneath the picture of the R.33 tethered to the Pulham mast appeared the inscription "Tested and Tried".

Tired but cheerful, members of the R.33's crew pose for a photograph before taking a well-earned rest after their eventful North Sea flight. Left to right are engineer W. H. King, leading engineer S. E. Scott, engineer Z. Little, rigger R. W. Dick, chief coxswain G. W. "Sky" Hunt, coxswain W. A. Potter and coxswain L. A. Moncrieff.
Dr P. Rawlence

CHAPTER EIGHT

A Dangerous Living

REPAIRS completed, the R.33 was brought out of the Pulham shed in which she had been housed since her exploit in April and took to the skies again on 5th October, 1925, to carry out pressure experiments connected with the design of the new giant airship to be built at Cardington, the R.101. These experiments involved taking readings of the pressures being exerted on the girders and the envelope of the airship during flight.

The first of these experimental flights, during which the airship was under the overall command of Major G. H. Scott, lasted more than nineteen hours. Flight Lieutenant H. C. Irwin was captain and the newly promoted Squadron Leader R. S. Booth was second pilot. The design team working on the R.101 project was on board; much of the information gleaned from the readings taken during the flight was incorporated into the design of that ill-fated craft.

Ten days later the R.33 took part in an experiment of a different nature. Seven years earlier thought had been given to the problems of defending airships against attack from fighter aircraft and trials had been carried out at Pulham with Sopwith Camels carried beneath the belly of HMA No 23; now in 1925 the idea of testing the ability of an aeroplane to detach itself from a trapeze under the airship's hull and then to attach itself again to the mother ship had come to the fore once again.

The R.33 had been fitted with a large trapeze structure amidships, to which was hooked a small low-wing monoplane which had been carrying out performance trials at RAF Martlesham Heath in Suffolk. The tiny de Havilland D.H.53 Humming Bird had been modified with a gantry above the forward fuselage bearing a long rod which curved at the front end; not surprisingly it was nicknamed "The parrot beak".

The first trial with the Humming Bird was carried out on 15th October. The pilot for the first attempt was Squadron Leader Rollo de Haga Haig, a Martlesham Heath test pilot. When all was ready the R.33 gently rose to 3,000 feet; at that altitude the signal was given that all was correct and the pilot pulled the release lever. The mechanism worked perfectly and the Humming Bird dropped away from under the airship's hull, started its motor while in a gentle dive and flew around the mother craft. The pilot then brought his small charge slowly up under the trapeze, matching his speed to that of the airship. At the crucial moment, however, there was a hitch and later there was some doubt as to whether the signal to re-engage had in fact been given. As the aeroplane came up with its "parrot beak" poised, it failed to engage the trapeze. The propeller smashed into one of the trapeze stay wires and was snapped as it cut into the wire. Taking immediate action, de Haga Haig disengaged the suspension gear and dropped down to glide motorless to the safety of the airfield below.

What should have happened was that the aircraft should have flown up to within about fifty feet of the airship, approaching from the stern; the suspension trapeze frame should have been lowered by a winch mounted in the lower hull of the airship. With the airship moving at a speed of about 49 knots, the aeroplane should have approached at a slightly greater speed and, taking up a gentle nose-up attitude, should have engaged the "parrot beak" guide, which slid into a springloaded slot where the aeroplane's frame would be secured. The winch would then have hoisted the suspension frame complete with aeroplane to a position under the hull where suitable pads were fitted to enable the plane's wings to be held secure.

A second attempt was made on 28th October, 1925, using the same aeroplane, now repaired. There was a different pilot, Flight Lieutenant Janor. With the R.33 moving along sedately at an altitude of 2,500 feet, the D.H.53 dropped away at a given signal and successfully flew above the ship before going round to the airship's stern and lining up to come up gently beneath it to engage the lowered trapeze frame. Again a slight error in relative speeds caused the monoplane to foul the trapeze, which was damaged, but once again fortunately the D.H.53 suffered no harm and was able to land at Pulham.

It was third time lucky on 4th December, when the same combination of airship and aeroplane crews flying at 3,000 feet and 45 knots successfully

The de Havilland D.H.53 Humming Bird L.7326 with the attachment known as the "parrot beak" designed to hook on to the attachment under the R.33. It was intended that the aircraft, originally designed as a light trainer, should act as a "ship's boat".   *Mr Roger Aldrich*

disengaged and re-engaged. This was the last flight of the R.33 for some months, as she was taken into the shed and deflated in preparation for overhaul.

One local resident recalls that this was not such a lucky day for one small lad who had been drawn to the air station by the excitement of this event. As the landing operations took longer than anticipated and he did not notice the onset of night because of the large number of landing lights which had been switched on to assist in the handling, he stayed on longer than prudent. When all was finished the lights suddenly went out and the young adventurer was left in

A de Havilland D.H.53 Humming Bird suspended under the R.33.
de Havilland Aircraft

almost total darkness, with only one light on the shed roof to give him any sense of direction. Scrambling over small hedges and through dank, wet ditches he eventually made the landing area and stumbled on to the railway line, whereupon he was able to stride the sleepers, fortunately in the right direction, and was thus able to find his way home. Doubtless many a reader has had such an adventure in his earlier life, and often also in the cause of aviation.

The Norwegian explorer Roald Amundsen had attempted for the second time to reach the North Pole by air on 21st May, 1925, using two Dornier Wal flying boats. Taking off from Ny Aalesund in Spitzbergen, one of the craft had been badly damaged as it landed near its polar destination. The mission was abandoned and the remaining flying boat landed back safely at Spitzbergen, without crossing the pole. Determined to achieve his objective, Amundsen looked around for new ideas. By coincidence one of his companions, Hjalmar Riiser-Larsen, was a qualified airship pilot who had carried out his training in Italy and was an acquaintance of Umberto Nobile, the Italian aeronautical engineer.

Word reached Riiser-Larsen's ear that Nobile's semi-rigid airship, the N.1, was about to be disposed of and he suggested to Amundsen that this would be an ideal conveyance for the polar expedition. Feelers were put out for the purchase of the airship, the money being put up by a rich American, Lincoln Ellsworth, and a deal was concluded with the proviso that although Amundsen should be the leader of the expedition, Nobile would command the airship, which was named *Norge* on 29th March, 1926. Benito Mussolini did not want the Norwegians to get all the credit for such an achievement, if it came off.

It was decided that when the expedition became airborne a stop would be made at Pulham before setting out towards the North. The *Norge* left Ciampino airfield near Rome on 10th April and made for Pulham.

Great crowds of people, some of whom had come by car from considerable distances around, gathered round the air station on 11th April and strained their necks and eyes as they scanned the grey and not very spring-like skies in hopes of seeing the airship arrive from Italy. Perhaps they hoped to catch a glimpse of the Norwegian explorer who, fourteen years earlier, had been the first man to reach the South Pole, but they would be disappointed; Amundsen was not on board the airship but had left Italy by ship some time before to prepare for its arrival in Scandinavia.

They needed considerable patience, for the *Norge* was late in arriving at Pulham. The airship crossed the Thames Estuary at about 2 pm and was not sighted at Pulham until 3.40, much later than she had been expected to arrive. And when she reached the air station there was further delay, as the *East Anglian Daily Times* reported next day:

> Several thousands of spectators witnessed the arrival of the *Norge*, which had made a non-stop flight of thirty hours. The *Norge* was docked in one of the great hangars with some difficulty and much delay. Coming from the South-east before a brisk Northerly wind, she was sighted from the aerodrome at 3.40. It was at once apparent that the landing would not be easy. Again and again she made for a certain position, and then had to tack again and again in wide circles without being able to make her landing ropes touch the ground.

When at last the ropes were grasped by the landing party the ship proved uncomfortably buoyant, and at least one man was lifted into the air until he was forced to release his grip on the rope. A witness from the Air Ministry described the arrival somewhat tersely:

> When we thought that it had made it, it rose again and circled round to have another attempt until eventually it did get down and was pulled into a shed, not without great difficulty, by over 100 men, mostly farm workers who had been swiftly recruited for this task. One of the passengers reported that the journey had been most uncomfortable and that the airship's commander, Colonel Nobile, had insisted on several circuits with the release of ballast which resulted in the craft gyrating up and down like a ping-pong ball.

Perhaps the exhaustion of the crew, a mix of Italians and Norwegians, was in part responsible for the problems experienced in bringing the airship down. Major Scott, who had been a passenger on the *Norge* on its flight from Italy, was suitably tactful when interviewed by a representative of the Press Association.

"The difficulty in landing was due mainly to variations in temperature and to the fact that after so long a journey the ship was not in good trim," he explained.

The difficulties in getting the ship down were the more embarrassing as the arrival was watched by Prince Olav of Norway and the British Secretary of State for Air, Sir Samuel Hoare. Colonel Nobile, who had been without sleep for seventy-two hours, spent little time dealing with the distinguished welcoming party, nor did he speak to reporters until he awoke next day from a twelve-hour sleep.

> In Rome, we had been waiting for a start at the earliest opportunity, and it would have been possible for me to go to bed on one of the nights, but I preferred not to do so because of the responsibility. It can be understood that last night I was very, very tired, in fact more tired than I have ever been in my life. I didn't want any food or drink, and did not have any when we came down, I just wanted to sleep . . .

Major Scott, in true British service tradition, had other things on his mind. He said his first need when the airship had landed was for a smoke and a drink. "The need for sleep came after, and it was a very real need, for in the *Norge* we had no facilities for rest. We had to stand up most of the time . . ."

There was time for an official meeting with Prince Olav and others on 13th April at the Old House, Harleston, before the *Norge* left Pulham the next day. Lifting gently from the Norfolk airfield, she gained height as she circled the air station and then set course towards Oslo, which was reached safely. In the end

The Italian airship *Norge* arriving at Pulham on 11th April, 1926, on her way from Italy to the Arctic. She left Pulham on the 14th for Oslo. *Mr Roger Aldrich*

Amundsen was beaten again in his quest to be the first to fly over the North Pole; two American airmen, Commanders Richard Byrd and Floyd Bennett, became the first men to look down on that desolate place on 9th May, 1926. They had not crossed the Polar icecap, having flown from King's Bay and then back again. Amundsen and Nobile did look down on the Pole on 12th May when the *Norge* dropped Norwegian, Italian and American flags. The *Norge* battled on through terrible weather conditions and after suffering all manner of near-disasters eventually alighted from its trans-Polar flight at 7 am on 14th May at Teller in Alaska, after a flight of over 3,000 miles; she was only fifty miles from her intended destination. This was a great achievement. Amundsen must have been bitterly disappointed to hear the news of the American airmen's triumph, but he was brave enough to carry on with his own endeavours which resulted in the first flight across the top of the world.

The visit of the *Norge* was recalled by Mr Charles Cutting, of Pulham Market, aged ninety-four at the time of writing. One of his duties as a civilian worker on the station was to ensure that the officers and men received their daily papers as early as possible each day, and he remembered delivering papers to Nobile while he was at Pulham.

A colleague of Mr Cutting's was Mr Percy Harker, who was in charge of the large water pumping installation on the airfield. Large quantities of water were required for the production of hydrogen by electrolysis, and as this water had to be as pure as possible, an equally large softening plant was part of the installation. During Royal Air Force days the villagers around the station enjoyed real soft water, but when the station eventually closed down and the plant was taken over by Depwade District Council the water returned to its former hard state.

A popular member of the air station staff was Mr Ernest Hubbard, a maintenance man who was responsible for the welfare of the upper parts of the huge airship sheds. Mr Cutting recalled having seen Mr Hubbard walking along a dangerous-looking catwalk between the two shed roofs more than once. With the enormous expanse of sheet roofing material covering the sheds it was almost a never-ending task to ensure that the sheets were all securely fastened. In their elevated position they were exposed to the high winds which swept across the site, and if any had worked loose and dropped down into the interior of the shed they could have caused tremendous damage to one of the ships floating down below. The ingress of water was another hazard and it was essential that the roof was kept as watertight as possible. One perk of this job was the excellent view that could be obtained of the surrounding countryside; on a clear day it was possible with binoculars to see the spire of Norwich Cathedral fifteen miles away.

Mr Cutting said that when he was demobilised from the Army during 1919 unemployment was rife in this mainly agricultural area of South Norfolk. To help these men the Army allowed them to keep their uniforms and their

The R.33 jettisons water ballast from the bows to correct her bows-down attitude as she comes in to land at Pulham. Sometimes the ballast was jettisoned over members of the landing party.

East Anglian Film Archive

greatcoats. If they were really desperate for money they could hand them in to the local Police Station, where they would be sold for cash and the money given in return. One of the few pleasures of life at that time was the fact that one could buy fresh herrings, in season from nearby Great Yarmouth, at twenty-five for a shilling.

Another very youthful veteran still at work in his Pulham Market garage business is Mr William Herring, always known as "Billy", who also has vivid memories of the days of the airships "up at the station". As the author and his wife stood and talked with him, they almost expected to hear the klaxon of the RNAS tender as it came through the village street calling the local folk up to the station to form a handling party, such was the descriptiveness of his memories. He was always glad to hear these calls to duty as he was paid five shillings a visit, and that was considerably more than one earned in the fields. Still very spritely, and working on a customer's motor-mower as he talked to us, he recalled that upwards of four hundred pairs of arms and legs were required to get one of the large rigids in or out of the shed; Billy pointed out that this could be a very uncomfortable task as sometimes the ship had to jettison water ballast as it approached the landing party, and this of course showered down from a height on to the men and women below.

His first duty came about in a peculiar way. He was out near the perimeter of the airfield gathering acorns to feed the pigs when he and the other lads with him heard the call for handling parties sounded; they ran over and were accepted. After this occasion they were always on the lookout for further calls; after mastering the non-rigids in the early days they graduated to the large rigids as they came along. The task was not without its hazards; one of the handlers was one day caught up in one of the trail ropes and carried aloft until he let go and fell to the ground — he was killed instantly. One or two others were more fortunate and survived such an experience; they usually received a small life pension for injuries incurred while engaged on these duties.

Being mechanically minded from an early age, Mr Herring always took a keen interest in the station's powerhouse housing the large diesel engines which drove the generators to provide electric power for the station, and in particular for the machine shop which turned out the many bits and pieces necessary to maintain the ships. The power plant, workshops and gas plant were all on the Rushall side of the site, while the sheds and airship facilities were on the Pulham side.

Mr Jack Bricer of the *King's Head* public house at Pulham St Mary recalled that in his father's barn a white owl had brought off a nest of youngsters; Major Scott on one of his visits to the hostelry had been shown the owlets by the landlord. He immediately took a fancy to them and took one of them back to the station where he kept it as a mascot and pet. The public house has a fine display of Pulham photographs in the bar parlour, and mine host is always ready to show interested visitors his relics of the airship days.

During the spring of 1926 the Government announced that the R.33's experimental programme had come to an end and that the airship would be shedded at Pulham; both the air station and the airship were to be put on a care and maintenance basis. It was not long before the station opened up for business again and the R.33 was recommissioned to take part in further experiments with the air-launching of fighter aircraft and for trials of the newly-constructed mooring mast at Cardington, erected for use by the R.100 and R.101, which were then being planned.

Instead of the diminutive D.H.53 Humming Bird, which it had been envisaged would be used as a means of communication in the same way that a warship used its boats for communication with the shore, the R.33 was now to be equipped with two of the RAF's most powerful fighters, the Gloster Grebe. The Grebe, which had a loaded weight of just over a ton, had come into service in 1923 when it replaced the wartime Sopwith Snipes. The two fighters were attached in tandem, one forward of the R.33's midships car and the other aft of it.

The combination took off from Pulham on 21st October, 1926, under the overall command of Major Scott, with Squadron Leader Booth as acting captain,

Experiments were carried out with the R.33 in 1926 into the flying off of Gloster Grebe fighter aircraft. Above two Grebes can be seen attached under the R.33's hull, and below is a closer view of the aircraft showing the method of attachment.   *Mr Roger Aldrich*

Squadron Leader E. L. Johnston as navigator and Captain Meager as first officer. Also on board was the Director of Airship Development, Group Captain Fellowes, and a crew of twenty-three, with the "flying side" under the command of Wing Commander Walsh. A further experiment carried out during this flight was into aerial acoustics, and this was under the direction of Mr Whateley-Smith.

While the R.33 was flying in the Pulham area at 2,000 feet the pilot of the rear-mounted Grebe, Flying Officer C. Mackenzie-Richards, started up the Armstrong-Siddeley Jaguar air-cooled radial motor; when it was warmed up the signal was given to cast off. The same procedure was then taken by the pilot of the second aircraft, Flying Officer R. L. Ragg. After he had released and successfully cleared the airship, the two fighters flew around the "mother" and then made for a local RAF station where they landed safely. The R.33's flight terminated at Cardington, where the airship was slightly damaged when she made a heavy landing.

The popular aviation weekly *Flight* sent their representative to Pulham to witness the operation. He wrote:

> A particularly interesting Service visit was to Pulham, again to witness the launching of Gloster Grebes from beneath the airship R.33 which had just recovered from a broken nose attachment upon breaking away from the mooring mast. We all stood anxiously waiting and wondering, not knowing what the R.33 would do when suddenly relieved of over a ton weight, the equivalent of 40,000 cubic feet of lift. The outcome was not spectacular, the R.33 carrying on its competent 30 mph way apparently unaffected. The first Grebe flown by F/O Mackenzie-Richards gained sufficient airspeed for control in the first 100 feet or so. The second Grebe flown by F/O Ragg had some starting trouble but eventually got away safely.

Two more Gloster Grebes, piloted by Squadron Leader Baker and Flight Lieutenant Shales, were flown off from under the R.33 after it had taken off from Cardington on 23rd November on its way back to Pulham. Also dropped on this flight were two parachutists, one of whom was Leading Aircraftman "Brainy" Dobbs of Martlesham Heath fame[17].

One of the R.33's last tasks was to try out several design structures in connection with the projected new airships, which were now in an advanced state of design layout. The veteran airship was put into the Pulham shed during November, 1926, for long-term storage; there she languished after metal fatigue had been detected in the framework, finally to be dismantled during 1928 after ten years' service with the Royal Air Force and 735 hours in the air. During her life R.33 had been a lucky ship, surviving being struck by lightning as well as being wrenched from the mooring mast and drifting over the North Sea, and she always had the respect of her crew.

The largest surviving relic of a British rigid airship is the forward portion of the control car of the R.33, which is on view to the public in the Royal Air Force Museum at Hendon.

During 1928 the massive No 2 Shed at Pulham Air Station was declared

The climax of the air-launching experiment as a Grebe flown by Flying Officer C. Mackenzie-Richards is released and banks away from the parent airship. It was followed later by the second Grebe which can be seen still attached in the forward position.   *Mr Roger Aldrich*

redundant to the station's needs. It was envisaged that the new breed of civil airships would operate from Cardington, where there was only one large rigid shed, and it was decided that the Pulham shed should be dismantled and transported to Cardington where it would be re-erected for use by the new ships. Work commenced on the dismantling, which was carried out by the Norwich contractors, Harry Pointer (Norwich) Limited; the massive structure was gradually denuded of its outer cladding, exposing the frames which in their turn were lowered to the ground, where they were all marked so that they could be re-erected in their correct order. A fleet of lorries transported the metal components to their new Bedfordshire home.

Of about the same dimensions as Pulham's No 1 shed, it was over 800 feet long, 180 feet wide and 130 feet high. As originally designed and erected it was a cantilever roofed structure with the main members bolted together, the whole building being clad with corrugated steel sheets. The large windscreens which were erected outside the opened doors were made of the same materials.

The largest components in the building were the gigantic doors which sealed the 180 feet by 130 feet opening at each end of the shed. Running in multiple tracks, these doors had many wheels in order to spread the weight over the largest possible area to reduce rail pressure and make their movement easier.

After the shed had been dismantled and transported to Cardington it was re-erected in an enlarged form in order to accommodate the new larger generation of craft. The door components were despatched to the contractor's yards in the North-east of England where they were re-designed and rebuilt for the new shed configuration. As the height of the doors had to be increased, so the undertracking had of necessity to be "beefed-up" in order to take the extra weight and also to be able to withstand the extra wind pressure on the enlarged surfaces. Another innovation incorporated during the rebuild was the introduction of mechanical power for the doors instead of the half-hour exertions on capstans by teams of heaving men. The practice of using the steam traction engine and the redundant tank had long since been discontinued. In their new form the doors weighed approximately 470 tons each. Some 4,000 tons of steel were used in the structure, which after re-erection covered an area of four and a quarter acres.

The original design must have been efficient, as after its twelve-year sojourn at Pulham, dismantling and re-erection at Cardington, the shed stands to this day on the latter site and is still used for housing lighter-than-air craft. The author well remembers spending several shivering hours within its confines, as do many other young RAF recruits of the Second World War, during the first few hours of his Service life.

Used for blimps during the early days at Pulham and later the rigids of wartime and post-war days at Pulham, it housed barrage balloons at Cardington during the Second World War and now proudly accommodates the helium-filled non-rigids of Airship Industries Limited.

While Pulham's No 2 shed was being rebuilt in enlarged form at Cardington work was proceeding on the giant R.101. Pulham was to have little to do with this project, but not far away in Norwich an old-established firm with considerable experience in the design and manufacture of all-metal structures was much involved. Boulton and Paul had been building aircraft of their own design for a number of years and had supplied the RAF with a medium bomber of metal construction, the Sidestrand, to a specification issued in 1924. It was to this firm, and to its technical director, John Dudley North, that the airship builders went for the design and production of much of the primary structure of the R.101[18].

And when the R.101 had been completed at Cardington she made one of her early flights over the county which had produced so much of her structure.

Leaving the mast at Cardington, she flew to North Norfolk and circled the Royal Estate at Sandringham where King George V and Queen Mary waved to the crew of the ship as she flew overhead. She then made her away along the Norfolk coast, flew over Sir Samuel Hoare's house at Northrepps (Sir Samuel was Secretary of State for Air), and then over Norwich as a tribute to the men of Boulton and Paul. Turning south, she overflew the air station at Pulham on her way back to her base at Cardington.

Pulham was at this time the home of a radio direction station which had been brought into service to give guidance to the R.100 and R.101 when they opened the projected civil airship service to India. The service never did get under way, but the station was able to carry out considerable work guiding civil airliners flying to and from the Continent.

The Film Archive Section of the Royal Air Force Museum at Hendon has some splendid film of this radio direction station guiding airliners of Imperial Airways, Sabena, KLM, Air France and Lufthansa into Croydon, then the airport for London. It looks crude by modern standards, with long strings with pins at their ends to indicate the tracks of aircraft they were directing in. Nevertheless it was effective. With airliners having an airspeed of between 90 and 140 mph the operators did have considerably more time to work it all out than have the air traffic controllers of today.

The R.101 rides on the Cardington mast, with the ex-Pulham shed in the background. The Cardington mast, designed for commercial operations, was fitted with a lift in contrast to that at Pulham, which had to be ascended by ladder. *Popular Flying*

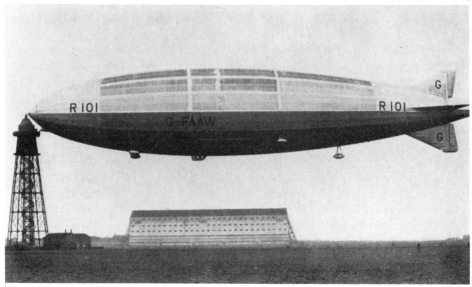

CHAPTER NINE

Fallow Field

THE AIRSHIP cause received a disastrous setback when in the early hours of 5th October, 1930, the R.101 crashed into the north-west ridge of the Bois de Coutumes near Beauvais in northern France during what was to have been her maiden flight to India. Of the fifty-four people on board only six survived the inferno as the giant airship with its five and a half million cubic feet of hydrogen was consumed by fire[19].

Among those who died were many of the top men in the British airship industry, some of them with close Pulham links. One of these was Major G. H. Scott, who at the time of his death was Assistant Director of Airship Development and had in the past commanded the Pulham Air Station; earlier still he had been chief experimental officer at Pulham. Another was Flight Lieutenant H. C. Irwin, who was well known at Pulham in connection with the R.33 and had been a member of the British athletics team at the Olympic Games in Antwerp in 1920; he had also represented Ireland and the Royal Air Force in other athletic contests.

With them died Brigadier-General Lord Thomson, who had become Secretary of State for Air the previous year. It was his insistence on being able to fly to India in the R.101 and to return to Britain in time for a forthcoming Imperial Conference that resulted in the R.101 starting for India on 4th October, 1930, considerably earlier than some experts had deemed advisable.

One of the politicians who died in the crash, Sir Sefton Brancker, the Director of Civil Aviation, was known to harbour doubts about the usefulness of large airships, which he regarded as no more than interim vehicles pending the development of large aeroplanes and flying boats which would carry the British flag over the Empire air routes. An aviator of long standing, he was remembered by many as a great practical joker; many a bystander was astonished when Sir Sefton, who was never seen without a monocle, would offer to swallow that eyeglass if he was wrong about any statement that he had made — and would then proceed to devour the glassy morsel.

Among the East Anglian residents who died was Squadron Leader F. M. Rope, who lived at Kesgrave, near Ipswich, and at the time of his death was assistant to Lieutenant Colonel V. C. Richmond, the Assistant Director of Airship Development (Technical), the man who headed the Cardington team responsible for the design and construction of the R.101. It was Squadron

Leader Rope, a member of an old Suffolk family, who evolved the brilliantly conceived harness for the gas cells of the R.101.

A small Roman Catholic chapel was built alongside the main Ipswich–Lowestoft road at Kesgrave, close to the farm where his wife lived, as a memorial to Squadron Leader Rope. Dedicated to St Michael, it is known locally as "the airship church". Inside hangs a beautiful model of the R.101, made as a contribution to the memorial chapel by the men of the Royal Airship Works at Cardington; it is lit during Mass by a concealed spotlight which casts a shadow of the airship above the altar. Also in the chapel is a stained glass window of St Michael, who has the head and face of Squadron Leader Rope, and a plaque at the door requests prayers for his soul. The celebrant at the Requiem Mass held in Westminster Cathedral on Friday, 10th October, 1930, was Squadron Leader Rope's brother, the Reverend Harry Rope.

Navigator of the R.101 on that fatal flight was Squadron Leader E. L. Johnston, who had earlier served in the R.33 and had been in the airship business for some years. He had been responsible for organizing the Guild of Air Pilots and Air Navigators, of which he was Deputy Master. His son, Wing Commander E. A. Johnston, was station commander at RAF Martlesham Heath in Suffolk during 1953.

One of the handful of survivors was Harry Leech, the foreman engineer, who had served at Pulham during the First World War. Another ex-Pulham man, chargehand engineer Mr Tom Keys, was among the dead, and so were chief coxswain G. W. Hunt, first engineer W. S. Gent, chargehand engineer S. E. Scott and chief wireless operator S. T. Keeley, all of whom had been in the crew of the R.33 when she broke away from the Pulham mast. Mr Keeley lived at Stuston, near Diss, only a few miles south of Pulham. And assistant chief coxswain W. A. Potter had lived at Yoxford, a little further south along the Norwich–Ipswich road.

It is said that chief coxswain Hunt emerged unscathed from the blazing wreck of the R.101 and was then heard to call out that he was "going back to get Wally", in other words his old friend assistant chief coxswain Potter, who had been a survivor of the R.38 disaster in 1921. Both died among the wreckage.

Much has been written about how the R.101 was despatched on her maiden flight to India without ever having been flown in bad weather and without even having carried out speed trials. The ship had been beset by problems: diesel engines selected for the R.101 had proved to be almost twice the calculated weight; servo controls to operate the control surfaces were either not fitted or were removed at considerable expense; a new midship section and an additional gas bag had to be added to give the craft added lift; and in the view of reliable experts the ship should not have set out on the Empire flight when she did.

The arguments will probably go on for ever, but those who wish to learn more of the unhappy story of the R.101 and the rivalry between that government-sponsored ship and the privately constructed R.100 should read Geoffrey Chamberlain's *Airships—Cardington*, published by Terence Dalton in 1984.

The private constructor, the Airship Guarantee Company, a subsidiary of Vickers, was headed by Sir Dennistoun Burney, with Dr Barnes Wallis as his designer and Nevil Shute Norway as chief calculator[20]. In his book *Slide Rule* Nevil Shute, as he is better known, says that most of the people responsible for the design of the R.101 were new to airship work, the crash of the R.38 in 1921 having killed most of the top Government designers. The R.38 herself had broken up, he suggests, because of the incorrect calculation of stresses imposed on the airframe — or perhaps because the proper calculations had not been made at all.

The result of the R.101 accident was inevitable. When a decision was made about the future of British airship operations it was a negative one. The successful R.100, which had proved her worth by flying across the Atlantic to Canada and back, was eventually sold for a mere £450 and was broken up for

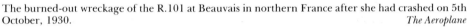

The burned-out wreckage of the R.101 at Beauvais in northern France after she had crashed on 5th October, 1930. *The Aeroplane*

117

scrap. She might have gone on to achieve great things for Britain in the lighter-than-air field, but she was given no chance.

With the decision to discontinue airship development in Britain all the money that had been spent on research and building was lost; so were the skills and the devotion that had created the great airships. Undaunted, the Germans carried on with their successful Atlantic crossings with the *Graf Zeppelin* and the *Hindenberg*, pioneering many new aspects of the operation of large rigid airships in all weathers over long distances.

The German airship expert, Dr Hugo Eckener, stated that the loss of the R.101 had not made the Zeppelin Airship Company alter its standpoint as to the ability of airships. He also added that the catastrophe of the R.101 would not have been so terrible in its extent if the airship had been filled with helium gas. The Zeppelin Airship Company had always adopted the view that helium should be used for passenger airships instead of hydrogen, and it would be a very graceful act if the American Government now agreed to place helium gas, of which America had plenty, at the disposal of international aviation. Mr Britten, chairman of the United States Naval Affairs Committee, announced that he would sponsor legislation to allow the export of helium gas as the result of the R.101 disaster. This had, however, not come about before the Second World War, and one of the last of the large rigid commercial airships, the Zeppelin Company's hydrogen-filled *Hindenburg*, was destroyed by fire as it came in to moor at the American airship base at Lakehurst, New Jersey, a few years after Mr Britten's statement.

Air activity of another kind came to Pulham during July, 1930, when a prototype biplane on a test flight from Martlesham Heath was forced to seek refuge on the flat expanse of the airship field. The aircraft was the Handley-Page H.P.34 Hare, serial number J.8622, an experimental biplane which had been built to Air Ministry specification 23/25. It was undergoing evaluation tests at the Aeroplane and Armament Experimental Establishment as a day bomber. An orthodox-looking unequal-span single-bay biplane, it was powered by a Bristol Jupiter nine-cylinder air-cooled radial engine driving a four-bladed wooden airscrew. The Hare, piloted by Squadron Leader Goodwin, took off from the heather-clad airfield at Martlesham Heath on 3rd July for a medium altitude climb as part of its handling trials. When it had reached an altitude of around 16,000 feet a piston seized in the radial engine, which stopped dead; the pilot was faced with the necessity of making a dead-stick landing in a suitable field. Glancing down, he saw the expanse of Pulham Air Station within gliding distance and put the aircraft down there without further damage.

After details of the forced landing had been communicated to Martlesham Heath steps were taken to get the stranded aircraft back to its base. This necessitated the removal of the seized engine and its replacement by another. The only engine available was fitted in another experimental aircraft, also at

Martlesham Heath, the Vickers Type 177 shipboard single-seat fighter. It was decided to remove the Jupiter XF from the Vickers Type 177, take it by road to Pulham, install it in place of the defective engine and fly the Hare back to the A.& A.E.E. This was duly carried out and on 14th July the Hare rose again into its natural element and arrived safely back at Martlesham Heath. The donor aircraft suffered as a result of losing its power plant as it was taken back to its maker's factory at Weybridge and from there passed into obscurity. Apart from the earlier aircraft activity connected with the airship/aircraft launching experiments this was the only aircraft movement from Pulham until a later incident during the Second World War.

One correspondent who visited the air station during 1932 recalls that the only activity there was at the radio station, which was still employed in giving directional bearings to commercial aircraft. The hydrogen gas plant was still intact, well preserved and painted, and a captive balloon was tethered on the airfield.

The Handley Page H.P.34 Hare J.8622. which made a forced landing at Pulham while on a test flight from the Aeroplane and Armament Experimental Establishment at Martlesham Heath in 1930.

Handley Page Ltd

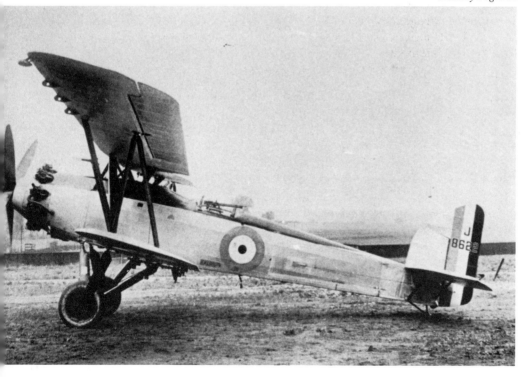

An Air Ministry Memorandum of March, 1937, shed some light on the position of men who had been engaged in airship grades.

> Airmen of the obsolescent trade of Rigger (Airship) will be remustered as Balloon Operators, Group II with effect from March 11th, 1937. Their service as Rigger (Airship) will count towards promotion and progressive pay in the trade of Balloon Operator as soon as possible.
>
> Existing airmen in the trade of Rigger (Balloon), Group III who are employed as instructors in balloon rigging for the new trade of balloon operator and are therefore unable to complete the necessary additional training for that trade will be remustered provisionally as Balloon Operators from the date at which the first trainees complete the training and are remustered as Balloon Operators.
>
> This order is a result of the formation of balloon units for the Air Defence of Great Britain.

Those balloon units were to become familiar to East Anglians between 1939 and 1945, when the port area of Felixstowe and Harwich and towns and cities such as Ipswich and Norwich were protected by balloon barrages. Some people even referred to the balloons as "pigs".

Barrage balloons were used to protect many potential target areas during the Second World War.

CHAPTER TEN

At War Again

Wto life again, though in the conflict ahead it was to play a very different role from that which it had played in the First World War.

During March, 1939, No 2 Maintenance Sub Unit was formed at Pulham under the command of Flight Lieutenant L. H. Anness, AFC, and when No 53 Maintenance Unit was formed just before the outbreak of war the original sub unit was incorporated.

No 53 MU at Pulham was part of No 42 Group, Maintenance Command, which was responsible for the storage and issue of a number of heavy commodities required by the RAF's operational units. Petrol, explosives of every imaginable kind, and all the bits and pieces associated with armaments were stocked by the Pulham unit. Among these bits and pieces were bomb pistols and fuses for detonating the main explosive load of bombs carried by the RAF's bombers and the tail units for the bombs, which were always stored as separate items.

All these stores had to have special containers to protect them from damage when in store and on the way to the airfields at which they would be employed, and Pulham played a unique role in connection with these containers. No 53 MU was the only such unit in the United Kingdom to receive, store, repair and re-issue all types of ammunition containers and boxes, which came to Pulham from operational stations all over the British Isles. A section was set up to deal with the necessary repairs when these cases and containers were received in damaged condition, and the sounds of hammer, saw and file were heard day after day as the work went on.

Several small huts were erected in a special fenced-off area, known as the "danger zone", for the storage of pyrotechnics such as target markers, signal cartridges for Verey pistols and flares of all descriptions. There was also a filling station for practice bombs of the smoke emitting type which weighted 11 lb and contained a liquid filling. No bulk quantities of explosives or large amounts of small-arms ammunition were ever stored at Pulham.

With the recommissioning of the station much of the equipment had to be renewed. Soon Pulham was again self supporting, with its own electricity generating plant, a water pumping station and an efficient sewage disposal unit.

German intelligence was undoubtedly aware of the renewed activity at

The *Graf Zeppelin* seen over the North Norfolk coast during a "goodwill" flight three years before the outbreak of the Second World War. The real objective of the flight was to observe British defences.

Mr G. Soar

Pulham in those last months of peace. During the Allied advance into Europe after D-Day a large number of aerial photographs of potential targets in the British Isles were found in a safe in a German headquarters in Brussels; among them was a photograph of Pulham Air Station taken on 9th April, 1939. Whether it was taken by a reconnaissance aircraft of the Luftwaffe or by a civilian aeroplane, possibly a Lufthansa airliner which had strayed from its accustomed course, is not known.

Such aircraft were not the only ones to be involved in espionage. During August, 1939, the recently-commissioned Zeppelin LZ-130 *Graf Zeppelin* carried out spying missions off the East Anglian coast with the intention of picking up signals from the radar towers which had been erected at Bawdsey and at other sites around the British coasts[21].

The airship was ideally suited for such purposes, for she could loiter just out of sight of land while her detecting apparatus was used to pick up signals from the new sites. The surveillance apparatus was under the direction of Dr Breuning, a young electronics expert.

On this occasion the airship's commander, Albert Sammt, took good care not to cross the coast. In 1936 the LZ-127, also named *Graf Zeppelin*, had made no effort at all to avoid crossing the coast when making "goodwill flights" over East Anglia, in the course of which she had passed slowly over many sensitive sites, including the RAF station at Martlesham Heath, then the home of the Aeroplane and Armament Experimental Establishment and engaged in testing aircraft such as the Supermarine Spitfire and the Hawker Hurricane, which were to play such a significant part in the coming conflict.

Pulham did have a role, albeit a passive one, in the early development of radar. The late Mr Arnold Wilkins related to the author how in the early days of radio-location experiments at Orfordness an aircraft from Martlesham Heath would fly under the direction of the Orfordness scientists towards Pulham, whose remaining airship shed provided a wonderful navigational aid for the pilot. As the equipment was developed the scientists were able to track the aircraft all the way to Pulham, watch it make its turn above the air station and then follow its return flight. In due course improvements in the equipment enabled them to track their quarry further afield; the aircraft then flew to Bircham Newton in west Norfolk, still passing within sight of Pulham.

During the early months of the Second World War a more powerful direction finding radio station was established at Pulham, where it operated independently of No 53 Maintenance Unit and outside the jurisdiction of the station commanding officer. This DF station, which operated round the clock, worked in conjunction with two other stations, position fixes being worked out from the intersection of signals from the three stations; these fixes were sent to the aircraft concerned by radio.

It is rumoured that one day a Luftwaffe pilot, speaking with a strong Cockney accent, asked for a navigational fix. When he received a reply indicating that the operators at the RDF station had rumbled him his further transmissions are said to have been an extremely rich example of true-blue invective.

Pulham's enormous shed was undoubtedly a landmark that could not be hidden from the eyes of Luftwaffe pilots, to whom it must have proved a most useful navigational aid as they approached from over the North Sea. Indeed, there was a rumour current in the early days of the war that the Luftwaffe used the Pulham shed as a target for fledgling aircrews on their first operational flight over England. Certainly the station was strafed on numerous occasions by German aircraft which dropped the odd bomb or two from time to time; as the months rolled by the number of holes in the shed multiplied, keeping a team of men busy patching them up.

The narrow gauge railway line which had served the airfield itself for several years came into its own during the Second World War, when it was called upon to carry all manner of materials across the site. The driver of the narrow gauge engine used on this line was Mr Sydney "Pop" Stannard, who made many friends and is still recalled by many who served at Pulham.

The narrow gauge line ran alongside the standard gauge spur which diverged from the Waveney Valley Line of the London and North Eastern Railway, there being a loading dock at the terminus of the standard gauge line at which goods could be transferred to the narrow gauge trucks. There was also a large covered shed at this terminus.

An official Great Eastern Railway route map bearing the date 25th December, 1919—the railways worked on Christmas Day before nationalisation—shows the track leaving the Waveney Valley Line near Pulham station and curving away into the air station, passing through two or three sets of gates. This mile-long branch was lightly constructed, and many residents recall seeing the occasional truck heeling slowly over as the track subsided beneath it. On one occasion all the wagons of a short freight train finished up leaning over as a long section of track sank beneath the train's weight.

The branch, which was owned by the Air Ministry, was served by the occasional pick-up goods train; it was never used by passenger trains. Locomotives were able to run round the trains by using a loop at the terminus. Another loop on the main line at the junction of the airfield branch allowed trains departing from Pulham to travel either to Tivetshall in one direction or to Beccles in the other.

In the wartime years the Waveney Valley Line, which in peacetime had been used as a diversionary route for passenger trains from the Midlands to the East

The masts of the radio direction finding station at Pulham and the remaining airship shed form twin landmarks in the Norfolk countryside.   *Mr R. Aldrich*

Coast holiday resorts, was busy with goods trains bringing ammunition and other stores to the bomber airfields hurriedly constructed for the United States 8th Army Air Force on both sides of the Waveney Valley. The line also had an important part to play in a wartime campaign to increase food production, sugar beet being loaded into wagons not only at the various stations along the line but also on the Air Ministry siding at Pulham. When the sugar factories at Cantley and elsewhere were working at full capacity wagons were diverted for these agricultural loads, which took precedence even over the RAF's own goods traffic.

The spur at Pulham remained in traffic until 1957. No 53 MU utilised it as

The terminus of the standard gauge line inside the air station. The Nissen building replaced an earlier wooden structure.
Dr Ian C. Allen

their main means of transport for heavy stores, the railway having obvious advantages over road transport for the carriage of potentially dangerous explosives.

The early forties was the time of great activity by the Luftwaffe, and its bombers ranged far and wide over East Anglia scattering their bomb loads on towns and villages alike. At times it was hard to conceive what the target was; far easier to feel that the bombs and bullets had been aimed at almost anything in general as long as it was in the British Isles. Farm labourers in the fields, postmen on their cycles in leafy country lanes, women hanging out their washing and the slow rural goods train wending its way along a single winding track were all fair game to the roving intruders. Not all got away unscathed.

Pulham lay under the path of Luftwaffe bombers making their almost nightly excursions to the industrial Midlands and the north-western cities and ports. The Norfolk countryside received many a bomb originally intended for the other side of the country, but jettisoned during the homeward flight. The

A barbed-wire entanglement and the concrete bases for a windscreen serving an early non-rigid airship shed can be seen in the foreground of this wartime photograph of the camouflaged Pulham hangar. Missing panels from the wall were blown out by blast from a bomb which exploded inside the building. *Mr Roger Aldrich*

most disturbing aspect of these activities was the continuous wail of the air raid sirens, resulting in sleepless nights and consequently hampered days at work.

The war came a little closer on 21st August, 1940, when a twin-engined Dornier Do.17 bomber from the Luftwaffe formation II/KG.3, one of three which had been lurking in the Norwich area, was shot down near Harleston and came down to earth in a wood at Conifer Hill, Starston, not far from the air station. The raiders had arrived about midday and while two of the original three had gone off on other business, the remaining one turned south and made its way towards Pulham. It was set upon by three Hawker Hurricane fighters of No 242 Squadron based at Coltishall flown by Flight Lieutenant G. S. Powell-Shedon, Sub-Lieutenant R. E. Gardner, a Fleet Air Arm pilot who had been seconded to augment the depleted ranks of the RAF's fighter pilots, and Pilot Officer J. B. Latta. As it was around dinner time many people were in the streets of the villages beneath to witness three parachutes open over the Weybread area as the crew members of the Luftwaffe bomber baled out. The pilot, Leutnant Heinz Ermeke, stayed with the rapidly descending bomber and managed to bring it down for a fast crash landing in a pasture at Starston, where in its wild career across the meadow it killed two ponies. Still skidding along at a fast pace it crashed into a spinney where it exploded. The resulting inferno was tackled by local firemen when they reached the scene of the crash, but they could do no more than confine the flames to the crash site. Leutnant Ermeke died in the crash.

The three Luftwaffe non-commissioned crewmen who had parachuted down landed at Weybread, where two of them were picked up quickly by farm workers in the fields. The third was taken prisoner by a farmer's wife, Mrs Ada Daniels, of Chancel Farm, Weybread, ably assisted by her young son, Ian, who was carrying his father's Home Guard rifle. Mrs Daniels took him to the farmhouse, tended his wounds and gave him a cup of tea, although he was covered all the time by Ian with the rifle. The dead pilot was buried in St. Margaret's Churchyard, Starston, personnel from RAF Pulham providing full military honours.

Next month, on Wednesday the 11th, all was calm on a Summer's day at nearby Eye when another raider roared down low and dropped three large bombs. Fortunately they failed to detonate, having been dropped at too low an altitude, but one of them bounced up from the street and passed through the open window of a bedroom over a shop in the town centre. It was a very lucky day for that small Suffolk town.

This was also the time of mounting invasion fears. Although Pulham was some distance from the coast, full precautions were taken to prevent any attempt at an airborne landing. The open stretches of the airfield were covered with suitable obstacles to deter any approaching troop transports, and defensive positions were prepared by locally stationed troops and the Local Defence Volunteers.

Pulham air station itself came under attack on 16th February, 1941, when a Luftwaffe bomber dropped down out of a murky cloud-laden sky and released its bomb load almost at roof level. The four bombs landed beside the old airship shed, which was being used at the time for shell filling and contained huge stocks of bombs. Little damage was caused.

A few days later a stick of five bombs straddled the shed roof, the first one making contact at one corner while the fifth hit the opposite diagonal corner. Fortunately the angle of the last two missiles was such that on striking the concrete shed floor they bounced up again and exploded safely outside after passing through the side walls. The last one exploded on the narrow gauge railway track, leaving the twin rails raised up in the manner of an upright horseshoe. The narrow gauge railway was not repaired and was never used again after this attack.

One of the shed's design features was that incorporated in the walls were detachable panels which were only loosely attached to the main structure. If a gas explosion had occurred when one of the ships was shedded the increased pressure within the shed would push out the panels and allow the blast to vent itself, thus saving the main structure from greater damage. The design of these panels was proved efficient, as on this occasion they detached as designed and the shed was saved from any great damage. Saved also were the airmen working in the shed, even those high up aloft on a catwalk in the roof; no casualties resulted from the attack.

The arrival of an aircraft at a airfield should not really be worthy of mention, but Pulham was no longer a flying field. A Supermarine Spitfire which had run into trouble over the North Sea and landed at Pulham during 1941 was the only aircraft to do so during the duration of hostilities. Both the Spitfire and its Czech pilot arrived safely; both were subsequently removed by road.

Flight Lieutenant S. E. Thorn, who was in residence from February to June, 1942, remembers:

> I was stationed at Pulham during the first half of 1942 after entering the Royal Air Force with a Direct Commission during December, 1941. After a brief posting to Bawdsey, Suffolk, I was posted to Pulham as adjutant. To my surprise the commanding officer, who was of Flight Lieutenant rank and whose name I cannot recall at the present time, I had known previously by sight. He had been in the Midland Bank at Palmers Green while I was in Barclays just across the road.
>
> One task was that during the end of April or early May a single cypher was introduced and each day I was required to send off a signal to show that I knew how to do it. I very soon got tired of making up messages and so one lunchtime I picked up a

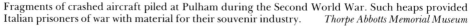

Fragments of crashed aircraft piled at Pulham during the Second World War. Such heaps provided Italian prisoners of war with material for their souvenir industry. *Thorpe Abbotts Memorial Museum*

copy of Shakespeare's plays and, glancing through, wondered if by remote chance there might be something appropriate for that day's signal. Almost immediately I spotted a quotation that left me in no doubt but to use it, it appealed to my sense of humour.

I made a note of the play, act, scene and speaker and the quotation was duly sent off. The next day as we were going into the farmhouse that was our mess, DRLS (Despatch Rider Letter Service) roared up and held out an envelope, saying "Signal, Sir". I took it, thanked him and he rode off. Opening the letter I found that I had been posted to a full Cypher Course at Oxford. The signal I had sent was "Thou must untangle this, not I, 'tis too hard a knot for me to untie."

I have a recollection that during the enemy raids on Norwich the airship shed was peppered with machine-gun fire through the roof and sides. It was said that the water ballast tanks were still full of water as they had not been hit.

Another incident comes to mind that was not without humour. The Duty Officer for some reason or other was not satisfied with the preparation of the food for the Airmen's Mess. He was not satisfied either with the answer he got to his question and countered it with another "Why?". Still not satisfied, he repeated, "Why?", and for a third time he expressed dissatisfaction. At lunchtime in the Officer's Mess a steak and kidney pie was placed in front of the commanding officer for him to portion out for us. From above the piecrust looked like this.

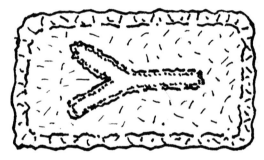

The Duty Officer immediately looked at Trembath, the cook, and said "What's the meaning of this?" Trembath looked blank and said "The meaning of what?" and received the answer "This Y". Trembath looked at him and said "Y, Sir? That's not a Y. I happened to have some spare pastry and just decorated the pie crust."

When I arrived at Pulham there was a dance band but no pianist, so I filled in. The rest were trumpet, sax, violin and drums. We played in surrounding villages; Brockdish and Long Stratton are two that I remember; and sometimes we had to take our piano with us, which we had previously learned to be necessary as in some halls the pianos were very badly out of tune.

With such a large open area available for storage it soon occurred to someone that this area could be used for the storage of dismantled or wrecked aircraft. Consequently the shiny heaps of cripples and wrecks grew daily as aircraft which had come to grief in the mid-Norfolk area were picked up by the salvage teams and dumped at Pulham. All these arrivals, mainly bombers of the US 8th Air Force, came in by road. Maintenance officers from the local bomber airfields became constant visitors to Pulham as they searched for usable components for their charges; many of the aircraft lying derelict at Pulham were the source of all manner of spares which could not be procured through the normal channels.

Another of Pulham's storage capabilities was discovered by Mr P. C. Sage, of Rougham, Suffolk, who remembers:

> On 4th January, 1944, I was sent to Pulham St Mary to collect a small load of thin metal strips which were called "Window". We now know that these were dropped over enemy territory to confuse their radar but at the time of my visit this was top secret. I believed that this was some of the first to be dropped and it was stored in the old airship shed along with many other instruments of war including what I think must have been the first "Block-Buster" bombs. The station was at that time under the protection of Air Ministry civilian police and appeared to be a top security station. At this time I was a member of No 115 Bomber Squadron with Avro Lancasters, based at RAF Witchford, near Ely, Cambridgeshire.

After Italy surrendered on 7th September, 1943, and changed her allegiance the many Italian prisoners-of-war who were working on farms in East Anglia became co-belligerants. They could not be returned to their homeland because of the continued German occupation of Italy, and many were drafted into Pulham where they were able to free British servicemen for more essential tasks. The ex-POWs were free to come and go as they pleased in the area when not on duty. As there were many skilled craftsmen among their ranks, the aircraft salvage dumps were Aladdin's Caves for suitable material for them to exercise their skills on. Rings, cigarette lighters, and cases, ashtrays and many other articles of this nature were fashioned and traded, while discarded ammunition boxes, of which there was a large store, provided the wood for all manner of carved items and trinkets.

With the arrival in East Anglia of the United States 8th Army Air Force Pulham Air Station was almost encircled by four of their bomber airfields, Thorpe Abbotts (Station 139) to the west, Hardwick (Station 104) to the north, Flixton (Station 125) to the east, and Metfield (Station 366) to the south. The first-named was virtually only just over the fence from Pulham; the construction firm of John Laing started work on that site during 1942 and it became operational in June, 1943.

The resident unit at Thorpe Abbotts was the 100th Bombardment Group (H), which was part of the 13th Combat Wing, whose aircraft carried a large white letter D in a black square on their fins. Flying the Boeing B-17F and G, the unit picked up the nickname of "The Bloody Hundredth" due to the very heavy losses sustained during operations over Germany. In one week the Thorpe Abbotts Group lost twenty aircraft and 200 crew members killed or missing[22]. The group comprised four squadrons, the 349th, 350th, 351st and 418th. During the course of operations they dropped over 19,000 tons of bombs and lost 177 aircraft. They were one of the last units to return to the United States of America after the Armistice.

The Pulham salvage dump was the last resting place of many a proud aircraft. Remains of a Pathfinder Lancaster and both B-17s and B-24s can be identified among the wreckage.

Thorpe Abbotts Memorial Museum

The Thorpe Abbotts airfield site was sold during 1956, but the former control tower has been made into a fine museum commemorating the exploits of the 100th, all the work being carried out by local aviation enthusiasts.

Several fine books tell the exploits of the USAAF during its stay in East Anglia and in particular of the deeds of those who flew from the four stations which surrounded Pulham. Within the confines of this history it would not be untoward to mention a few incidents which occurred within the Pulham environment. The nearby railway station at Diss, on the main LNER line from Ipswich to Norwich, saw the arrival of large numbers of replacement combat crews, many of them destined for Thorpe Abbotts where it seemed that their stay was of only short duration. On 8th October, 1943, the base lost seven ten-man crews, and another twelve crews two days later.

Not all these losses were in the air; on 5th January, 1945, a day when Winter had laid hold on the countryside, disaster came from the sky but multiplied on the ground. Out of the overcast sky, as the result of a mid-air collision, a screaming B-17 from another base dived into the Thorpe Abbotts bomb dump, where on impact its two 2,000 lb bombs detonated with a tremendous roar.

Villagers in the area, used to the almost constant noises of war, realised that this was something different and wherever possible opened their criss-crossed plaster-striped windows in order to minimise further damage; base staff fled from the impending holocaust which would emerge from the rising cloud of oily black smoke and blood-red flame. They did not have to wait long, as further eruptions scattered debris around the surrounding snow-covered countryside. Several hours later the fires were subdued and there was a gradual return to the base; it is remembered by many residents that the local police had quite a job rounding up base staff who had taken refuge in the local hostelries.

Fourteen days later the cloudbase was down to "no bird flying" level when a B-17 emerged out the murk and flew in a direct line for the control tower. Realising his predicament, the pilot swung the low-flying bomber violently away from the vital building. It slid at speed into tents which were normally occupied by men of the maintenance staff. For some reason or other they were empty at this time except for the base cat, which beat a hasty retreat. Catching fire, the B-17, named "Heaven Can Wait", burned for a while before the bomb load detonated, destroying another three B-17s.

This Boeing B-17G Fortress 230796 of the 100th Bombardment Group made a forced landing in the Pulham area on 30th December, 1943. It was the end of its flying career after thirteen missions.
Thorpe Abbotts Memorial Museum

CHAPTER ELEVEN

Doors Closed

A FTER the dust of the Second World War had settled and all the wartime
airmen and the Italian POWs had departed, No 53 Maintenance Unit
carried on its work at Pulham with a greatly reduced staff, assisted by two
detachments based at the former USAAF airfields at Flixton, near Bungay,
Suffolk, and Seething in Norfolk.

The work was more or less of a cleaning-up nature, as the enormous heaps
of aircraft salvage were gradually reduced to smaller portions and then carried
away by road and rail to the smelter's furnaces — swords into ploughshares, as it
were. Large stocks of armaments still had to be carefully looked after; some of
them had to be sorted out for disposal. General tidying up was also the order of
the day, with wartime airfield defences to be dismantled and many of the smaller
temporary buildings to be taken down.

Reminders of the residence of Italian POWs at Pulham can be seen at the
Norfolk and Suffolk Air Museum at Flixton. Using what materials they could lay
their hands on, these clever craftsmen made numerous items which still remain
in the area as treasured relics. Mr and Mrs Kent of Needham who worked at the
air station during the war were given a biscuit barrel, cigarette box and cigarette
case by the "residents"; the first two items were made from discarded
ammunition boxes and the cigarette case from aircraft scrap. They donated
these items to the museum for display to the public so that all can see for
themselves the type of skills these men from Southern Europe used.

During 1948 work began on dismantling the huge No 1 Shed, a landmark
on the East Anglian skyline since it had been erected in 1917. The task was
carried out by the Norwich firm of Harry Pointer (Norwich) Limited, the large
workforce being under the supervision of Mr T. J. Williamson.

The first task was to remove the many hundreds of sheets of corrugated
steel which covered the structure and the massive doors. In order to reach up
into the spidery girders of the roof high-reaching mobile cranes with 200-feet
jibs were employed as well as power winches and other sophisticated equipment.
As the outer cladding was removed the large girderwork webs which supported
the roof weight could be seen. The gigantic doors were taken to pieces where
they stood, being too heavy to be removed in their entirety. Soon the area
surrounding the shed was covered with great masses of sheet steel and girders,
and large heaps of irregular lengths of strip steel girderwork.

When the shed was finally dismantled many hundreds of tons of steel was sold for scrap; it was transported from the site by a fleet of contractor's lorries taking it to Norwich and other places.

Pulham's former No 2 Shed still stands at Cardington, and those who wish to see better for themselves what these huge sheds looked like can still do so by visiting the Bedfordshire site.

During 1948 the radio direction finding station at Pulham ceased operations. The equipment was transported away to other stations and its personnel dispersed.

During the nineteen-fifties the Norwich to Harleston freight trains were hauled by an ex-Great Eastern Railway Class D.16 Claud Hamilton 4-4-0 tender locomotive, a J.19 Class 0-6-0 locomotive and tender or a diminutive J.15 Class 0-6-0 tender locomotive. On the return run from Harleston the engine always ran round the train at Pulham in order to work up the airfield spur, where once again it ran round its train in order to be at the correct end of the wagons for the return journey to Norwich, via Tivetshall. With the rationalising of railway services all over the British Isles, the country districts of East Anglia lost many of

The skeleton of the Pulham No 1 shed is revealed as demolition men begin stripping off the steel sheeting in 1948. *Mr Roger Aldrich*

In British Railways days, an N.7 tank engine brings its train to a halt on the air station spur. On a sleeper in the foreground can be seen a plaque marking the limit of Air Ministry property.

Dr Ian C. Allen

their old-established services. The Waveney Valley Line, which had served the community since 1855, closed to passengers on a wintry 5th January, 1953. The last passenger train from Tivetshall Junction to Beccles was hauled by Class F.3 2-4-2 tank locomotive No 67128[23].

Freight traffic continued for a while, although the runs up the airfield spur became less frequent. The track was, due to lack of maintenance, becoming rather loose, and in consequence only locomotives with light axle loading were allowed up the spur; one in particular seemed to collect this duty, Class J.15 No 65471, whose tall funnel could be seen as it gently puffed up to the dock at the end of the spur. Another visitor was Class N.7/3 tank No 69679. As the loads tailed off so their visits became less and less frequent, until all freight traffic ceased on the Waveney Valley Line on 18th April, 1966.

At the present time most stations and crossing keepers' cottages remain and the former route is easy to follow from Pulham Market to Beccles. A stretch between Homersfield and Earsham has been made into a fine road to link the villages in the Waveney Valley, and at one spot the new road runs almost alongside a former station platform.

Men of the Air Ministry Police who carried out security duties at Pulham. *Mrs V. K. Bailey*

Doctor D. P. Rawlence of Pulham Market looked after the medical needs of the district for over thirty years and in the course of his practice came to know many of the men who worked at the air station. It was through his good offices that the author and his wife were able to visit many of these wonderful old gentlemen and hear their stories of the days of the airships up at the station. We have already heard of "Billy" Herring and Charlie Cutting; another of long standing was an Air Ministry policeman, Mr George Taylor, who did not retire until 1960 after having served in that branch since 1939. This force did valuable service in policing the air station site and thus released servicemen for more exacting tasks.

No 53 Maintenance Unit continued its work on a very limited scale through the nineteen-fifties, but as the once-gigantic heaps of wrecked aircraft were slowly reduced so the number of men required to do this job grew smaller. On Friday, 23rd August, 1957, the *Norfolk and Suffolk Journal* reported "Pulham's airship days will be long remembered. Famous station is closing down early next year."

> There have been rumours for several months that the station was to close soon but the definite announcement will be received with regret in South Norfolk. For many people it will mean that they will have to find fresh work, although some with "established" jobs may be given work elsewhere.
> In more recent years the station has been used mainly as a Maintenance Depot, staffed almost entirely by civilians.

136

The blow fell in February, 1958, when No 53 Maintenance Unit was disbanded and the station closed as an RAF establishment. The airfield surface had for some years been given over to grazing and where many of the former buildings had stood only flat concrete pads remained. Great fears of unemployment were rampant in this area of almost exclusive agricultural occupations; fortunately as one door closed so another one opened when new light industrial concerns opened up in the Harleston area, and these were able to absorb much of the redundant manpower.

The Air Ministry severed its last links with Pulham Air Station on 20th July, 1962, when the 762 acres bought by the Government before the First World War and turned into an airfield were sold by auction by Apthorpe's at Diss Magistrates' Room. The selling price was £57,250. One parcel comprising 735 acres had been occupied and farmed by the West family of Oakley, near Diss, since it was an airfield, and this was bought for Mr Peter West, son of Mr Oliver West, for £48,000.

History is still revealed even when we think that it has passed us by. During 1982 a very historic and valuable find was made in the Pulham district by local aviation enthusiasts, members of the Anglian Aeronautical Preservation Society. Three members of the society had been carrying out a survey of Second World War crash sites during 1981, and after one excursion called in at a teashop at Banham, Norfolk, for refreshment. The chairman of the society, Mr Dan Engle, of Brandon, casually remarked to the proprietor that they had been working on aeroplane crash sites; a lady who was in the shop volunteered the information that a local house might interest them. It was discovered that a local farmer, a Mr Rout, had built the house at about the same time as a renowned airship had been broken up at nearby Pulham. Feeling that the delicate light alloy tracery of girders would be useful in his new garden, Mr Rout bought the girders and transported them to Banham. For almost five decades they gave support to climbing roses and hosts of other flowers.

With the permission of the present resident, Mrs Joanna Smith, members of the society, with their Director of Operations in charge, sought out these treasured relics and after a short time identified them as the remains of the Italian-built S.R.1, whose story is told in chapter five.

"We were surprised to see it in such good condition, it seems as if the vegetation protected it," said Mr Engle.

On a fine day during the Summer of 1984 the author and his wife visited Mr and Mrs Duncan West at their Upper Vaunces Farmhouse, fronted by a beautiful large pond, bubbling with almost every breed of duck. Standing high on the plateau which looks out over the Waveney Valley and the twin villages of Pulham, this fine building mingles with a cluster of trees, the only ones for some distance around. Mr West took us on a conducted tour of his airfield farm and we traversed roads which had once carried military vehicles of all types and ages,

137

Above: Standing on the concrete apron of No 2 shed, the author looks out to where the concrete bases of the windbreak are hidden by a line of bushes.

Below: Upper Vaunces Farm, which became the Officers' Mess on the establishment of the Royal Naval Air Station, has now returned to its original use as a farmhouse.

past sites of buildings, now only patches of concrete among the tall waving grasses.

Licensees and owners of the site for many years, the West family again farm the plateau with arable crops, and Mr Duncan West appeared as interested to learn about the site as we were to see it for the first time. We passed slowly by the crumbling brick and concrete platform of the railway unloading dock with the remains of the transit shed that had succumbed to the winter gales of two years earlier. The trackbed was barely visible but could be distinguished by the lower growth of bush and weed, which found it hard to push upwards through the compacted ballast. Stout posts leaned at wayward angles, posts which had supported hinged gates spanning the track; the fireman of the locomotive would have had to descend from his steaming mount to open them, and the guard would have had to vacate the warmth of his coal-stove-heated guard's van to close them.

High on this treeless plain the Summer breeze blew chilly. It was not difficult to imagine what the lancing bitter easterlies of midwinter could have done to the ill-protected bodies of First World War airmen. After what seemed a considerable drive the shed area was reached; immense flat stretches of concrete, the floors of the sheds, and at each end the bolts which had once held the door rails could still be seen. In both floors were ringbolts recessed into the concrete to serve as holding-down points, and the ducts which had held the hydrogen pipes for gassing the ships could still be seen. In the floor of No 1 shed there were still the wooden sleepers, laid from end to end of the shed, which had held the rails used to guide the rigids into the shed. Still serving a useful purpose, the concrete floors were the base for very large animal-feed silage clamps. On a tall sandy bank alongside the shed area numerous rabbits bobbed in and out of their burrows; one wondered if the gipsy-like character of yesteryear would emerge from the tall bushes and make his catch.

Although the sheds are gone there still remain long lines of massive concrete bases to which the windscreens were bolted. Hedges have long since grown up around these indestructible relics.

Just across the old road from the sheds stood a brick building which had housed the silicol gas plant—a replacement for the original plant destroyed by an explosion in 1917. Although it had clearly been used to accommodate cattle one could still see where extractor fans had been fitted beneath two of the windows to remove air from the room housing the hydrogen generator and so prevent any leaking gas from reaching the electric motors in the adjacent compressor room. Across the field stood another similarly built structure of mellowed red brick. Almost alongside this was a brick building, weathered by wind, sun and time; on its upper storey was a circular lookout, probably an early type of control tower. Three large hip-roofed sheds of the usual military type, corrugated sheet-clad construction and large doors, completed this side of the former airfield, which is now predominantly occupied by the installations of the Anglia Water Authority plant. Further down the slope stood a pair of cottages which at one time doubled as the Officers' Mess; a curl of blue woodsmoke from its chimney indicated present-day residence. It was intriguing to view these buildings in the flesh, as it were, after studying them on photographs in order to try to reveal some of their secrets.

As we walked and talked Mr Duncan West, who with his wife Victoria is restoring the wonderful farmhouse, told us that in the course of their labours they discovered that several of the original oak doors carried numbers and other designations, leftovers from their days when they housed officers of the RNAS and the RAF. Out on the airfield the wind rustled the crops and turned the long grasses to alternate waves of silver and green. Three large black sheds, of modern build, stand in line across the field, continuing the line of the old railway; these appear to be all that is left of the RAF's Second World War activities. Other items which remain despite Mr West's endeavours to remove them are large patches of broken concrete, which will probably remain to baffle future generations. Bare patches of ground show that in some places, especially near the gas plant, crops are reluctant to grow as the result of chemical contamination by the waste from the gas plant over the years.

With the wind sighing and a combine harvester roaring dully as it swathed a distant cornfield in ever-decreasing circles, it was not too difficult to imagine one heard the approaching rumble of a large rigid as it approached the station. Soon we shall be able to see the long, slender streamlined hull with its red, white and blue roundel on the bow as the airship noses down to pick up its mooring on the mast in the centre of the field. Equally easy, if concentration is complete, to distinguish the clatter of a Crossley tender as it goes about its duties, and likewise the asthmatic cough of an LNER J.15 goods engine as it struggles up the spur with its wagons of assorted freight. To the believer all things are possible; here, on the spot where so much happened over the years, surely nothing is impossible.

Gone are the huge rigids, gone are the blimps, but hope springs eternal. Down at Pulham's sister station, Cardington, gas-filled airships do still fly, and they are taken in and out of Pulham's former No 2 Shed. Voices are heard in the land that a new generation of airships could be the heavy lift carriers of the future, the containerships of the skies, filling a gap in the air transport field. If this dream were fulfilled it would doubtless be because Pulham laid down the rules and established the fundamental principles of lighter-than-air craft.

References and Notes

1. The grass sowing details are from the records of T. W. Gaze and Son, Diss.
2. Duralumin is an aluminium base alloy containing 3.5–4.5 per cent copper, 0.4–0.7 per cent magnesium, 0.4–0.7 per cent manganese and up to 0.7 per cent silicon. It has a tensile strength, after forging and heat treatment, of 25–28 tons per square inch.
3. Raleigh, Sir Walter, and Jones, H. A. *The War in the Air*. Clarendon Press, 1922–1937.
4. Chamberlain, Geoffrey. *Airships—Cardington*. Terence Dalton, 1984.
5. *East Anglian Daily Times*, 28th June, 1917.
6. Higham, Robin. *The British Rigid Airship, 1908–1931*. G. T. Foulis, 1961.
7. Kinsey, Gordon. *Seaplanes—Felixstowe*. Terence Dalton, 1978.
8. Gamble, C. F. Snowden. *The Story of a North Sea Air Station*. Oxford University Press, 1928; Neville Spearman, 1967.
9. Ibid.
10. Williams, T. B. *Airship Pilot No. 28*. William Kimber, 1974. Meager, George. *My Airship Flights*. William Kimber, 1970.
11. Kinsey, Gordon. *Seaplanes—Felixstowe*.
12. Williams, T. B. *Airship Pilot No 28*.
13. Abbott, Patrick. *Airship*. Adams and Dart, 1973.
14. Chamberlain, Geoffrey. *Airships—Cardington*.
15. Gamble, C. F. Snowden. *The Story of a North Sea Air Station*.
16. Barnes, C. H. *Short Aircraft since 1910*. Putnam, 1967.
17. Kinsey, Gordon. *Martlesham Heath*. Terence Dalton, 1975.
18. *The Leaf and the Tree*. Boulton and Paul Group.
19. Chamberlain, Geoffrey. *Airships—Cardington*.
20. Morpurgo, J. E. *Barnes Wallis*. Longman, 1972.
21. For a full account of the early days of radar, see Kinsey, Gordon. *Bawdsey, Birth of the Beam*. Terence Dalton, 1983.
22. Freeman, Roger. *The Mighty Eighth*. Macdonald and Jane's, 1970.
23. Shrewring, Colin. *Steam in East Anglia*. Becknell, 1980.

APPENDIX ONE

Airship Types Associated with Pulham

NAVAL No 4. PARSEVAL TYPE. 1913.
Non-rigid. External wire suspension to car which was attached to a large fabric reinforcing sleeve running around the base of the envelope; further fabric straps ran fanwise around the remainder of the envelope to spread the load. Of German design but British built, Nos 5, 6 and 7 with enclosed cockpits were used for training duties only. Original built in Germany as PL-18 and redesignated No 4 after being bought by Great Britain during June, 1913. Three more ordered but due to outbreak of war never delivered. No 4 was the first airship used on active service, on 16th August, 1914.
Length: 275 feet. Diameter: 49 feet. Volume: 300,125 cubic feet.
Gross lift: 20,400 lb. Useful lift: 6,174 lb. Engines: Two Maybach 170 hp.
Speed: 37 mph.

NAVAL No 5. 1917.
Developed version of Parseval design, British built.
Length: 312 feet. Diameter: 57 feet. Volume: 364,000 cubic feet.
Engines: Two Renault 240 hp water-cooled motors. Speed: 53 mph.

BETA II. NAVAL AIRSHIP No 17. 1912.
Early non-rigid constructed for the Army and used in early Army exercises; transferred to RNAS at outbreak of hostilities.
Length: 116 feet. Diameter: 26 feet. Volume: 42,000 cubic feet.
Engine: One Clerget 50 hp rotary air-cooled motor. Speed: 35 mph.

GAMMA II. NAVAL AIRSHIP No 18. 1914.
Non-rigid airship constructed for Army use to Willows design; transferred to RNAS before outbreak of war. Originally based at Farnborough.
Length: 169 feet. Diameter: 34 feet. Volume: 101,000 cubic feet.
Engines: Two Inis motors, of 40 hp each. Speed: 30 mph.

DELTA. NAVAL AIRSHIP No 19. 1914.
Early non-rigid airship constructed for the Army and originally based at Farnborough; transferred to RNAS at outbreak of war.
Length: 198 feet. Diameter: 39 feet. Volume: 173,000 cubic feet.
Engines: Two White and Poppe motors of 100 hp each. Speed: 44 mph.

SEA SCOUT. 1915–1917.
Non-rigid with external wire suspension to car. Steering by rudder bar connected to vertical rudder at trailing edge of fin. Elevator control by twin elevators on trailing edge of horizontal stabilisers. Suspension wires terminated at Eta patches, so named after those designed for Admiralty Airship No 20 which was the former Army airship *Eta*. This patch comprised triangular pieces of fabric, laminated together and attached to the outside of the envelope; at the pointed end a large D-shaped wire ring was attached and the bridle wires passed through the ring and were then pulley-blocked to the main suspension cable. Pilot and wireless operator were accommodated in an aircraft fuselage of conventional design and from there steering, engine controls, elevators and gas and air valves were controlled. Twin cockpits were open; later modified to carry three.
Length: 143 feet. Height: 43 feet. Diameter: 27 feet 9 inches. Volume of envelope: 65,000 cubic feet. Volume of ballonets: 6,000 cubic feet (2). Lift: 1,236 lb. Engine: One Renault 75 hp water-cooled or Green water-cooled motor.
Endurance: 16 hours at 40 mph. Over 150 built. Other versions are listed below.

S.S.1. 1916.
Non-rigid built by Armstrong Whitworth Limited during 1915. Length: 100 feet. Diameter: 26 feet. Volume: 39,000 cubic feet. Engine: One Renault 70 hp. Speed: 40 mph.

S.S. A.W. 1916.
Non-rigid built by Armstrong Whitworth Limited, 1916. Length: 143 feet. Diameter: 30 feet. Volume: 70,000 cubic feet. Engine: Green or Rolls-Royce 100 hp. Speed: 50 mph.

S.S. M.F. 1916.
Non-rigid fitted with Maurice Farman fuselage. Length: 143 feet. Diameter: 28 feet. Volume: 60,000 cubic feet. Engine: One Rolls-Royce or Renault 82 hp. Speed: 45 mph.

S.S.P.1. 1917.
Non-rigid, developed version of previous Sea Scouts. Length: 143 feet. Diameter: 30 feet. Volume: 70,000 cubic feet. Engine: One Green or Rolls-Royce 70–100 hp fitted as a pusher, hence "P" in designation. Speed: 53 mph.

S.S. TWIN. 1917.
Further design extension of the S.S.P., this version having two engines. There were plans to build a fleet of 115 of this successful type, but by the end of the war only thirteen had been completed and the rest were never built. Length: 165 feet. Diameter: 49 feet. Volume: 100,000 cubic feet. Lift: 1,600 lb. Engines: Two Rolls-Royce Hawk water-cooled motors of 75 hp each. Crew: 5.

S.S. ZERO. 1917. Sometimes designated S.S.Z.
Designed by Lieutenant, later Squadron Leader, F. M. Rope and Warrant Officer Righton. Boat-shaped gondola for crew of three. Royal Navy took delivery of 66 of these craft.
Length: 143 feet. Diameter: 32 feet. Height: 44 feet. Volume: 70,000 cubic feet. Petrol capacity: 204 gallons. Oil capacity: 4½ gallons. Water ballast: 28 gallons. Maximum speed: 48 mph. Endurance: 16 hours at 48 mph; 40 hours at 20 mph. Cruising speed: 34 mph. Armament: Lewis gun; 3 × 100 lb bombs. Line dragged in the water relayed underwater sounds up to the airship. Engine: One Rolls-Royce Hawk of 75 hp.

COASTAL. 1915–1917.
Tri-lobed Astra-Torres envelope with control car suspended close up beneath envelope to strongpoints inside the envelope where the triangle of lobes met. Here the suspension cables were attached to a jackstay from which lines ran out to the tops of the three lobes as well as to fabric screens between the ridges. Crew usually six: pilot, wireless operator, steering coxswain, second pilot, navigator and gunlayer.
Overall length: 195 feet. Height: 52 feet. Width: 39 feet 6 inches.
Volume of envelope: 170,000 cubic feet. Volume of ballonets: 51,000 cubic feet.
Engines: Two 150 hp Sunbeam water-cooled motors, one tractor, one pusher.
Speed: 52 mph. Armament: 2 Lewis guns; 4 × 100 lb bombs.
Machine-gun position on top of envelope reached by canvas tunnel up through envelope.
Typical load: Fuel for 11 hours (about 180 gallons).
        2 × 100 lb bombs.
        Water ballast, 315 lb.
        Crew six.
Twenty-eight of this type were built and commissioned in the RNAS, plus four built for Russia and one for France, a total of thirty-three.

COASTAL C 'STAR'. 1918.
Developed from Coastal in the light of operational experience. Envelope and car suspension as Coastal.
Length: 218 feet. Width: 49 feet 3 inches. Volume: 210,000 cubic feet.
Lift: 3,086 lb. Crew: As Coastal. Speed: 60 mph. Engine: One Fiat 260 hp water-cooled motor. Ten of this type were built and commissioned.

NORTH SEA. 1917–1918.
Tri-lobe envelope similar to Astra Torres built up of 2,500 shaped panels in the three lobes. Suspension as Coastal. Enclosed cockpit and completely enclosed cabin; engines suspended on gantries at the end of a walkway from the cabin. Engineers' compartment between engines.
Length: 262 feet. Diameter: 56 feet 9 inches. Volume: 360,000 cubic feet.
Lift: 7,384 lbs. Load: 8,400 lb. Engines: Two Rolls-Royce 250 hp or two 260 hp Fiat water-cooled motors. Maximum speed: 58 mph. Cruising speed: 43 mph.
Crew: Ten in two five-man watches. Entered service February, 1917.
Sixteen built. N.S.11 established endurance record of 61 hours 30 minutes.

S.R.1. 1918.
Semi-rigid of Italian design bought by Admiralty. Built at Ciampino, Rome. Served at Pulham throughout its life in Great Britain.
Length: 269 feet. Diameter: 59 feet. Height: 87 feet. Volume: 441,000 cubic feet.
Ballonets: 200,000 cubic feet. Disposable load: 6,800 lb. Weight empty: 15,873 lb. Useful lift: 13,090 lb. Engines: Two Itala Maybach 200 hp; one SPA 220 hp. Speed: 50 mph. Crew: 9.

HMA No 9. 1916.
First British rigid airship to fly, built by Vickers Limited. Cylindrical form with blunt bow and stern. Used basically for training and mast mooring experiments. Metal construction, fabric covered. Swivelling propeller mountings.
Length: 526 feet. Diameter: 53 feet. Volume: 866,000 cubic feet in 17 cells.
Engines: Two Wolseley-Maybach 180 hp; one Maybach 250 hp aft. Later four Wolseley-Maybach of 180 hp water cooled. Scrapped summer, 1918. Flown 198 hours.

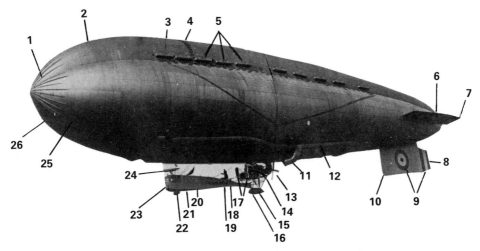

The component parts of a non-rigid airship:

1 Bow stiffeners
2 Upper lobe of envelope
3 Upper gun position
4 Rope ladder from gun position to fuel tanks
5 Fuel and water tanks
6 Horizontal stabiliser fin
7 Elevator
8 Rudder
9 National insignia
10 Lower vertical fin
11 Air scoop to ballonets
12 External trunking to ballonets
13 Four-bladed propeller (one of two)
14 Water-cooled motor (one of two)
15 Engineers' car
16 Engineers' car understructure and landing bumper
17 Radiators
18 Walkway from control car to engineers' car
19 Gun position
20 Sleeping accommodation
21 Navigation and wireless cabins
22 Control car landing bumper
23 Control section
24 Rope ladder from control car through envelope to upper gun position
25 Lower lobe of envelope (one of two)
26 Flexible outer cover of envelope

HMA No 23. 1917.
Rigid, built by Vickers Limited. Designated "23" Class. Swivelling propeller mounts. Engines contained in three cars. Metal construction, fabric covering. Similar in external form to No 9.
Length: 535 feet. Diameter: 53 feet. Volume: 942,000 cubic feet in 18 cells.
Power: Four Wolseley-Maybach 250 hp. Later four Rolls-Royce Eagle V.12, 280 hp.
Speed: 52 mph. Cruising speed: 40 mph. Ceiling: 3,000 feet. Useful load: 13,228 lb.
Bomb load: four 100 lb bombs. Crew 17. Hours flown, 321½ hours.

HMA No 24. 1917.
Second ship in "23"-Class. Details same as No 23. Hours flown, 164 hours.

R.26. 1918.
Built by Vickers Limited during 1918 and used mainly as an experimental mooring craft.
Length: 535 feet. Diameter: 53 feet. Volume: 942,000 feet. Engines: Three Rolls-Royce Eagle 200 hp and one Maybach 200 hp. Speed: 55 mph.
Hours flown, 197 hours 35 minutes. Struck off charge, March, 1919.

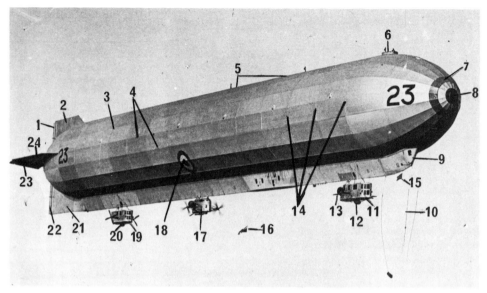

The component parts of a rigid airship:

1 Upper rudder
2 Upper vertical stabiliser fin
3 Outer fabric covering of hull
4 Longitudinal framework members
5 Walkway along top of hull
6 Upper gun position
7 Bow section
8 Mooring attachment
9 External keel section
10 Mooring ropes
11 Forward control car
12 Landing bumper
13 Forward motors and airscrews
14 Circular frames
15 Union Flag
16 Ensign
17 Midships power car
18 National insignia
19 Rear control and power car
20 Landing bumper
21 Lower vertical fin
22 Lower rudder
23 Elevator
24 Horizontal stabiliser

R.32. 1919.
Built by Short Brothers Limited at Cardington. Reinforced plywood girder webs similar to German Shutte-Lanz designs, with fabric covering. Streamlined control car forward on bottom surface of envelope. Used to train United States airship crews.
Length: 614 feet. Diameter: 65 feet 6 inches. Volume: 1,553,000 cubic feet.
Lift: 16½ tons. Engines: Five Rolls-Royce Eagles 250 hp. Speed: 65 mph.
Hours flown, 260 hours.

R.33. 1919.
Built for the Royal Navy by Armstrong Whitworth Limited at Selby. Based on German Zeppelin L-33. Designed for extended oversea reconnaissance. Metal construction, fabric covering. Nineteen cheese-shaped gas-bags spaced within transverse frames and kept apart by longitudinal girders. One engine in each amidships wing car and two in

centreline car, one tractor, one pusher. Gun platform on forward upper hull and in tail cone. First flight 6th March, 1919. Re-registered as civil aircraft, G-FAAG, 1920. Most successful British rigid airship. Mainly based at Pulham. Survived several dangerous situations including being struck by lightning. Spent over 150 hours on Pulham mast. Length: 643 feet. Diameter: 79 feet. Volume: 1,950,000 cubic feet. Useful lift: 58,100 lb. Engines: Five Sunbeam Maori 250 hp 12-cyclinder water-cooled. Maximum speed: 62 mph. Cruising speed: 45 mph. Fuel: 4,200 gallons. Oil: 2,300 gallons. Water ballast: Three tons. Crew: 22. Cost: £350,000. Hours flown, 800 hours. Dismantled 1928.

R.34. 1919.
Based on German Zeppelin L-33 design. Built by Beardmore Limited at their Inchinnan Works, Scotland. Semi-streamlined form. Metal construction, fabric covered. Basically same as R.33. Reversible airscrews on amidship cars. Made first two-way crossing by air of North Atlantic.
Length: 643 feet. Diameter: 79 feet. Volume: 1,950,000 cubic feet. Power: Five 270 hp Sunbeam Maori water-cooled engines. Speed: 62 mph. Fuel: 4,900 gallons. Oil: 2,300 gallons. Water ballast: Three tons. Cost: £350,000.
Hours flown, 500 hours. Flew into Yorkshire hill on 28th January, 1921, and badly damaged; taken to Howden and broken up.

R.36. 1921.
Based on German Zeppelin L-48. Built by Vickers Limited. Metal construction, fabric covering. Last airship built for Admiralty. Originally to military specification but converted for commercial duties. Construction started 1917, first flew 1921. Re-registered as civil aircraft G-FAAF. 30 passengers, 1 ton of cargo.
Length: 672 feet. Diameter: 80 feet. Volume: 2,101,000 cubic feet. Weight: 70,068 lb. Engines: Three 350 hp Sunbeam Cossack 12-cylinder water-cooled; two 260 hp Maybach M6 six-cylinder water-cooled (from L-71). Cost: £350,000. Max speed: 65 mph. Cruising speed: 51 mph. Hours flown, 80 hours. Suffered mooring accident at Pulham, 21st June, 1921. Broken up, 1926.

R.38. 1921.
Built by Short Brothers Limited at Cardington. First flight, 23rd June, 1921.
Length: 695 feet. Diameter: 85 feet 6 inches. Volume: 2,784,000 cubic feet.
Useful lift: 45½ tons. Weight: 25,982 lb. Ceiling: 22,000 feet. Engines: Six 350 hp Sunbeam Cossacks in three power cars. Maximum speed: 71 mph. Duration: 65 hours at 65 mph. Carrying out trials prior to being transferred to United States as ZR-2, broke up over River Humber, 24th August, 1921. Flew 56½ hours.

R.80. 1921.
Built by Vickers Limited as only solely British-designed airship to date. Intended for RAF Airship Service. Engines of German design. Streamlined hull form and smaller than previous designs. Fully streamlined control car. First flight 20th June, 1920.
Length: 535 feet. Diameter: 70 feet. Volume: 1,260,000 cubic feet. Lift: 15 tons. Ceiling: 16,400 feet. Range: 6,400 miles. Max speed: 70 mph. Cruising speed: 50 mph. Weight: 52,416 lb. Crew: 20. Engines: Four 230 hp Wolesley-Maybach six-cylinder water cooled. Armament: 2 pounder rapid fire gun: 2 Lewis guns on top; 2 Lewis guns in tail cone and others in gondolas: 8 × 230 lb bombs. Flew 73 hours. Dismantled 1925.

L-64. ZEPPELIN. (Maker's No LZ-109). 1920.
German naval airship surrendered to Great Britain during 1920 and flown to Pulham from North Germany. Never flew after arrival at the air station. Latest development of the Naval V-type designed for long-range bombing operations. One of the few German airships not wrecked by their former crews.
Length: 644 feet 5 inches. Diameter: 78 feet 4 inches. Volume: 1,977,360 cubic feet.
Engines: Five Maybach IVa motors of 240 hp. Speed: 74 mph.

L-71. ZEPPELIN. (Maker's No LZ-113). 1920.
German naval airship surrendered to Great Britain during 1920 and flown to Pulham from North Germany. Never flew after arrival at the air station. Last type developed by the German Naval Airship Division before the Armistice. Type X "Super Zeppelin". Designed for long overseas operations including the proposed bombing of the United States of America.
Length: 693 feet 7 inches. Diameter: 78 feet 4 inches. Volume: 2,196,282 cubic feet.
Engines: Six Maybach 260 hp VIb six-cyclinder water-cooled motors.
Max. speed: 73 mph. Ceiling: 22,970 feet. Range: 3,730 miles. Fuel load over 30 tons.

N.1 "NORGE". 1926.
Semi-rigid of Italian design purchased by Roald Amundsen for trans-Polar flight.
Length: 348 feet. Diameter: 64 feet. Volume: 654,000 feet. Load: 18,243 lb.
Lift: 18,240 lb. Empty weight: 28,660 lb. Engines: Three 250 hp Maybach M6 IVa six-cylinder water-cooled. Speed: 70 mph.

The Why and Wherefore of Airship Operation

by Norman Peake

THE relatively primitive aeroplanes of 1915 were not really suitable for patrolling and submarine-spotting over the open sea. Their fuel capacity restricted their range, and their speed (below 100 mph, but still twice that of airships) and vibration meant that continuous observation from the open cockpit was difficult. Engine failures usually meant emergency landings (impossible on the sea), and these were not infrequent.

Non-rigids (except for the later S.S. Zeros, S.S. Twins, C Stars and North Sea types) also used standard aeroplane fuselages, but devoid of wings or tailplanes. Their slower speeds meant even more engine failures from overheating, due to less efficient slipstream-cooling, but when the engine did stop the ships remained airborne as free balloons, and the mechanic could usually repair the engine (for which a kit of spares was always carried); even chewing-gum sometimes served to mend cracks in fuel or cooling pipes. An airship's slow speed (anything from stationary to 45 mph) meant that it could keep station with warships or slower merchantmen; and from an altitude of 800 feet or so the confused effect of waves was lost, and submarines or tethered mines could be spotted as easily as in a millpond. Wireless equipment could also be more easily carried than in an aeroplane, and was much used for reporting mines, submarines, etc. And of course their range was limited only by the capacity of their fuel tanks (usually attached to, or even in, the envelope) and the endurance of their crew, which often exceeded eight hours.

It was for these reasons that the Admiralty pressed so hard to get them. While they became sitting ducks to attacking German seaplanes operating from Belgium later in the war, these never penetrated the Irish Sea or Western Approaches, nor even the western side of the North Sea, nor over southern coasts.

Most former airshipmen of the First World War that I have met enthused about their mounts, and have remained devotees for the rest of their lives despite taunts from heavier-than-air fliers. Leslie Murton, of Norwich, now (1988) a sprightly eighty-nine years of age, remembers his local football team visiting Pulham Air Station in 1916 to play against the station team; so impressed were they with the airships they saw after the game that three of the team promptly enlisted in the airship service. Leslie, who served as coxswain in S.S. Twins (though not from Pulham) was, at the age of eighty-two, afforded the honour of piloting the Goodyear airship *Europa* from Yarmouth to Norwich on the occasion of her visit.

Why Hydrogen?

Hydrogen—the lightest gas known—was first isolated by Henry Cavendish at Cambridge in 1766. Black then tried to levitate pigs' bladders inflated with it, but failed because of their weight. By 1782 an Italian, Cavallo, was causing inflated soap-bubbles of it to rise to the sky, and by 1783 large balloons of varnished fabric were bearing men into the air, where they drifted like the clouds themselves wheresoever the air currents took them.

Inventors soon foresaw that if only balloons could be given a fish-like shape, and a means of propulsion, then they could swim through the air just as a fish does in water. Thus was the dirigible balloon conceived, though it became practical only when lightweight petrol engines arrived around the turn of the present century.

Near the Earth's surface, 1,000 cubic feet of air weighs 75 lb, whereas a similar volume of hydrogen weighs only 5 lb. So 1,000 cubic feet of hydrogen is said to provide a "lift" of 70 lb—but, of course, it needs to be confined in a container, which itself has weight. Typically, a balloon of (say) 20,000 cubic feet capacity might weigh 500 lb (the weight of its gastight bag plus its retaining net); this would then leave 900 lb of "lift" over to support a stout wicker basket, the passengers with their food, etc., and necessary ballast (bags of sand).

But at 8,000 feet (say), the air pressure (and hence its density) is only two-thirds of that at the Earth's surface, and, since all gases expand as the pressure is reduced, 1,000 cubic feet of air at that altitude will weigh only 60 lb—the same amount of hydrogen around 4½ lb. The lift there is thus only about 55 lb/1,000 cubic feet, or approximately four-fifths of that at the surface. If the balloon was full on release it would by that altitude have lost one-fifth of its hydrogen through its open "neck"; the lift will be inexorably reduced as it ascends until it balances the weight. Ascent will then cease.

To descend, yet more gas will need to be released (via a spring-loaded valve at the top of the bag, operated by a long cord down to the basket), and as descent occurs the hydrogen (now less than four-fifths of the original) will be further compressed. If the descent were not controlled in some way the balloon would strike the earth with a mighty thud, so ballast has to be jettisoned as the earth approaches.

A rigid airship is really nothing more than a row of net-encased balloons (called "cells" and usually numbering between fourteen and twenty) within a rigid frame of streamlined shape covered with weatherproof fabric. The frame itself carries fuel tanks, engines, passengers and ballast, being supported by the "balloons" within it. German Zeppelins later in the First World War normally set out with their cells only two-thirds full to allow for expansion as they consumed fuel and ascended. Conversely, the non-rigids (the "Pulham Pigs") had no framework but a limp fabric envelope which relied upon the gas within being under slight pressure (only that of, say, a domestic gas supply) to maintain its streamlined shape—aided by stiff canes bonded to the fabric at the bow to prevent the nose being blown in by wind pressure when flying at speed.

Like the rigids they could, if need be, set out only two-thirds full of hydrogen, the other third being occupied by airfilled bags within termed "ballonets", stitched to the underside of the ship's interior. The air would be forced out of these as the hydrogen occupied all the space available, at which point the ship was said to be at "pressure height". Any further ascent would entail loss of hydrogen through relief-valves. However, as a non-rigid descended, and the hydrogen became compressed, air had to be forced back into the ballonets to maintain the pressure in the envelope, and hence its shape. This was done by having air-scoops in the slipstream(s) of the propeller(s), although a separate "blower" was carried for use when the propellers were not functioning.

If, as sometimes happened, the ship had gone well above pressure height the ballonets might not be large enough to make up for the loss of hydrogen once it descended, and a bent or buckled envelope, with the car at some uncomfortable angle, could result. Much the same would happen if the envelope had been holed by bullets or small tears (although if fired at from below only the ballonets were likely to be punctured, and those could be kept inflated by the slipstream or blower, or even both). Pulham folk recall seeing ships looking like bent bananas returning from patrol—they usually got home. Should the reader wonder how it was they remained airborne, it must be pointed out that during a patrol they would consume many gallons of fuel, so despite losses of hydrogen they were normally lighter on their return than at take-off. In the event of a mishap early on in a flight, fuel could always be dumped as "emergency ballast".

Since there were ballonets fore and aft, a non-rigid ship could be kept trimmed (ie. horizontal) by releasing air from one ballonet and forcing more air into the other. Judicious moving of the elevators (hinged to the horizontal tailplanes) could also be used to force a ship's nose up or down in flight, so that it could "fly heavy", aided by dynamic lift with its nose up, or descend to the ground with its nose down while yet too light to do so under static conditions. This latter was always aimed at. A pilot's last action was to cut engines and drop ropes. Once these had touched ground (to "earth" the ship, which often acquired a massive electrostatic charge, which could give a severe electric shock), they were seized by the ground crew, and the pilot would "ballast up". That is, he would release enough ballast to tauten the handling ropes. The ground crew would then pull the ship down and prepare to hook on sandbags as each member of the crew stepped off, thus lightening the ship. The crewless but slightly buoyant ship could then be "walked" into the shed. The bigger rigids needed a large ground crew, and to minimise the number required were secured by the nose to a short tripod mast atop an army tank—the after part of the ship often being weighed down with heavy artillery wheels.

Wind (usually present at Pulham!) was the biggest hazard during docking or undocking, and huge windshields (looking like giant elongate cricket sight-screens initially of wood, or of corrugated iron sheeting, were erected in front of the shed doors. It was soon found that nasty eddies developed on their lee sides. To limit these, alternate panels were removed or replaced by open slatting along the top and at the outer end. Timber struts buttressed their outer sides, while stout wire ropes anchored to rings set into concrete blocks secured them against wind pressure. Manoeuvring a ship sideways on to the wind, when it was not within these shields, could be a very tricky business.

Once the airship was within the shed, minor repairs were done by cementing on patches. But if major repairs were needed, requiring the ship's deflation, an empty envelope called a "nurse-balloon" (often an old patched one, no longer considered fit for flying duties), held down by an "inflation net", was brought alongside and the hydrogen bled into it from the ship needing repair.

The envelopes always leaked to a degree, despite being made of two layers of rubber-coated thin cotton fabric, cemented together by a third layer of rubber. The outer

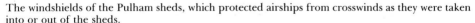

The windshields of the Pulham sheds, which protected airships from crosswinds as they were taken into or out of the sheds.

151

Still surviving in 1988, the brick building which housed the silicol gas plant at Pulham. This replaced the original silicol plant, which had exploded in 1917.

coating was further "doped" with a varnish containing aluminium dust which minimised absorption of the sun's heat by day (and cooling by radiation at night); it also rendered the ship less conspicuous against a bright sky. Hydrogen losses through leakage and other causes meant that an S.S. ship would need "topping up" with from five to fifteen thousand cubic feet per week, so the hydrogen demand at a station like Pulham was considerable.

Hydrogen Generation

In the early days of ballooning, hydrogen had been made by the action of sulphuric acid on iron filings or zinc in lead-lined barrels—the acid spray being removed from the gas by allowing it to bubble through successive barrels of water. Even so, it still contained malodorous hydrogen sulphide and residual acid which damaged the fabric. By 1910 less unpleasant processes had been developed, the earliest of which was the "silicol" process.

Silicol was a man-made compound of iron and silicon. When silicol was slowly added to a strong caustic soda solution a stream of fairly pure hydrogen was emitted as fast as safety and the size of the equipment allowed. The gas then passed through a tower down which water trickled, to remove caustic soda mist and to cool it. It was piped directly to a gasholder, which merely served as an intermediate "buffer"; gas was drawn from the gasholder into a Reavell compressor which forced it into large horizontal cylindrical gas tanks of high-tensile steel. These contained the hydrogen at 600 lb per square inch. A group of them could later be connected by a manifold, whence the hydrogen passed through an expansion valve into large diameter hoses (called "gas trunks") for inflating envelopes or the cells of rigid ships.

Initially a standardised "portable" silicol plant was provided to stations like Pulham, but with an output of only 2,500 cubic feet per hour it was not really adequate for more than one airship. The next installation was an electrolytic plant which produced hydrogen by passing an electric current through a dilute caustic soda solution. Oxygen was produced simultaneously, but at Pulham the oxygen seems to have been merely vented to atmosphere. The output of this plant is not recorded, but it was not likely to be substantially greater than the earlier silicol one. But it was clean, and safer, and could be run with little bother for twenty-four hours a day so long as the diesel generators did not break down; it also produced very pure hydrogen.

By mid-1917 a "fixed" silicol plant of much larger capacity became available capable of producing up to 10,000 cubic feet per hour. Tricky and dangerous to operate, it had the advantage of almost instant availability to cope with a sudden demand. Great care was needed to operate it, and the by-product sludge which had to be dug out at the end of a "run" was very unpleasant, and caustic. If the silicol was added when the caustic solution was too cool, hydrogen evolution was sluggish; but as the reaction itself warmed the solution up the production of gas could become dangerously rapid, leading to an explosion and the scattering of strong caustic soda.

The *Admiralty Hydrogen Manual* (revised issue, 1919) contained warnings about wrong operation of silicol plants. A reference to an explosion having occurred probably related to the Pulham plant, which exploded at midday on 19th April, 1917, killing two. It was the policy in such manuals never to identify any particular station.

The Germans used a cheaper method, called the Messerschmitt process, of passing steam over heated iron turnings in a red-hot tube (originally a gun-barrel). A British process developed from the water-gas plants used by gas companies to augment their supplies at peak demand times was eventually installed at Pulham. In this process, coke was mixed with five times its weight of quicklime and brought to red heat by firing in a stream of compressed air. Once up to temperature, steam was blown through, and hydrogen thereby produced. For the chemically inclined, the reaction (put simply) was as under:

$$2H_2O \; + \; C \; + \; CaO \; \longrightarrow \; 2H_2 \; + \; CaCO_3$$

| Steam | Coke | Quicklime | Hydrogen | Limestone |

This plant had an output of 14,000 cubic feet per hour, but unlike the silicol and the electrolytic processes (which were retained) could not be started up quickly. Nor was it economic to run it for only a short period, though in the long term it was by far the cheapest.

In addition, hydrogen was also purchased from firms which produced it as a by-product at Wolverhampton and at Runcorn. It arrived on rail wagons in large cylinders weighing around 7 cwt apiece. Despite the contained hydrogen being at 1800 lb per square inch, most of the weight was that of the cylinder itself, and they were very unpopular with railwaymen. Each cylinder yielded only 400 cubic feet of hydrogen, so very many were needed. In fact, by 1918 no fewer than 88,000 were in use throughout Britain. The metallic "clangs" as these were manhandled around the station are remembered by those who lived in nearby Pulham Market.

APPENDIX THREE

Visit to Pulham by Members of Parliament
Friday, 17th June, 1921

THIS hitherto unpublished document is indicative of the then current euphoria about the future of airships as vehicles for tying together more closely the bonds of Empire, following the defeat of the Central Powers.

While the figures quoted for the dimensions of R.36 are perfectly accurate, those for its anticipated performance are wildly optimistic, and are far more important for what they do *not* say.

In fact, the R.36 was an "improved" and lengthened R.33 type, but with a lighter framework based upon that of the Zeppelin L-48, which had been brought down at Theberton, Suffolk, in 1917. But the L-48 had been designed especially for high-altitude bombing, and strength needed at ordinary altitudes had been sacrificed to achieve "height climbing"; her builders even recommended specially cautious use of her rudder and elevators at low altitudes. The "two forward wing cars" of the R.36, referred to, had merely been transferred at Pulham from the German LZ-71 (which had been surrendered there in July, 1920). Their Maybach MB IVa engines had been designed especially to provide maximum power *only* at high altitudes.

Interestingly, the R.36's very spartan furniture—collapsible tables and light wickerwork chairs—was that later re-used in the ill-fated R.101.

On the day of the visit, forty-nine MPs were taken for a flight lasting an hour, which took them to the coast and over Norwich. The ship need have carried very little fuel, and the weather was fine. Only four days later her nose was badly damaged by a taut mooring cable which had snagged as she overshot the Pulham mast after a flight.

CIVIL AIRSHIP G – F.A.A.F. (R.36).

Constructed by

SIR WILLIAM BEARDMORE'S WORKS,
INCHINNAN, GLASGOW.

DESCRIPTIVE NOTE FOR MEMBERS'
OF PARLIAMENT VISIT TO PULHAM
ON FRIDAY 17th June, 1921.

CONTROLLER OF INFORMATION
CIVIL AVIATION DEPT.,
AIR MINISTRY.

The first British-built Airship adapted for Commercial purposes is the R.36, her Civil registration mark being G.F.A.A.F.

She was designed by the Admiralty more than three years ago for naval duties and is a progressive development on earlier types of Airships, but does not embody the marked improvements in design which have been elaborated during the past year. She has been constructed by Messrs William Beardmore & Company Limited at their Inchinnan Airship Works near Glasgow.

Construction was begun in the early part of 1919 following the completion and handing over of R.34. Completion was deferred owing to changes in Airship policy.

The ship is 672 foot in length, which is approximately 30 feet more than the length of R.34. The maximum diameter of the ship is 78 feet 9 inches.

The ship has a maximum cubic capacity of slightly more than 2,100,000 feet of hydrogen gas which gives a nominal lift of 63.8 tons.

The maximum speed is 65 miles an hour, its normal cruising speed being slightly over 50 miles an hour. It has a maximum range of action of more than 4000 miles. The economic range varies according to the numbers of passengers and freight carried.

The gas-containing hull comprises a skeleton streamline framework of polygonal cross-section built of light metallic girders. This framework is divided into chambers in which drum-shaped gasbags – of which there are 19 – are enclosed. The hull is covered with sheets of doped cotton stretched tightly over the framework.

Each gasbag has an automatic gas release valve and some are also fitted with a hand-controlled valve, in order, if necessary, to discharge gas while landing or to alter the trim of the ship.

In the inside of the bottom of the hull there is a structure, which runs the complete length of the ship, containing all the petrol tanks and water ballast bags and a pathway which provides access from one part of the ship to another.

The ship is fitted for mooring at a mast and at the extreme bow there is a trap-door, opening outwards, which enables passengers and crew to pass, when the ship is moored, to and from the mooring-mast platform.

R.36 is fitted with six cars, five of which are designed to take power units, the sixth being the passenger car, the forward portion of which is used as the control car.

Two of these are wing cars placed near the bottom of the ship, each of which contains a 260 h.p. Maybach engine which actuates, in each case, a small direct-drive two-bladed propeller. The passenger car is placed almost amidships and opposite its centre are fitted two more wing-power cars each of which contains a 350 h.p. Sunbeam "Cossack" engine.

The fifth power car is on the centre line of the ship towards the stern and also contains a 350 h.p. Sunbeam "Cossack" engine. Each of the three Sunbeam "Cossacks", actuate, through reduction gear and a clutch, a large two-bladed propeller. These power units, therefore, give a total of 1570 h.p. which is substantially more than was fitted in R.34.

In the control car are situated all the arrangements for manoeuvring the ship and varying its speed, the telephones and voice-pipes for communicating with various parts of the ship and the releasing arrangements for dropping the mooring and control ropes. Centred here, too, are the navigating instruments including those for taking astronomical observations at night, or when the ship is flying above the clouds. A wireless cabinet, both for telegraphy and telephony, is also installed in this car.

Four large fixed stabilising fins are fitted at the tail of the ship, two vertical, and two horizontal. To the trailing edge of each of these large fixed fins is fitted a small balance moveable plane. The two vertical moveable planes, which are operated from the control car, cause the ship to turn to left or right, according to will. The two horizontal moveable planes, which are also operated from the control car, govern the height at which the ship flies.

An entirely new departure in British Airship construction is the fitting of a passenger car which has been designed to accommodate 50 passengers. The car is 131 feet long.

The car is divided by a passage way which runs down the centre. On each side are cabins which are furnished with beds for two passengers, a table, and chairs.

The colour scheme selected for the furnishings is light blue, the effect being harmonious and pleasing.

The general arrangements of the cabins is such as to provide each passenger with a clear view both inside and outside.

The cabins are divided off by curtains at night which may be drawn back during the day and the beds folded up.

The car is fitted with a cooking galley and a pantry which are situated in the centre of the ship. Each is furnished with the necessary cooking apparatus and other equipment.

Good washing & lavatory accommodation is also provided.

Crew.

A normal crew of 4 officers and 24 men is carried.

The officers consist of:-

> The captain,
> 1st Officer, pilot.
> 2nd Officer, pilot.
> Engineer Officer.

The crew consists of:-

> 2 Coxswains,
> 7 Riggers,
> 13 Engineers,
> 2 Wireless operators.

In large ships such as R.36, the crew is divided into watches which take alternative spells of duty and rest, as is the old established custom of the sea. The only exception to this is the captain who is not necessarily continuously on duty. Thus, when the flying is difficult he remains on duty in the same way as a steamship captain remains on the bridge when approaching the coast or in bad weather, and when the flying is straightforward he goes off watch. The remaining members of the crew usually keep watch for four hours on and four hours off. The 1st and 2nd officers of the airship take command under the captain in alternate periods of watch-keeping as on board H.M. ships. The riggers correspond to the seamen in the Navy, the 1st and 2nd coxswains being the two senior riggers. The group of riggers is divided into two watches, one under each coxswain, and their duties during flight usually comprise height control, steering (lateral control) and watch-keeping in the keel.

In their periods off watch the crew take their meals etc in the quarters in the keel, which are furnished with mess tables and all necessary conveniences, including a gramophone. Hammocks are slung between the girders along the keel.

Performance.

Overall dimensions.
{
Length .... 672'2"
Diameter .... 78'9"
Height .... 91'7"
}
Volume or capacity in cu.ft .... 2,101,000.
Gross lift in tons 63.8
Number of engines 5
Total Horse-power 1570
Maximum Speed .... 65 m.p.h.
Lift available for fuel and freight. .16.0 tons.
Petrol and oil per 100 mile journey. .0.65 tons.

R.36, with this performance, and allowing an ample margin of spare fuel in case adverse winds are encountered, would carry:-

(1) *To Stockholm*   ø 30 passengers and 2 tons of mails or goods or *extra* passenger baggage in 20/24 hours.

(2) *To Switzerland*   ø 40 passengers and 2 tons of mails or goods or *extra* passenger baggage in 12/15 hours.

(3) *To Marseilles*   ø 30 passengers and 2 tons of mails or goods or *extra* passenger baggage in 15/18 hours.

(4) *To Egypt*   ø 30 passengers and 1 to 2 tons of mails or *extra* passenger baggage in about 72 hours.

ø In addition to the weight of a passenger and his clothes, an additional allowance of 100 lbs. per passenger has been made for hand luggage.

On each of the above routes a considerable saving of time is effected compared to other forms of transport – particularly in the case of Egypt. At the same time it should be remembered that the main function of the Airship is long-distance transport and the saving on a typical airship route of the future will be very marked e.g. England to India where the airship voyage would occupy approximately six days as compared with the fastest overland and mail route of 21 days.

Glossary

Aerofoil.	A plane shaped so as to produce an aerodynamic reaction as it moves through the air.
Aerostat.	Any lighter-than-air craft, not necessarily navigable; this includes kite balloons.
Aerostatics.	The science relating to the upward lift of balloons and airships.
Aerostation.	The practical use of aircraft receiving lift from gas or hot air.
Air bottle.	Container for compressed air used for starting large aero-engines.
Air cooled.	Usually engine designation. Engine cooled by its passage through the air as opposed to cooling by water in a water jacket.
Airscrew.	Any screw propeller which moves an aircraft, whether as a pusher propeller, propelling from behind, or a tractor, pulling in front.
Aneroid.	A barometer arranged to indicate barometric pressure and height above sea level on a dial.
Balanced rudder.	A control plane hinged more or less centrally to relieve the pilot of the full loads when in action.
Ballonet.	A bag in the interior of an airship or balloon designed to hold air to maintain the shape of the envelope.
Balloon.	An aerostat with no motive power. Employed either to drift with the wind or moored as a stationary observation post.
Bay.	That part of an aeroplane or airship that is contained between any four struts or two frames.
Biplane.	An aircraft with two superimposed mainplanes.
Blimp.	The nickname for all small non-rigid airships. Several explanations are offered for this term, ranging from the military vernacular for the Type B, which was referred to as a "Limp Bag" and then shortened to "blimp", to an expression used by a Royal Navy officer during December, 1915, who flipped the envelope of an inflated airship with his finger and remarked that the sound was pronounced "blimp".
Blower.	A mechanical fan used to maintain pressure in ballonets.
Bow.	The front end of an airship's hull.
Bracing.	The system of wires or struts employed to hold parts of an aircraft's structure together.
Canvas.	A fabric made of coarse cotton thread, a term frequently employed erroneously for the fine linen fabric covering of aeroplanes.
Capacity.	The ability to contain. Generally the volume of gas contained in an airship or the internal volume of an engine cylinder.
Car.	Aeronautically the nacelle of an airship.
Ceiling.	See **Limiting height**.
Centre of gravity.	That point in an aircraft's structure at which it would balance on a point.

158

Clutch.	A mechanism designed to engage or disengage at will the driven parts of a mechanism from the source of power.
Direct drive.	A term generally used of an airscrew to indicate that it is fixed direct to the engine crankshaft instead of being driven by a train of gears.
Dirigible.	Any aerial vehicle dependent on gas for its lift and which can be navigated through the air.
Dope.	Special varnish usually with a cellulose base for tightening the fabric covering of an aircraft.
Drift.	Flight path taken by an aircraft away from its desired course due to the effect of wind.
Elevator.	Horizontal hinged flap at the tail of an aircraft for raising or depressing the tail section, causing the aircraft to dive or climb.
Envelope.	The fabric gas container of a non-rigid airship or the hull covering of a rigid airship.
Fabric.	Woven material, usually fine linen, which forms the covering of aircraft.
Fairing.	A light wooden, fabric or metal covering attached to the main structure to give it a streamlined shape.
Fairlead.	A metal guide, usually with a wheel, for retaining control cables along a structure to their termination.
Fan.	Either the cooling fan used for an aircooled engine or the blower of an airship—but never an airscrew.
Fin.	A fixed vertical surface usually placed in front of the rudder or rudders of an aircraft.
Gas bag.	The treated fabric containers in a rigid airship or the envelope of a non-rigid airship.
Gas plant.	Plant where lifting gas, hydrogen, was produced for filling airships.
Glide.	The controlled descent of an aircraft from any altitude with the engine at rest.
Gondola.	The hanging car of an airship.
Hangar.	A large shed used for housing aircraft, so called because airships when deflated were suspended by straps from the roof of the building.
Hover.	To remain motionless in the air.
Hydrogen.	The lightest gas known, and used for the purpose of lifting lighter than air craft.
Kite balloon.	A captive balloon with cylindrical envelope kept rigid by internal air ballonet and balanced so that it will fly head into wind. Usually used for observation purposes.
Limiting height.	The altitude at which an aircraft ceases to climb.
Mast.	Structure to which an airship is moored.
Motor.	A common expression for an internal combustion engine.
Nacelle.	Literally, a cradle. Applied to the car of an airship or the streamlined fairing of an engine.
Non-rigid airship.	An airship in which the shape of the envelope is preserved by the pressure of air and gas it contains.
Power plant.	The engine or engines of an aircraft.

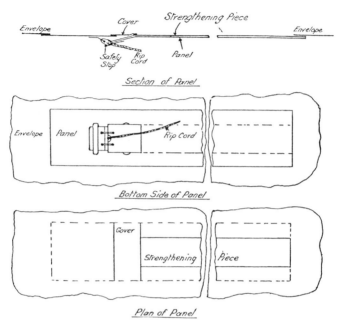

Details of the ripping panel of a Sea Scout airship.

Pressure height.   The altitude beyond which further ascent would involve loss of hydrogen.

Ripping panel.   Panel on the outer skin of an envelope which can be detached to allow the rapid release of gas to destroy lift.

Rudder.   A vertical flap, hinged in such a way that the pilot can steer with it to give the craft directional control.

Semi-rigid.   An airship with a non-rigid structure but stiffened by a keel or a long spar along the greater part of its length, with the nacelle or car suspended from this keel instead of from the envelope.

Stabiliser.   A term for the fixed horizontal tailplane of an aircraft which gives longitudinal stability.

Streamline.   A body designed to offer the minimum resistance to the airflow by presenting a blunt rounded front and a taper to the rear.

Trail rope.   A rope or cable trailing from an airship or balloon to enable ground handling and sometimes to aid stability.

Valve.   A device to admit or shut off gases in an engine or the gas bags of an airship.

Zeppelin.   Rigid airship of German design used mainly by the German Navy and built by the Zeppelin Airship Company. Used extensively for bombing raids on Great Britain during the First World War.

General Index

Index of Aircraft and Airships

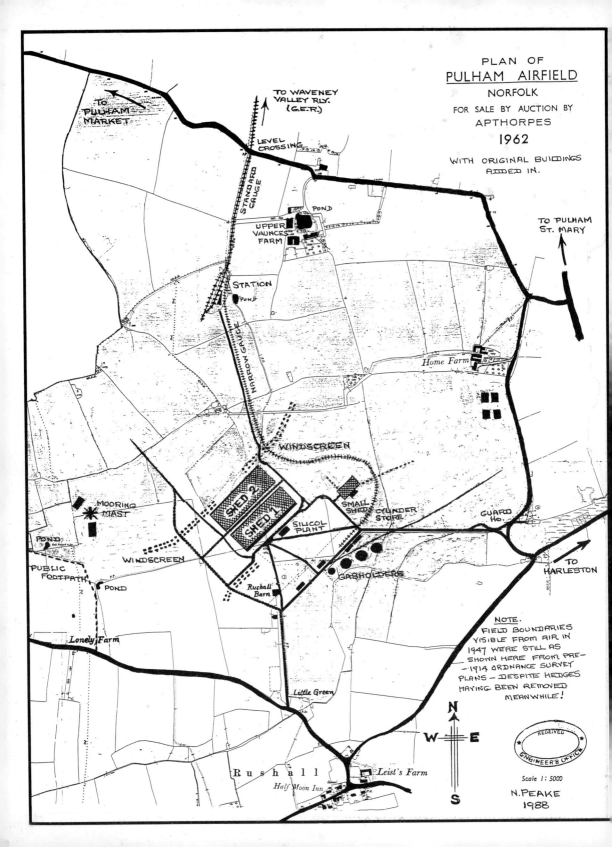

PLAN OF
PULHAM AIRFIELD
NORFOLK
FOR SALE BY AUCTION BY
APTHORPES
1962
WITH ORIGINAL BUILDINGS
ADDED IN.

TO WAVENEY VALLEY RLY. (G.E.R.)

LEVEL CROSSING

TO PULHAM MARKET

TO PULHAM ST. MARY

STANDARD GAUGE

POND

UPPER VAUNCES FARM

STATION

POND

NARROW GAUGE

Home Farm

WINDSCREEN

SHED 2

SHED 1

SMALL SHED

CYLINDER STORE

GUARD Ho.

MOORING MAST

SILICOL PLANT

POND

WINDSCREEN

GASHOLDERS

TO HARLESTON

PUBLIC FOOTPATH

POND

Rushall Barn

Lonely Farm

Little Green

NOTE.
FIELD BOUNDARIES
VISIBLE FROM AIR IN
1947 WERE STILL AS
SHOWN HERE FROM PRE-
-1914 ORDNANCE SURVEY
PLANS — DESPITE HEDGES
HAVING BEEN REMOVED
MEANWHILE!

N
W E
S

RECEIVED
ENGINEER'S OFFICE

Scale 1: 5000

Rushall
Half Moon Inn

Leist's Farm

N. PEAKE
1988